Torquere Press Novels

Achilles' Other Heel by Tulsa Brown • *Bareback by Chris Owen*
Blasphemy edited by M. Rod • *Broken Sword by Emily Veinglory*
Bus Stories and Other Tales by Sean Michael
Catching a Second Wind by Sean Michael
The Center of Earth and Sky by Sean Michael
Chance Encounters edited by M. Rode
Cowboy Up edited by Rob Knight • *Date Night by Kathleen Dale*
Dust and Violets by Mike Shade
Farr Anderson Lane by Kathleen Dale
Fine as Frog Hair by Sean Michael
Fresh Starts edited by Rob Knight • *Gemini by Chris Owen*
A Gentleman of Substance by Julia Talbot
Gods and Monsters by Sean Michael • *Honor Bound by Wheeler*
Scott Jumping Into Things by Julia Talbot • *Lassoed by BA Tortuga*
Latigo by BA Tortuga • *The Long Road Home by BA Tortuga*
Manners and Means by Julia Talbot • *Monsters edited by Rob Knight*
Mysterious Ways by Julia Talbot • *Myths edited by Rob Knight*
Naughty edited by M. Rode • *One Degree of Separation by Fiona*
Glass Out of the Closet by Sean Michael • *Perfect by Julia Talbot*
Playing with Fire by Sean Michael • *Post Obsession by Julia Talbot*
Rain and Whiskey by BA Tortuga • *Second Sight by Sean Michael*
Shifting and Shifting Too edited by Rob Knight
The Sound of Your Voice by David Sullivan
Stress Relief by BA Tortuga • *Tempering by Sean Michael*
Three Day Passes by Sean Michael • *Tripwire by Sean Michael*
Wheel of Fortune by Julia Talbot
Where Flows the Water by Sean Michael
Winning Hand by Sean Michael

chris • owen

bareback

Torquere
Press

TOP SHELF
An imprint of Torquere Press Publishers
PO Box 4351
Grand Junction, Colorado 81502

Copyright © 2003 by Chris Owen
Cover illustration by KL Gaffney
Published with permission
ISBN: 1-933389-19-2
www.torquerepress.com

First Torquere Press Printing: September 2003

Printed in the USA

Dedicated to my husband

                         --C

By Chris Owen

One

—◆—

Jake twisted the wire around the screw head and cut it with a snap of the wire cutters. Wiping sweat from his forehead, he squinted into the sun, looking down the field toward the big house, and cussed under his breath. Where the hell was Tor? The bastard was supposed to be helping fix the fencing in the backfield. They had to move fifty head of cattle in here in the next day or so, and the storm last week had snapped wire all over the place. Jake cursed again, not seeing any sign of anyone, much less Tor, coming to lend a hand. He put the tools in the back of the truck and moved to the next break.

Jake was just finishing up the south end of the field when he heard hooves coming up, nice and steady. He stood and leaned back on the fence post, watching Tor ride up. Damn, but he looked good on horseback. Jake hated that Tor looked good at any time. Sure, the man was a good hand to have around, but the most arrogant son of a bitch Jake had been cursed with in a long time. No matter how dark Tor's hair, or how strong his back, Jake wasn't about to put up with the shit Tor could bring with him just by entering a room. Besides, the man was just begging for a fight. Jake wasn't about to let him have it.

Tor swung down from the saddle and patted the horse hard on the flank, murmuring softly to the animal before taking his sweet time sauntering over to the fence.

"How's the work going?" Tor asked, checking out the latest fix.

"Slow. Could have used a hand about three hours ago. Still have the east side." Jake moved to the truck and got a water bottle, drinking deeply. "Where the hell were you?"

Tor grinned at him and slapped his thigh, raising dust from the denim. "Missy wanted me, now, didn't she?"

Jake rolled his eyes. Of course. Missy. Barely eighteen and trouble in boots. Thought she was queen of the damn world, prancing about in tight jeans and tiny shirts, teasing the hired hands and torturing the young lads with a hell of a lot of 'look, but don't touch'. Figured she'd go for Tor. Thirty-three, dark and strong, not a kid by any means. Sure she would find something for him to do.

Jake snorted. "Watch yourself. Boss finds out you're messing with the Princess you'll find yourself out of work and less your balls."

Tor stared at him and laughed. "Christ, Taggart, what kind of fool do you take me for? No way in hell I'd play with that little girl. I was helping her break her filly. Boss was there, even." He smirked, then said, "You know what she named that horse of hers? Pegasus. Pegasus, for Christ's sake. Calls her 'Peggy'. What the hell is it with that family and names? You know what 'Missy' is short for?"

Jake grinned and nodded slowly. Together they said, "Mississippi," and started laughing.

When they finished laughing at the name the Boss had seen fit to curse his vixen daughter with, they moved to the next piece of fence and started working.

Jake thought that the ranch was about to burst. Too many hired hands, too much work, not enough time. They were getting the last of the hay in and trying to get cattle ready for auction, so there were extra hands everywhere. Everyone was bone tired, working from sun up until long past dark, breathing in the dust and heat and smell of each other. Nowhere to sleep, really. So many people around it was a matter of grabbing a blanket and bunking in the loft, or out on the grass if the night was clear, on the porch if it wasn't. Most nights men just fell where they saw a flat spot and slept like the dead. A body could sleep well like that, tired from work, smelling sweet grass, listening to someone else snoring close by. And if the occasional slick sound of hand on flesh came your way, well, you did your best not to know where it was coming from. Even in close quarters a man deserved as much privacy as the darkness would provide.

But tonight wasn't a good night for sleeping. The air was electric and everyone was on edge. If it rained they'd have to wait for the hay to dry before putting it up, and they were so close to being done Jake could taste it. He moved through the barn, listening to the men talk quietly, everyone falling silent when the first roll of thunder sounded. Far away, but damn, if it rained…

Jake left the barn, a rough blanket over his arm. He didn't want to be surrounded by the stink of so many men, didn't want to feel the worry crawl over his skin. He'd spent enough time on the land to know that if it rained, it rained. Not much they could do about it tonight; hoping it wouldn't was the best they could do.

He was heading out behind the barn to find a soft piece of grass when Elias called out to him. He stopped walking, waited for the other man to reach him.

"You seen Tor?" Elias asked.

Jake shook his head. "Not since early morning. Boss sent him to town in the old truck. Haven't seen him since he got back, but I've been hauling bales all day."

Elias scrubbed at his face, the stubble on his jaw rasping. "That's the thing. He never came back, the bastard. We need that truck tomorrow. It may be a piece of shit, but it's got wheels and a bed. Fuck." Elias stalked away, calling out to someone else, still looking for Tor.

Jake stood looking at the sky, cursing. Yeah, they needed the truck, but why the hell hadn't someone clued in hours ago? Why did it take dark and oncoming rain before someone had to go looking for the jerk? And where the hell was he? Tor was a smartass, and too damn stubborn for his own good, but he wasn't a shirker. Tor wouldn't just take off in cutting season, and he certainly wouldn't steal a truck.

"Damn." Jake passed the blanket to a passing hand and stomped onto the porch, rapping at the door before pulling the screen open.

Missy answered, for once not wearing anything more revealing than her mother would. She looked tired, and Jake realized she must have been putting up hay all day, too.

"Jake. What's up?" she asked, managing to pull off a tired version of her come fuck me' smile.

10

"Your daddy around, Missy?"

"Somewhere. Hold on. Want to wait in the kitchen?"

He shook his head. "Cooler out here, I expect."

She nodded and closed the screen door, letting the light from the hall spill out. In a few moments her father came out and Jake straightened up.

"Taggart? Something going on?" The man looked serious, his eyes creased at the corners.

"Not really, sir. Or, maybe. Tornado's not back. I'm going out on River to look for him. Just wanted you to know."

"Goddamn…yeah, fine. Go get him. I swear, if that man isn't injured or stuck with four flat tires, I'll break his legs. After the hay is in and the auction's done. Of all the times to have a man gone…" The Boss glared at the sky. "Rain coming. Take a tarp and try to keep dry. With luck, the lightning will pass us by, but it'll be wet before morning. Better take food, too; if Tor's been out all day he'll be hungry. Idiot."

Jake nodded and went to saddle River, loading up the saddlebags with a first aid kit, plenty of water and feed, food and blankets. He tied a couple of tarps on and headed out, following the only road to town, cursing the dark and wondering how he'd spot the truck if Tor had decided to go across land. If the truck had gone off the road, or had a flat, someone would have stopped to help.

Jake rode for almost two hours, watching the sheet lightning light up the sky from over the horizon. Looked like the storm was moving off to the west of them; Boss was right, they wouldn't get the lightning, but they'd get the rain. As if the rain had been waiting for him to admit it to himself, the clouds suddenly let loose, fat drops hitting him with cold smacking sounds. The rain took only moments to get heavy, and as Jake crested one of the few hills in the area he saw a flicker of light to the east. Peering through the rain he was pretty sure it was a campfire, so he turned River off the road and headed toward it.

Before he was even halfway he was soaked to the skin and the fire was out, unable to withstand the onslaught of rain. Without the fire to guide him, he could only hope he was heading in a direct path to where it had been and he slowed River down, letting the horse pick his way through the field, making sure the animal didn't step into a hole or slide on the mud.

Jake thought he must have gone past the fire, or even imagined it, he'd been making his way for so long. Lightning flashed, this time a little closer; the storm was turning. He kept moving forward, and the next flash brought him an image of the truck, just to the left and about seventy feet away. He swung River gently and headed over.

As he dismounted and tried to soothe River, skittish from the storm, Tor appeared on the other side of the truck, bobbing up like a jack in the box.

"Took you fucking long enough," Tor yelled, his voice muted by the rain.

Jake froze, incredulous. Tor came around the front of the truck, wet clothes stuck to him and covered in mud. It would have been amusing, if not for the fact that Jake was just as wet. Tor's attitude was making a bad night worse, and Jake was too tired, wet and plain fed up to coddle the bastard.

"I've been out here for fucking hours! Where the hell were you?" Tor roared.

Jake pulled his arm back and let fly, catching Tor's jaw with a neat right. Tor fell, though Jake was pretty sure it was because he slipped on the mud and not because of the punch.

Tor lay in the mud, staring at him. Jake watched him for a moment and then turned back to River and started unsaddling him. Tor was a horseman, and Jake knew that if they were going to have a fight—and it looked like they were—Tor wouldn't start up while Jake was working with the animal.

He tossed the saddle over the side of the truck bed, and rummaged in the saddlebags for dry feed. He gave River a couple of apples and some water, keeping an eye on Tor, who was now standing, shaking with anger. Jake decided it was a good thing he was mad at Tor, because shit, the man was soaked, everything clung to him and he looked hard and lean and completely touchable. Yeah, best to be pissed at the jerk when he looked like that.

Jake stepped away from River and advanced on Tor, who didn't wait for a written invitation. Tor lunged at him and they slipped in the mud, falling backward. Jake had a moment to realize that Tor was on top of him, then a fist landed on his shoulder with a painful smack and they were grappling with each other, rolling in the mud, blinded by the rain and flying muck. They fought without any finesse, most punches missing their mark entirely, tangled in flailing arms and restricted by the cling of wet material.

As they rolled away from the truck Jake got a knee down for leverage and gripped Tor by the shoulders. "What's wrong with the truck?" he grunted, as Tor pushed back and they rolled again.

"Fuck, I'm not a mechanic. You tell me." Tor was on top of him again, and there was no way Jake was going to let that happen. Not if he wanted to avoid Tor knowing what he was doing to Jake, anyway. Jake kicked out with his right leg and hauled hard with his left arm, throwing Tor off. They scrabbled to their knees and swung at each other again, water running down their faces, mud caked in their hair.

"Fuck," Tor swore as Jake's fist connected with his jaw again. "Leave my face alone, you bastard. Not my fault I'm prettier than you."

Jake gave him a tight grin and launched a fistful of mud into that pretty face, then spun on his knees and ducked as Tor retaliated with a handful of his own.

Things deteriorated after that. Jake figured that when two grown men start flinging mud at each other instead of fists it was pretty clear the fight was over. All that was left was to figure out who won.

He got to his feet and started scraping mud off his arms, leaning against the truck. Tor moved to his side and Jake glanced at him, then ducked, fast, seeing the unexpected roundhouse flying to his head.

"Jesus, Tor! What the hell's gotten into you?" Jake demanded, stepping neatly to the side and grabbing at the arm that sailed over his head. He held fast to the wrist, twisting it up and back, forcing Tor into the side of the truck. Jake was well and truly pissed. Working off some steam was one thing, but that was just uncalled for.

"Figured I owed you one. You hit me first," Tor said over his shoulder.

"Bastard. I hauled bales all day and was gonna catch some sleep when I found out you were still gone. Shit, Tor. After dark, two hours in the saddle looking for you, fucking lightning and rain and muck and the first thing you do is swear at me. Fuck you." He pushed Tor hard against the truck and moved off, heading into the rain and God only knew where.

He peeled his coat off as he walked and tried to run his hands through his mud-slicked hair. "Shit." He stopped walking and turned back to look at the truck. The saddlebags were in the back. Saddlebags meant blankets and water and dry food. He stalked back to the truck, watching Tor, who didn't look too happy to see him coming back.

The rain wasn't letting up. Tor tipped his head back and starting dragging mud out of his dark hair with strong fingers, letting the water wash as much of it off as possible. Jake stood at the front of the truck, watching, unable to look away and hating himself for it. It wouldn't have been so bad if he actually liked Tor, but the man was irritating and arrogant and had just made damn sure that Jake was a mess. So Jake was pissed to find himself watching Tor wash mud off in the rain and getting harder than he'd been in a long time. Including the time he'd accidentally seen Tor skinny-dipping.

Tor finished with his hair and dropped his hands to his shirt, unbuttoning it. He looked up and Jake tore his gaze away, but not soon enough.

"Problem, Taggart?"

"Yeah. The blankets are in the saddlebag. Saddle's next to you. I don't want to eat any more mud, and I don't trust you enough not to hit me again if I go over there."

Tor finished unbuttoning his shirt and lifted a hand to wipe water off his face. He sneered at Jake and half turned away, saying, "You're safe enough. C'mon around." Jake walked forward, untucking his own sopping shirt, watching as Tor peeled his off and leaned on the truck, undoing his belt.

Jake kept walking because the only other choices were to either moan and fall to his knees or run away.

Jake dug out the blankets and made a dash for the cab door, throwing them inside before they could get soaked. He turned around, ready to strip off his muddy, soaked clothes, and smacked into Tor, who had come up behind him.

"What the hell are you—" he started, grabbing at Tor's shoulders to keep from sliding over in the mud. Tor grabbed back, big hands catching him at the waist.

"Sorry. Just trying to get in and get dry."

Jake willed his fingers to let go, but as Tor hadn't let go either he didn't rush it. He made sure they both had their footing in the slick mud and then eased off, careful not to push. Tor let go a moment later and took a cautious step back.

"You're not getting in there with wet clothes and mud on you. You'll just soak the blankets and then we'll be as bad off as we are now." Jake's gaze flicked down Tor's body, taking in the defined abs and the open jeans, saw bare feet. He glanced in the back of the truck, saw Tor's boots, covered in mud. They'd be wrecked by morning.

"So, what? We get naked?" Tor asked.

Water dripped off Jake's hair into his eyes. He rubbed it away and said, "Well…yeah. Problem with that?" His hand came away from his eyes and suddenly Tor was right there, close and hot, hands back on his waist.

"Nope. You?"

Jake froze, unsure of what exactly was happening. Then Tor's mouth was on his, a hungry tongue was sliding its way in, and Jake's brain decided that it had somewhere better to be. The hands at his waist slid around to his back and Tor was pulling him in.

Jake wasn't about to be seduced like some schoolgirl. Not by a man who used the unlikely name of Tornado, not by anyone. He stood as firmly as he could in the mud and tore his mouth from the kiss, staring into too dark eyes. As his hands made their way into Tor's wet jeans he said, "This doesn't mean I like you, you know."

Tor threw his head back in the rain and laughed, the sound turning to a moan as Jake's rough fingers found the head of his cock and swept over it. "Oh, Christ."

Jake worked his hand as far into the clinging denim as he could and wrapped it around Tor's thick shaft, pumping as well as the tight fabric would allow. Tor groaned and thrust his hips into the stroke, almost slipping in the mud. Jake turned him, pressing him into the door of the truck, and gripped Tor's cock a little tighter, his other hand trying to push Tor's jeans down and out of the way.

"Like it like that, Tor?" he said. "Hard and fast?"

Tor didn't answer, just started undoing Jake's shirt. The wet cotton was plastered to his chest and Tor had to push it out of the way with every button he managed to undo. The process would have being entirely too frustrating for Jake except that with every button undone, every bit of skin revealed, Tor's mouth moved over him, licking and sucking, leaving a trail of tingling nerve endings.

When the shirt was finally undone, Jake let go of Tor and dragged it off, tossing it into the back of the truck. He leaned against Tor again, kissing him hard, their teeth clashing.

Tor finally pushed him off and licked his swollen lips. "Strip down, Taggart. Get the muck off."

Jake put a hand on the truck for balance and yanked one of his boots off, sending it into the back of the truck with his shirt. As he bent to get the other one off, he looked at Tor and moaned, seeing him leaning against the truck, pants gone now, stroking himself in the rain. Water ran down his chest and arms, his legs were spread to brace himself in the slick mud and he was pulling himself in long, hard strokes.

Jake tried to take his boot off without taking his eyes off Tor and fell over.

"Fuck." Jake lay on his back, propped up on his elbows and looked at Tor. Tor didn't even bother trying not to laugh, though how he managed to laugh his ass off and keep stroking that beautiful cock, Jake wasn't sure.

Sighing, Jake sat up and pulled the other boot off and leaned back again. He figured he couldn't get much dirtier, so he may as well do this the easy way. He undid his belt and started getting his jeans undone, then realized that Tor had stopped laughing. He glanced up and met Tor's heated look, the intensity on the man's face burning into him. "Oh, shit."

He couldn't get his pants open fast enough, his straining erection making the job that much more difficult. With a gasp and a soft sigh he managed to push his soaked jeans past his hips and his cock practically jumped into his fist. He leaned back and thrust his hips up to meet his hand, gripping himself tightly as he watched Tor jerking off. Jake wriggled in the muck, working his pants off as he stroked himself, feeling his balls pulling up.

His breath was coming in ragged gasps and he knew he was going to shoot soon. He squeezed the base of his shaft hard, trying to stave off the inevitable, but Tor beat him to it. With a sharp cry, Tor fell to his knees, hips snapping back and forth as he fucked his hand. Jake watched as Tor screamed out a slew of nonsense and shot, come hitting Jake on his legs and belly, and then Jake was over the edge, coming in jerky pulses, spraying his own chest.

Jake was still shaking with the aftershocks when Tor was on him, rubbing against him and taking his mouth in a hungry kiss. Jake moaned, not caring that he was lying in mud, getting his brain twisted by the arrogant bastard who drove him to the end of his patience about twice a week.

"Christ, Taggart, you're hot," Tor hissed in his ear as he moved over Jake. "Drive me out of my fucking skull, the way you walk around, just handling shit like you know it all."

"I do know it all. You just don't get that," Jake replied, thrusting his hips up into Tor's.

Tor groaned and slid down Jake's body again, the maneuver made easy by rainwater, mud and come. He licked at Jake's cock and then rolled off.

"No way I'm fucking in the mud, Taggart. Up you go." Tor pushed himself up to his feet and held a hand out to Jake.

Jake looked down at himself and raised an eyebrow. He didn't blame Tor in the least; messy was an understatement. He let Tor pull him up and they stood in the rain, scraping as much dirt off themselves as they could, then let the rain take care of the rest. They moved hands over each other, wiping the water to where it was needed, feeling taut muscles strain and flex.

Jake felt Tor's hand move down his back and tensed, not sure if he was going to get turned around for another mind melting kiss or if the games were progressing. The only thing he was sure of was that no one's cock was going in anything other than a mouth without a condom, lots of lube, and a very thorough examination for mud.

"What's up?" Tor said, moving his hand away.

Jake turned and looked at him, saying, "Me. Get in the truck, Tornado."

Tor smirked and reached for him, pushing him up against the truck, his hand stroking Jake's erection to fullness. "Yeah, Taggart. Truck." Then his mouth was on Jake's again, tongue owning him. Jake moaned, giving himself over to the man, his hips thrusting lazily into Tor's hand.

Tor let go and opened the truck door. "After you," he grinned.

"Bastard." Jake moved, climbing into the truck and pushing the blankets out of the way. He leaned back and watched Tor get in, eyes following the water trail down the leanness of Tor's body to the dark thatch of hair at his crotch.

Jake let his hand move to his own shaft again, needing to feel some friction, some contact. He moaned softly when the door closed against the rain and it was just him and Tor in the truck, the rest of the world shut out. He closed his eyes and let himself go, riding the slow build of need, feeling it gather at the base of his spine.

He felt Tor move his leg, spreading him wide. He opened his eyes and watched as Tor's dark head dipped low, felt Tor's tongue on the tip of his erection. He shifted a bit, giving the man more room to work, and was rewarded by the sudden, all encompassing heat that surrounded him, the wet mouth taking him in, nice and deep.

"Oh yeah, Tor, like that."

Tor moved a little, then pushed down, taking in more, worked his tongue around the head and started to suck. Big hands held his hips, not letting him thrust as Tor moved up and down on his cock, and Jake couldn't have that. He let Tor have his way for a while, let himself get so hard it hurt, lost in the feeling. He hissed when Tor pushed at the slit at the tip with his tongue and Jake just about crawled out of his skin when he felt teeth on the upstroke. When he felt himself getting close, though, he pried at Tor's hands, forcing them off his hips. Tor resisted, like the bastard he was, and Jake finally resorted to talking him into it.

Hands on Tor's head, Jake said, "Tor, just let me. I'm not gonna hurt you, not gonna push. Just let me."

Tor slowed his sucking, but finally relinquished his grip on Jake's hips and Jake immediately took control. He held Tor's head exactly where he wanted it and started to thrust into that smart mouth, watching Tor's face, feeling his cock hit the back of Tor's throat and pulling out before he could gag. He thrust fast and hard, careful not to go too deep, and Tor started moaning, making those gorgeous needy sounds Jake didn't know he loved until he heard them.

"Fuck, Tor, so good. Just...fucking...perfect."

Tor reached down and took his own cock in one hand, pulling hard and fast.

"Tor, shit, gonna come," Jake gasped, and then Tor was off his dick and up his body, lips on his neck sucking hard as they thrust, grinding their cocks together.

"Taggart, you fucking bastard. I've never let anyone do that. No one. You better be fucking worth it."

Jake was coming then, covering them both in a hot, sticky mess. "Better than anything you've ever had, Tor. Promise," Jake said, sliding his hand in the puddle, getting it slippery. He wrapped his hand around Tor's cock and started to pull, loving the way Tor moaned into his ear, the way Tor's legs were shaking, hips thrusting into him.

"Come for me, Tor, c'mon, I wanna see you—"

"Jake—" Tor groaned, and with a shudder spilled into Jake's hand.

Jake grinned at the drugged look on Tor's face and kissed him soundly.

"Fuck, that was...I don't know what the hell that was," Tor finally said.

"That, Tornado, was Jake Taggart. Now shift your ass so I can get at a blanket. We gotta figure out how we're getting back to the ranch."

Two

―――――◆◆◆―――――

Jake was about ready to collapse. They'd spent two days moving cattle while waiting for the hay to dry, and tomorrow morning they would start back on the bales. The end was in sight, though; the hay should only take a day and half, one day if all the extra hands stayed on. But for now all he wanted was something cold to drink and his bed.

As he crossed the yard from the barn to the bunkhouse he absently counted the bodies scattered over the grass. Lot of men sleeping out. Granted, it was hot as hell, but he'd figured some of them at least would sleep in the tents on the front lawn, or in the barn itself. He shrugged, not really caring; he knew his bed was his and he had every intention of having a mattress under him instead of rocks and grass. Until he opened the door and felt the temperature increase about ten degrees.

He stepped into the kitchen and swore, immediately peeling off his T-shirt. Elias was just coming down the hall from his own room, carrying a blanket.

"Stayin' in here, Jake?" Elias asked, dumping the blanket on the kitchen table.

"Not anymore. Christ, it's got to be over a hundred degrees in here." Jake moved to the side, leaving room for Elias to pass him, and he heard the kitchen door bang open.

Elias said, "How 'bout you, Tor? Sleeping out tonight, or you want the whole house to yourself? I'm heading for the lawn and Jake's not stayin' in this heat either."

Jake stopped moving.

Tor swore. "Damn, it's hot in here. No way I'm staying. But it's getting real crowded out there, boys." He stomped through the kitchen toward the fridge and Jake leaned back against the wall, watching him. Tor looked…hot. Jeans and boots, no shirt, sweat making a path down the center of his chest to his waist. Hot.

Jake had spent a lot of time in the last few days wondering if he was losing his mind. He didn't sleep with guys he worked with. Well, that wasn't quite true; there had been a couple of guys over the years that had been agreeable to an arrangement of sorts, and a couple more that had been more long term, if one defined long term in weeks and a short series of months.

But he didn't sleep with guys he worked with, who he also didn't like much. Which was where the possibility of losing his mind came in, what with part of his brain pointing out some disconcerting truths. Like the fact that what he'd always called "arrogance" in Tor he called "self-confidence" in himself, and that Tor's pushy nature was not unlike his own take charge attitude.

22

Plus the man looked hot. And had an amazingly kissable mouth. And it had been a long fucking time since Jake had been with anyone, let alone someone who could make his blood boil like Tor could. It had to be either incipient insanity or too much work in the heat.

Elias was standing in the door, swinging it back and forth to make a draft. "We got how many in tonight, Jake? About twenty-five?" He was peering out to the front lawn, counting bodies.

Jake watched Tor get a bottle of water from the fridge, then lean back against the counter, head tipped back and throat working as he drank it in big, greedy gulps.

"Thirty-three. The bunch that came up for the day were too tired to drive back tonight." Jake felt his cock start to get hard, watching Tor's throat. He let his hand drift down, rubbed at his stomach.

"Damn," Elias said. "I can see ten from here…"

Tor stopped drinking, opened his eyes and saw Jake watching him. The dark eyes flicked over Jake and then raked up and down, finally settling on Jake's groin. Jake tried not to grin when Tor blinked, and Jake took a quick, shallow breath when those eyes got even darker and Tor ran a hand across his own chest, pinching at his nipple. Tease.

"…seven still on the porch…"

Jake let his hand move farther down and turned what should have been a simple adjustment into a long, hard stroke on his cock. Tor's eyes flared.

"…there's just not enough grass. You'd think, out here in the middle of nothing, there'd be enough room to sleep out in privacy. There's gonna be close to twenty men out behind the barn tonight."

Jake rocked his hips into his hand and let his head fall back against the wall. Tor's own hand move down, tracing a light path on the inside of his waistband and groaned.

"Yeah," Elias agreed. "With you there, Tor. Oh well, standing here won't make it easier to find a spot." Elias grabbed his blanket and stepped out, letting the screen door slam closed.

Tor advanced on Jake in three long strides and Jake sent a warning look to the screen door and the open kitchen window. Tor frowned and sat at the table, nice and close. Just two guys in their kitchen, having a quiet talk—if one ignored the way Tor's hand was teasing a path up the inside of Jake's thigh.

"Where?" Tor asked.

"Back orchard. Ten minutes."

Tor looked thoughtful and nodded, his hand moving higher. "We need some stuff."

Jake pushed away from the wall, into Tor's hand for a moment before moving away and heading down the hall to his room. "Got it covered."

"You better, if you want to use it," Tor's voice called from the kitchen. Jake rolled his eyes and went in his room.

He stripped the blanket off his bed and shoved it into his rucksack, then added another from his trunk. Crossing to the side of the bed he opened the drawer of his nightstand and reached in, then paused. Shit. He looked at the foil packets scattered in the drawer, wondering how many he should take. Two would be just fine, three would be better, but it wouldn't do to give Tornado a bigger ego than he already had. Fuck it. He grabbed a handful and was about to shove them into the bag when a thought struck him.

He sat on the bed, dumping the handful of condoms on the sheet. How long had it been? The fact that he had to check the expiration dates told him that it was way beyond too long.

Finally, blankets, rubbers and lube all packed up, he left the house, grabbing a bottle of apple juice on the way out. He crossed the yard and passed Tor, standing with Elias, who was still lamenting the lack of privacy.

"G'night, Jake."

"Night, Elias."

Tor didn't say anything.

Jake walked past the barn, greeting those who called his name. He passed the last of the hired hands and put on a burst of speed walking fast, long legs moving him toward the apple trees. He worked his way through the orchard, glancing back now and then to see how far he was from the others, and pressing on.

When he was sure that they would be out of earshot he dropped the rucksack and spent a couple minutes clearing fallen apples from the ground, then spread out one of the blankets. He sat down, watching for Tor as he pulled his boots off and then stripped out of his jeans. Not much point in being coy.

Jake lay back on the blanket, using his bundled up jeans as a pillow. He rubbed a calloused hand over his chest, listening for Tor, but hearing only his own breath. Spreading his legs, he moaned softly. If he wasn't so horny he would have just fallen asleep. But he was horny, so he let a hand move down to cup his balls and started squeezing, rocking his hips a bit, just letting the need build. He was just getting lost in the feeling when he heard someone coming and looked toward the house. Tor, walking up fast, wearing nothing but sweatpants and sneakers now.

He started moving his hand a little faster, brushing his thumb over the swollen head. Tor didn't even stop moving, just walked over and fell on top of him, pushing Jake's hand away and replacing it with his own while his mouth started sucking and licking at Jake's neck.

"Christ, yes, Taggart, that's it. No messing around, just get to it," Tor said, moving his mouth to find Jake's.

Jake kissed him hard, one hand on the back of Tor's neck, the other inside the back of the sweatpants, kneading at that tight ass. They were writhing together on the blanket, humping like teenagers, and it felt fabulous. Jake worked Tor's pants down past his hips and gasped when Tor's erection hit his own.

"Jesus. Need you. Now," Jake said in a voice so hoarse he hardly knew it as his own.

"What're you waiting for, then?" Tor rolled off him and Jake reached out, grabbing for a condom and the lube.

He tossed the rubber to Tor and spilled lube onto his fingers. "Open that, will you?" he said, slick fingers sliding between Tor's ass cheeks, loving the way Tor moved toward his hand, up on all fours.

"How the hell am I supposed to do that when I'm leaning on my hands?" Tor said, shifting back to kneel instead. Which, to Jake's great delight, forced Tor down onto his waiting fingers. "Oh fuck, yes!"

Jake worked his fingers into Tor's ass, waiting while Tor fumbled with the foil. He moved one, then two fingers deeper, brushing against Tor's prostate, making Tor moan. Jake grinned, then slid his fingers back out a bit, letting Tor concentrate long enough to pass the condom back to him.

One handed, Jake rolled the rubber on, his hand stretching Tor's ass, working the lube in. Tor leaned forward again and thrust back, making those lovely wanting sounds Jake remembered so well from the night in the truck. He added a third finger and then Tor was rocking back faster, fucking himself on Jake's hand, and Jake couldn't take it any longer.

He slid his fingers out and moved up, guiding his cock to Tor's ass. "Ready for me?"

"Bastard. Just fuck me, will you?" Tor ground out, trying to move back.

"Just had to ask, Tor. Just had to ask." He pushed in, burying himself in one long, slow thrust. "Oh, sweet Lord. So tight. God, Tor, so good."

Jake started thrusting, trying to keep his rhythm slow, but he had been so long without feeling that heat, that pressure, he couldn't last long. He began to thrust faster, using shorter strokes, barely pulling out at all before slamming back in and he could hear whimpers and grunts, wasn't sure if they came from him or Tor and didn't care.

"Shit, yes, Jake. Harder, fuck me. God, just fuck me..."

Jake thrust harder, fingers digging into Tor's hips, his own hips pistoning back and forth, watching his cock slide in and out of that beautiful ass.

"Tor, gonna come. Christ, it's been so long, so good, Tor..."

Tor groaned and thrust back, hard. "Touch me, Jake, please. Need to come, please..."

Jake pried a hand off Tor's hip and moved it down, fisting the hard cock he found waiting. Tor was like a rock, dripping pre-come and so ready to blow that Jake wondered how he'd managed to hold off this long. He stroked Tor hard in time with his thrusts and Tor cried out, a loud yell that meant nothing other than "Oh yes!" and Jake's hand was hot with Tor's come.

He buried himself deep in Tor's ass, riding out the contractions of Tor's muscles, then began to move again, letting the seize and release milk his own climax. His cock pulsed and throbbed, shooting come out for so long that he wouldn't have been surprised if Tor had managed to get it up again before he was done.

Finally he leaned over Tor's back, gasping for air. "Shit. That was—"

"Just what I needed," Tor finished. Then Tor's arms gave out and they sprawled on the blanket.

———•◆•———

Jake and Tor were passing the bottle of apple juice back and forth, not saying anything. Jake felt calm, relaxed and really sleepy; almost content. He watched Tor finish the juice and grinned a little.

"What?" Tor asked.

"Nothing." Jake lay back and kept smiling at Tor, mostly because he was well and truly fucked, but also because Tor looked like he was going to go nuts trying to figure out what Jake was thinking.

Tor lay back as well and stared at him, trapping Jake with his eyes. "C'mere," he said softly.

Jake paused for a minute and then rolled onto his side, facing Tor, who reached over and pulled him in, wrapping an arm around his back and kissing his forehead.

Jake moved even closer, pushing into the embrace and wiggling until he was stretched out along the lean body. If he could have, he would have purred.

"Thought so," Tor chuckled. "You're a snuggler."

"Shut up," Jake said, snuggling in a little more.

Tor laughed again. "Hey," he said softly.

Jake moved his head back and looked at Tor, wondering what he was going to say. Tor didn't say anything, just moved his own head down and kissed him, soft and oh so fucking sweet. It went on for ages, never deepening, just a slow and gentle caress, Tor's lips soft and full, teasing and playful, but not hungry.

Jake went with it, couldn't do anything else. He trailed his fingers gently down Tor's spine, and back up, using enough pressure not to tickle, but no more. Once more down Tor's back, tracing the shape of his muscles, then down his hip and thigh. He stroked Tor just as sweetly as the man was kissing him, and he felt Tor's tongue trace his lower lip, the kiss starting to deepen.

They lay like that for long minutes, hands petting and stroking, tracing lines and patterns, tongues exploring and tasting, but not devouring. Slowly, Tor began to move his hips, the thrusts as gentle as every other motion, and Jake felt himself stir.

Jake met Tor's thrusts, but didn't increase the pace, just let everything be lazy and soft, even if their cocks weren't. He sighed softly as Tor's erection got harder against his hip and he felt the first drops of pre-come leave a trail on his skin. He wondered what it tasted like and started to shift, to move down and take Tor into his mouth, but Tor held onto him, breaking the kiss only long enough to say, "No. Just…like this. Like this."

Jake stayed and kissed Tor, falling into the taste of the man's mouth. Apple juice, a very faint trace of beer, and just Tor. The smell of him, sweat and earth and sweet grass and animals. The feel of him, hard muscle overlaid with smooth skin and the heat they were creating.

When Jake came it was with a soft sigh and he dug his fingers into Tor's side while he shuddered and then relaxed, kept the movements of his hands and hips smooth until Tor followed him, groaning quietly with his own orgasm.

Tor reached behind himself without letting Jake move away and grabbed the other blanket, tossing it carelessly over them. They were still kissing when Jake fell asleep.

Three

It was late. Really late, Jake knew, and he was still awake, going over every pissy little thing he had done wrong in the last twenty years, and then some of the big things. It was one of those nights when no matter how hard he tried he couldn't let go of the sick feeling in his stomach, couldn't stop himself from digging at old wounds.

He tossed and turned in his bed, half expecting to hear a chorus of voices yelling in the dark, waiting for lights to flash on and angry men to drag him out of bed. He knew it wasn't going to happen, hadn't happened in over a dozen years, but some nights it just felt like it should.

He got out of bed and went to the window, naked except for his boxer shorts. His room faced the backyard, which meant there wasn't anything to see except acres of open land and a few trees. The moon was up, fat and full, and he watched a cloud cross it, not noticing. His mind was on another moon, not quite as round, and not there. Further south, different time of year, and hard walking. Couldn't get a lift to save his life, like every truck that passed knew where he'd been, or just knew better than to pick up a skinny kid with not even a rucksack. Only thing he had in his pocket that night was a letter from his momma, the only one she ever sent him.

So they tell me you're sick now, playing with boys. Always thought you were odd. Don't worry about us, Jakey, we'll do just as well without you.

Jake turned from the window and took a book off the shelf by the bed, not even looking at the title. He held it for a minute and slammed it back in, forgetting for a moment that he wasn't alone in the house. He froze and listened hard to the sounds the house made at night. He could still hear Elias snoring, not much chance of stirring him up before dawn. Kip was out, said he was going to stay at Beth's for the night. Tor...well, thinking about Tor wasn't the mental torture he was currently engaging in. Thinking about Tor was becoming more and more a way to relax. And that worried him.

There was a soft knock on the door and he said, "Yeah, c'mon in," knowing it was the man himself.

The door swung open and Tor came in, wearing only a pair boxers.

"Sorry. Didn't mean to wake you," Jake said, keeping his voice low.

Tor shut the door behind him and shook his head. "Didn't. Not with that anyway. I've been listening to you toss about for an hour, at least." Tor came in and swung himself into the chair in the corner, just looking at him.

Jake sighed. "Yeah, well. One of those nights, you know?"

Tor just nodded at him, his dark eyes serious. Jake wasn't sure what to say. It wasn't that he didn't want to talk to Tor, it was just that he didn't want to talk. Tor nodded again, like he'd made a decision, and stood up.

"Lie down, Taggart. On your belly."

Jake raised an eyebrow, but turned and lay down on the bed. Tor climbed on after him, onto him, straddling his hips, and started working at Jake's back with strong fingers. He didn't say anything, just kneaded the muscles until Jake started to relax, and kept on going for ages until Jake felt like he was made of Jell-O. Jake closed his eyes and started to drift off.

"Better?" Tor whispered in his ear, his hands slowing.

"Mmmph."

Tor chuckled quietly and leaned forward again, kissed his shoulder blade. "G'night, Jake." Then he got off him, got off the bed.

"Stay."

Jake knew in that instant that Tor wouldn't stay, that he would just go quietly, and that everything would feel different. He knew that in a few days, or in a week, they would steal a moment somewhere and get off together, and that it would feel too strange, too unlike the way it was supposed to be. That it would change everything forever, and that he had just crossed a line they both knew was there and that wasn't supposed to be crossed, and that he had just fucked everything up unless he could open his mouth right then and say something, anything, to take it back and smooth it over and—

Tor was back on the bed with him, wrapping a strong arm around Jake's chest, pulling him close. Jake smiled and shifted even closer, hooking a leg around Tor's and wrapping his own arm around Tor's back.

"G'night, Tor."
"Go to sleep. Idiot."
"Mmmph."

———————◆◆◆———————

When Jake woke up it was the gray of early dawn and he knew Tor was wide-awake by the insistent nudge of a hard cock on his hip. He opened an eye and saw Tor ginning at him.

"Finally. Thought I was gonna have to go jerk off in the shower."

Jake groaned and closed his eye again, snuggling down, hoping to get more sleep.

"C'mon, Taggart, show me what you got." Tor rolled them over and braced himself on his arms, leering down at Jake.

"Sleepy."

Tor shook his head and grinned. "Your cock's not. Tell you what, you sleep through this and I'll let you do me any way you want next time."

"How 'bout I get into this and you let me do you any way I want next time?" Jake thrust his hips up and snickered when Tor groaned, grinding back onto him.

"Yeah, whatever, just get naked." Jake noted that Tor already was, and wondered only briefly when that happened. Didn't matter, he decided; he was just glad that it was true.

"Get off me, then."

"God, you're pushy." Tor rolled off him and Jake skinned off his boxers, throwing them in the corner with Tor's, then pointed to the nightstand.

By the time Tor managed to get a rubber and the lube out of the drawer Jake was flat on his back, stroking his cock with a tight fist, feet planted so his legs were spread wide. He knew he looked like an utter slut, but hell, Tor had woken him up.

Tor just raised an eyebrow and tossed the condom in his face. "Hold that." He swatted Jake's hands away. "That's mine."

Jake was going to laugh until Tor bent down and took him in his mouth, swallowing him almost to the root. "Oh, shit..." Jake bucked up into Tor's mouth and almost crawled out of his skin when Tor started sucking on him. He was doing a swirling thing with his tongue and sucking so hard Jake wondered if he was still going to have a dick when Tor was done.

"It's like...a fucking tornado!"

Tor came off his cock with a grin. "That's my name."

"Suits."

"Don't you forget it."

"Won't. Do it again."

"Nope, got other plans for you," Tor said, opening the lube. "Just keep quiet. Don't want Elias barging in, wondering why you're screaming your fool head off."

Elias. Right. And now there were strong, slick fingers making their way between Jake's ass and balls and oh yes, it had been far too long since he'd felt that. Jake moaned softly as Tor pushed in, thankful it was only one finger when he felt the slight burn.

"Jesus, Taggart. You sure you've done this before? I haven't felt anything this tight since...fuck, I can't remember."

Jake relaxed and felt fire build at the base of his spine. "It's been a while. Told you that."

Tor moved his finger in and out and added another with a hiss. "So tight...Christ, Taggart, how long?"

Jake sucked in air as those wonderful fingers found his prostate and shifted down, trying to get them to brush against it again.

"How long?" Tor asked intently, moving his fingers out.

Jake shook his head. "Can't think, just, please, Tor…"

Then there were three and Tor was fucking touching his sweet spot. Not pushing, not moving, not brushing it. Just. Touching. Jake was all over the bed, trying not to be loud but losing it anyway, needing more. His hands were fisting the sheets and he tossed his head in frustration.

Tor moved his fingers away and said, "Still got that rubber, Taggart? Open it up for me."

Jake stared at him, trying to think. Oh, right. He found the foil packet and managed to get it open without tearing the condom, which he figured was a small miracle, and passed it to Tor.

Tor eased his fingers out and put it on, then lifted Jake's legs to his shoulders, guiding his cock to where Jake wanted it most.

"How long, Taggart?"

"Fuck, I don't know. Spring…"

Tor started to push into him. "Oh God, Jake, so fucking tight. You have no idea how good you feel."

Jake just thrust his hips, trying to get Tor to hurry up and fill him.

"Spring? Shit, man, that's only—what, four months?" Tor was still taking his sweet time sliding in, but the strain was showing in the way his arms were tense, the way the muscles on his abdomen flexed.

"Spring of two thousand…"

Tor pushed all the way in and sighed softly, then leaned over to kiss Jake's chest. "Two thousand and what?"

"Just two fucking thousand. Now, will you fuck me?"

"Two and half fucking years? Oh, hell." Tor started to move. "Man, this isn't going to last, you feel so good. Gotta just do it…"

Jake didn't bother replying, just started bucking up. Tor grabbed his hips and slammed into him, hitting his gland on every thrust, grinding into his ass and soon they were lost, fighting to keep quiet but Jake was loving the noises, the words, the way Tor was losing it completely and swearing he'd never felt anything so good.

Then there was a fist on his cock and Jake shoved his own hand in his mouth to keep from screaming as he came, shooting all over them both, feeling the hot come hit his chest and belly. Tor shuddered and swore, then Jake could feel him coming in his ass, thick, hard cock pulsing in his body and making him feel so fucking connected to the world.

———◆———

Tor was still lying on top of him.

"What are you doing?" Jake asked. He was actually curious. Tor wasn't sleeping, and his breathing was back to normal. He was just…lying there.

"Lookin' around. How long you been here?"

Jake glanced around the room. "Thirteen years." There wasn't much to show for the time. Lots of books. Some magazines. No family pictures, like the others had. Just…regular stuff. He didn't really need much.

"What's that?" Tor asked, moving his head slightly.

Jake smacked him lightly. "What's what, idiot? Can't see where you're looking."

"Fuck off. Top shelf of the bookcase."

Jake looked, knowing what Tor was talking about. "Lego."

"Lego?"

"Lego."

"Isn't that for little kids? My niece, Susie, loves the stuff." Tor raised his head and smirked. "She's six. What the fuck are you doing with Lego?"

Jake pushed Tor onto the floor and stood up, walking to the shelf, only a little stiff. He grabbed one of the boxes at random and handed it to Tor, saying, "Take this. Put it together. Take it apart. Put it back in the box and give it to me. Then we'll talk about if Lego is only for kids."

Tor stood up and took the box, then looked at Jake. "You're serious. You want me to play with kids' toys?"

Jake moved forward and stood close to him, and slowly licked Tor's neck, from collarbone to ear and then along his jaw to his mouth. "I'll let you play with all my toys, Tor."

Tor moved forward and kissed him, none too gently, and they heard Elias' alarm go off.

"Fuck."

"Later."

"Often."

"Get out of my room."

"Yeah, I'm going."

But they were still kissing. Finally, Jake moved Tor to the door by pushing him with his body and they broke apart.

"See you in the barn."

"Yeah. Get out." Jake kissed him once more and opened the door and pushed him into the hall.

Four

The Boss knew how to throw a party.

Jake figured he might just have found his fun when he wound up with Ben Knox on top of him during a pick up game of touch football. The "'touch' part was being blatantly disregarded in favor of a slow, subtle grind. When Ben was hauled off him, Jake met his eyes and grinned before standing up and walking to the fence to take a break.

"Who's that?" Tor asked, suddenly appearing beside him, his eyes full of laughter, his smile slow.

Jake blushed, he knew he did. "Who?" he asked, watching the game.

Tor laughed softly. "The guy who was humping your leg while looking like he wasn't."

Jake looked at Tor again, trying to gage his reaction. He had no idea if fun with Ben would fit into whatever the hell it was he and Tor had going. However, Tor seemed amused and a little turned on; certainly not pissed. Thank God. Jake didn't need the stress, and he had no real idea if they had rules he was supposed to know about.

"Name's Ben Knox," he said. "From Stafford's place."

Tor nodded and grinned. "And?"

Jake rolled his eyes. "And what?"

"What's he like?" Oh yeah, Tor was loving this. Bastard.

"No idea," Jake said, then winced as Ben wound up on the bottom of a pile. He'd sort of had plans for the parts of Ben that were currently getting smushed.

Tor was staring at him with one eyebrow raised, waiting. Jake sighed and said, "We've been missing each other for about four years now. Never managed to get past a two minute groping session before being interrupted. Last time was more than a year ago, at the auction."

Tor threw his head back and laughed. "Jesus. That's unbelievable."

Jake had a hard time believing it, too. Every time he and Ben got within talking distance something would happen, and then nothing would happen. It was a challenge now.

"Yeah. Sucks. Or not." He shrugged one shoulder and contemplated getting back in the game. Lots of chances for getting under Ben out there.

Jake fucking loved touch football.

Tor laughed again. "You aiming to fix that tonight?" he asked.

"Depends," Jake said, deciding to stay where he was as Ben started to limp toward them.

"On what?" Tor moved away a little, but his arm came up to rest on the fence behind Jake's shoulders.

Another cowboy moved away from the spectators and slid into step with Ben.

"On how you feel about threesomes. Or four, as the case might be," Jake said lightly. He was gratified to hear Tor's calm shatter with a sharp hiss. "That's Ben's man. Name's Jeff. Nice guy."

And he was. Jeff was also one of the sexiest men Jake had ever seen, tall and built, classically handsome. Ben was a little shorter than both Jeff and Tor, almost exactly the same height as Jake, more fair haired and country than Jeff.

"Jesus," seemed to be Tor's only reply as the cowboys reached them.

Jeff smiled at Jake and shook his hand. "Long time, Taggart."

"Has been, yeah. This is Tornado. Tor, this is Ben and Jeff."

The men all shook hands and quietly assessed each other.

"So, you two…?" Ben asked, waving his hand between the two of them.

"Have spent some time looking for dark corners," Tor replied, his voice even.

Ben grinned and nodded, then very thoroughly looked Tor up and down. Jeff did the same, one of his hands turning Ben slightly so his body shielded them from onlookers. That done, Jeff very casually reached out and ran a finger along Jake's thigh, watching Tor's eyes.

Tor shuddered. Ben grinned.

Jake grinned, too, watching as both Jeff and Tor untucked their shirts, letting the tails hide their approval of each other and the situation.

"So, this gonna happen?" Ben asked. "Or is someone about to appear with forms to fill in? A sick horse? Sudden rain?"

"Can do it in the rain," Tor said. "Trouble is where. Lot of people around."

Jake snorted. "Not a problem. Riverbed."

Tor blinked. "Yeah. Okay. Need stuff."

And just like that they were walking, all four of them, toward the bunkhouse. Jake watched Ben closely, feeling a little like if he blinked too slowly Ben'd disappear.

Jeff saw him and grinned. "Relax. He'll be impossible to live with if this don't happen—I reckon me and Tor can take care of the details."

Tor laughed and walked faster. "Don't even need a list. Blankets, food, rubbers and lube."

"Water and juice," Jake put in as they climbed the steps.

"Ah, yes. The juice. Never forget the juice," Tor said, stepping to the side as Jake tried to smack him.

"Beer?" Jeff asked, as they moved through the kitchen.

"Can if you want," Jake said. "I don't drink. Don't care if you do."

Tor winked at him. "And I don't 'cause he doesn't like the taste."

"No beer, then," Ben said with a grin. "I plan on lots of kissing."

Laughing, the four of them made their way to the back of the house and Tor turned into his room to get the condoms and lube, while Jake headed into his own for blankets.

Jake had barely stepped into the room when the door slammed behind him and Ben had him pressed into the wall. "Hey," Ben said. Then his mouth was on Jake's and they were thrusting against each other, fast and furious.

Jake moaned and opened his mouth wider, Ben's hand sliding over his ass and pulling him even closer. Jake arched his back, driving himself into Ben's body, aching already. He could feel Ben's cock, hard and long, fitting just right along his hipbone. And just like that he was going to come.

"Christ," Ben whispered.

Jake was about to agree, when the door opened and Jeff looked in. "Told you they started without us."

Jake whimpered as Ben was pulled away, Jeff's big hand tugging at Ben's shirt. "Cool it. Going somewhere to play, another ten minutes won't kill you. But I might if you get this going here. Too many people, yeah?"

Ben rolled his eyes, and said, "Yeah." He didn't sound very apologetic.

"Fuck," Jake muttered, trying to catch his breath. Tor just laughed at him and took a quick kiss before moving to strip the blanket from his bed.

"Get the food, Jake."

Jake sighed and got the food.

It took them about ten minutes to walk to the riverbed, which was five minutes less than it usually did. They seemed to be rushing.

"So, the chances of anyone showing up here are what?" Jeff said, turning Tor by the elbow and stepping close.

"None."

Jake watched as Tor lifted a hand to the back of Jeff's neck and pulled him close for a kiss, their mouths wide and tongues plunging deep. Jeff grabbed Tor's ass, grinding against him, and Jake's cock throbbed.

"Hot, huh?" Ben asked, standing close enough that Jake could brush against him.

"Oh yeah." Jake hadn't really thought much about what it would be like to watch Tor with someone, and now he just wanted to see it again. "Come on, we're almost there. Just gotta climb down the rocks and around the bend."

Tor and Jeff seemed as reluctant to break their kiss as he and Ben had been, but they did it. The four of them walked down the dry riverbed, each one unbuttoning his shirt while juggling blankets and the rest of the supplies. Patience was in short supply.

Jake tossed the blanket he'd been carrying onto the ground and utterly refused to look at Tor or Ben as he toed off his boots. He had no intention of coming in his jeans, and if he looked at them he'd touch them. That would lead to other things, including coming in his pants.

So he spread the blanket and got his boots off, eyes fixed on the ground. He could hear someone kissing, by the sounds of it Ben and Jeff, then there were hands at his waist, and Ben was turning him, peeling the shirt from his back.

"Need help?" Ben said, his hand working Jake's jeans open and his mouth latching onto Jake's neck.

Jake just closed his eyes and went with it, his back arching as Ben got a hand around Jake's cock and started stroking him. His own hands were on Ben's shoulders, in his hair, clinging to the man. They moved together, hands sliding restlessly over skin and pushing fabric away, Jake finally gathering enough brainpower to get Ben naked as well, before they toppled over onto the blanket.

"Christ, you're going to drive me insane," he said, gasping as Ben bent his head to lick and bite at his nipples.

There was a sound of agreement to his left and he glanced over to see Tor and Jeff, still fully clothed, making out on the other blanket. Their hands were busy, plucking at nipples and kneading denim clad pricks, but they seemed to be in no rush to get undressed. He grinned at Tor and turned his attention to Ben, sliding a hand over Ben's thigh and rolling them over so he was on top.

Within seconds Ben was gasping as Jake ground into him, their erections pressed tight together. Ben was hard and leaking, his cock hot alongside Jake's. Jake kissed him again, sweeping his tongue through Ben's mouth and sucking on his lower lip.

He broke the kiss when a hand landed on his back, another on his thigh. "Here," Jeff murmured, dropping rubbers and lube next to them. "Give us a show."

Ben grinned and winked at Jake, his hips still rocking. "How do you want me? Had a long time to think about it, Jake. What's your favorite?"

"For you? Hands and knees. Gonna nail your ass hard."
Jake felt Ben's cock twitch and knew he'd guessed right.
Total bottom. It made him growl a little, made him ache to
sink into Ben's body.

Ben rolled over when Jake let him, his back arching
into Jake's hand as he teased a finger down Ben's spine to
his ass. "Need it deep, Jake."

Jake ran his hand over Ben's ass in appreciation. Firm
and smooth, it was a great butt. Best one he'd seen at the
Boss's party four years ago, when this had all started, and
now it was, waiting for him. He reached for the lube and
slicked his fingers, bending to lick Ben's spine.

He heard a moan and looked at the other two, shirts
gone. Tor was sitting in front of Jeff, his jeans undone, and
both of them were stroking Tor's cock slowly. Jake grinned
and pushed two fingers into Ben to a chorus of low groans.

Ben was hungry, moving back onto him. Jake shook his
head and let Ben go for it, let him fuck himself on Jake's
fingers for a couple of strokes as Jake managed to get a
rubber on one handed. Tor whispered something to Jeff and
Jake looked over to watch them kissing, still playing with
Tor's dick. His own cock jerked in response and he curled
his fingers inside Ben.

"Jesus." Ben dropped his head between his shoulder
blades. "Jake, please."

Jake nodded and eased his fingers out, then shifted
closer, positioning his cock at Ben's tight hole. "Want it,
Ben?"

Ben surged back and Jake pushed. "Oh, fucking hell,"
Jake moaned. Ben was tight and hot, his body making way
for him easily.

"God, yeah," he heard Jeff hiss.

Jake grabbed Ben's hips and thrust in deep, pulling out
completely before slamming back in, changing the angle.
Rough and hard, he gave Ben what he asked for, listening
to the broken words as he plunged in and out of the man's
ass.

Ben screamed when Jake nailed his gland, his head snapping back and his entire body shuddering. Jake groaned and did it again, hitting the same spot over and over. Ben was hot around him, his body tensing and clutching at his cock, and Jake felt like he could do this for hours.

Ben, though, was losing it, going wild on Jake's cock. He was pushing back, taking Jake as hard as he could, hips bucking. With a grin, Jake slid a hand around to Ben's dick and stroked him once from root to tip.

"Oh fuck, yeah, gonna shoot," Ben said, his voice rough, and Tor groaned beside them.

Jake gasped as Ben's ass clamped down around him and the prick in his hand pulsed. Tor came at the same time, and Jake watched as Tor's head fell back on Jeff's shoulder, his spunk spilling over Jeff's hand. Jeff groaned and shifted, thrusting into Tor's back, and by the way his eyes rolled back Jake figured he'd shot his load as well.

Jake bit his lip as Ben's muscles rippled around him and started fucking him again, slow and easy, just nudging at Ben's sweet spot and stroking his cock. The shallow thrusts, and gentle rocking were somehow more intense, more powerful for Jake. Or maybe it was the scent of sex, the look of Tor and Jeff peeling off the rest of their clothes and exchanging lazy kisses.

"God, you're going to keep me up," Ben whispered.

Jake grunted. "Gonna fucking try. Four years, Ben. You're coming for me again."

Jeff crawled over in front of Ben and kissed him, hands sliding over Ben's back. "Want some help, cowboy?"

Ben nodded and Jeff eased him up a little, so he was mostly in Jake's lap, still riding Jake's cock. Jake wrapped an arm around Ben's waist and pushed into him with his hips, biting down on Ben's shoulder as Jeff bent his head and started sucking Ben off.

"Christ." Tor lay down beside them, watching. "Fucking gorgeous, Taggart."

Jake moaned, watching Jeff suck Ben's cock. Then Jeff's fingers were sliding back, presumably over Ben's balls, and back further. Jake felt Jeff tease at him, sliding over his cock as he pushed into Ben and he tensed, fire racing through is blood.

"Oh fuck, Jeff."

Tor moaned softly, stroking his erection back to life, and Jake pushed harder, feeling Jeff's fingers and Ben's ass tight around him. When Jeff's hand moved back further, tugging his balls gently, Jake knew he was going to blow.

With a grunt he thrust deep into Ben, and Jeff went one better, pushing a thick finger into Ben's ass along with Jake's cock. The extra pressure was all Jake needed and he came hard, crying out as his balls emptied in powerful spurts.

Ben screamed Jeff's name and his hips snapped as he came in Jeff's mouth, his second orgasm making Jake weak as everything was wrung out of him. He fell back onto the blanket as Jeff and Tor managed to ease Ben off him, legs shaking.

Tor curled around him, kissing him possessively. "Fuck, that was hot, Jake."

Jake grunted and kissed him back, still panting. Tor pulled away far enough to let Jeff in, and Jake kissed him as well, letting hands stroke over his sides as he came down. Jeff grinned into the kiss and backed off, stopping long enough to kiss Tor quickly, too.

For a few minutes the four of them just lay there, catching their breath as Jake and Ben recovered. Jake could feel Tor shifting restlessly, still curled around his back. Tor's cock was hard, nudging against him instantly.

"You've got to be kidding," he said with a grin. "I'm dead. Go away."

Tor snorted. "C'mon, Taggart. Give me a hand, here."

Jake rolled onto his belly. "No way."

"Even better," Tor said, and Jake saw him reach for the lube.

Jeff and Ben laughed, moving slowly against each other, and Jake groaned. But he spread his legs a little, willing to let Tor in. When Tor's fingers slid over his ass he moaned softly, waiting. His skin felt over heated, sensations sharp as they were layered on top of the aftershocks from fucking Ben.

When Tor pushed a finger into him they both hissed.

"Fucking tight," Tor whispered, moving carefully as Jake relaxed. It was a good thing he'd come, relaxing was easy. Soon Tor had another finger in him, opening him smoothly.

Jake closed his eyes and lifted his ass, rocking back. He blocked out everything but the feel of Tor's fingers, the fading burn as he was stretched; he could hear Ben and Jeff kissing, hear the soft noises Tor was making, but most of his attention was on Tor's fingers and his own filling erection.

Tor hit his gland and Jake moaned, body shuddering.

"That's it, Jake." Tor did it again, long fingers moving, massaging his sweet spot until Jake was almost—but not quite—ready to beg.

The fingers disappeared and Jake moaned again, feeling empty. Tor laughed quietly and Jake heard the tearing of the condom wrapper and Ben's own chuckle turn to a sigh. He would have looked over to see what Jeff was doing, but Tor was there again, the blunt head of his cock resting at Jake's hole.

"Please," Jake gasped, hips rocking as he pushed himself up onto his elbows.

"Please what?" Tor teased, not moving.

"Fuck me," Jake groaned, still trying to move back.

"Like this?" Tor asked, one hand on Jake's hip, the head of his cock pushing in slowly.

Jeff groaned and Jake pushed back, wanting more.

"Or like this?" Tor pushed in, sliding in a little deeper and pulling out again.

"Tor!" Jake was gasping, Tor's cock stretching him, but not going deep, not where Jake needed it.

Tor gave a strangled groan and thrust in, splitting Jake open and plunging deep.

"Fuck, yeah!" Tor stayed deep in him, hands tightening around his hips. "Oh hell. Don't move."

Jake couldn't not move. He jerked on Tor's cock, his stomach clenching, hips rocking as he tried to get more.

"Jesus, Jake. I'm gonna pop if you keep that up."

"Don't care," Jake gasped. "Just fuck me. Please? God, Tor, need it—"

Tor growled and pulled almost all the way out, then slammed into him again. Jake grunted and gasped for air as Tor set up a brutal rhythm, nailing him hard. It was a wild ride, and it couldn't last long, Tor was too far gone, but it was good. Good enough that Jake was starting to feel his own orgasm build when Tor cried out and froze, his cock pulsing as he came.

Tor eased out of him and Jake rolled over, hand going to his cock as Tor started kissing him. Close, but not close enough and Jake was willing to take care of it himself.

He'd just started pulling himself off when a strong hand closed around his wrist and Ben said, "No way, man. Enough bodies here that you'll not be wanting."

Jake looked at him through heavy lidded eyes, feeling drugged. "Yeah? You're gonna take care of me?"

"The man said there's lots of bodies here," Jeff said, settling between Jake's thighs. "Wanna fuck you, Jake."

Ben only waited for Jake's nod and Tor's whoop before he grabbed condoms. He passed one to Jeff and another to Tor with a happy smile. "Going to make this a full fledged, orgy, boys, and Taggart's the main dish."

Jake blinked.

"What's the plan?" Tor asked, sitting up. His eyes were locked on Jeff's cock as the man slid the rubber on and lifted Jake's thighs.

"Oh, it's nice," Ben purred, opening a third condom. "Jeff's gonna fuck him. You're gonna suck him. And he's going to suck me."

Jake shuddered, the image alone sending him into overdrive. "Hurry," he said hoarsely.

"Not a problem," Jeff said with a grunt as he pushed in. "Oh fuck, you're tight."

"Told you." Tor rolled the rubber he was holding over Jake's prick, stroking firmly as Jeff sank in. "This'll only be the third time Jake's taken a cock in two and a half years."

"Thanks," Jake said. "Need everyone to know that." He groaned as Jeff moved deeper. The man wasn't as thick as Tor, but he was longer, pushing deeper. "Oh God."

"Nice, yeah?" Ben asked.

Jake couldn't answer, Tor's mouth was on him, and Jeff was fucking him and he was suddenly very short of both breath and thought. He was, however, fully aware of Ben straddling him and the hard cock teasing at his lips.

"Suck my cock, Jake."

He opened his mouth and let Ben in, tongue teasing over the fat head. Ben moaned and pushed in slowly, setting a nice, easy pace, which was about all Jake could handle. Jake's lips slid over the rubber, the taste of the latex quickly become secondary to the feeling of thick, hard flesh filling him.

Jeff nailed his gland hard, and Jake groaned, his hips thrusting back. Tor was sucking him in deep, mouth tight around his dick, and Ben shuddered when Jake moaned, thrusting harder.

Jake gave it all up. Sensations slammed into him with every lick, every thrust, every sound. He was being well and truly used and he loved it. Jeff was plowing into him, harder and faster, going so deep Jake ached, crying out around the cock in his mouth with every thrust. He could feel Tor's tongue and lips, and every moan Tor made. Someone was playing with his nipples, pinching and twisting them until his back was bowed, his body on overload.

What little thread of control Jake had snapped. He was writhing, begging with his body, sucking Ben as hard as he could as his hips rocked between cock and mouth, his orgasm building like white heat. He felt his cock swell, knew he was going to shoot his load, and he cried out.

"Fuck, yeah, Jake. Come on me. Come for us." Jeff's voice was harsh, and Tor's moan was like lightning around him. He started to shoot, wailing around Ben's prick, his hips bucking.

Ben groaned and came, his cock pulsing on Jake's tongue, both of them jerking as their climaxes roared through them.

Tor sucked him, wringing everything out of him, every shudder, moan and gasp Tor could get, before backing off and ditching the rubber. Ben had moved away, sprawling on the ground beside them. Jeff…well, Jeff was still fucking him, and as soon as the others were out of the way he bent down and kissed Jake hard.

"Stunning," Jeff murmured. "Oh shit. Gonna—" With a long groan Jeff came, burying himself in Jake's ass as spasms wracked his body.

Jake couldn't move. He didn't want to. What he wanted was Tor to curl up with, sleep, something to eat, and more sleep. What he got was Tor wiping him off, Ben passing him water, Jeff dropping one more kiss on his mouth, and then Tor's arms around him. With a happy sigh and slight wiggle that might have been called snuggling, Jake fell asleep, listening to the others tease him about being too tired for round three.

Ben woke him up with a shove and a far-too-happy-for-this-early-in-the-morning voice. "Jake, you're missing the show."

Jake pried an eye open, entirely unwilling to face the day. He was sore and tired and why was Ben there, anyway? He remembered when he got his other eye open.

Jeff and Tor were going at it like nobody's business, all roaming hands and open mouths as they fucked. Jeff was pushing hard into Tor, holding Tor's legs up and open, while Tor was curled nearly in half so he could shove his tongue down Jeff's throat.

It was surreal. So Jake did the only thing he could think of. He reached over and grabbed a couple more rubbers and tossed one to Ben. "C'mon. No way we should miss this."

Ben grinned, one hand still stroking his hard-on, the other reaching for the foil packet. "What are we doing?"

"Daisy chain." Jake rolled a condom onto his own wood and stood up. "Me in Jeff, you in me. Jeff in Tor."

"Fucking hell, you are," Tor said. "Can you even walk?"

"Fuck off, I can walk fine. And I can fuck just fine, too." Jake knelt down behind Jeff, popping the lid on the lube. "How 'bout you, Jeff? Want it?"

Jeff stopped pounding into Tor, or at least slowed down enough that Jake could push a couple fingers into his ass. "Oh yeah. Ain't gonna last long, though."

Ben laughed, suddenly behind Jake and snatching the lube away. "Don't gotta be long, just gotta be hard, baby."

Tor gave up.

Jake finger fucked Jeff for a moment, hissing at how tight he was. Right, Ben was a bottom; willing to jump into the chain, but Jake would bet that Jeff took it up the ass fairly infrequently.

He stopped when Ben's fingers started sliding down his own crease, teasing at his hole. Jake slicked his cock fast and moved into position, waiting until Ben breached him to push forward.

"Fuck," Jeff hissed, and Jake had to agree. Tightest heat around him, fingers in his ass—it was fucking unbelievable.

He eased into Jeff slowly, holding onto Jeff's hips to keep him still. When he was deep inside, Jake looked back at Ben and grinned. "Anytime you're ready."

Ben grinned back and took a fast kiss, then the fingers slid out, leaving Jake momentarily empty. Ben's cock nudged at him and he moaned softly; he might be able to walk, but that didn't mean he wasn't well and truly fucked.

"Okay, Jake?" Ben asked seriously.

"Yeah, just…just go slow for a second."

Ben did, easing into him gradually until all four of them were joined.

"Jesus fucking Christ." Jake wasn't sure who said it, but he agreed entirely.

"Okay, Ben. Let's go." Tor's voice was tight and Jeff was already shuddering. Wasn't going to take long at all.

Ben bit down on Jake's shoulder for a second. "Thanks," he whispered. Then he pulled back, his hands on Jake's hips pulling Jake out of Jeff a little as well. Jake barely had time to register the sensation before Ben thrust in again, forcing Jake deep into Jeff.

All four of them gasped and swore.

Surprisingly, it only took two or three strokes before they found a rhythm, the four of them working together, moving more or less smoothly—for about three more thrusts, then things got wild. Tor cried out as Jeff pounded into him, with Ben and Jake's weight behind him, and Jeff—who'd probably been damn close to coming anyway—swore and started shaking harder. Jake was swept along, Ben nailing his prostate and cursing in his ear about how fucking hot it was, how tight Jake's ass was, and then the air was filled with the smell of fresh spunk as Tor shot his load.

Jeff wailed, his ass clamping down around Jake's prick, pulling Jake over the edge with him. Lights flashed behind Jake's eyes as he came, the sounds of Jeff and Ben around him as they alternately cried and grunted with effort, hips still slamming into him from both sides.

The edges of his vision blurred a little, and Ben whispered, "Oh shit. Oh fucking shit—" and the cock in Jake's ass throbbed, reminding him that he was more than slightly tender. He could have sworn he felt each pulse, every twitch; and then it all faded as they fell into a sweaty pile of limbs, each man trying not to hurt the others as he aimed for a soft spot to die.

Ben pulled out slowly and Jake stifled a whimper, but not before Tor heard it and shot him an evil look. Jake rolled his eyes. "I promise I'll nap all day today, okay? Be fine for the dance."

"Not worried about the dancing, Taggart," Tor said with a grin.

Jake rolled his eyes. "Yeah, whatever. Right now though, I can think of a few other things more important than the state of my ass."

Ben laughed weakly and wrapped an arm around Jake's waist. "Like coffee."

"Food," Jeff added, reaching for a water bottle.

"Shower," Jake said firmly.

"Sleep." Tor extracted Jake from Ben's grasp and curled around him. "Sleep first. Then food. Then walking. Then showers. Then more sleep."

Jake kissed him and agreed wordlessly; snuggling was good for an hour or so. He gave Ben a smile and Jeff a wink, then wedged his head into the crook of Tor's neck. Sleep was very good.

Five

The Boss always called the big barn dance a reward for a year's hard work, but this was the first year that Jake even came close to agreeing with him. Usually the dance was an event he made his way through by telling himself that it would be over in 'X' many hours, and life would return to normal. The first four years Jake was on the ranch he didn't even come out of his room for it, convinced that there was no way in hell he'd make it through a weekend full of that many people, that much booze around, and that much noise, without drinking.

He didn't think the Boss had even noticed that he wasn't there; after all, there had to be more than a hundred people in the yard, tents everywhere, trucks parked three deep all along the lawn. But then, about a week before the party in Jake's fourth year there, the Boss had just asked him if he was going to join them this year. Jake had shaken his head and said, "Not this year, sir. Maybe next." And the Boss had nodded and let it drop.

Over the years, and with a certain amount of trial and error, Jake had worked out what his endurance was. The first afternoon, when people started arriving and there were the sounds of happy greetings and the bands warming up, was fabulous. The early evening, when people sat around in tight circles, or moved from group to group talking to everyone they knew was fun. It wasn't until full dark, when the music was loud and the voices grew louder with too much drink that it got rough. Even that had changed over the years, though. Early on, it was a dread of wanting to join them in their excess, the burning need for a bottle of his own that drove Jake to his room. Now it was just a need to be away from that many drunken people. The booze itself didn't faze him anymore; he didn't even notice the beer in the fridge of the bunkhouse unless it was in front of his apple juice. It was just the idiocy that came with it that got to him after a while. He still found the second day a trial.

But right then it was just dusk and Jake was feeling fine. It was a big gathering, over a hundred and fifty people, since most started bringing their families and camping out. He was wandering around, talking to people he didn't see that often, meeting new faces, and generally just enjoying being social. He liked the sound of the band, liked the smell of the food; it was going to be a good night. The beer was just starting to flow and he figured it would be a couple of hours before he would really want to be somewhere else.

He knew that his tolerance was high this year due to actually missing the first night completely. Spending the night on the riverbed with Ben and Jeff had been much more enjoyable than trying to make his way through the Boss's party. He even thought that his body was almost fully recovered, if not quite normal. Jake was just as glad; as much as he had enjoyed the night before, and that morning as well, he just wanted to settle back tonight, be apart from it all.

He was talking to a rancher from a spread south of theirs when Elias wandered up and asked to have a quick word with him.

"What's up?" Jake asked, as they walked up toward the stables.

"River. I was just feeding the horses and saw him favoring one leg. No one told me anything about it, so I just thought I'd mention it."

"Damn," Jake said. "Nothing wrong with him this morning. Anyone have him out this afternoon?"

Elias just shrugged, and said, "Don't know. Listen, I didn't even take a close look, just thought I'd tell you, seein' how you seem to favor him. I could ask around though, if you want."

"No, don't worry about it. I'll take a look; you just go have some fun. No sense getting all twisted if there isn't anything wrong with him."

Jake headed into the stable and made his way down the row of stalls, stopping at River's.

"Hey, baby, how're you doin'?" he asked the horse as he stepped in. River looked up at him very seriously and Jake laughed.

"Right then. Not talking to me. Got it. Just want to check you out, 'kay?" He moved carefully around the horse, sliding his hand gently up and down each leg. "So where do you hurt, baby? Not seeing anything…shift a bit would ya?" He coaxed the horse to move to the side and watched his hooves, not seeing anything. He moved to the other side and shifted him again, then saw the horse dance a little on his front left.

"What we got here, River? Let me see, c'mon." He examined River's leg and then guided the horse to lift it up so he could take a look at the hoof itself, and saw a nice chunk of rock wedged tight against the shoe. "Well, damn. That's gotta hurt." He stroked River's flank and moved off to the tack box to get a hoof pick, swearing under his breath.

He was working at the rock, talking quietly to River when he heard footsteps approaching. He didn't really think anything of it, there were people everywhere and if Elias had mentioned River to anyone, someone would have come up to lend a hand or at least see what was up.

"S'okay, baby, I got you. Gonna get rid of this for you and make you feel much better. That's it, you'll be fine in no time, River. I'm right here, baby..."

"You talk to your women that way, Jake? Must work just fine."

Jake glanced up at Missy and smiled politely. "Not often, no."

She smiled at him and held out her beer can. "Drink?"

"No, thanks." He dropped his head and went back to River's hoof, wondering how long he could drag it out before River had enough and kicked him out of the stall. Jake really didn't want to be anywhere with Missy, and hiding behind a horse was fine with him.

"You got nice words, Jake. Would work just fine on me."

Jake could hardly miss the offer and winced. Boss's daughter, half his age, half drunk, coming on to him. Yeah, this was good. He didn't say anything; if he opened his mouth the only thing that would have come out of it was the truth, and he didn't think she'd take well to being told that he thought that anything would work just fine on her.

"Women like to hear those pretty words, you know. Trust me. Talk like that to a girl and she'll be all over you."

Jake did glance up this time, and saw her flattening the front of her dress to her belly, showing off her breasts to him. She took another drink from the beer can and smiled at him.

"Your momma know you're drinking?"

She laughed. "Lord, no. Last time was more than enough for her—all right for anyone else, but not her precious little girl." Missy rolled her eyes. "Said that if I got drunk again this summer she'd have my hide—and she didn't say what she'd do with it."

Jake nodded and looked back down at River's hoof. "So that's why you're up here? Hiding from your parents?"

"Started that way," Missy said lightly. "Now I'm thinking the company is better here than at the dance."

Jake didn't know quite how to reply to that. "So, what happens if someone sees you drinking up here and decides to tell your momma or your daddy?" he asked, wanting to change the subject to something that didn't involve him.

He looked up in time to see Missy shrug. "I'll just say it's yours, no big deal. Not like I ain't been yelled at before, anyway."

Jake smiled then, a huge happy grin. "You do that, Missy." If there was one man on the planet who wouldn't believe that, it was her daddy, and he was pretty sure her mother wouldn't buy it either. She'd be in more trouble for the lie than the beer, he figured.

"So, you going to ask me to dance later, Jake?"

Laughter came from behind her and she spun around, almost falling over.

"Taggart? Dancing? Not likely, Missy." Tor grinned at her. "Taggart's good on horses, but the man has two left feet. Barely makes it from the kitchen to his room each night." Tor glanced at Jake over the top of Missy's head and Jake grinned at him, making a mental note to thank him later.

58

Missy leaned into Tor and Jake's grin grew.

"So, how 'bout you, then, Tor? Dance with me, hold me in your arms?"

Jake almost lost it, seeing the look on Tor's face—sort of confused and terrified at the same time.

"Ah, no, I don't think so. I'm too old for you, Missy. Why don't you go and find some nice young fella to have your fun with?" Tor tried to back away from her, but she followed him. Jake was still grinning, and Tor was trying to kill him with his eyes.

"You're not as old as Jake," she pointed out.

"Taggart's too old for you, too. Look, just take your beer and go find some hard stud to see to you, okay?"

She stiffened and stepped back from Tor. "It's not my beer. It's Jake's. And if you tell my folks any different—"

Tor's face went hard and he stood a little taller. "I'll not lie for you, little girl. You want to drink, that's fine, but you don't lie to me about it, you don't lie about Taggart about it, and you don't threaten me. Stop this shit now, or not only does your daddy find out about the beer, but he also hears about you catting after the hands, two at a time."

She paled. "He won't believe you."

"He'll believe me." Jake's voice was quiet, but she heard the truth in it and stared at him, her eyes wide.

"Why would you do that?"

"You think it's nice to have a girl throw herself at you like that? Then see her turn right in front of you and try to get into another man's pants as well? That kind of thing will get you a world of pain, Missy." He softened his voice and smiled gently at her. "Now look. Just take your drink, go down to the party, and try to have some fun. There's lots of fellas around, and I'm sure at least three quarters of them are panting to ask you to dance. Just go have a good time, Missy and don't fret about us. We're not going to say anything."

She looked at him, her face flushed and then nodded sharply. She turned and left the stable, moving fast and not even glancing at Tor.

When she was gone Jake sighed and leaned back on the wall, looking at Tor. "Did you just defend my virtue?" he asked with a grin.

"Fuck off." Tor looked hugely offended.

Jake laughed and put the hoof pick away.

"What's up with River?"

"Just a rock in his hoof." Jake smacked the horse's flank and then rubbed the spot he'd hit. "You'll be fine, won't you, baby? Yeah, I take good care of you."

Tor made a noise that sounded like it came from deep in his chest and Jake glanced at him. Tor just looked back, with a slight smile, but Jake saw his eyes grow dark and felt himself respond. "You going back down to the party?" he asked.

Tor shrugged. "Not much to do there, 'cept avoid Missy and drink. Think I'm done. You?"

Jake figured his effort at this year's dance was as good as it was going to get, and if Tor wasn't going back to the party then there wasn't much point to him sticking around, either. "Yeah, think I'm done." He came out of the stall and headed toward the stable door. He got about four steps before Tor grabbed his arm and he found himself pressed up against the back wall of an empty stall.

Tor's mouth was hungry and hot, and Jake grinned into the kiss. "Wanna go somewhere quiet?"

Tor nodded, his tongue still trying to get down Jake's throat, and his hands cupping Jake's ass and pulling him close. Jake could hear the music from outside, the sounds of a hundred and fifty people less than thirty feet away. It was dangerous and stupid and the hottest thing he'd experienced in—well, a day at least. He was thrusting his hips into Tor's, not able to stop himself. Tor was hard against him, lean body pressed tight, cock trying to rub right into his skin through the denim.

"Shit, Tor, ease off or I'm gonna come in my jeans."

Tor shifted, shoving his thigh between Jake's legs, and that was all it took for Jake to start on the way to release. He was humping Tor's thigh and tasting Tor in his mouth, feeling strong hands on his ass, listening to the noises Tor was making and the racket from outside; flying.

Then there was another sound, far too fucking close, boots on the hard pack of the stable, and a voice calling out for him. "Jake, you in here?"

Tor whimpered into Jake's mouth and threw himself away, leaning against the wall and trying to disappear into darkness of the corner.

Jake swore and wiped at his mouth, knowing he looked like he was just being fucked into the wall and tried to adjust himself, moving to the stall door. He looked out and saw the Boss, heading into the tack room.

Oh fuck.

Jake moved out of the stall as fast as he could, and back into River's, draping himself over the stall door to hide his rather stubborn erection.

"Right here," he called out, and the Boss came back out of the tack room and looked around, finally spotting him.

"How's the horse?" he asked, walking up.

"He's fine, sir. I don't want him out until tomorrow night, though. Whoever had him out today didn't check his hooves for rocks, and he's most likely a little tender." Jake shifted his weight, wishing his damned hard-on would just go away.

The Boss nodded and looked closely at him. "You okay, son? You look a little flushed."

Jake looked away and then back at the man. "Fine, really. I think I'm done with the party for this year, though. Gonna go out to the fields, I think, camp out."

The Boss smiled at him. "You do that. Take Lug, if you want. And don't rush back in the morning, there's going to be a lot of hung over cranky people around." The Boss turned to leave and then glanced back at him. He paused for

61

a second and came back. "How you doing these days, Jake? Really?"

Jake smiled. "I'm just fine, sir. Thanks for asking." It gave Jake a warm feeling in his stomach whenever the Boss did something like that. If Jake had family at all, it was this man.

They said good night and then the man was leaving, and Jake collapsed against the stall door, the tension in his body finally getting to him.

"Oh hell, that was close," he said as Tor came out of the other stall, looking pretty fucking relaxed. Jake glared at him. "Bastard. Least you were quiet about it."

Tor just grinned and looked pleased with himself.

Jake went to the tack room and got Lug's saddle. "You coming out with me?"

"Fuck, yes, don't be an idiot. You saddle him, I'll go get some stuff from the bunkhouse. Back in five minutes." Tor took off and Jake just grinned, heading for Lug's stall.

When Tor got back, Lug was ready to go and they started stowing the mountain of stuff Tor had brought into the saddlebags. Blankets, feed, apples, water. Then Tor started handing him the rest: bread, cheese, three bottles of apple juice, bag of cookies, condoms, lube, another blanket, and something wrapped in foil.

Jake raised his eyebrow and Tor said, "Apple pie, of course."

They led Lug out the back of the stable and Jake said, "Wait, forgot to sign him out. Hold on."

They had a system for the horses, so if anyone went looking they would know where the animal was. It was just a small chalkboard in each stall, and when a horse was taken out the hand either wrote "field", if the horse was out to pasture, or just the hand's initials if they were out for a ride.

Jake went into the stall and marked a "T" on the board. That was easy—Taggart/Tornado. No problem.

When he went back out Tor was already mounted, so he grabbed the back of the saddle and swung up behind him. "Where we going?"

"Know a spot. Won't take long."

They rode for about twenty minutes, Jake feeling slightly odd being behind Tor and not holding the reins. He couldn't remember the last time he'd ridden with someone else, and it took a bit of getting used to. They worked into a rhythm though, and Jake started to get bored, not knowing where they were headed and not having to pay attention to the land or guiding the horse.

He wrapped one arm around Tor's waist and started unbuttoning Tor's shirt with the other hand.

"Hey. What do you think you're doing?" Tor asked, a smile in his voice.

"Getting started."

"'Kay. Just checking."

They rode for another ten minutes or so in silence, finally stopping in a field of sweet grass. They dismounted, spreading out the blankets, and then settled Lug in with his feed.

It was different this time, Jake knew. Before, they had pretty much just run from people so they could get off, hunger and need and lust driving them. That was there this time too, but they weren't rushed, they weren't desperate to be naked and writhing and touching. It may have been overload from the day before, or simply the growing easiness of being in each other's company.

Jake sat down on the blanket and pulled off his boots, Tor sitting beside him, stripping off his shirt. Jake looked around them and smiled. "Pretty here."

Tor glanced at him as he pulled off his boots. "You've never been here?"

"'Course I have, just not at night. It's…nice."

Tor nodded and lay back on the blanket, one arm crooked behind his head, looking up at the sky.

As Jake took off his shirt, Tor asked, "You ever think about leaving here? I mean the ranch, not the country. Buy yourself some land of your own?"

"Nope." Jake lay down next to him and said, "Like my work. Like the ranch. I don't want the headaches of running a spread, don't need the pressure. Just want to do what I'm doing."

Tor looked at him and nodded. "Yeah, I get that."

"Besides," Jake went on, "it's not like I'll ever have to worry about supporting a wife and kids."

Tor chuckled. "Yeah, I get that, too." Then he sobered and said, "She's gonna figure it out, you know."

"What? Who?"

"Missy. She's either just gonna decide we're queer out of spite for tonight or she's actually going to think and get it right. I mean, hell, Taggart, you've been here for thirteen fucking years. How many women you brought around?"

Jake nodded slowly. He knew Tor was right, and that if Missy wanted to, she could start all kinds of shit just by talking to the right people.

He rolled over and looked at Tor, staring into those brown eyes. "What'll that mean for you?"

Tor shrugged. "Couple bar fights, maybe a tussle with some of the hands. Nothing I haven't gone through before. You?"

"Not much. Boss knows, has since I got here. Couple of the others know, figured it out on their own. Nobody says anything, never had a real problem."

Tor nodded again and looked at the sky. "Might be different if she figures that we're…" He stopped and gestured with his arm.

Jake didn't know what to call what they were either, so he let it slide and just lay on the blanket, looking at Tor. "Hey."

Tor turned his head to look at him and Jake leaned over, kissing him softly. He brushed his lips on Tor's, then pressed in a little, teasing his lower lip and sucking gently.

Tor brought a hand up to the back of Jake's neck, holding him there, deepening the kiss. Jake relaxed into it, letting Tor's tongue slide into his mouth, tasting him.

He moved closer on the blanket and wrapped an arm around Tor's waist, just holding him. They kissed like that for a few minutes before Jake pulled away. "Better?"

Tor grinned at him. "Yeah. But now I'm worked up again."

Jake laughed, and felt his cock jump, going from half-mast to full in about three seconds. "You're easy."

Tor leered at him, eyes focused on Jake's crotch. "So are you. Strip 'em off, Taggart."

They both peeled off their jeans and stretched out on the blanket, tangling their legs together as they started to rock. Jake's mouth was hungry now, sliding over Tor's collarbone and neck, leaving a trail of open mouthed kisses and licks.

Tor started moaning and pushing against him with his hips, hands on Jake's back, holding him tightly. "Want you. Want you inside of me, Taggart."

Jake sucked on the soft skin just below Tor's ear, then whispered, "I can do that."

They separated, Jake reaching for a condom and the lube, Tor lying on his back, letting his thighs fall apart. When Jake moved between his legs Tor pushed himself up on his elbows and they kissed again, long and slow.

Jake felt like he was melting.

Still kissing Tor, Jake slicked his fingers and slid one in, teasing the soft skin around Tor's entrance with the others. He smiled when Tor moaned into his mouth and slid two more in at once, sinking into the warmth of that body and stroking gently, loving the way Tor moved with his hand.

Tor's kiss was getting hotter, tongue dancing now, instead of just stroking, so Jake eased his fingers out and rolled the condom on. He moved closer to Tor and entered him with one long, slow thrust, burying himself in the soft, tight heat.

"Oh yes," Tor breathed into his mouth.

"Feel so good," Jake sighed as he started to move, slowly at first, then a little faster, a little deeper.

Tor broke off the kiss, his head falling back. "Jake…God, what you do to me. Feel so good."

Jake closed his eyes and moaned, moving his hips faster and moving a hand to Tor's shaft, stroking him in time with their movements.

"Tor…Tor, look at me."

Tor opened his eyes and lifted his head. Jake smiled at Tor and winked, then dipped his head to kiss him. As he bent over he changed the angle of his thrust slightly and felt Tor shudder. He thrust again and again, hitting the same spot, feeling Tor lose his rhythm and pick it back up again, before he lost it for good and just rode it out as Jake took him over the edge.

"God, yes," Jake said, feeling Tor come in his hand, ass clamping hard around his cock. "Yes, so good."

Jake came deep in Tor and stayed there, hips rocking nice and slow as they came down. When he started to soften he grasped the rubber and eased out, kissing Tor and sighing softly. He got himself cleaned up and lay down on the blanket, drawing Tor into his arms and kissing Tor's face lightly.

They curled around each other, lying quiet and still. Jake listened to the insects and the frogs, feeling peaceful and warm, letting random thoughts wander in his mind as his hand stroked Tor's side and down his thigh.

He wasn't sure what the hell was going on with him and Tor, but he damn well knew that they were past the "getting off together and that's all" stuff. Tor could still piss him off by times, but that was okay. Wouldn't be Tor if he didn't.

Tor shifted a little and smiled at him. "Nice night to be out."

Jake nodded. "Love this piece of land. Have since I got here."

Tor rolled onto his back and stretched. "How old were you then? Twenty-two?"

Jake nodded, and looked at the sky. Lots of stars, and the quarter moon was low and bright.

"What did you do before you got here?" Tor asked.

Jake paused. So fucking easy to say what he always did, leave it open ended and move on. But it was Tor asking and even if they were past the just fucking stage, Jake wasn't sure if the truth was a good idea. He glanced at Tor and then watched the sky again, drawing in a deep breath.

"Time," he said the word as a sigh.

Tor didn't freeze so much as just...stop. He was perfectly still, not even breathing. Jake waited.

"Time. Jesus." Tor didn't move and Jake didn't say anything.

Then Tor was on top of him, kissing him hard before sliding off and wrapping strong arms around him, nuzzling at his neck.

"Shit, you were just a kid," he said into Jake's shoulder.

Jake nodded. "Just a kid. With a messed up life and making all the worst mistakes." Then he started to shake.

"Shhh...I'm here, I've got you...shhh." Tor's arms were strong around him, his voice low, breath soft and warm on his skin. Jake felt himself calm, growing still and Tor was still there, still holding onto him, making soothing noises.

When they were quiet and still again, Tor kissed his shoulder. "Didn't have to tell me."

"Yeah. I did."

They lay on the blanket for a couple of minutes and Jake waited for Tor to ask what Jake had done. He was pretty sure that Tor would happily just let it go and not bring the subject up again, but there were sometimes things that needed to be said. A man could go to jail for a lot of things.

"How long?" Tor asked, not looking at Jake.

Jake swore to himself. That wasn't the question he had anticipated, and one that could only bring more questions. Hard ones.

"Five years of an eight to twelve sentence."

Tor pulled away from him a little, and now he did meet his eye. "That's a long time, Taggart." Not Jake.

Jake nodded slowly, feeling himself close up inside. Damn.

"That makes you seventeen when you went in. Transferred to adult court."

"Yeah."

Tor sat up, still looking at him. "Long sentence. This wasn't pissy little shit that kids pull, was it?"

Jake rolled onto his stomach. "No. Wasn't." He waited a heartbeat and then said, "Fuck, Tor, just let me tell you what I did." Having Tor sitting there running through crimes in his head, making his eyes distant, was starting to make a knot in Jake's belly.

Tor shook his head and looked away. When he looked back his eyes were softer again and he leaned forward, dropping a kiss on Jake's back.

"Tell me," he murmured.

"Armed robbery is what they finally settled on, and threatening bodily harm. Was drunk, had been for days. Running wild, trying to live outside my skin and needed money, had a boot knife." Jake was staring at the blanket, the words feeling like sand in his throat. "Took out a convenience store, threatened the girl working there with the knife. Scared the crap out of her. Got picked up the next morning, still drunk."

Tor lay back on the blanket, tilting his head to look at him. "Long sentence for that, Jake."

"Yeah. My lawyer said that the girl was pregnant. She lost the baby. They weren't sure what they were going to do with me until they got my psych results. Doctor said I needed help to get out the bottle and had potential. But the only way they could keep me in the program was to put me away for more than two years. So they charged me with intent to harm and told me to plead guilty."

Tor nodded slowly.

"When the judge saw the charges and the guilty plea he called me a born trouble maker who had most likely pulled this kind of stuff before and not been caught. Said he couldn't sentence me for anything else I had done, but by Christ he could for what I'd been caught doing. Gave me the maximum, and that was it.

"Did the time, did the detox and the other programs, school and shit like 'life skills', did everything they said. Got out and my parole officer brought me up here, asked the Boss to take me on as day labor. And here I am."

Jake lay his head down on the blanket and tried to breathe. Tor was still beside him, and Jake felt like he was floating somewhere, caught between currents. Nothing he could do now but wait for Tor to decide.

He let his eyes close and listened to the frogs. He may have fallen asleep, but he doubted it, he was too keyed up now, too tense to just drift off. A voice in the back of his mind was cussing him out for saying anything, but his gut was telling him that he'd done the right thing. A man can't make good choices without all the information. He may not like what Tor decided was best for himself, but he'd be able to shave in the morning without fear of his reflection.

Finally, Tor moved, a strong hand on his back, soft mouth at his ear.

"Idiot." Then Tor was kissing him, his body hard and insistent and promising that things were going to be all right.

They slept hard, tangled together under their blanket, and in the morning they got cleaned up a little better before they got ready to go back to the ranch. Jake felt good. So good that it wasn't until they rode into sight of the ranch that he realized they were about to out themselves. Tor had the same thought, apparently, as he reined Lug in and turned in the saddle.

"Not sure I'm ready for this part," he said.

Jake shook his head. "Know I'm not. Not with over a hundred people there. You walking in or am I?"

Tor grinned and kissed him on the mouth, fast. "I am. Boss told you to take Lug."

They dismounted and Tor got a blanket out of the saddlebag, along with a bottle of juice. "See you later on, Taggart."

Jake just grinned at him and rode toward the stables.

Six

The first time Jake got called to the Boss's office that week was two hours after he rode in from spending the night of the dance camping out with Tor. He was in River's stall, checking out the horse's sore hoof when Elias came up and said, "Boss wants you in the main house, now. If not sooner."

Jake glanced at him and raised an eyebrow. "What's up?"

"Hell if I know, I just happened to be on the porch when the window flew open and he hollered for someone to find you. If I were you, I'd hustle. He's not in a great mood."

Jake walked to the house, wondering what was going on. He'd only been called into the house like this a few times, and each time it had been something to do with one of the other hands. He walked through the front door, stood outside the Boss's office and rapped on the doorframe, waiting until beckoned to enter.

Tor was standing at the window, looking out, but Jake saw the silent acknowledgement of his presence in the way Tor's shoulders loosened a little even though the rest of his posture remained ridged, hands clenched at his sides.

The Boss was sitting on a couch, leaning forward to look at Missy, who was curled up in the armchair, looking upset. She glanced up at Jake and gave him a small smile, but Jake could see smug triumph in her eyes.

He felt a hard knot start in his stomach, and glanced at Tor again. He hadn't turned from the window, still wasn't looking at Jake.

A sound from behind him made Jake turn. The Boss's wife was standing against the wall, glaring at Tor. Jake figured if looks could injure then Tor would need an ambulance right about then.

"Jake, maybe you can clear something up for us," the Boss said.

"I'll try, sir," Jake said, his confusion coming through in his voice.

"Seems Missy here had a bit too much fun last night—"

He was interrupted by a snort from his wife, who had turned her glare to her daughter.

"—and I wanted to know where she got the beer—not that it was hard to find around here last night. I was more concerned about the fact that she didn't actually make it into the house last night and when she did turn up she was…well, not fit to receive company. Now, she's telling me one thing, and Tor's telling me another. Trouble is, I can't find anyone who can say where either of them were last night."

Jake felt the knot in his gut tighten and he looked at Tor's back, hoping for some kind of hint. Tor didn't move a muscle.

"Missy says she was in the loft drinking with Tor most of the night. Tor says he wasn't there. Now, I'd just let it drop, but—"

"But if he's been getting my daughter, a child more than ten years younger than him, drunk, and doing God only knows what, I want it dealt with." Yeah, Missy's momma was pissed.

The Boss held up a hand. "Now, let's not get like this. Point is, Jake, no one I've asked saw either of them all night. Missy says one thing, Tor says another. I won't be doing anything to anyone without proof. 'Cept you, Missy, I got the proof you were drunk after you were told to mind your behavior, and I'm fairly sure that the rest of your clothing will turn up at some point. We're just so proud of you."

The glare he gave her surprised Jake; he'd been sure that Missy had her daddy wrapped around her littlest finger. Missy seemed to shrink a little under the weight of it. Jake looked at Tor's back again and saw him clenching his fists.

The Boss turned his eyes to Jake. "Tor says you know where he went last night."

Jake stood very still and looked the Boss in the eye, not seeing anything there but the man who'd taken him in, the man who knew all about him. He wasn't accusing or searching, he was just…asking.

"Tor?" Jake asked, looking at the Boss.

When Tor spoke his voice was low and even. "Just tell him the truth, Taggart."

Jake nodded sharply and looked at Missy. "Tor was out in the fields with me last night."

Missy snorted. "Yeah, right."

As soon as the words left her mouth she looked stricken. Her mother rounded on her and Jake tried to make himself small in the wake of the woman's anger. She didn't even say anything, just stood in front of Missy and stared at her.

Finally the Boss said, "Missy, apologize to Tornado. And you will tell your mother where you were last night."

But Missy wasn't the sort to cave that easily. "What, you're just going to believe him? Jake says he was out in the field and you say, oh, okay?"

Tor moved. He spun from the window and stalked across the floor to her chair and stood in front of them all. "What do you want, Missy? You want to see the goddamn condom wrappers? I was with Jake last night, rode out on Lug."

There was a second of absolute silence and then several things happened at once. Missy's jaw dropped open. Her mother gasped and put a hand to her mouth. Jake flushed and thought about dying, and decided against it. Tor moved back to stand next to Jake. The Boss let a slow smile cross his face as he looked at them.

Everything was still for a moment and then the Boss looked at Missy.

"Yes, I think I believe them. Now we have a new problem, young lady. You just outed a man who didn't want to be outed. I think you had best keep it to yourself, and seeing as how you seem to have it in for the man, I'm not sure if you will."

Tor made a noise in his chest and everyone looked at him. "Don't care. She can tell who she likes. I can handle it, but I think it might be a good idea to restock the first aid kits. Gonna be fist fights."

"Not on my land there won't be." The man's voice was hard. "See Missy? That's what these men have to deal with. Threats of violence, and sneaking away. You got anything to say?"

Missy looked at Jake and Tor, her eyes wide. "I didn't…I didn't know. I thought you were just being mean."

They didn't say anything. Jake glanced at Tor and saw pain in his eyes. Fuck.

Finally they were allowed to leave, Missy swearing she wouldn't tell anyone and that she would never lie about anything so stupid again. They didn't speak on the way to the bunkhouse and when they got there, Tor went to his room and closed the door.

Seven

The first fight happened two days after the party, and if it had to be blamed on anyone, Jake figured it was ultimately himself.

The Boss had asked just about damn near everyone on the ranch if they had seen Missy or Tor during the dance and most had figured Tor had been a dog and would soon be hitting the road for fraternizing. Then nothing happened; Tor was still there and Missy was walking around for two days in a sulk.

So people talked. One of the regular hands said that Tor had been off on Lug, had signed him out with a "T". Someone else said no, Taggart had been on Lug, Boss had said so. A bunch of them put two and two together and came up with eight, figuring that the bunkhouse was the new Sodom.

Which made Kip pretty pissed. Elias wasn't too happy, either.

The first Jake knew about it was when he went into the stable to check River's tack box for a missing harness. Tor was sitting on the floor, leaning up against a stall door and trying to stop the blood flowing from a cut under his eye. Elias was standing close by, sporting a blackening eye, and Kip's nose looked smashed. The two hands who'd started it all were sitting in the stall, looking pretty bad.

Jake froze. "What the fuck happened?" he asked the group in general.

No one replied, so he went over to Kip and took a look at his nose. "Yep, busted." He moved to Elias, who waved him away and Tor didn't even look at him. Best not to even ask him how he was.

Jake opened the stall door and looked down on the two men he'd worked with for the last three years. "Can you walk up to the house okay?"

"Get the fuck away from me, you cocksucking freak."

Jake just nodded his head. "Right. I'll just bring the Boss here, then." He turned and went to the house, stopping on the way to throw up from anxiety and a wash of dark memories he chose not to dwell on.

The Boss fired the hands without any hesitation, and he and Jake patched up the other three, though Tor made sure that Jake didn't even get near him.

Jake hated what he saw in Tor's eyes. Misery and dread.

Kip decided that he was going to spend the night at Beth's and took off as soon as his nose was set. Tor had disappeared as soon as he'd cleaned out the cut on his face, and Elias followed Jake back to the bunkhouse.

They sat at the kitchen table, Jake with his juice and Elias with a can of beer.

"Is it true?" Elias finally asked.

"Which version? 'Cause the one where I fucked him over the saddle and called him a stallion doesn't even bear thinking about."

"Fuck, Jake…"

Jake sighed. "Look, think about it. I've been here longer than you, you ever see me date a girl? Hell, yes, I'm gay. Tor's been here for more than two and a half years, you ever seen him with a girl? What do you think?"

Elias just nodded and looked embarrassed. "So, you two…together?"

Jake met his eye and said, "He hasn't said more than three words to me since yesterday, so I think I'll pass on answering that."

"But you were…the other night…"

"That's really not any of your business." And how Jake hated to say it. Elias was a friend, someone who wasn't actively trying to make his life hell. He'd gotten into a fight along side Tor, even if it was mostly to defend himself from disgusting accusations. But Jake had no clue what was going on with himself and Tor anymore, and didn't really want to talk about whether or not they were sleeping together.

Elias just nodded, and they sat in silence for a bit. Jake felt like he was going to crawl out of his skin after a while, and went out to sit on the porch of the main house.

It was a quiet evening, not many people about now that the heavy labor of hay and auctions was done. Pretty soon Jake was more or less alone and he watched evening come in, listening to the crickets and the frogs, watching the stars come out.

He didn't hear Tor approach until he was on the porch, and didn't say anything until Tor sat down next to him.

"How's the cut?"

"It's nothing."

Jake nodded and went back to watching the stars. "You done thinking?"

Tor nodded. "Yeah. Fucking sucks, you know?"

"Yep."

"Been thinking about what you were telling me the other night." Tor was staring at him, and Jake turned to look at him.

"Yeah?" So, maybe being in prison years ago did matter, and having this shit on top was just too fucking much. Jake felt a little numb, but met Tor's eye. "What about it? More questions?"

Tor shook his head. "No, not like that. Just...it took a fuck of a lot for you to tell me."

Jake nodded, not sure where this was going.

"And I was thinking that maybe it would be okay to tell you some stuff. About why I've been twisted since Missy pulled her stunt, why I was so fucking ready to fight."

Jake looked at Tor then turned his gaze to the sky. "Don't have to tell me anything you don't want to, Tor. Not some game of trading secrets." He looked at Tor again and hoped he was doing this right. "But if you want to tell me something, I'm going to listen. Just don't want you to—"

"Fuck, Taggart, I'm not saying I want to have a goddamn heart-to-heart. I'm saying that if this is gonna work between us then you can know some stuff about me that others don't. Stuff I want you to know."

Jake let a smile ghost across his face. "Yeah. Okay. Let's go home and see if Elias runs from any room we happen to be in together."

Tor snorted. "Living in that house is gonna be fucking insane after today. Kip...he's a good kid, but I don't know if I can take him staring at me all the time."

They started walking to the bunkhouse. "Just ignore it. He'll stop after a while, when he sees we're not going to try to seduce him. Or give him a free show."

Tor laughed. "You don't want to make out in front of the TV on Saturday nights? I'm hurt."

Jake chuckled and smacked him on the head. "Idiot."

When they went into the bunkhouse Elias was in the living room watching TV. He looked up and nodded to them, his eyes curious, but he didn't say anything other than to ask Tor how his cut was feeling.

"Not bad. Had worse," Tor said as he settled on the couch.

Elias nodded, then shook his head. "Damn idiots."

Jake sat in the easy chair and the three of them watched TV for a few minutes in silence. Jake glanced up when Tor got up and left the room, and flat out laughed when he came back carrying the box of Lego Jake had given him.

Tor sat on the floor and dumped the box out, then started sorting the pieces by size.

"What the hell are you doing?" Elias asked.

"Relaxing."

Jake watched Tor for a while, thinking that you could tell a lot about a person by the way they played with Lego. Tor had sorted all the pieces by color and size before he even glanced at the instructions, and when he started assembling the lunar module, he did it exactly by the directions, step-by-step. After he was done he held it up to Jake and Elias for approval. When they acknowledged the masterpiece he took it apart and put the pieces back in the box.

Tor picked up the box and looked at Jake. Then he shook his head and said, "Damn," spilling the contents out once more. This time he paid no attention to color at all, snapping the little bricks together rapidly, going only by the shape of the pieces.

He worked at it for a few minutes, not looking up at the other two, who by now had abandoned the TV entirely and were watching avidly.

Tor held up a brick to Jake and said, "Need more of these, man."

Jake got up and went into his room, grabbing one of the larger sets off his shelf. By the time he got back to the living room Elias was sitting on the floor helping Tor build. He handed the new set over and Tor dumped it out on the floor, tossing the directions back in the box with a grin.

Jake sat in the chair and watched the two men play with a smile. Over the next hour they fitted pieces together and rearranged things to their liking, saying little to each other but grinning lots. By the time they finished they had used two more sets and had built the weirdest looking castle Jake had ever seen, using Lego from two space-themed sets, one fantasy set and a set based on a front-end loader.

They were exceedingly pleased with it. They were less pleased with Jake's strict instructions that every piece had to find its way into the correct box when they were done.

Jake finally gave his approval to the clean up and Elias stood up, wincing as he stretched.

"Sore?"

"Yeah, pulled a muscle in my shoulder trying to kick those damn bastards' asses."

Jake thought for a brief moment then cautiously said, "You gonna freak if I offered to put some of that backrub stuff on it for you?"

Elias snorted. "I'm pretty sure you're not lusting after my fine bod, Jake. You want to help, I've no objection."

Jake grinned. "Yeah, your body's safe from me."

He got the tube of ointment and Elias took off his shirt, letting Jake rub the stuff in. It smelled vaguely like toothpaste and Jake worked the knot out of Elias' shoulders while the other man groaned in appreciation.

"Thanks, Jake. Feels better," Elias said. "I'm gonna go take a shower and crash. See ya both in the mornin'."

"G'night, Elias," Tor said. "And thanks. For earlier."

Elias grinned. "Haven't been in a fight for years. Nice to know that I still have what it takes."

"Yeah, your black eye makes you look tough," Tor said. "Real dangerous."

"Fuck off," Elias tossed over his shoulder as he left with a cheery wave.

Jake looked at Tor, still holding the tube. "How about you? Strain anything?"

Tor grinned, nice and slow. "Wouldn't say no to a backrub." He stood up and peeled off his T-shirt and Jake swore.

"Goddamn. That has to hurt." Tor's left side was sporting a huge bruise, from just under his ribs to down below the waistband of his jeans. "Ribs okay?"

Tor shrugged. "They don't seem tender. But yeah, the bruising is a bitch. Jon kicked me, nice and hard. Couple of times."

"Fuck. God, Tor, it looks nasty. I think we've got something for bruises. Let me go look, I'll be right back." He turned to get the first aid supplies.

"Uh, if I'm going to be stripping down so you can put shit on the bruise I'm going to my room. Don't fancy getting doctored in the living room."

Jake nodded. "Sure, whatever. I'll meet you there. Be right back."

When he knocked at Tor's door a few minutes later it swung open and he went in to find Tor, naked and lying on his belly on the bed. Tor's back had more bruises, though none as big as the one on his side. Jake rubbed arnica cream into the dark patches and told Tor to roll over.

"Let me take care of this big one, then you can get some sleep," he said.

Tor nodded his head and rolled over.

"Holy fuck."

The bruise went down past Tor's hipbone, around to the front of his groin and down the inside of his thigh, in assorted shades of purple and black. Jake felt ill. Standing out, amid the riot of dark colors was a scar, a thin white line from the tip of his hipbone, down on a diagonal following his pelvis. It looked like someone had tried to cut his cock off.

Tor didn't say anything, just studied the bruise with disinterest.

Jake put arnica cream on his fingers and started to smooth it into the discolored tissue. "I'm surprised you can walk."

"So'm I, now that I see it. Felt bad, but I didn't think it would look like this. Fucking jerk had cowboy boots on. Tried his best to get my balls."

Jake traced the scar with a fingertip. "And this?"

"One of those things I could tell you about," Tor said, his voice quiet.

Jake nodded and gently rubbed more cream into the bruise. When he was sure that all of the dark patches had been treated, he put the top back on the tube and stripped, climbing onto the bed with Tor. He lay behind Tor, pulling the man to his chest, the way Tor had held him in the field.

For a long time they didn't speak, then Tor said, "Remember what you said about trying to live outside your skin? Well, I had a fucking death wish. I was running, any place I could get to, for about a year and a half. Was twenty-one, and just couldn't…well, I couldn't stay. So I took off for Texas, hit New Mexico for a while, Arizona. Wound up in Mexico.

"I was in this pissy little town, hanging out in the only bar, doing nothing but sitting and drinking for about a week. Days I would be out in the sun, walking, or sitting or whatever. Just not…thinking. Nights I'd sit in the bar, drink beer and watch people."

Jake nodded and rubbed his hand absently over Tor's stomach.

"Was a kid there, nice looking boy, about eighteen or so. He caught my eye one night and gave me the once over, cruising through the language barrier, you know? And I've got this 'fuck, whatever' attitude, so I just nod my head and follow him out."

Tor stopped talking and swallowed hard. Jake just stroked his stomach again, and kissed his shoulder.

"Went out behind the bar, real fucking romantic alley. He's going down on me, sucking me off nice and slow, and then there's six guys on us, screaming and hitting and fucking losing it. Kid got hit in the head and one guy picks him up and takes off. Turns out it was his brother, and they were out for my blood. Saw the kid checking me out the day before and decided that I was the devil. Had a knife and fucking near killed me, trying to cut off my balls."

"Jesus Christ."

"Yeah. I was screaming bloody murder, literally, and a bunch of people came out to see what was going on. They ran off and I fucking got the hell out of there as soon as I could stop the bleeding. Not sticking around in some Mexican backwater hospital. Went to my sister's place in Texas. Lived on penicillin for a while, hoping the cut wouldn't get infected. Figured that my death wish was gone when I realized I didn't want to die like that. My mom—she just about killed me, anyway. Her heart's not so good and she says I scared about four years out of her."

Jake kissed his shoulder again. "What were you running from?"

Tor sighed and shifted a bit, moving his hand to hold Jake's. "A ghost." He raised Jake's hand to his mouth and kissed his fingers. "So when those jerk-offs went after us this afternoon, I couldn't just back away. Fucking hate gay bashers. Won't let it happen again."

Jake nodded. "Yeah. Can see that."

They lay quietly for a long time, then drifted off to sleep. Jake woke up at the sound of Elias' alarm and eased out of the bed, trying not to wake Tor. He bent and kissed the man's forehead before going to his own room.

Eight

The second time Jake was called into the office that week was the day after the fight, and it was only a routine conversation. The hands had been eating lunch on the porch and the rest had just taken off to clean up when the Boss called him into the house and handed him a stack of brown envelopes. "Can you take these to the bunkhouse on your way?"

"Sure, sir. Not a problem." As he walked he flipped through the stack looking for his. Every day when the mail came in from the post office the Boss sorted it into envelopes for each hand. The Boss firmly believed in a man's right to privacy, to the extent that he didn't think anyone needed to see what the hands got in the mail. If he could have, he would have had the postmaster separate if for him.

Jake had always thought that kind of funny, seeing as how if there were ever more than four full time hands living on the ranch, two had to share a room. However, mail was sacred to the Boss, so…brown envelopes.

Jake went into the house and put the other three envelopes on the kitchen table, taking his into his room. Seed catalogue and the results from the physical all the hands had been through a few weeks back for the ranch's insurance. It said exactly what he thought it would. He was a healthy male of thirty-five, with no illnesses, heart problems, viruses or anything else. He tossed the letter on his nightstand and went back to work.

Late in the afternoon he was just heading into the hay barn when he heard someone coming up behind him, fast. He turned his head in time to see Tor stride past him.

"Tor—"

Tor didn't stop, but he did turn around and grin, walking backwards. Then he stopped and whacked Jake on the chest with an envelope, pushing it into his hands, and ran into the barn.

Jake knew what it was before he opened it. Tor's physical results, stating that he was clean and healthy. It was also an invitation, if Tor's grin was anything to go by. He stood in the yard reading the letter, momentarily bothered by the fact that the letter was addressed to someone named Mark Flynn. He never figured he'd be fucking a guy whose real name he didn't even know.

Jake stuffed the envelope in his pocket and went into the barn, looking for Tor and not finding him. "Where are you?" he called out.

"Here. C'mon up and see me." Tor's voice came from the back of the loft and Jake headed up the ladder, knowing he was going to find a naked and horny man waiting for him.

He moved to the back of the loft with a bit of struggle; the place was full of bales, he couldn't figure out how Tor had managed to find a spot that wasn't right out in the open.

He hadn't.

Tor was leaning up against a pile of bales, naked and hard, stroking his cock and grinning like an idiot.

Jake shook his head and stripped off his T-shirt, then pressed up against Tor, kissing him hard. "Nice news."

"Yeah. Saw yours…went looking for it. Get naked, want to taste you."

Jake didn't wait for a second invitation, stripping down fast, sighing when his erection was free of his jeans. He was barely naked when Tor was on him, pushing him onto his back and swallowing his cock.

"Oh, God yes!"

They were sprawled out on the hard bales, lying on their clothes, shirts and jeans saving their backs from the prickly hay. Jake moaned as Tor licked at the head of his prick, tongue dancing as it teased over him. He shifted around, turning until he was lying underneath Tor and able to return the favor, licking at Tor's shaft like a starving man at a banquet.

Tor was making needy sounds deep in his throat as Jake took him in, the sounds traveling up his spine and making him moan around Tor. Jake felt like he was drowning in the sensation, feeling Tor's mouth on him, sucking him hard and long, sliding up and down in deep pulls. Tor's tongue rasped on his cock, and the wet heat of the man's mouth was so fucking good.

He sucked at the head of Tor's cock, playing at the slit with the tip of his tongue and Tor's noises got louder and even more needy and hungry. When Jake opened up and sucked him in, Tor bucked and started moving, fucking his mouth.

Jake rolled Tor's balls with his fingers and opened his throat as much as he could, Tor's need making him ready and willing to do anything to bring Tor over. Tor was licking at his cock with every movement, taking him in deep and playing with his balls. Jake groaned and grabbed Tor's hips, pulling Tor into his mouth as he swallowed around Tor's cock, his own hips thrusting up into Tor's hot mouth.

Tor began to shudder and Jake felt himself getting close, the taste of Tor's cock, the smell of his sweat and musk taking him higher than ever before, and knowing that there wasn't any need to stop, no need to lose that sweet mouth around him, drove him over. With a strangled cry around Tor's prick Jake came, shooting deep into Tor's mouth, feeling Tor swallow it all.

Jake was still coming when Tor thrust down into his mouth once more before freezing, then jerking hard as Jake tasted hot come in his mouth, in his throat. He swallowed, not letting Tor stop moving, his hands still guiding Tor in and out as he sucked Tor dry.

Jake kept sucking and licking, shuddering with his own orgasm as Tor licked at him, cleaning him off. Jake calmed, felt himself relax, but he kept working Tor, teasing him, not letting his cock soften.

Tor released his prick with a kiss and moaned, moving his hips and sliding in and out of Jake's mouth. They twisted again, so Jake was on top, teasing Tor with his mouth and hands. Jake licked at Tor like he was an ice cream on a hot day, then moved down drawing one of Tor's balls into his mouth, sucking gently.

"Oh yeah, Jake. Feels so good, tastes so good."

Jake hummed a little, loving listening to Tor. He licked along Tor's scar, sucking gently, trying not to make the bruise from his beating worse, but still acknowledging the scar and the more recent pain. Tor moaned softly.

"Yes, please, Jake, want you. Want to be in you."

Jake felt his cock twitch is response, the thought of that lovely cock in him without a goddamn barrier. He kissed his way up to Tor's mouth and plunged his tongue in, fucking Tor's mouth. Tor was reaching around him, searching through clothes but not letting his mouth go, his hips pushing his cock into Jake's. Jake felt himself start to get hard again and rubbed up against him, friction doing its job on them both.

Tor finally found what he was looking for and Jake thanked everyone he could think of that it was lube. With a groan of pure lust Tor flipped him over and draped him over a hay bale, ass high.

"God, you are so fucking hot, Jake. So sexy. Love your ass, so fucking tight." Tor slid two slick fingers into Jake and scissored them, moving in and out only a few times before leaving him empty again.

"Tor, God, Tor, need you."

"Right here," Tor said in his ear as Tor slid his cock into Jake.

They both groaned as Tor pushed in deep.

"Oh fuck, Jake. So good."

"Oh God. Oh God, just…just stay. No, move. Oh fuck…"

Tor laughed and started moving, sliding out real slow before going deep again. They moved together, Jake's hips moving back to take him in, picking up speed.

"You look so hot, laid out like this. Want to fuck you over and over."

"No objection. Oh God! Right there!"

Tor chuckled and changed his angle to hit Jake's prostate on every thrust, speeding up as he did. "Know what I'm gonna do, Jake? I'm gonna make you fucking scream. Maybe not right now, but I'm gonna have you so hot for me that you'll beg me to do this. And then I'll fuck you through the wall."

"Christ Tor, gonna come if you keep talking." Jake groaned again as Tor's cock hit his sweet spot.

"Know what I want to do to you, Jake? I want to tie you up. Want you spread out and begging for me, not able to move. What do you think, rope or one of the leather harnesses?"

"Oh God, yes!" Jake screamed and came, shooting hard and long. Tor hadn't even touched his cock.

Tor cried out as Jake spasmed around him and Jake felt Tor's warmth flood him, felt Tor's cock throb and pulse.

They lay draped over the bale until Tor got his breath back, then Jake felt Tor slide out of his body and he whimpered at the loss. Tor pulled him down onto his lap and kissed Jake, nice and slow, mouth hot and wet.

"Fucking amazing."

"Yeah. Christ… You really want to tie me up?"

Tor grinned at him, eyes dark and wicked, making Jake shiver.

Nine

The third time Jake was called to the office was at the end of the week and he went into the house wondering what the hell was going on now. He hadn't spent so much time in there since he'd first been on the ranch and the Boss was trying to find out exactly what his problem was.

When he went in there were two men with the Boss. New hands, to replace the ones who had been fired for attacking Tor.

"Jake, this is Tommy and Kevin. They're starting in the morning. This is Jake Taggart, my foreman."

Jake offered his hand and the one named Tommy said hello.

Kevin grinned and said, "Call me Hound. Everyone does."

Jake smiled and nodded, then looked at the Boss when he said, "Hound's going to be moving into the bunkhouse. Thought you and the others would like to sort out who's going to be sharing a room, and then late tomorrow you all can shift the furniture around."

Jake stared at him. When they had to share before it was simply a matter of letting the last one hired know he had a roommate and trading rooms around until the biggest room had two beds.

The Boss was looking him the eye and Jake clued in. Right, two guys in a room. Boss's eyes were telling him Hell, if you two are sleeping together might as well share a room, right? There was always the whole 'new guy shares a room with the gay cowboy' thing, too—Tor was last one hired and it may not be a good idea to stick him with a green hand, now that everyone on the ranch knew that he was gay.

But fuck, that wasn't a great idea.

Jake nodded and said, "I'll tell them. We'll get it sorted, sir."

He walked slowly to the bunkhouse, not sure how to approach this. Tell Tor first? Tell them all that Tor was getting a roommate and go from there? He was pretty sure that him sharing a room with Tor would lead to more fights, and damn it all why did this have to happen now? Jake wasn't sure if he was ready to be actually living with Tor, and he was damn certain that Tor didn't want to be living with him.

Maybe it would be easiest to tell Kip that he was getting a roommate. It was the only way that things would stay peaceful, as long as Kip didn't kick up a fuss because he was senior to Tor.

When he got to the bunkhouse the other three hands were all sitting in the kitchen having supper.

"What did the Boss want?" Elias said as Jake got a plate for himself.

Jake sat down at the table and started eating. "Hired two new hands. Some guy named Tommy, looks good on paper, should work out okay."

Tor looked up. "What about the other one? Not so good?"

Jake shook his head. "No, he should be fine, too. Name's Hound. He's moving in with us."

There was a chorus of groans from everyone.

"There goes my private bath," Elias said with a scowl.

"Yeah, you've got the biggest room," Kip said. "So, who gets to share with the new guy? Tor?"

Jake looked at Tor and met his dark eyes. "Yeah, if he wants to," Jake said, looking away when Tor looked surprised.

"That a good idea?" Tor asked, raising an eyebrow. "Things are pretty stirred up, and I don't think I like the idea of the new guy freaking when he finds out about the shit that happened this week."

Elias snorted. "Hell, don't know why we're even talkin' about this. The only thing that makes sense is for you two to share. Not like everybody doesn't know. And I don't like the idea of people talkin' about who's sharing beds in here." He got up and went to the fridge.

"Damn it, Elias, it isn't that easy," Jake said.

Tor looked at him and said, "Why the hell not? He's right, not like everyone doesn't know."

Kip sputtered a little and went red. "Umm, I think that if you two are…together…then you should share. Don't see why not."

Jake rolled his eyes. "You want to live with every girl you've slept with, Kip?"

"Well, yeah."

Tor grinned. "Virgin before Beth, right?" Kip glared at him, and Tor looked at Jake. "I think maybe we should take this somewhere else."

Jake nodded and got up to go before Elias stopped them.

"Look, I don't know what the deal is with you two, and outside of getting in fights with idiots, I don't want to. But if Kip or me winds up sharing a room with anyone I'm gonna be pissed. 'Cause every night I'm gonna be thinkin' that there is an empty room in this house and if you two are gonna be fucking sneaking around in the mornings to find your own beds then it's not fair to us. Go get yourselves sorted, but think about it." Elias nodded at Tor and left, heading into the living room.

Jake sat down again, slowly. He hadn't thought of it that way. A glance at Tor told him that he was in deep shit if he didn't say something fast. "Fuck. Tor—"

"Man has a point, Taggart," Tor interrupted. "Look. The whole fucking ranch knows about the other night, right? And they know that the Boss isn't gonna stand for shit. Aside from the fact that it makes sense to have the two gay guys who happen to be fucking—" he looked up as Kip fled the room and shook his head, "the two of us sharing a room if one needs to be shared, it might actually make things calmer around here if dumb asses don't think that we're panting after everything in jeans."

Jake nodded slowly, trying to understand. "So, we share a room and everyone just gets comfortable with the idea that we're together and then everyone goes on their merry way?"

Tor leaned back in his chair. "Pretty much. Fuck, it's not like we haven't been living in the same house for almost three years, Taggart."

"It's not the same, and you know it."

Tor sighed and stood up, then walked to the door. "Whatever. Fuck it. Let me know where I'm sleeping tomorrow night if you get the chance." The door closed behind him with a bang and Jake was alone in the kitchen.

He listened to the TV in the other room and the deafening silence from Kip and Elias until he couldn't take it anymore. He stood up and cleared off the table, throwing his supper away and wrapping the other plates with foil, then he did the dishes, taking his time drying them. Tor didn't come back.

Jake leaned on the doorframe between the kitchen and the living room until Elias looked up. "Gonna go find him?" Elias asked.

Jake sighed and looked at the floor. "Not sure he wants me to."

Kip snorted and shrugged. "He'd be more pissed if he did want you to find him and you didn't."

Jake looked at him and nodded. "See you later."

When he got to the stable he found that Lug's stall was empty and the black board was scrawled with a huge "Tor", underlined twice. Jake shook his head and got out River's tack.

He rode for about an hour, just wandering around, before he found Tor. Lug was happily munching on apples and Tor was sitting in the middle of a field, apparently watching the stars. Jake rode up and gave River his own apples, then sat down next to Tor.

"I'm goin' to my sister's," Tor said. "Let you figure out where you stand."

Jake wasn't sure what to say, so he said the first thing that came to mind. "Don't go."

Tor looked at him, frustration evident in his face as his jaw twitched. "Why the hell not? I mean it's pretty fucking clear that you don't know what you want right now. Maybe some space will help."

Jake shook his head. "Fuck, Tor. How the hell are you so sure what you want? Christ." He just couldn't understand why Tor was so adamant about this, so eager to just move ahead at what, for Jake, was a blinding pace.

Tor's eyes were dark and serious. "Just do. Make up my mind and go as far as I can. Knew what I was doing when I kissed you the first time."

Jake blinked. "What?"

When Tor laughed it was without humor. "Wanted you, didn't I? Waited for months, trying to see if you were even interested in men." He looked at the sky and growled. "You think I didn't see the way you looked at me? Not fucking blind, Taggart. Knew you were into it." He was angry now, his voice rising, and Jake was glad for the privacy of the country.

"Before me, apparently," he said, his own voice quiet.

"No, you just had more will power than I thought. Set you up with that skinny dipping thing, you know." Tor actually leered at him a little, talking in a normal tone.

"The hell you did!"

Tor nodded. "Did. And it still took me getting practically naked in the rain and shoving my tongue down your throat before you'd react."

"Shit. I had no fucking clue."

"Yeah, I get that now. We're at different points here. So, I'm just gonna go. Come back in a bit and see what's what."

"No." Jake shook his head.

"Jake—"

"Tor, just shut up. My turn. The last time I shared a room with anybody was in prison. I've never…I mean, hell, I've never even considered this. It's…new. Do me a favor though and don't take off. Just stay. Give me a couple of hours, instead of a couple weeks. You're a pushy bastard, should be able to do that."

Tor was silent for a few moments, not looking at him. Then he stood up and started to walk away, toward Lug. "Not gonna comment on sharing a room with me being like it was in prison, Taggart. But the rest? Yeah. Let me know in the morning. You want time, you got it. I can still go to Becky's."

Jake sat for a long time in the dark, trying to figure out what the hell had just happened. When he finally rode back to the ranch, Lug's stall was still empty and Tor was nowhere to be seen. Elias and Kip looked up when he came in, but didn't say anything, didn't ask any questions.

Jake didn't sleep much that night.

Ten

When he headed to the barn the next morning he was sleepy and cranky and wondering where the hell Tor was. He'd knocked on Tor's door and then looked in when he was greeted by silence; Tor hadn't been back the night before.

Jake was kicking up dust with his boots as he crossed the yard, then he looked up at the sound of someone riding in, fast. Tor was on Lug, and Jake watched them approach with a sick feeling in his belly.

"Taggart, we got fences down and cattle looking for new homes. Get the boys and let's ride!"

Jake nodded and started bellowing orders, then headed to the house to tell the Boss.

Before long every hand was scrambling for horses and trucks and heading out, following Tor's directions. When they got to the fence line, Jake, Elias and the Boss started examining the breaks while the rest got to work herding the cattle and driving them back onto the ranch property.

It was a hard morning. No one was exactly sure how many animals had wandered off until Tor managed an accurate head count and came up twenty short. Tor took the new hands and they rode off in search of missing cattle, and Jake went over to the Boss and Elias, who were examining one of the breaks while a couple of other men attempted a quick fix.

"What happened?" he asked as he walked to them.

Elias pointed to the wire and wood fencing and spit on the ground. "Cut. Fucking fence was cut in at least four places."

Jake swore and the Boss looked about ready to hunt down the culprits himself.

"Think they'll find the cattle?" Jake asked.

The Boss shook his head. "Nope. Gone, I think. I'm going back to the ranch to make some phone calls." He started to walk to his truck and paused, raising a hand to his eyes. "Somebody's comin' up," he said, pointing to a truck approaching from the direction of the ranch.

Missy pulled up in a truck, bringing lunch for the hands. She offered Jake a tentative smile and then turned to handing out food and drink to the hands, making sure that everyone was fed. Her father smiled at her when she wasn't looking.

He moved to Jake's side while they ate. "You lot get the new room arrangement made?"

Jake blinked. He hadn't even thought about it since they had headed out in the morning. "Uh, yeah, I think so, sir."

"Good. Hope it all works out for you," the Boss said before moving away.

They set some food aside for Tor, Tommy and Hound, then went to work repairing the fencing and moving cattle.

It was almost three in the afternoon when Tor and the others appeared, bringing nineteen animals with them, looking pleased with themselves. They moved the cattle into the fencing and accepted congratulations from everyone before settling into their late lunch, then they helped with the fencing.

It was a long, hard day, and Jake was the last one into the bunkhouse at suppertime. He walked into the kitchen to find Elias, Kip and Hound sitting at the table and Tor leaning against the kitchen counter. They all looked at him as he entered.

"So," Hound said, "how does this work? I share with the last one hired, right? So that's Tor?"

Tor's eyes were hot on him, and Jake saw Elias and Kip lean back in their chairs, waiting.

Jake shook his head, still looking at Tor. "Usually. But not this time. Kip, you keep your room. Elias, you take mine. Hound, you get Tor's. Tor and I'll take the big room."

Jake heard Kip sigh and Elias chuckle, but it was on the outside of his awareness. All that he really knew was that Tor's eyes were dark and then he was pushed up into the fridge as Tor kissed him hard, tongue invading Jake's mouth. Jake did the only thing he could think of, which was to put a hand at the back of Tor's neck and hold him there, kissing back.

"Holy shit," Hound said. "They're..."

"They're making me lose my appetite," Elias said.

Jake pushed Tor away and flushed, more embarrassed than he could remember being in a long time.

"I think I can live without seeing that again," Kip said.

Jake looked at Hound, who was staring at them with wide eyes. "This gonna be an issue?"

Hound blinked and said, "What? Oh, no. My brother has a boyfriend. Just didn't think you two were the type is all. My brother is all arty and stereotypical."

"You two better not keep me up all night," Elias growled. "I need my sleep. So help me God, if I hear that fucking bed so much as squeak I'll make sure you get salt in your coffee."

Tor nodded. "Right. No squeaking. Best leave lots of floor space." Then he turned and headed to his room. "I'll clear my stuff out, Hound."

Jake felt rather shell-shocked. But he thought he might be happy.

Eleven

It took about three hours for them to get everything into the right bedrooms, including stopping for supper and The Great Nightstand Hunt. Everyone had a nightstand, so it just stood to reason that Tor would move his into the large bedroom. Except that meant that his old room was without one, and no one could remember if there had been another one when they had had to share rooms before.

Hound was really good about it, saying he didn't really need one, but the others insisted he did. They were wandering around the house looking for stray tables that would do when there was a knock at the door.

The Boss was a firm believer in the fact that the bunkhouse was home for the hands, and not a place that he could just wander into uninvited, so he waited patiently for someone to open the door for him.

The entire bunch of them trooped out to let him in, Jake rolling his eyes. Every time he turned around since they started the hunt for a nightstand he was bumping into Tor, who never failed to make the most of it. He'd been groped, squeezed, kissed and nuzzled. Not that he really minded, but it was making it hard to concentrate on the mission.

The Boss stepped into the kitchen and greeted them all individually before asking, "So, are the room arrangements all sorted out?"

"Yes, sir," Jake said, stepping away from Tor a little.

The Boss didn't seem to notice, but Elias did, and he rolled his eyes. "Life is just getting strange here."

The Boss looked around and finally sighed. "Jake, do you guys need the other bed brought down, or not?"

Jake felt himself blush again and the others laughed. "Uh, no, sir. We're good. But we're looking for another nightstand. Can't remember if there was another one or not."

The Boss pointed to the kitchen phone, which was on a nightstand being used as a table. "There you go. Good night, all."

The Boss left, closing the door gently behind him while Jake and the others stared at the phone. Tor walked over and picked the phone up, moved it six inches so it was on the end of the counter, and pointed to the stand. "There ya go, Hound. Now, I am going to bed." He turned and walked toward the hall, slowing only long enough to grab Jake by the belt loop and pull him along.

Jake didn't say anything, but the others laughed and Kip said that he was going to go stay with Beth if they didn't calm down soon.

Tor dragged him into their bedroom and spun him around, slamming the door shut before pressing him up against it. "Want you," Tor growled in his ear, he hands already untucking Jake's shirt.

"Never would have guessed," Jake said as he dipped his head and started sucking at Tor's neck. "God, you're so pushy."

"You keep saying that." Tor got Jake's shirt pushed up and ran his fingers over Jake's chest, his hips pressing tight into Jake's groin. "Shut up."

"Kiss me, then."

They devoured each other's mouths, hunger building fast as they rocked together, Tor pushing them up against the door with his body. Jake felt like he was starving, needing more and needing it now, his cock impossibly hard in his jeans. Tor's hands were everywhere, pinching his nipples and then cupping his ass, pulling him even closer.

Tor's mouth was hot and wet, claiming Jake's for his own, then moving down to Jake's jaw and neck, harsh sounds of want and need spilling out. Jake moaned, thrusting his cock into Tor's, rubbing hard. He tried to undo Tor's belt but as soon as his hands were at Tor's waist, Tor gasped and pleaded with him, a ragged breath that sounded like "Please".

Jake turned his hand and forced it between their bodies, stroking Tor through his jeans, moving lower to cup and squeeze his balls. Tor thrust into his hand, clutching at Jake's ass, mouth hungry at his throat. "Oh God, yes, Jake, so good. Fuck, I'm gonna come like this."

Fire raced up Jake's spine at the want and need in Tor's voice and he bucked, his cock hitting the back of his own hand. He stroked harder and felt Tor shudder, felt Tor's body stiffen against his own, and then Tor was moaning in his ear. "Oh shit, oh shit. Fuck, now, please Jake."

Jake's hips were liquid, moving his own shaft against his hand as he stroked Tor, and then Tor was coming, soft hungry sounds in his ear, and Jake shuddered too, groaning as he came.

They leaned against the door panting. "Oh fuck. That was intense," Tor said into his neck.

Jake laughed shakily. "Not sure I can walk. Hell, I haven't come in my jeans since I was a kid."

Tor kissed him, deeply and thoroughly, and Jake felt himself start to respond already, his cock twitching.

"Shower," Tor said. "Then bed."

Jake nodded, more grateful than he'd expected to be that their new room had a bathroom attached. They made their way to the bathroom on shaky legs, pulling off sticky clothes as they went. Tor got the shower going while Jake admired him; Tor's long body, strong and lean, tanned skin gleaming with sweat. Tor's bruise looked awful, moving into the brown and yellow patches that meant that it was healing. Then Tor stepped into the shower and held his hand out to Jake.

Jake took his hand and got in the shower, quickly washing come off, and then settling for the soothing heat to do its job and relax them both. They washed each other carefully, using soap-slicked hands to memorize each other's skin, to glide over muscle and bone.

Tor moved behind him, put him in the spray, quickly and easily washing his hair, strong fingers massaging his scalp. Jake was pretty sure he was in heaven.

When Jake was boneless and relaxed, Tor washed his own hair and Jake used his hands to follow the soap bubbles down Tor's chest, fingers gliding over dark nipples and tracing the edge of the bruise. Tor's cock was filling and growing, and Jake admired it briefly before taking it in his hand to feel the weight of it, to feel it grow. Long and thick, the skin as smooth as warm butter, Jake needed to taste it.

He slid down the wall, trailing licks and kisses on Tor's body, tasting soap and water and the muted flavor of Tor. He took the semi-hard shaft in his mouth, all the way in, and cupped Tor's balls in his hand, gently rolling them between his fingers as Tor's cock swelled and grew, filling his mouth.

He sucked gently at first, tongue flitting over the skin, then harder. He danced his tongue over the tip of the head, playing quickly with the slit. He didn't stay there, knowing that it was the fastest way to make Tor come, but started licking and kissing along the shaft, pulling it into his mouth with quick sucks that made Tor groan.

Tor's hands were on his head, fingers twisting in his hair, and Tor was moaning soft words that Jake could barely hear over the fall of the water.

"Yes, so good, Jake. You're so amazing, you should see yourself. So hot."

Jake moved down to suck at Tor's balls gently, his hand wrapped around the shaft, pumping it lightly. When Tor groaned and started pushing into his hand he moved back up and took Tor into his mouth again, settling in to suck, to make Tor fly apart.

He teased with his tongue, licking and playing, then started sucking on the head, lips sealed just below the crown, his tongue pressing into the slit carefully. Tor bucked and Jake felt a hand drop to his shoulder, the other twisted in his hair so tight it was pulling almost painfully.

"Fuck, Jake, yes. So right. God, I need you."

Jake bobbed his head, taking Tor in deep, sucking hard, feeling the thick cock hit the roof of his mouth before sliding back to hit his throat. He was making his own needy sounds now, needing to give Tor this, needing to hear Tor's words. His own prick was hard and throbbing, aching to be touched.

He put both his hands on Tor's hips, holding Tor steady and he worked faster, long sucking pulls that had Tor groaning and trying to thrust deep into his throat. He looked up at Tor, saw glazed eyes hot on him and moaned. Tor was just so perfect like that, water around him, his face lost in pleasure.

Jake wanted him that way forever.

He closed his eyes and took Tor as deeply into his mouth as he could, felt the head of Tor's cock at his throat and relaxed, trying to take him in further. When he swallowed Tor cried out his name and came, filling Jake's mouth and throat with seed. Jake swallowed, the taste of Tor sending his senses reeling, the sound of his name echoing in the bathroom driving him insane.

He sucked at Tor gently, bringing him down, not willing to give up that feeling of Tor's cock in his mouth. He stroked at Tor's hip with one hand, lowering the other to his own aching shaft and pulled at himself hard, coming after only a few seconds.

"Oh Christ, Jake." Tor slid down the wall and gathered Jake into his arms as best he could, given that they were in tight quarters. "You're amazing." They kissed gently, Jake sharing Tor's flavor with him.

"Didn't think you were going to say yes," Tor said quietly. "Figured you'd put Hound in with Kip."

Jake kissed him and met his eye. "You would have left."

Tor nodded. "Yeah. I would have."

"Couldn't have that. May not be entirely ready for this, but you leaving...didn't want that."

Tor kissed him again. "Bed now? I think we're almost out of hot water."

Jake tried to stand up. "Yeah, bed. If we can get there."

Twelve

Jake was not a morning person. Of the many things that sharing a room with Tor was teaching him, the most persistent was that Tor *was* a morning person. Jake was never sure how he was going to wake up, except that there was going to be a hard cock pressing on him somewhere. Sometimes Tor was just rubbing up against him, slow and easy, and sometimes harder, with more urgency. Other times he would wake up with a hand on his own morning erection and on a few occasions the hot wetness of Tor's mouth. Once, he had woken from a very deep sleep, before the light of dawn, with Tor already sliding inside him.

This particular morning he was awakened by words.

"Hey. You awake yet?"

"No." Jake tried to roll over but discovered that they were hopelessly tangled together, legs wrapped around each other and arms tossed over waists and necks.

Tor chuckled softly. "You are so. I can feel you."

"You could feel me from the next state. You always know when I'm hard." Jake's eyes were still closed, his voice husky with sleep.

"Yeah. Stay where you are. I've got an idea."

Jake groaned. That sounded slightly ominous to him. But he didn't move, other than to kiss Tor's jaw.

He felt coolness on his skin when Tor moved his arm, reaching back for something. He heard a snap and smiled to himself. Tube of lubricant opening, if he wasn't mistaken.

The arm came back, but lower, Tor's hand caressing his ass. Tor shifted his legs, pushing Jake's apart slightly and Jake gasped when slick fingers entered him.

"God, you're still so tight," Tor whispered.

Jake just grinned and clenched his ass.

Slick fingers moved in him and Jake moaned, giving himself over to the feeling. They were rocking together on the bed, erections hard against each other, skin damp with a light sweat. Tor smelled of musk and soap and Jake kissed and licked at Tor's neck and chest, sucking on one dark nipple until it was hard and stiff.

Tor moved hard against him, fingers probing and seeking in Jake's ass. "Want you to fuck me, Jake. Want to ride your cock," Tor said, voice hard and sharp with need.

Jake opened his eyes and looked at Tor. "Uh, yeah, okay. Sure. Oh yes, there —but, umm…I thought you were getting me ready—"

Tor gave him a wicked grin and then the fingers were gone, leaving him empty and slightly disappointed. Then something cool and slick and solid was sliding into him, something smooth and hard that wasn't part of Tor. He was being stretched, but not filled, and then the pressure lessened, the stretch receding but not going away entirely.

"What the fuck is that?" he asked as Tor moved on the bed untangling them and stretching out beside him, hands roaming over Jake's chest and belly, tongue licking at his nipples.

"Butt plug." Tor bit lightly at Jake's nipple and moved a hand down to Jake's balls, cupping them and squeezing gently. "C'mon Jake, want you in me."

Jake was confused and surprised and, well, he admitted to himself, not a little turned on. He shook his head and reached for the lube, gasping as the plug moved in him. "Oh God."

Tor grinned. "Yeah."

Jake shook his head and started stroking himself as he tossed the lube to Tor. "You do it."

Tor's eyes widened and then he smiled, appreciation in his eyes. "Right. Turnabout." Tor lay back on the bed and drew up his legs, planting his feet flat on the bed. He slicked both his hands with the lube and closed his eyes with a soft sigh, starting to stroke his cock and play with his balls.

Jake leaned back on the headboard, stroking his erection with a lazy fist, watching Tor. It was the hottest thing he had seen since their first night in the rainstorm. Tor was arching into his own hand, the hand on his balls moving lower to tease at his hole. His finger would dip in and then back out, and he would tug at his balls. He was teasing Jake, and Jake knew it.

Jake moved his hand faster and carefully reached for the lube, trying not to move too much. He moaned when Tor finally slid two fingers into his ass and watched, eyes wide as Tor worked his cock with one fist, thumb playing over the head while his fingers went deep and moved, twisting slightly as he reached.

Tor gasped and jerked up into his fist, eyes flying open. He stared at the ceiling and moved his fingers faster, fucking his hands. "Fuck, Jake, please…need you in me, gonna fucking come like this."

Jake squeezed the base of his cock hard, the need in Tor's voice making him breathless. "More, Tor. Another finger. Let me watch."

Tor shook his head and groaned. "No, want to come with you in me." But Tor didn't slow his hands and Jake watched him ease a third finger into his hole. "Oh shit, Jake!" Tor swept his thumb over the tip of his cock again and pressed the slit, a harsh needy sound escaping his chest as his hips thrust his cock into his fist and then down onto his fingers.

Jake's breath was coming fast as he watched Tor fucking himself, and he knew that Tor was about to shoot. He watched for a couple of seconds longer, saw Tor's balls pull up tight and saw the strain in Tor's legs. He opened the lube and slicked his cock, moving fast to push Tor's hand off his cock and then he took Tor's shaft in his mouth, moaning as the movement jostled the plug in his own ass.

"Fuck! Oh shit, Jake!"

Tor came in shuddering jerks, still thrusting onto his hand, and up into Jake's mouth. As soon as he'd shot his load Jake was off his cock, a hand on the one in Tor's ass, easing Tor's fingers out, and thrusting his own cock in.

"Now I'm gonna fuck you," Jake said, kissing Tor hard, pushing his tongue into Tor's mouth in time with the thrust of his hips. He fucked Tor hard, fast deep strokes, and he could feel Tor's ass clenching around him, as Tor's orgasm faded. Tor's tongue was devouring his mouth, pushing his own tongue out of the way as Tor sought out the taste of himself.

"Fuck, so hot, Tor. So fucking good." Jake groaned into the kiss, lost in sensation.

Tor moaned and thrust his hips up, even as he pulled his legs back further, opening himself to Jake. Tor shuddered softly and moaned, "There Jake, right there. Fuck, feels so—oh Christ, yes!"

Jake moved faster, hitting Tor's gland with every stroke, feeling himself get close. "Tor, 'm gonna come."

"Yes, please, Jake. Come for me, do it, please, oh fuck!"

Jake cried out, coming hard, deep in Tor's ass. Tor whimpered and kissed him, almost sobbing.

"Tor, oh God." Jake was shaking and Tor wrapped strong arms around him, holding him tightly.

"Right here."

They held each other and kissed deeply, moving slowly together as Jake softened inside Tor. Finally Jake moved back a little, slipping out, and then collapsed on Tor again.

They were silent for a while, wrapped together on their bed. Tor moved a hand to stroke along Jake's spine, then down between his ass cheeks to touch the butt plug. Jake gasped softly and shifted, expecting Tor to take it out.

"How's it feel?" Tor asked.

Jake shifted again. "Intense. Wild."

Tor chuckled softly. "Give it time. Gets better."

Jake lifted his head warily. "What do you mean?"

"Leave it there. Until say…lunch."

Jake shook his head. "Nope. Don't think so. Can't. I'll be a mess."

Tor kissed him. "Leave it there. Until lunch. I'll fuck you into the wall if you do."

"And if I don't?"

Tor shrugged. "Fuck you into the floor, I suppose. But I'd like it if you left it in for a bit."

"Why?"

"Just so you know. All day long, or until lunch, I guess. Just so you know every fucking second of the morning that I'm gonna do you. So you think about me all the time."

Jake shook his head again. "How am I supposed to work if I'm thinkin' about that? And what makes you think I don't do that already? And I don't think I can even walk."

Another shudder rolled through him at the thought of trying to walk with the plastic in his ass, brushing against his sweet spot all day. Fuck, he'd be coming in his jeans.

Tor laughed. "There's a contradiction in there somewhere, I know it." He kissed him again. "Leave it in?"

Jake found himself nodding. "Yeah. Until lunch. But you better do something real special for me."

"Will."

Thirteen

Jake was fairly sure he was going insane. The damn plug in his ass had turned him to jelly within an hour and he'd had to take a moment at mid morning to sneak into the bunkhouse and jerk off. He found himself obsessively checking his watch as the morning wore on, and finally, thank God, it was almost lunchtime.

Jake finished up in the barn and silently thanked whoever was in charge of his life that he hadn't had to ride a horse. He walked to the bunkhouse, impossibly hard in his jeans. The anticipation alone was making him throb.

"Jake!"

Jake groaned to himself and changed direction, heading to the Boss, who was standing on the front porch of the main house. "Yes, sir?"

"How are things working out, Jake?" the Boss asked, just as casual as could be.

"Fine, sir. Thanks." And would you please just let me go so I can get off? Please?

"Just making sure." The Boss glanced around the yard and suddenly grinned. Jake looked over, following his gaze, and saw Tor making his way to the bunkhouse, looking intense and rushed. "Here. Mail. Have a good…lunch."

Jake felt himself blush and nodded sharply, practically snatching the brown envelopes from the Boss before heading once more to the bunkhouse. He flipped through them and saw that there wasn't any mail for himself, but Tor's envelope was thick. His sister was most likely sending the latest batch of photos in the "watch grow" show.

He walked into the kitchen, empty except for Tor, and kept walking, tossing the envelopes on the table except for Tor's.

"You got mail," he said, thrusting the package into Tor's hand and pressing him up against the wall. He licked Tor's neck and said, "Need you. Now."

Tor grinned. "How bad?"

Jake ground his cock against Tor's erection and kissed him hard, tongue going deep, hoping that his willingness to make out in the kitchen when anyone could walk in was an indication of how much. Apparently it was, 'cause Tor broke the kiss and grabbed his hand, then dragged him down the hall to their room.

Tor pushed him into the room and onto the bed, then knelt on the floor reaching for one of Jake's boots. As he pulled it off he said, "You lose the boots and your pants. Then we'll see what I can do for you."

Jake didn't say anything, just undid his belt. When Tor got the boots off, Jake was out of his jeans faster than a bull out of the chute. Tor grabbed him at the waist, flipping him so he was bent over the edge of the bed, legs spread.

With one strong hand on Jake's back Tor caressed an offered ass cheek and said, "Push, now. Just a little."

Jake pushed gently and felt a slight stretch as the plug was forced past his entrance. Then it was out and Jake was oddly sorry, felt slightly bereft of the pressure he'd had all morning.

Then *oh holy hell, and fuck, yes* there was something else, something wonderful and new and hot and wet. Tor's tongue licking gently at the sensitive flesh and oh God, that was just right. Jake clutched at the sheets on the bed and willed himself not to come. He'd never felt anything like this, had never had any idea that it would feel so good. He'd heard about it, of course, but had never done it, had never had it done to him.

Tor's tongue teased and licked at him and Jake thought he could very well die from the pleasure of it. Then that tongue was inside of him and that was just so much better. His balls and cock were throbbing, and he was twisting the sheets in his fists, moving back onto Tor, needing more and getting it.

They were almost silent. Jake was past speech, the sensations too intense and too different for him to articulate anything. Tor's usual soundtrack was missing, but Jake found that its absence was making everything more powerful. All of his senses were screaming at him; all he could feel was Tor's tongue fucking him, all he could smell was Tor's sweat and the bed linen in his face, all he could hear was the sound of his own breath and Tor's belt buckle and zipper being undone.

Tor wrapped a fist around Jake's cock and stroked him hard. Jake was quivering, so close to release that he could practically feel his come traveling from his balls up into his cock, then Tor's tongue was gone. Jake almost whimpered, but before the sound was even fully formed Tor was pushing into him, stretching and filling and just making everything so fucking right.

Tor entered him with one smooth thrust that brushed against his prostate and Jake was coming hard, shooting all over the side of the bed. Tor froze, buried deep, until Jake's initial spasm had passed then slid out a little before pushing back in, nice and slow, brushing his gland again. Tor's hand was still working his cock, stroking and pulling gently, teasing his orgasm out.

Tor fucked him, slow and even thrusts that hit his sweet spot every fucking time. Tor's hand, working magic on his prick, keeping him hard. Tor's body, leaning over his and Tor's lips, kissing his back. It went on forever and not long enough. Jake felt like he was whole and flying to pieces at the same time, never wanting this to end but needing it to before he lost his mind.

Tor's voice, finally, in his ear. "Wanted to make you come again, Jake. Wanted to do this right, do this so bad. But, shit, I can't hold it together. Just gotta—"

And then there was Tor's cock, slamming into him hard, and Jake didn't know that he needed it like that until it happened. He rode Tor, fast and hard, and arched his back when Tor grabbed at his shoulders for leverage, pushing into Jake so much harder and deeper than before, and Jake came again, not shooting as much, but the feeling spiraling so much longer, rising each time Tor hit home. Jake couldn't cry out, couldn't breathe, could barely process anything until he felt Tor come, felt Tor's cock throb inside him, felt the heat flooding him.

They were both breathless and gasping for minutes afterward, exchanging long kisses and touches. Jake finally scrapped himself off the floor and went into the bathroom to clean up, leaving Tor to strip the bed of its sheets.

Jake looked in the mirror and smiled. He looked completely well fucked. He looked happy. He looked like he needed a nap. However, there was another half day of work to do, so he went back into the bedroom and got clean jeans on while Tor cleaned himself up. Jake noticed that Tor wore the same stupid grin he'd just seen in the mirror.

He was getting fresh sheets on the bed when Tor came over and picked up the brown envelope that they'd tossed on the floor. "Hey, pictures! Sit yourself down, Taggart. Gonna show off my pretty princess."

Jake just grinned and sat on the bed, wrapping himself around Tor and kissing him on the neck. He belonged right where he was, and if he were pressed for the truth Jake might have been forced into admitting that he liked looking at Tor's family pictures. It made him feel connected to a family, even if it wasn't his.

"Now, this is Susie at the pool…Susie in the pool…Susie crying 'cause she doesn't want to leave the pool…" There were about twenty-five pictures of the six year old in the batch, and Tor was in proud uncle heaven.

They were almost through the stack when Tor flipped the latest "Susie at the pool" picture over and froze.

The photo was of a young man, about twenty or so, Jake guessed, with fair hair and blue eyes. He was caught in profile, looking at something off camera and smiling slightly, as if he weren't sure if he was amused or annoyed at what was going on. Tor traced the boy's features with a finger, hand shaking slightly. Jake shifted to look at him, but Tor's eyes were fixed on the photo.

"Is…are there anymore?" Tor whispered, handing the rest of the pictures to Jake.

Jake flipped through them quickly, seeing only Susie. "No, it looks like that's the —oh, wait, here's one."

The second picture was of Tor and the young man. Tor looked like he was nineteen or twenty, lean and lanky, hair too long. They were wrestling and Tor had the boy pinned down, was smiling over his shoulder at the camera. The boy was laughing. Tor's eyes were dark, dark, dark, and Jake knew the look. Tor was getting off on wresting with this man.

The Tor beside him was lost in the pictures, looking at one and then the other, touching the boy's face.

Jake studied Tor for a moment, feeling lost. He had no idea what to say, or what to do. Tor was completely shut off from him now, and Jake felt like he had just been thrown.

"Who is he?" he asked softly, not touching Tor, not wanting to intrude, just wanting to remind Tor that he was there, goddamn it. To save a piece of the feeling he'd just lost.

Tor blinked and looked at him. He carefully put the pictures down on his nightstand and said, "Doesn't matter. Let's get some lunch, right? Then back to work."

Tor stood and left the room without looking back.

Fourteen

Jake watched Tor ride off after lunch and sighed, feeling confused and worried and just plain out of sorts. Tor hadn't said anything over lunch, had just gone back to work in silence, his eyes distant. Jake was pretty sure that Tor hadn't even known what he'd eaten.

It was late when Tor came back to the bunkhouse, and the others had almost finished supper. He came in and fixed himself a plate, ate standing at the counter. He answered direct questions, but offered nothing, and the look he gave Jake said only "stay away".

They had gotten into an after supper routine, the five of them, based on the fact that working together and sharing a house meant far too much time together. Kip would stay in the kitchen, on the phone with Beth, Elias and Hound would watch a little TV in silence, taking turns with the remote, and Jake and Tor would separate for a while. Usually Jake would get a book or magazine and head to the porch to read, or go to the stables and check the horses. He didn't know what Tor did, but he suspected that he just took a nap to rest up for the morning. How else could he be so damn awake that early?

But this time Tor just rinsed his plate and went to their room, closing the door behind him. They all heard the door lock.

"What's up with him?" Elias asked, brow raised.

Jake shook his head. "Hell if I know. He got something in the mail today that has him a little upset."

Kip and Hound were looking at him, Kip worried and Hound all sympathy.

"What?" Jake asked, feeling brittle and defensive, his voice gruff.

Hound raised his eyebrows. "Man, you just got locked out of your fucking room. He's more than a little upset."

Jake stood in the kitchen while the others cleared up, and then he went to sit on the porch of the main house. He'd been there for about an hour when the door to the house opened and the Boss came out.

"Evenin' Jake."

Jake looked up at him as the Boss levered himself up on the wide railing. "Sir. Nice night."

The Boss laughed softly. "No one around, son."

Jake smiled. "Right, Doug. How was your day?"

The Boss looked at him, his eyes twinkling. "Not as good as yours if I read the signals right at lunch time," he teased.

Jake looked down at the porch and sighed. "Yeah, well. Lunch had its moments. The rest of it, though…not really good."

The Boss made a noise and Jake looked at him. "What, you too? Hell, if I get any more sympathy I'll get a sugar high. He's got a mood, that's all. Nothing to worry about."

"That why you're out here brooding?"

"I don't brood."

"Sulking then."

"Shit." Jake leaned back and looked at the man in front of him.

The older man just looked back, not saying anything for a long time, then he sighed. "Okay, you don't want to talk about it. I can understand that. But think, Jake. When was the last time you had a relationship? Three years? More? You gotta decide what you'll take and what you won't."

Jake shook his head. "It's not like that. He's not pissed at me, he's just working through something, and he doesn't need my help. Pretty sure I couldn't help anyway. And it's been a damn sight longer than that, Doug, and you know it."

The Boss sighed again. "Richard. Fucked you over pretty big, didn't he?"

Jake laughed. "That wasn't a relationship. That wasn't even a convenience. That was a guy trying to get rid of a woman and then finding out he liked it. Just didn't like me, is all. Trust me, I wasn't too upset to see him leave."

"You were pretty twisted at the time, Jake," the Boss reminded him. "You worked sixteen hour days for a week."

"It was hay season!"

The Boss grinned. "Yeah, well, it's not now, so if you start putting in extra time I'm gonna worry." He stood up and crossed to the door. "You go home now, and try to straighten this out, Jake. If he matters to you."

Jake sat on the porch, wondering why everyone suddenly felt the need to tell him how to deal with Tor. They didn't get that the locked door wasn't a rejection of him, just a statement of needing to be alone; they didn't seem to understand that there were some things a man needed to deal with on his own.

Then he wondered why he felt sick to his stomach, and lonely, and hurt.

Eventually he went back to the bunkhouse and watched TV with the others. When he walked in three sets of eyes looked at him and Kip said, "He's not been out yet."

Jake just nodded and sat down, staring at the TV, ignoring the looks the others kept giving him. When the ten o'clock news came on Hound went off to bed. Jake watched the news with the other two and when they heard the bedroom door unlock and open, Jake ignored the sharp looks he got. Tor didn't come out, but at least Jake knew that he didn't have to sleep on the couch.

Kip nudged his leg with a foot. "You just gonna sit here?"

"Yep."

Kip sighed and rolled his eyes. "Fine then. I'm going to bed; if ya'll fight don't wake me up. And if you make up, for God's sake be quieter than you were this morning. Christ, that was enough to make me want a smoke."

Elias laughed as Jake flushed and sank down in his chair. "Kip, I'm telling ya, you need earplugs. I got mine three days after they started sharing a room. Sleep right through it now."

Kip smacked Elias on the shoulder as he moved past. "Yeah, and you sleep through your alarm too." Then Kip was gone and Elias and Jake were left to watch the news in peace.

Elias went to bed at eleven without a word, for which Jake was grateful. He turned off the TV and sat for a few minutes then gave in to the inevitable and went down the hall to the bedroom, turning off lights as he went.

Tor was lying on the bed wearing his jeans and facing the wall. The bedside light was on and Jake could see the photos, still on the nightstand. Tor didn't look at him as he stripped off his shirt and went to brush his teeth, didn't say anything.

Jake lay on his back on the bed, following Tor's lead and leaving his jeans on. He reached to flip the light off and Tor rolled over, staring at the ceiling.

"What time is it?" Tor asked, his voice hoarse.

Jake looked at him, taking in the drawn face and tired eyes that wouldn't look at him. "Little after eleven."

Tor sat up. "I gotta make a phone call." He stood and left the room, and Jake waited until the kitchen light came on before following him.

Jake stood in the hall, leaning on the smooth, cool wall, feeling only slightly guilty about eavesdropping. He heard Tor pull a chair across the floor and dial a number. Eleven digits, long distance.

"Hey, it's me. Sorry to call so late… Yeah, got the pictures today, Susie's lookin' fine. Thanks for sending them… Not sure when, I'll try to get away for a long weekend next month, maybe… Yeah, I'll call her, swear. Listen, where did you get those other pictures… Jesus, Becky, what made you think that was a good idea? The woman has dealt with enough, I'm sure that you showin' up and asking for pictures wasn't something she… No, Becky, it's not fine. She blames me, she hated me and you opened it up for her again… Just 'cause she asked about me doesn't mean that she's happy I'm not wasting my life in Mexico… Yeah, okay, if you say so. But I still think that it was a mistake to talk to her about me… Shit, what do you think? Do I sound okay? …yeah, it's been a long time, but that doesn't mean it gets easy, you know? …God, don't cry, Becky. I know you didn't mean to hurt me. I know you were just trying to give me back a piece of him, but God, you should have warned me, or something. I've been out of it all day… No, it'll be okay, I'm sorry. I shouldn't be talkin' to you like this… I love you, too. I'm sorry… No, things here are fine, work is good. Got a new housemate though, so I gotta share a room… Taggart… Yeah, him. He's still annoying… That is none of your business, little girl… Shut up… I said shut up…hanging up now… 'Kay, love you, hug Susie for me… G'night."

Jake went back to the bedroom and lay down on the bed, staring at the ceiling.

Tor came in and gave him a steady look. "You gonna sleep in your jeans?"

Jake let a smile flit across his face. "Not unless you are."

Tor rolled his eyes at him and sat on the edge of the bed. He picked up the pictures and looked at them once more, then sighed and opened the drawer of his nightstand and dropped them in. "Get naked, Taggart. Don't want to have to fight with buttons in the morning."

Jake rolled off the bed and got undressed, then crawled into bed, waiting for Tor. When Tor was naked and in his arms, Jake let himself sigh softly before turning off the light.

"G'night, Tor."

"G'night, Taggart."

Jake woke up to pitch black and the sound of Tor gagging in the bathroom. He lay still for a moment, letting himself come fully awake, and he realized that Tor was alternating between dry heaves and sobs that sounded like they hurt like hell.

Jake swung out of bed and went into the bathroom, ignoring Tor's gestures for him to go away. He knelt down and wrapped his arms around Tor's waist, held him through the heaves. He felt Tor's stomach muscles clench and twist as his gut tried to force something up, and he felt the tension in Tor's body when nothing came.

Tor was fighting him, gasping when the heaves paused. "Get the fuck out, Taggart, just leave me alone."

"Can't do that." Jake held Tor, stroked his back and shoulders, let one hand work at the stomach muscles still trying to force Tor's body to do something it couldn't. Tor was crying now, giving over to the sobs and just letting his body shake and quiver.

It felt like hours before Tor's gut decided that there really wasn't anything to bring up and stopped spasming. Then Tor was just crying, which was almost worse. He clung to Jake and cried into his shoulder, tears running down his face and Jake's chest, moans tearing from his throat and desperate sounds that Jake could only imagine sounded like a broken heart.

When the tears stopped, Jake helped him up off the floor and into the bed, held him the rest of the night, wide-awake while Tor slept.

Fifteen

For the first time since they started sharing a room they just got out of bed in the morning. Tor kissed Jake before they left the room, and they started their day.

The Boss took one look at Jake's tired eyes and sent him to town to get some parts for the old truck. "Don't think you're up for much in the heavy labor department today," he said as he passed a list over. "Just get this stuff, have some lunch in town, and c'mon home."

Jake nodded and climbed into the cab of the nearest truck and headed off. It was a nice day to drive, and the forty-minute trip into town gave him time to think. He knew that Tor had been sick in the night because of the pictures and memories that they had brought back. He knew that the pictures were of someone Tor had loved very much. And he was sure that the boy was dead, and that he was the ghost that had sent Tor to Mexico. What he didn't know was what to do about it.

Jake thought about the whole thing for a while, shivering when he thought about Tor in the bathroom. He hurt so much and there was nothing Jake could do to help. He had never been in love the way he imagined Tor had loved the man in the pictures. He only knew that Tor was in pain, and Jake wanted it to go away. The only way he could think of to help that happen was to do what he had done the night before; hold Tor when he cried, be there when he needed someone. If he had to be a willing body for a time, then he would. He just wanted Tor whole again.

He reached town and went directly to the supply store, parking out back where he knew he'd have to load the parts. He walked around to the front of the store, noting that at this time of the day there should be a fair number of men about; this was the place to go for a quick cup of coffee and morning gossip.

He walked in and moved to the counter, ready to hand the list over and then grab a cup and sit with the boys for a few minutes. He was halfway there when the silence hit him like a wall, each voice falling quiet as his presence was noted. Then the whispers started. He caught a few words, enough to make his jaw clench and his heart pound hard and fast in his chest.

Faggots. Fucking in the barn. Bunch of... Gillian's spread. Tornado. Taggart.

Jake felt his back tense and his stomach turned to lead before settling. He knew that if he didn't handle this right there would be trouble, and lots of it. Not just for him, but for Tor, the other hands, and the Boss. Hell, for anybody having anything to do with the ranch.

He ignored the men as best he could and went to the counter, standing there until Dave Prince, the owner, couldn't ignore him any longer. The man came over and stood in front of him, his eyes cold and hard.

Jake put the list down on the counter and slid it across. "I think Mr. Gillian called this in yesterday or this morning. Is it almost ready to go?" Just be polite and leave. Get the stuff and go home.

Prince nodded. "Yeah. He didn't say he was sending you in for it though."

Jake ground his teeth. "Didn't know until this morning. He thought I might like a trip to town. Besides, I've been picking stuff up here for more than a decade."

The man nodded. "Uh huh. But not anymore, Taggart. Tell Doug to send someone else next time. And not that Tornado fag, either."

Jake just nodded his head, inwardly giving up hope of reasoning with the man. Some people just couldn't be talked to.

"Heard you had some trouble out there a few weeks ago," a voice said behind him.

Jake turned and looked at Steve Whalen. "Yeah. Worked out, though. Patched up the hands worth keeping and let the trouble go."

"Some of us think that Gillian let the wrong ones go."

Jake was reaching his breaking point and he knew it, so he made himself stand very still, concentrated on keeping his hands relaxed. "How long you known me, Whalen?" he asked, his voice low and smooth.

"Not nearly fucking long enough, and too long as well. Get out of here, Taggart. Get your parts and go back to the ranch. We don't need you spreading your filth here in this town. This is a nice place, Taggart, and we aim to keep it that way."

Jake nodded and glanced at Prince. "Stuff out back?"

Prince nodded and said he'd charge it to the ranch account. "Just go, Taggart."

Jake left.

As he walked toward his truck he could feel bile rising in his throat. He forced it back and concentrated, knowing that he wasn't away safe and sound until the truck was loaded and he was on the road. His hands were clenched into fists now and he could feel rage and fear and shame warring in him.

Just don't throw the first fucking punch, Taggart. You hit first, you are one fucked ranch hand. If you gotta fight, make them hit you first.

He rounded the edge of the building and tensed, knowing they were there. Whalen and someone else, what the hell was his name? Pete? Peter Neale.

Whalen swung first and Jake ducked, but not fast enough, catching the punch high on his cheekbone. He moved away, fast, trying to get to the truck, trying to get out of it without fighting back. But Neale was there, and then there was blood in his mouth from a split lip, or maybe a broken tooth. Didn't matter. He was on the ground and he had to get up. He rolled to his feet and was greeted with a fist in his eye and God, that hurt.

Jake fought back, hating them, hating himself and hating the whole fucking world. He hated these goddamn pricks, he hated Tor's sister for fucking him up, he hated Tor for not being there, he hated the Boss for sending him into this hell hole and he hated the man in the pictures for holding Tor's heart.

But mostly he hated the fighting. Hated the way flesh felt when he hit it. Hated the sounds men made when they rolled in the dirt trying to kill each other. Hated the way a jawbone felt against his knuckles as it broke.

Then someone was pulling them all apart and rough hands were slamming him against the truck.

"Get the fuck out of here, Taggart. Now."

Jake was pushed again and the others were helped up, someone holding Whalen back as he screamed obscenities at Jake. "Fucker broke Pete's jaw. Let me go!"

Jake got in the truck and headed home.

Sixteen

———◆◆◆———

Jake glanced at his watch as he climbed out of the truck in front of the bunkhouse. It was only eleven thirty and there wouldn't be anyone in the house, thank God. He could get cleaned up and then go see the Boss, tell him what happened and why the parts they needed were still in town.

Jake pulled open the kitchen door and walked in, unbuttoning his ripped shirt as he went. He was three steps in before he realized that the kitchen was full. The four who lived there and two other hands were having omelets for lunch.

"What the fuck happened to you?" Hound was out of his chair and following him through the kitchen.

"Nothing," Jake said, heading to the bedroom.

There was a squawk behind him and he assumed that someone had grabbed Hound by the collar and hauled him back, because the footsteps following him down the hall were Tor's.

He went into the bedroom and sat on the bed, finally getting the ruined shirt off. He glanced up when the door slammed shut and met Tor's eye.

"What the flying fuck happened, Taggart?" Tor's eyes were snapping, his face flushed and his chest thrust out as he leaned on the door.

"Fight. Seems that we aren't welcome in Dodge anymore." Jake stood up and threw the shirt into the corner and paced the floor, anger rising again. He snapped a fist into the palm of his hand and swore. When that didn't make him feel any better he went into the bathroom and looked at his face.

Split and swollen lip. Black eye. Bruised cheekbone. Not very pretty. Tor was standing behind him and there were strong hands on his back, rubbing at his shoulders.

"What happened?" Tor's voice was quieter now, and Jake dropped his head, letting Tor work the tension out.

"Had a discussion in the store. Went back to the truck to load up and got jumped by Steve Whalen and that Peter Neale guy. They hit me some and then I hit back. Someone broke it up and now I'm here."

Jake moved back into the bedroom and sat on the bed again. He looked at his pants, dirty and ripped, but fixable. Scratches and bruises on his arms. Scrape on his chest. "Fuck," he said under his breath, and then Tor was holding him and letting him shake and twitch and be angry and jumpy and scared.

There was a knock on the bedroom door and Tor said, "Go away. He's fine."

The Boss's voice came. "Jake, I need to come in. Now."

Jake looked at Tor. He had never heard that tone of voice before, not in thirteen years. They sat straighter on the bed, but Tor didn't let go of him entirely. As Jake called out to let the Boss know he could come in, Tor kissed his collarbone before shifting away slightly.

When the door opened there were three men waiting to come in. The Boss and two cops from the sheriff's office.

Tor's arm tightened around him and Jake looked at the floor.

"Jake? Are you okay? Do you need a doctor?" The Boss sounded concerned and gentle, his voice forcing Jake to look up at him.

"I'm fine, sir. Black eye, bruises, a few cuts. They didn't do any real damage."

Jake tore his eyes away from the Boss and looked at the cops. "You want a statement?"

One of the cops nodded and the other stepped forward. "We'll have to do it downtown, Mr. Taggart. Someone reported the fight in progress and we're taking you all in. Apparently, you broke Mr. Neale's jaw, and you might face battery charges. As it is, you'll be arrested and processed, but if you can make bail by the end of the business day you can be home by supper."

Tor swore under his breath and didn't let go. The cop who was still standing back looked at them and his eyes widened a little, then he nodded slightly.

Images slammed into Jake's mind: bars, and mattresses that were too hard and narrow, and the stink of too many men in one place for too long. He felt sick, so sick he was sure he was going to throw up. He tried to stand, but Tor wouldn't let go, so he said, "Tor. Bathroom, now."

Tor finally clued in and let Jake go, and as Jake bolted Tor was with him, holding him as he puked up fear and anger and dread.

Jake wiped his mouth. "Fuck, we spend a lot of time in here. I'm never sick. But since I started up with you I'm fucking throwing up all the time, or holding you when you do it."

Tor looked startled and then laughed, a harsh brittle sound that made Jake wince.

Jake brushed his teeth and went back into the bedroom getting a clean shirt. The cops were off to one side talking quietly. As Jake buttoned his shirt the Boss came over.

"I'll call Becket. Your bail will be posted as soon as they have the paperwork ready."

Jake was stunned. "You don't even know what happened, and you're sending your lawyer to take care of me?"

"I know you. That's enough."

Jake nodded his thanks at him and moved toward the cops, ready to go back to town. Tor moved in front of him.

"Gotta go, Tor." Jake's voice was low.

Tor nodded and put his hands on Jake's waist. "I know." He kissed him, slow and sweet, and Jake let him, not caring who saw.

He needed it.

"I don't want to go," he whispered.

"I know."

They broke apart and Jake turned to the cops, ignoring the uncomfortable looks on their faces. "All right then, let's go."

Jake led the way through the house and out into the yard. A glance told him that if everyone who lived and worked there wasn't standing around watching, it was damn near it. He paused, fighting the urge to just turn around and go back into the bunkhouse. He didn't want to leave in handcuffs.

Bobby Hearn caught his eye and nodded at him. Jake nodded back. Bobby was a good man, and Jake was pretty sure that the marks on his face were telling him and everyone present the story they needed to hear.

The Boss stood next to him and said, "Becket will meet you in town. We'll get you home as soon as we can, Jake."

Jake nodded at him and said, "Thank you, sir."

He walked to the cruiser and waited while one of the cops opened the back door for him. Everyone in the yard was silent and still, so when Tor spoke everyone heard it.

"Jake."

Jake looked up and saw Tor standing in the doorway of the house, tall and strong, arms across his chest. They stared at one another for a long moment, telling each other things that they didn't have words for.

"See you at supper," Tor finally said.

Jake nodded and got in the back of the car, hating the sound when the door slammed shut. He watched Tor go back in the house and knew that anyone who wasn't watching him sitting there was watching Tor's back as he disappeared.

The drive to town started out silent, the two men in front not saying anything at all. The younger one, the one who had started to figure him and Tor out before they'd made it perfectly obvious, was driving. The older guy eventually turned around and looked at him.

"You wanna talk about it, Mr. Taggart?"

Jake smiled a little. "Aren't you supposed to record it, or something? Don't get me wrong, I'm willing to talk about it, just don't know how gossipy you want me to be."

The man laughed and said, "Well, let's just wait then. How 'bout I talk to the kid here and you listen? Sort of telling my partner what I think?"

"That'd be fine, sir."

The cop shifted around in his seat so he was facing sideways, letting Jake hear as best he could over the noise of the road and the static of the police band radio.

He glanced back at Jake and addressed him directly, before turning to the driver, who was wearing a small grin. "So, me and Luke here, we were just getting ready to find us some coffee and a nice piece of pie this morning when

136

we get a call about a fight goin' on behind Prince's Parts and Supply. Well, that was a surprise to us, 'cause we've never had any sort of trouble there before. So off we go. Except when we get there all we find is a pile of people standing around and two guys looking pretty banged up. 'There's our fighters,' I say to Luke. But I'm wrong, it seems. These two, they were fightin' all right, but not with each other. They say a cowboy was in and was starting a fuss about the prices and crap like that and he got so he needed to leave. They say they walked him out and he didn't much take to their help.

"Now, I'm writing this down and I'm looking around and I'm seeing stuff that doesn't add up. Why would a hand be kicking up about prices? He's not paying for it. And I see the box with Gillian's address. So he didn't even load the parts. And then there's the fact that the two twits can't get straight which one of them got hit first. So I go talk to Prince. All he'll tell me is that yes, there was a discussion in the store and that the cowboy left when asked. Won't tell me what it was about.

"We have to go pick the guy up, Neale's got a broken jaw and we have a complaint to deal with. So we call for another cruiser to transport the two we have to the hospital and then the lock up, and we head out to Gillian's to pick up one Jake Taggart."

Jake was looking out the window by this point, just taking it all in. The cops weren't watching him now, and he shook his head a little. At least the idiots didn't have time to get up a decent lie.

"We're driving, trying to get it straight in out heads, and then the information request on Taggart comes through. Got a record for intent to harm, with some other charges tacked on."

Jake stared out the window, feeling ice in his gut.

"Thing is, he's been out of jail for a damn long time and never got in any more trouble that we know of. So when we get to the ranch we talk to Gillian, who is pretty upset to think that his number one man has been fighting. By the time we find Taggart cleaning himself up in his room, we find out that Doug Gillian is just pissed that Taggart could be hurt."

The cop turned in his seat again and looked at Jake, who forced himself to meet his eyes.

"Was gonna ask you why they tried to beat you up, but then your man let us know, didn't he?"

Jake looked out the window again. "Yeah, I guess he did." His voice sounded hollow to his own ears, like he was talking from the bottom of a cave.

"Well, we'll just take the statement when we get to town, then. Try to get you home in time for supper."

Jake swallowed hard, his throat suddenly constricted.

They took his official statement at one of the desks in the office, with Becket right there. He'd been waiting when they'd rolled into town, checkbook in hand to pay Jake's bail. Jake told them his side, keeping his anger under wraps, his voice as even as he could. When he was about done and ready to sign the paper they laid in front of him, a door opened and a doctor came out.

"He's got the pain meds into him, and they wired his jaw at the hospital," the doctor said to the deputies. "Do you really have to keep him here, though?"

The cops nodded and said, "If he wasn't admitted he's ours until his bond is posted. Hopefully we can get a judge to sign them all off this afternoon, and clear them out. Mind you, if any of them insist on pressing charges…"

The doctor shook his head. "I don't know what happened; Neale's pretty banged up. Not sure he's gonna press charges though—he wouldn't even tell the guys at the hospital what started the fight, and usually we can't shut them up."

The cops smirked. "He's most likely none too proud of it."

The doctor looked puzzled, but just left a bottle of pain pills with them and left.

Becket stood up. "Now, let's go see if we can round up a judge, shall we?"

Jake was put in a cell, immensely relieved that there was a drunk tank in a room separate from the main cells. He was pretty sure that being in the same room as Whalen and Neale wouldn't be good for anyone. The cops apparently thought so, too.

He waited for hours before finding out that of the three judges the town employed, one was in court and one was returning from vacation to cover for the third, who was in the hospital. He would have to stay the night.

He ignored his supper when it was brought to him. The thought of food made his stomach ball up and he knew he'd never keep it down all night. He was being surrounded and assaulted by crushing memories of the time he'd spent in prison, and when sleep finally came he had nightmares.

He dreamed of long hallways that led to dark corners where a man could be hurt. He saw himself in a cell with Tor outside talking to him, but he couldn't hear. He dreamed that the man in Tor's pictures was with him in the cell and they were fighting, the man/child holding something important in his hand that Jake needed, but he couldn't see what it was. He dreamed that Tor was sick in the night and needed him, and he couldn't get to him in time to stop Tor from dying of the pain in his belly and his heart.

He woke up covered in sweat, thinking about Tor. Tor was alone too, fighting his own memories. And Jake couldn't help him from where he was, and he was supposed to be home for supper. Tor would be mad, and oh God, how did it get so fucked up when less than two days ago they were on the bed, fucking and happy.

Jake wrapped the blanket tight around himself and waited for morning.

Seventeen

Becket dropped Jake off at the ranch around mid morning the next day.

Jake went into the empty house and headed straight for their room, needing desperately to take a shower and get out of the clothes he'd slept in. He walked into the room, his shirt already gone and his pants undone, longing for hot water. He'd shower, then find out where Tor was. He needed to know that Tor had gotten better sleep than he had.

He was almost to the bathroom when he saw the envelope on the bed. On his pillow, actually, with his name written on it.

He sat down and stared at it, not wanting to read what was inside. He felt a tickle in his nose and swore. No goddamn way was he going to cry over a letter. No fucking way, not after the last two days.

He pushed a hand through his hair and reached out for the envelope, tearing the side open carefully. He sat on the bed and read, his heartbeat racing in his chest, his arms feeling numb with the weight of the single piece of paper.

Jake,

I gotta go.

Can't take this shit, can't deal with you getting hurt, me getting beaten up, people hating. Can't deal with the damn pictures, can't stand thinking of you in that place.

I'll be back.

Tor

Jake put the letter back in the envelope and stripped off his clothes and went to take his shower. He stayed in until the hot water ran out and stayed in a while longer. When he began shivering more than he was shaking, he got out and dried off. He dressed and went to the office.

The Boss wasn't there, so he just sat in the easy chair and waited.

He heard a door open behind him and listened to the careful footsteps. "When did he leave, Doug?"

The Boss sighed. "Last night, when it was clear you wouldn't be home. He asked me for some time off and just left. I couldn't make him stay, Jake."

Jake nodded. "I know. How much time?"

"He didn't say."

"Goddamn him."

The Boss didn't have an answer for that.

"He take a truck? Horse?"

"No. Just put on a jacket and walked down the lane. He looked bad, Jake. Like he was lost."

Jake stood up and left the office, heading to the porch. The Boss followed him, saying, "Jake, he'll be back."

Jake stopped, but didn't look back. "Yeah."

He went back to the bunkhouse and lay on the bed. He was too tired to sleep, so he stared at the ceiling for a while and finally rolled over to Tor's side of the bed and opened the drawer of his nightstand. The pictures were there, which made him feel better. He took them out and looked at Tor's younger self, noting all the differences and similarities. He turned the photo over and saw that someone had written on the back. *Me and my boy*. Not Tor's handwriting. He flipped the other picture over, but it was blank.

He sighed and put them back, feeling a wash of guilt at the snooping. He lay on Tor's side of the bed, inhaling the scent from his pillow until he thought he would go mad and finally levered himself off the bed.

He wandered around for a bit and went into the stable. He talked to River, groomed the horses that looked like they could use it, and finally started cleaning stalls. He was just finishing up when a quiet voice behind him said his name, and he turned to look at Bobby Hearn.

"Hey." Jake wiped the sweat from his forehead with the back of his hand and leaned on the shovel he'd been using.

"They treat you okay in town? I mean last night." Bobby looked concerned and worried, and Jake felt guilty for making everyone edgy.

"Yeah. It was…well, it was awful, but the cops were okay to me and they tried real hard to get me home last night."

Bobby leaned on the stall door and sighed. "Took Julie out for supper last night."

Jake raised an eyebrow at the change of topic. "I'm sure she liked that."

"She did. What she wasn't so keen on was all the talk around us, 'bout how two of the town's favored sons turned out to be jerk offs who pick fights with people outside honest businesses." He looked Jake in the eye and gave him a tight smile.

"Yeah," Jake said slowly, "not too many people care for that as dinner conversation." He wasn't exactly sure what Bobby was trying to tell him, other than the town actually seemed to know who had started the fight, and that it wasn't him.

Bobby sighed and ran a hand through his hair. "Jake…shit. Julie, she's got close family in the same sort of situation you're in. And she's real upset about what happened to you, and the more I listen to her the more I understand. It just ain't anyone's business, and now the whole freaking town knows, and it just ain't right."

Jake nodded. "No, it isn't. But that's the way we have to play it now."

Bobby growled in frustration. "Look. It isn't any of my business either. Just want you to know that Elias and Hound and me, we're doing a lot of talking to people here. Makin' them see that it doesn't matter. That it's just you and Tor, and to stay out of it. People in town, well, we can't do anything about them. This ain't the most accepting part of the world, you know that. But most of 'em had no idea who you were anyway, and there were some who were talkin' like they had half a clue in their heads. Not sayin' that everyone is going to be understanding or anything, and I know that there'll be hell to pay, but there's at least some who seem to be keeping a level head."

Jake looked at Bobby and shook his head, not knowing what to say.

Bobby seemed to understand, and he nodded his head and started away. "Anyway, you tell Tor that I said hey, and we got your back."

"Yeah, I will. If I see him."

Bobby stopped and glanced back. "If you...? Fuck. Where is he?"

Jake leaned the shovel against the wall and crossed his arms, head tilted back to stare at the ceiling. "No idea. He left last night."

"Well, goddamn. You okay?"

"Nope."

"Need anything?"

"Yeah. But unless you know where he is, I won't ask for any more favors." Jake looked at him and held out his hand. "You're a good man, Bobby. Thanks."

Bobby shook his hand and nodded again. "Anytime, Jake. Hope he's home real soon."

After Bobby left, Jake went back to the bunkhouse and took another shower. He was dizzy in the heat and suddenly realized he hadn't eaten any more than his breakfast in two days.

He went to the kitchen and ate supper with the others, thankful for the subdued conversation. He answered the questions about the night before, reassured them that no one was pressing charges, and that it was all over. He had a brief argument with Hound, who wanted Jake to press charges himself, but when Jake pointed out that he didn't want to be a public spectacle, Hound reluctantly backed off. After supper he went to his room and collapsed, fully dressed, sleep falling over him like a blanket.

He woke up to hear someone knocking insistently at the kitchen door. He groaned and rolled over, but the knocking didn't stop, so he got up and made his way through the dark house to the door, glancing at the clock on his way past the living room. Three in the morning.

He flipped on the light and opened the door to see Bobby.

"What the hell are you doing here?" he asked, rubbing at his eyes.

"Got something for you in the truck." Bobby looked pleased with himself, so Jake leaned out and peered into the darkness, trying to see into the lighted cab.

"Jesus. Where did you find him?" Jake was already moving to the truck, had to see if Tor was all right.

"At a honky-tonk out in the middle of fucking nowhere. I got there about nine thirty. He'd just been cut off and he wasn't too happy about it."

Jake stopped walking. "He pass out? If you brought him back here and he didn't want to come, he's just gonna leave again."

Bobby shook his head. "Nah. I talked to him for a long time. Well, he babbled, I listened and poured water into him, then coffee. He went on and on about family and kin, and how he couldn't take the pressure of everyone knowing your business, and how it hurt to think about you in a cell. When he finally started looking like he was gonna puke I took him out and let him. He's not drunk anymore, but he's well into hung over."

Jake started toward the truck again, and Bobby called out, "He's cranky. Be careful."

Jake opened the door of the truck and looked at Tor. He looked like shit, but he was at least awake and looking back.

"You pissed at me?" Tor asked finally.

"Yep."

"Real pissed?"

"Yep."

Tor looked away for a moment then back. "Fixable?"

Jake looked at the sky and sighed, then leaned on the open door. "Depends," he said quietly. "You gonna leave again?"

Tor looked out the windshield and Jake waited, every muscle tight. The question was simple, but it laid it all out and Jake had to know. Could they even attempt to untangle the damage that the last few days had done? Was there any point in trying, or was it just easier to back away now, stay out of each other's heads and just deal with their own shit?

Tor turned and got out of the truck, Jake backing up to give him space. They stood facing each other and Tor reached a hand out to Jake's face, feeling the air around him but not touching before drawing his hand back and curling the fingers into a fist. "Can't promise you forever," he said, his voice husky. "But no, I'm not leaving."

Jake felt himself relax and Tor must have seen some of the tension drain away from him because he stepped forward and put a big hand at the back of Jake's neck and pulled him close, kissing him deeply.

Jake could taste the coffee and booze, but under it was sorrow and anger, pain and desperation. He kissed him back, not bothering with being gentle, inviting Tor to taste his own worry and fear.

When they broke apart Tor whispered, "Can we go inside now? I really need to—I need to be next to you."

Jake simply said, "Yeah."

They went into the bunkhouse, past a grinning and tired looking Bobby Hearn.

"Take the morning off, Bobby," Jake said, as the door closed.

He turned off the light and heard Bobby call out, "Damn right I will!" before he and Tor walked down the hall and into their room.

They went into their room and looked at each other for a moment. Jake wasn't sure what the next step was, he just knew that he wanted to be with Tor right now, and not let him out of his sight.

"I, um, I gotta take a shower," Tor said.

Jake nodded and they stood there for a moment longer.

"This is stupid," Tor said, rolling his eyes. "C'mon. Get wet with me, will you?"

Jake grinned and started to unbutton his shirt.

They went into the bathroom, leaving a trail of clothes behind them, and got the shower going. The room filled with steam within moments, Tor setting the temperature as hot as they could stand it, and they got in.

They washed each other carefully, not speaking, just letting their hands talk. Jake wanted to push his body against Tor's, hold him and lean on him, let himself get lost in the heat of the room, and the sound of Tor's heartbeat.

But he didn't know how. He didn't know what the rules were anymore. So he ran his hands over Tor's back and around to his chest, soap slicked hands gliding over muscles he knew so well now. And Tor let him.

Tor turned in his arms and pressed a kiss on his mouth, a tentative touch that turned into something desperate. Jake couldn't stop, couldn't get control of what he wanted to do, and he was pretty sure that it wasn't what they needed, but oh God, it felt so right to be holding this man, feeling Tor's skin on his own.

They kissed and touched and soon they were just clutching at each other, hands roaming and rough, leaving no quarter for tenderness. Jake needed to let Tor know, somehow, how it felt to find him gone. He needed Tor to know that it couldn't happen again. When he pushed Tor into the wall and bit Tor's chest, he was claiming. He didn't know if Tor got that, and he didn't really care at that point.

Tor was just as demanding, hands on Jake's hips and ass, tugging him in close and kissing him roughly, biting at his neck. Their hips were grinding with a rhythm that said "now" and "harder".

Jake pushed Tor harder into the wall, dropped a hand to their erections and wrapped it around both of them, holding them tight together. As he stroked with a strong fist he tangled his other hand in Tor's wet hair, pulling him in for a deep, rough kiss that said as much as he could manage.

He let everything out in that kiss. The fear from the night before, the dread of Tor leaving, the anger at the bastards who hurt them both. And he let out the pain caused by Tor shutting him out and the need to know about the man in Tor's past. He let out the tightly held emotions that he held for the man in his arms, and when he was done he was coming, hips jerking with his release.

Tor followed him moments later and they stood in the steaming water, trying to come back to themselves. Jake lifted his head from Tor's chest and saw Tor's tears mingling with the water from the showerhead. He laid his head back down and held onto Tor as he cried, wishing that they were in bed and not standing up in the goddamn shower.

Tor's chest began to heave as he gulped in air. Jake held Tor tighter and lifted his head again, bringing Tor's head down to his own shoulder so he could comfort Tor. When the shudders eased off and Jake was pretty sure that the tears were gone, he said, "Tor. Gonna turn off the water and take you to bed, okay?"

Tor didn't reply and Jake reached one hand out as best he could to turn off the water. They got out of the shower and Tor reached for a towel, drying his hair and face. They moved to the bed, still wet and dripping, and lay down, Jake wrapping himself around Tor, not letting the man have a chance to retreat into himself again.

They were silent for a while and then Tor whispered, "Were you okay last night?"

"No. I had nightmares. About prison. About you. I didn't sleep much. I was worried about you. I wondered if you were sleeping, if you were sick again. If you were okay."

"I wasn't. Had nightmares too. Dreamed about you getting hurt, about you in jail and being locked away where I couldn't find you. I looked and looked and I couldn't find you, it was like a maze. But I found Kin and that was worse."

"Kin?"

"Yeah," Tor breathed. "Kincaid. The guy in the pictures."

Kincaid. Bobby said Tor was talking about family and kin, but maybe it was just Kin.

"Tell me?" Jake didn't want to have to ask. But he had to know, no matter how much he hated the asking.

Tor nodded and made a weak noise that Jake couldn't decipher. It sounded desperate; needy and sad. Tor didn't say anything for a long time, and when he did, Jake could feel him shaking and knew that the tears were back. Jake held him tighter and listened to Tor's voice, tight and harsh with uncontrolled emotion.

"He's dead. He's fucking dead and it still hurts, and oh Christ, how I could have forgotten how much I needed him? Dead and gone and always a kid and fuck he should be alive and happy and I let myself forget."

Tor talked. He told Jake about how Kin was smart and funny, and how they had been best friends from the time they met at fourteen, and how it turned into more when Tor was sixteen. How they had been happy and solid and forever, and how everything was bright and clean, the way it can only be when you are young and naive. And he told Jake how Kin died, run off the road by a too tired trucker. Kin had been on his little Honda bike, nothing fancy, just something he'd fixed up for himself, and the trucker came around a turn at him, straying over the line and going too fast, and Kin never stood a chance. Kin had been twenty-one.

Jake listened and held onto Tor in the dark, felt Tor's heartbeat against him. Tor had finally stopped shaking, was feeling more solid in his arms, and when Tor fell silent, nestled in Jake's arms, Jake held him tighter.

There was so much Jake could have said, about how Kin would have wanted him to go on and be happy, how Kin wouldn't like him to be like this, so long after he had gone. But he didn't, because Tor knew it, and what was the point in saying shit like that? Tor didn't need to hear that; but Jake wasn't sure what it was that he did need.

All that Jake knew for sure was that Tor had lost Kin and taken off, wandering around until he wound up in

Mexico, almost dying there. And then he had gotten on with his life. What he hadn't done was grieve.

"Tor, you didn't forget. You can't forget. It hurts, and that's okay. You still gotta get through the pain. Time doesn't make the process easier until you deal with the pain. You didn't forget him. You just started up your life again without really dealing with losing him."

Tor didn't say anything for a long time and Jake thought that he'd fallen asleep. "How do I do that? How do I let him go and not forget?"

"You got any of your old friends? Ones who knew him, I mean. Someone you can talk to about him, someone who can listen to the raw stuff while you work your way to talking about the good times?"

Tor shook his head slowly. "No, they–they all moved on, left the State, or just grew away."

"How about Becky? Can she help?" Jake offered up his last suggestion tentatively, not sure how it would be received, given that it was Becky who had started the avalanche.

But Tor nodded. "Yeah, she'd listen. She'd sort of have to, wouldn't she?" Then he chuckled and the sound sent Jake flying.

"Yeah, I guess she'll have to," Jake said, trying to keep his voice light, but even to him it sounded tight and hoarse. He couldn't help it, the sound of Tor's voice relaxing, the stress easing out of the long body next to him was making him feel light headed and hopeful despite himself.

Tor turned then, looking at him for the first time since they were in the shower. Jake could see how dark Tor's eyes were, felt desire start to build in the pit of his stomach. When Tor rolled on top of him and bent down to kiss him, Jake moaned softly and then they were rocking together, the movement gentle and sweet and so perfect it made him shudder.

Tor's kiss deepened and they grew hard alongside one another, heat growing and spreading until Jake thought he would come just from the feel of Tor's mouth on his.

"Want you," he murmured into Tor's mouth, spreading his legs so Tor settled lower on him.

Tor groaned and shifted, mouth swiping at Jake's collarbone as he reached into the nightstand for lube. Jake sucked at the skin just below Tor's ear, biting down as strong fingers slid inside him, working the lube in. Then Tor was filling him, long slow thrusts that burned and sparked and made him need more.

They moved together slowly, hands moving wherever they wanted, stroking arms and backs, moving to cradle faces and then clutch at hips, which were picking up force. They never stopped kissing, whether it was mouths together or Tor exploring Jake's chest, or Jake feasting on the soft skin at the base of Tor's neck.

They moaned softly as sparks started to light fires and their need grew into something that they couldn't cage. Tor began to thrust deep into Jake, finding Jake's prostate and staying there, pushing insistently until Jake groaned and thrust back, unable to take anymore, needing release.

Then Tor's hand was on Jake's swollen and leaking cock, tight fist pulling him with every thrust, and Jake was coming, calling Tor's name as he arched his body and drew his legs back, pulling Tor even deeper into him.

Tor cried out and pushed in, thrusting as deep as possible twice more before coming, and Jake could feel the tension in every part of him that was touching Tor, could feel all of the muscles around him and on him ripple as Tor rode out his pleasure.

Tor eased out of him after long moments and they curled around one another, kissing softly, lips and tongues speaking and sharing.

Jake was on the very verge of falling asleep when he heard Elias' alarm go off. Six a.m. "Oh fuck," he moaned.

Tor huffed into his chest and fell asleep. Jake smiled at him and tried to figure out how he was going to explain to the Boss why Bobby, Tor and most likely himself would need the morning off. He was still trying to get the phrasing right when he heard Elias' bedroom door open across the hall and heard Elias mutter, "Welcome home, Tor, you big fucking noisy idiot."

He started to laugh and heard Elias laughing along with him.

Eighteen

Tor spent the next week fluctuating between depression that would send him to the phone to call Becky and an apparent need to reassure himself that Jake was still home and not in jail. When he got in those moods Jake would roll his eyes and kiss Tor until the man was breathless, all the while trying not to get giddy at the thought that he was important enough for Tor to worry about while he worked through his grief.

The calls to Becky were mostly short; Tor seemed to know exactly what he needed to say and he would talk in short bursts and then listen for a while to Becky. He would tell her he loved her, and they would hang up; then he would go to the bedroom for ten or fifteen minutes. If the call was a long one, as the first one had been, he would nod his head at Jake and they would both go.

Jake would just sit with him and let him be. Tor didn't cry anymore, but he seemed to be thinking a lot, and he had nightmares. Jake would wake up in the middle of the night to find Tor thrashing in their bed, or sitting up staring into space. Then he would gather Tor into his arms and hold Tor until they could sleep again.

Work was a trial. Everyone kept watching them, and it was hard not to get upset. Jake knew that it would stop eventually, but for now the others seemed to need to look and assess them, both together and separately. Jake and Tor talked about it, and Jake started to make sure that they had stuff to do that would keep them apart most of the time. He hated sending Tor off every day and he worried that he was being possessive.

The hands would at least talk to him as they always did, which was good, even if they did stare sometimes, and there was no change at all with Elias, Kip, and Hound. They were always the same, ready to bitch about the dishes or who's turn it was to take out the garbage, or how much hot water two guys can use if they shower together. And there were always the volume complaints.

Jake felt sort of odd the first time he and Tor got caught on the couch watching TV. Tor was leaning back on him and Jake had one arm over Tor's shoulder, sort of rubbing at his chest while they watched. It was easy and comfortable, and they were together. When Kip and Hound came in Jake tensed, ready to move his arm so Tor could sit up. But Tor just grabbed his hand and held him where he was.

Kip just rolled his eyes and sat in the easy chair and Hound stole the remote. Jake was surprised that it was that easy.

Near the end of that God-awful week Jake went to see the Boss.

"Don't think you should send me or Tor to town for the next while, Doug."

The Boss looked at him and leaned back in his chair. "Your call, Jake. But I've never known you to run before."

Jake shook his head. "Not running. Just not up to being a spectacle for the entire town. Bad enough here."

"What do you mean?" The Boss's voice was low and dangerous. "You getting hassled here? On my spread?"

"Not as such, no. Just taking some time for everyone to adjust. Think about it, you and a couple of others knew about me. But everyone else…they're just going along in their happy worlds and the next thing they know the number two man on the ranch is fucking one of the hands. Then they're living together. And there's fights, and jail, and—shit. It's just going to take a bit for things to settle down."

"But no one's saying anything to you?" the Boss persisted.

"No. Well, Elias says that we use too much hot water, and Kip says that Tor wakes me up too damn early in the morning, but other than that, it's okay." He stopped while the Boss laughed, then added, "Guys are just looking. Trying to see what they missed that would have pointed us out. But Tor, he's dealing with other stuff right now, and I don't want him going to town and getting into trouble."

The Boss just nodded and agreed not to send either of them on town runs until they were ready. Jake thanked him and went to the stable to saddle River. He had a fence line to survey.

155

Nineteen

It was Lego night in the bunkhouse. Jake, Tor, Elias and Hound had every box open and the pieces were spread out all over the living room. They sat on the floor, happily clicking bits together while Kip sat on the couch in wide-eyed astonishment.

"Y'all are serious?"

Tor gave him a withering stare. "Do we look serious? C'mon Kip, loosen up. This is how real men relax."

Hound laughed and put wheels on the tractor he was making. Then he added a computer console.

They played for a couple more hours, trying to use all the pieces. They finally made a wall with the last of the bricks and took turns battering it with their vehicles, trying to assault Elias' castle.

Kip answered the phone when it rang and held the receiver out to Jake. "Boss for ya."

Jake stood up and took the phone, leaning on the wall to watch the battle. "Hello?"

"Hey, son. Come on up to the porch for a minute. I've got something to tell you."

Jake watched as Tor's big rig smashed the wall and crashed into the drawbridge. "Yeah, sure. Be there in a minute."

He hung up and told the others he'd be back in a bit and headed out. He was still smiling to himself when he got to the house, thinking about how much fun it was just to play kids' games with the others. Hound had never really grown up, he didn't think, but it sure was nice to see Tor play.

His smile faded when he saw the Boss. He was sitting on the bench outside the kitchen door, his eyes serious, every line in his body tight. Jake walked up and sat down next to him, looking out over the yard.

"What is it, Doug?" he asked quietly.

The Boss sighed. "Got a phone call a few minutes ago. Woman asking for you, said her name was Melissa Taggart."

Jake closed his eyes and leaned his head back on the wall. "What did she say?"

"Said she's your sister. That she found the number here in a box of stuff at her mother's. She was real upset, Jake. Said she'd been told you were gone. She thought you were dead."

Jake nodded. That made sense. Momma would have told her that. Hell, to Momma he was dead.

"She called up and said she was looking for you, wondered if you were still here. I said you were, but that I wasn't about to give out the number to the bunkhouse until

I talked to you. She said that was fine, and she gave me her number for you. Said that she'd really like to talk to you, but she'd understand if you took your time calling her up. She asked if you were doing well."

Jake could feel his chest tighten up and he thought that the unreality of the entire conversation was the only thing keeping him sane. He nodded again, but couldn't think of anything to say.

The Boss handed him a slip of paper. "Here's the number. And Jake?"

Jake looked at him and knew what he was going to say. "She's dead, isn't she?"

"Yes, son. Miss Taggart was clearing her house when she found the number. I think your momma's been gone for a couple of months now, though she didn't give me a date."

Jake folded the paper with 'Lissa's number on it carefully and put it in his pocket. "Thank you, Doug. Means a lot, you telling me like this. Not giving her the number and all, too."

The Boss nodded and they sat in silence for a bit, until Jake stood up and offered his hand. "Thanks again. I'm gonna go back now. We've got Lego to put away."

The Boss stared at him for a moment and then shook his hand. "You okay?"

"Yeah."

"G'night, then." He went into the house and Jake walked home.

When he went into the living room the boxes were all lined up and the others were trying to match pieces to sets.

Tor looked up at him and grinned. Jake offered a passable smile in reply, and sat on the couch, occasionally adding a piece to a box before giving up and going to their room. He left the door open and turned on the light before lying on the bed to stare at the ceiling.

Tor came in about three minutes later and closed the door. "What happened?"

Jake looked at him, and there must have been something desperate in his face because Tor didn't waste anytime lying down and wrapping up around him. "Tell me. It's okay, whatever it is. We'll make it okay."

"My sister called."

Tor blinked at him. "You have a sister?"

Jake started to chuckle, stopping before it could really get started. "Yeah. Two. And a brother."

"Well, shit. When was the last time you talked to any of them?"

"God, must be near eighteen years now. I left home when I was sixteen, talked to them on the phone about three months before I got arrested. Hell of a long time, either way."

Tor held him a little tighter and kissed his shoulder. "Long time is right. Why'd she call?"

"Momma died." Tor closed his eyes tight and Jake could see the conflict in his face. "It's okay, Tor. You don't have to say you're sorry, or anything like that. Woman threw me out and told my family I died, apparently. 'Lissa found the number for here in Momma's things and damn near had a fit, if the Boss was telling anything near the truth. She thought I was dead."

Tor kissed him, soft and slow. "Did you talk to her?"

"No. Boss gave me her number, though. She wants me to call."

Tor nodded. "You gonna?"

Jake shrugged. "Not tonight, that's for sure."

Tor nodded again. "So what are you going to do tonight?"

Jake rolled into Tor and offered his mouth for another kiss. "You."

"Works for me."

Jake kissed Tor slowly, the touch of his lips and tongue gentle, almost feather light. His hands slowly worked at Tor's clothes, baring his chest and belly. Tor moved under his touch, shifting to provide Jake with better ease of movement, but not to rush or hurry him.

Jake needed to do this at his own pace. He needed to feel Tor's skin under his hands and mouth. He needed the reassurance of this body and of the whispered words he only half heard. He needed the warmth and the touch only this man could give.

Jake needed.

He lingered over Tor's body, watched muscles play under his hands as he stroked smooth skin. He dropped kisses on Tor's chest and he bit at Tor's shoulders. He spent ages licking and suckling at the soft skin of Tor's inner thighs, listening to Tor's breathing change and catch, drowning in the unending wash of words that poured over him.

Strong...good...yes...hot...please...breath...give...sexy ...all...there...need...now...yours...please, oh please Jake...

Jake lifted his head and met Tor's eyes. He needed. He stood and stripped his own clothes off, Tor's eyes never leaving him. He lay on the bed and gathered Tor into his arms, kissing Tor deeply, letting his hunger out, letting Tor feel how very much he needed.

They rolled over and Jake settled himself between Tor's legs, arms braced. He stared into dark eyes as he entered Tor's heat, drew emotion and need from Tor's mouth as he moved.

When Jake came it was with a groan and a sob half torn from his throat. Tor met him with a sigh and a tight embrace, holding him in strong arms until morning.

Twenty

- - ◆ - -

It took Jake a week to decide to call his sister. He hadn't told anyone but Tor what was going on, so managing to find a chance to use the phone without anyone in the bunkhouse was a problem until Tor pointed out that the Boss would let him use the phone in the office if he only asked. Jake looked at him, honestly startled that the thought hadn't even occurred to him.

He walked to the house just after supper and knocked on the door. When the Boss came to see him he simply said, "Use your phone, Doug?"

So he was sitting in a fine leather chair at an empty desk with only a worn slip of paper in front of him. He sat for several minutes before finally picking up the phone and dialing. He hadn't been this nervous in years.

The phone stopped ringing at the other end with a cheerful hello. A young voice.

"Hello," he said, his voice sounding odd to his own ears. "I'm looking for Melissa Taggart."

There was a short pause, then a cautious, "This is 'Lissa."

Jake froze for a moment, wondering what to say next, his mind blank. "It's Jake."

"Oh Lord. Jake…I…oh God. You're really alive."

"Yes, ma'am. I am."

There was brief pause and then 'Lissa laughed. "You call me ma'am again and we'll really have an issue."

Jake grinned into the phone. "Yeah, okay."

"I want to say 'So, how are you?' but that's just…weird. God, it's good to hear your voice."

"Yeah. And I'm fine." Jake was still smiling. "Thanks for giving my Boss your number. And for knowing it would take a while for me to call. I didn't…I didn't think you'd be wanting to hear from me. Thought that you'd be just as happy to have me gone."

"Jake, honey, we never had the chance to–to even know that you were out there somewhere. When you left…and then that last phone call. It was bad, Jake. Then you died— well, you didn't die, but we thought you did. Oh God. There's just so much to tell you, so much to ask."

"Kinda hard on the phone. 'Lissa, I just want you to know that I'm real sorry I left you and Cath there. I was…hell, I was sixteen and drunk all the time. Wasn't thinking about you much, you know? Different now."

"I know. It'd have to be different now, it's been so damn long and so many things have changed. Listen to me, now. I want to ask you to do something, and I want you to think about it before you let me know."

"I'm here."

"I've been thinking a lot, waiting for the phone to ring. It's been a long time and we both have more to tell than a phone call can manage. Would it be okay if I wrote to you? Told you what happened after you left? Then you could write to me, and it might be easier to tell a piece of paper than a voice, if you know what I mean. Easy to skip stuff on the phone, easy to miss things when you're jumping from topic to topic."

Jake had started nodding as soon as she said *letter*. Easy to tell the whole truth when you knew you wouldn't actually hear a voice saying, "faggot" or "con". Easier to get it all out and start with an honest opening.

"Yeah. That's good."

"Really?" There was a smile in her voice, something relaxed and hopeful.

"Yeah. You got the address here?"

She did, and she gave him hers. Then he cleared his throat and glanced at the clock. "I gotta go real soon, 'Lissa. Just want you to know that I'm real glad you called. And I'm sorry if you miss Momma. I know it's hard for you, but she never did give me a chance to be who I was, and I won't lie and tell you I've been missing her all these years. But I'm sorry if you do."

She didn't say anything for a moment and Jake was about to apologize when she said, "Hon, I do miss her. But just 'cause she was my momma. I know she did something real bad to you, and I'm sorry for that. But thank you for even thinking of me missing her."

"Yeah. Will you write soon?"

"Tonight. I'm gonna call Cath right now, tell her you called me. She'll be over the moon."

"Tell her hi for me. And tell her…if she wants to talk to me that'd be good. But maybe she can wait a bit? Read the letter I'll send you?"

"I'll tell her. Jake, thanks for calling."

"I'm glad I did. Good night, 'Lissa."

"Good night, Jake."

When Jake got back to the bunkhouse he went into the living room and looked at the three hands watching TV. "Where's Tor?"

Hound waved his hand to the back of the house. "Your room."

Jake turned to go and got three feet down the hall before a chorus of "Keep it down tonight!" sounded behind him.

"Oh, shut up," he called back to them, grinning as he heard them laugh.

He walked into the room and Tor stood up. He'd been sitting on the edge of the bed, elbows on knees, just waiting.

"You okay?" Tor asked immediately, standing up.

Jake smiled at him and moved into his arms. "Yeah. Was good." He grinned then, feeling a little giddy. He thought he might be bouncing.

"Uh, Jake?"

"What?"

"You're bouncing."

"Thought so. Want me to stop?"

"Uh, not so much that as maybe bounce a little closer." Tor pulled him in so the bouncing turned into rubbing and Jake moaned a little then grinned wider.

"Can do that," Jake said, bouncing them to the bed. "Make some noise, yeah?"

"Yeah."

Twenty One

Jake and Tor had spent the morning on horseback, checking some of the herds. It was a job Jake enjoyed; the day was warm and sunny, and the nearest cattle were all where they were supposed to be. Looked like a good day.

They rode back toward the house, taking their time. There wasn't any rush, it was almost lunchtime and they would get a chance to just sit still for a while before starting the afternoon's rounds. Jake looked at Tor and smiled to himself. Man looked fine on horseback.

"What are you grinning at?" Tor said.

"Nothing. Just admiring your seat."

Tor shook his head and tried not to laugh. "Admire away, then. Just don't get any ideas, not a chance at being alone today until after supper."

Jake looked at the emptiness around them. "Um, Tor. We're kinda alone now."

Tor blinked and gave him a crooked grin. "Yeah. But we won't be for long. Close enough that someone can hear you screaming and then we'll have lots and lots of company."

Jake felt himself blushing furiously and stared straight ahead. "Shut up," he ordered, trying not to think about how they'd been caught only a few days before, in the middle of fine outdoor orgasm at the riverbed. The kind of orgasm that left them both hoarse from screaming, in a panting, trembling mess. Caught by what felt like half the ranch.

"Oh come on, it was funny. Even at the time it was funny."

"Doesn't mean I want to do it again. Well, I want to do that again, just without the audience, and I told you to shut up!" Jake glared at his lover, who was about to fall off his mount if he kept laughing that hard. "Christ."

Tor finally got some control back, though he looked like he could start laughing again at any point. "Think Elias has recovered yet?"

Jake grinned. "Been four days. Hell, I haven't recovered yet, not sure if he ever will."

Tor laughed again, and Lug expressed his displeasure by tossing his head.

"You tell him, Lug. Big jerk acts like he didn't have anything to do with it."

"Oh, I had something to do with it, all right. Show you how much later. Bet I can make you scream longer next time, too."

Jake shivered. Yeah, that would be good. Had to find somewhere else, though.

They rode into the yard and put the horses in the pasture before going to the bunkhouse. When they went in Elias was sitting at the table with a huge sandwich in front of him. He glanced up at them as they crossed to the fridge and said, "Mail's here. Put yours in your room."

Jake looked at Tor and chewed on his lower lip.

Tor said thanks to Elias and put a hand on Jake's shoulder, squeezing slightly. "I'll make lunch, you go see if there's anything exciting in the mail."

Jake gave him a small smile and went to their room, picking up the brown envelope with his name on it. Light, no catalogues this time; all Jake ever really got was catalogues and the odd magazine. He ripped the end open and looked in at one letter.

He sat on the bed and looked at the handwriting, thinking it was odd that the only way he knew it was from family was by the return address. He didn't know 'Lissa's handwriting. He opened the letter and lay down on the bed to read.

Dear Jake,

God, I never thought I'd get the chance to write that. So many years...

I spoke to Cath after I got off the phone with you last night. Well, after I stopped crying. I'm not usually one given to crying fits, but after we hung up, I guess it just all kind of hit me. Made it real, you know? Cath is as confused and upset as I am, and asked me to pass her address along to you. I'll write it at the bottom for you. She also asked me to tell you that she will understand if you take some time before contacting her—this is very emotional for all of us. She'll wait to read your letter.

Jake—she's a good kid. Well, if twenty-seven can be a kid.

So. As near as we can figure it, you left home for whatever reason—I say ~~Daddy~~ our father finally went too far, Cath reckons it was Momma. At any rate, you left and

167

then there was some sort of trouble and they either couldn't or didn't help you out.

Jake, they told us you were dead. Not that you were gone and not coming back, but that you were dead. Killed in a drunken wreck with your 'no good' friends.

They wouldn't tell us why they didn't bring you home to bury you. Now we know. At the time we thought it was 'cause funerals and burying cost money.

God, Jake. What happened? Where did you go, and why didn't you come back?

Family—I assume the only ones you care to hear about at this point is the immediate family.

I'm well. Thirty-two, married, divorced, one son. He's ten. Doesn't look a thing like his daddy, thank God. I'll send a picture next time, if you want. I named him Jacob.

Cath's twenty-seven. Never married, works for a bank in some sort of investment field I don't understand. She went to college on scholarships. Smart girl, our Cath is. But she's shy of men—and I don't mind that one bit.

James. Well, James is James. Thirty-seven and just like our father. Don't think I need to say anything else. He has three children at last count, but I haven't talked to him in a couple of years, so it could be more. Cath has, she might know. He drinks too much, doesn't work enough and has never bothered to marry any of the women who have his kids...more luck to them, I say. Three kids, three moms.

James and I don't see eye to eye on much.

Momma died nine weeks ago.

Daddy died six years ago.

I don't really know how to end this, Jake. I want the chance to get to know you again, if you're willing.

Lissa

Jake folded the letter and put it back in the envelope, then took it back out and read it again.

A nephew. A sister who went to college. A sister who wanted to know him.

Family.

Jake closed his eyes and tried to turn his mind off. He wanted to think about the warm feeling in his belly for a while before he had to ruin it all by writing his own letter. How much would 'Lissa want him in her life when she found out everything? Would she even let him see Jacob, just once, before she said that it was a mistake? That an ex-con and a homosexual wasn't a suitable relative for her boy, and it would be best if they stopped now?

Jake told himself he was looking for trouble where there wasn't any, that he could at least tell her the truth about himself and let her decide based on the facts. And suddenly he knew that he was going to tell her about Tor; not just that he was gay, but that he had someone. That he was happy.

He got off the bed and went to the kitchen for lunch, the letter safely tucked away in his nightstand. He gave Tor a warm smile and when Elias was at the sink washing his hands, he leaned over the table and kissed the man.

Tor blinked. "Uh, thanks?"

"You're welcome."

Tor grinned at him, and Jake smiled back.

Twenty Two

Dear 'Lissa,

Not sure where to start. I'll just shoot off your letter and add on later.

Thank you for the letter. And for calling Mr. Gillian in the first place. Man's the closest thing I've had to family in thirteen years. It's...nice to have a chance to add to that.

I remember Cath as a tiny little bit with too much hair and a dirty face, and a missing tooth. I will write to her, but not yet. Can't yet. Having a hard enough time with this one.

Tell her that I am thankful for the chance, and that I have her address. It's just going to take me some time. Tell her I'm sorry.

What happened. Lissa, I'm just going to put it out here, tell you the truth. I figure if you don't like it, or if it's too much, then we can just go back to our lives. At least you'll know that I'm alive, and I'll know that you didn't hate me before.

When I was sixteen I had enough of Daddy's fights and words and fists and was just going to go. Momma said I should go to Aunt Jess', work in her store for board, you know? So I went, just happy to be out of the house.

I was drinking a lot then. Been drinking since I was twelve, so no, I really didn't spare a thought to you and Cath being there still. I'm sorry. I'll never forgive myself for that—it's the start of a long list.

Went to Jess' and that was okay for about a week. Worked in the store and drank, wandered around the town at night. No one paid me much mind, certainly didn't try to start any fights. Days it was just me in the store, or me and Jess, or me and the other part time guy. Did as I was asked, and I like to think that I didn't give much lip, but knowing me I probably did.

The other guy, he was a bit older and hell of a lot more open about stuff he'd done. For all the shit I'd caused at home or at school I didn't talk about it much. He talked. About people he'd met, fights he'd had, people he'd slept with. He was Big Trouble and I was Little Trouble trying to be Big.

By that time I'd figured out I'm gay, and I think maybe Momma had a clue. Daddy did. That's why he beat me that last time, though he swore he'd not tell Momma, said it would break her heart to have a fag for a son.

Jess walked in on me and Big Trouble making out in the storage room. Said I wasn't welcome and if I wanted to see the next day, I'd best clear out before Uncle James came home. So I left. Hit the streets and was happy to go.

Got into some trouble—bar fight—and got picked up. The police called mamma and told her I was in the lock up. She said 'keep him', and I was just as happy.

Got a letter from her the next week through General Delivery at the post office. Jess had told her what she'd seen and Momma said that you all would be just fine without me and not to bother coming home.

Drank a lot, got in more trouble. Needed money and made the biggest mistake of my life. I robbed a small convenience store at knife point, got ripping drunk and arrested. A variety of circumstances saw me serve five years of an eight to twelve sentence in a medium security prison. Best thing that ever happened to me, though what got me there wasn't so good.

Got sober there, and learned a lot. When I was twenty-two I was pretty much sent here by my PO. It wasn't a condition of my parole that I stay here, exactly, but Mr. Gillian saw something in me, I guess, and he took me on. Been here more than a dozen years and it's home.

That's the worst of it, but I can pretty much guarantee that jail time isn't why Momma told you I was gone. She just didn't want me around after she found out I'm gay. Can't change your mind, if that's how you feel, but I won't hide it, either.

Got a partner, too. He's a cowboy here on the ranch, and a good man. His name is Tor; well, that's short for Tornado, and yeah, he's got a real name too. I've never used it; don't think I've ever heard anyone use it. If it matters, it's Mark Flynn. He's got family in Texas, though he's been in these parts for a bit now.

Reckon that's all the shocks I have for you right now.

I've changed, 'Lissa. I'm sober, I work hard, and I have nice life here. Be nice to add blood family to the one I'm building, but that's up to how you take all this, I guess.

Sorry to hear James isn't on level ground. Saw it happening when I left, but didn't have any way to stop it.

Sorry I missed Cath growing up. Tell her I'm proud of her. Show her this letter, too, and if she still wants to she can write.

I've missed you, 'Lissa. Tried not to think about y'all for a long time. Usually it worked, but there's always been this sore spot that was supposed to be full of memories I never had a chance to make. Maybe that's my fault, maybe I should have tried harder to track you down when I got out. I'm sorry.

Sorry I've missed ten years of Jacob, too. Not sure how to tell you how much it means to me that he has my name. Even if you only named him that 'cause I was dead, it's an honor I'll not forget.

Ball's back in your court, sis. Think you can take an ex-con gay brother on? You got room for that kind of baggage?

Take care,

Jake

PS. I really would love a picture of Jacob if you can see your way to sending one.

J

Jake folded the sheaf of papers and sighed. It wasn't right, it wasn't perfect, but he was beginning to the think that the perfect letter wasn't going to be an honest one. Telling her the truth was more important.

He addressed the envelope and shoved it into the outgoing mail, burying it under Hound's letter to his brother and Elias' latest monograph to his mother. When he turned around Tor was leaning on the doorframe looking at him.

"You get it done?" he asked.

Jake grinned. "Finally." The grin faded and he added, "It's hard, you know? Trying to balance too much at once with just enough?"

Tor walked to him and put a hand on his waist. "Yeah. I bet it is." He kissed him softly. "You tell her about me?"

Jake kissed him back, less softly. "Yeah. One thing I didn't even debate about. She wants me, she gets us both."

Tor looked surprised, then stunned. His expression finally settled on the one Jake called "Oh, I am so getting laid" and he pulled Jake a little closer. "Didn't have to."

"Yeah, I did," Jake said, his voice getting hoarse.

Tor kissed him, the hand on his waist slipping around to the small of Jake's back, holding him close. Tor had just started to grind against him when the kitchen door opened and Hound came in.

"Oops, sorry guys," he said, walking quickly past them. "You really should put a sign up or somethin'. You'll give Elias a heart attack."

Jake watched Hound disappear around the corner into the living room. "He's never gonna forgive us for that thing at the riverbed, is he? He blushes every time he sees us."

Tor shrugged and licked Jake's neck. "He'll deal. But the kid has a point. Bedroom?"

Jake forgot about Hound and groaned softly, pushing Tor back. "It's that way."

Tor walked backwards, arms still looped around Jake. "Know where it is, Taggart. Just making sure you don't strip me naked in the kitchen."

Jake kissed him again, pushing him against the wall. "Oops. Thought we were at our door," he said, one hand going to Tor's fly. "Besides, you didn't complain last time I started something in the kitchen."

"Wasn't anyone…oh, yeah, like that…home then and it was the middle of the night, not the day. Oh shit. Jake. Bedroom."

"It's over there," Jake teased, not moving.

Tor got a determined look in his eye and Jake froze. Too far. Now he was really going to get it.

Tor pushed him back by the shoulders and slammed him into the wall on the other side of the hall. Jake barely had time to regain his balance before Tor had his jeans open and one hand wrapped around Jake's cock, pumping him firmly.

"Now. You wanna blow here in the hall where any of them can see, or you wanna go lie on the bed like a good cowboy and let me do you right?"

Jake didn't even have to think about it. "Bed."

"Right then." Tor let him go and stepped back, pointing the way.

Jake went, happy he knew the right answers to the really hard questions.

Twenty Three

Over the next two weeks Jake felt himself grow more and more out of sorts. The work was slow around the ranch and he had more time on his hands than he really liked; more time to think and more time to wonder why he hadn't heard back from 'Lissa yet.

Tor didn't say anything about it, just made sure that Jake didn't have time to sit still for too long. They rode in the evenings until it got too cool or dark, or they played with the Lego. Some nights Tor would just make him talk, about the ranch, or the upcoming holidays, or when Kip would finally ask Beth to marry him.

Jake appreciated it, but he still waited for the mail each day with growing depression. He didn't realize he would feel the rejection so strongly. He'd gone almost twenty years without a family, he thought he should be used to it by now.

He was just heading into the barn to take River out for some exercise when the Boss came out of the big house with the familiar brown envelopes in his hand. Jake watched him walk toward the bunkhouse and pass the envelopes over to Hound, still not wanting to hope and having to anyway. With a sigh he headed back to the bunkhouse; he might really need to take River out if he got that sick, sad feeling again.

When he went in, though, Hound was just sorting them out and he absently handed a thick envelope to Jake. "Here you go, Jake," he said, wandering out of the kitchen with his own mail.

Jake sat at the kitchen table, barely glancing up as Tor came in. "I got mail," he said softly.

Tor stood behind him and rested a hand on his shoulder.

Jake dumped the envelope out on the table. Two catalogues and a thick envelope from 'Lissa. Without a word he picked up the envelope and went to their room. Tor followed for a couple of steps, then Elias called him. Jake looked back and got an apologetic look, followed by an encouraging smile.

"I'll be in as soon as I can. Besides, you don't need me hanging over your shoulder while you read."

Jake nodded. "But you'll be in?"

"Of course."

Jake settled himself on the bed and tore open the envelope. A letter from 'Lissa. One from Cath. And one from Jacob folded three times and addressed to "Uncle Jake" in pencil crayon. Jake blinked and his heart lurched. He put it to the side, picking up Cath's letter first.

Dear Jake,

I just wanted to send a short note to let you know that I read the one you sent to 'Lissa.

Love you, big brother. Never stopped.

I don't care if you're with a man. That sort of thing has never been an issue for me—I'm the strange one in this family. Mamma and Daddy were always set against it, and James too…but I never saw the point. So you'll get no hassle from me. As long as he's a good man and treats you right, he's welcome.

The other? Was a long, long time ago, hon. You've made the changes you had to and stuck by them. That's the end of it.

I would love it if you would call me, Jake. Want to get to know you.

Cath

Jake read it three times before setting it aside, and even as he unfolded the one from 'Lissa he kept glancing at it, like he thought it would go up in flames. Maybe he should just call Tor and make sure it said what he thought it did. He shook his head and looked at the letter in his hands.

Dear Jake,

Sorry this one took time to reach you—I had to wait for Cath's to get here, and Jacob really wanted his say as well.

Since you're being so honest I guess I better be, too.

Can't say I'm surprised you went to prison. You were heading that way, I know. I am sorry it happened though—no one likes to think that their brother went to such an awful place. And I can't help thinking that you're leaving something out, just 'cause it seems like a long time to serve for the crime, but I'm willing to let that go.

I'll let it go because it was so damn long ago and you aren't the same person now. You aren't the boy who left us. And I'm glad of that—the boy who left was the one who did that bad thing, and I'm glad you grew out of it, got your eyes opened. I'm glad you got the help you needed, even if I am sorry we couldn't be that help.

I'm glad you're a good man, Jake.

I'll admit to having a harder time dealing with you being gay. I was raised by the same people you were, so you know the prejudices I'm fighting here. I am fighting them, though, Jake. I lost you once over this, I'll not do it a second time. It may take me a bit of work, but I'll not be cutting you off from me or my boy because you're in love with a man.

I trust you when you say your Tor is a good man. I'm glad you have someone like that. Someone you can count on.

I told Jacob, and he's really what set me right about this. He just kind of blinked at me and said, "So? When can I see him?"

God, I love that kid.

Anyway. If you're still willing to try to patch our family together we're ready for you. We'll meet you more than halfway, Jake. We've missed you and we'd be damn fools to give you up on purpose.

The holidays are coming up in a few weeks and the better part of me is crying out to invite you for Christmas— Tor too—but the smarter part is telling me it's too soon and that Christmas is stressful enough. Would you be willing to see me and Cath and Jacob in the spring? Maybe the five of us can meet somewhere for a long weekend.

Call me. Anytime.

'Lissa

Jake set the letter down on top of Cath's, his hands shaking. They wanted him. His sisters wanted him back. All the years he'd tried to push them out of his mind, all the times he'd felt angry and alone ate at him, made him want to scream. He picked up the last letter and unfolded it, letting two photos drop into his lap.

The first was a studio shot, looked like a school picture. Jacob's wheat-colored hair stuck up in the back and his shirt was smudged. He had a wide, beaming grin that showed the very devil and his blue eyes glittered with laughter. He didn't look much like Jake remembered 'Lissa, but he could see some of James in him, around the cheekbones. He could see himself in Jacob's brow and hair and ears.

The second was 'Lissa and Jacob together, sitting on a couch, smiling happily. Jacob's hair was still sticking up, though his shirt was cleaner. He was a scrawny little thing, and 'Lissa was, too. She was slim and had long dark, curly hair, blue eyes glowing with happiness. She looked…wonderful. She had some of their mother in her, but that was just fine. She had more of their grandmother than Jake had ever thought, and he could see three generations of his kin right there in her face.

He didn't bother wiping the tears from his cheek when he started to read Jacob's letter.

Dear Uncle Jake,

Momma told me you're alive and I think that's just so cool. Like you were gone and now you're ours again. It made Momma cry, but she says that's because she's happy. Is that weird?

She also told me you did a bad thing a long time ago and you paid the price for it. She says that it didn't matter anymore, that you growed up. Good for you.

Momma seemed a little upset to find out you have a boyfriend, but I told her that Kelly at school has three dads and it works out fine for her. She had a Ma and a Daddy first, then they got a ~~divau divors~~ split up and then she has a Ma and a Dad, and a Daddy and a Da. She says her Daddy and Da don't fight at all and they look silly when they kiss and stuff, but other than that it's good.

Can you ask Tor if I can call him Uncle Tor? Are you guys sort of married? I'd like to, if he says it's okay.

Can we see you in the spring?

Love
Jacob

Jake was curled around his pillow when Tor came in.

"Shit. What did they say?" Tor sounded near panicked at the tears.

Jake sat up. "They said—hell. Jacob wants to call you Uncle Tor."

Tor stared at him. "He what now?"

Jake nodded happily. "He wants to know if we're—" he reached for the letter and quoted, "sort of married. And he wants to call you Uncle Tor if you say it's okay."

Tor sat down on the bed looking shell-shocked. "Uh, yeah. That'd be cool." He looked at Jake again. "So, it's good?"

"It's good." Jake leaned up and kissed him. "It's good."

Tor kissed him back. "I got mail too. From Becky."

"Yeah?" Jake asked, looking for another kiss.

"She wants us to go for Christmas. My mother wants us there."

Twenty Four

———◆◆◆———

Tor had already threatened to turn the truck around and deliver him back to the ranch twice so Jake just stared out the window and bit his lip as they got closer to Texas. It wasn't that he didn't want to go to Becky's for Christmas, he did. He just wasn't sure if he was up to meeting Tor's mother.

He was lost in thought, contemplating the amount of stuff they'd brought for a four-day trip, and deliberately not thinking about what he would say to Tor's mom, when the truck veered sharply and Tor hit the brakes, stopping at the side of the road.

"Gonna tell me what the problem is, Taggart? Getting too far to just turn around now. You don't want to do this I gotta know now." His tone was far gentler than his words, and when Jake turned his head to meet Tor's eyes he found them to be even softer than his tone.

"Not that. Want to do this; wouldn't have come this far if I didn't."

"So? Talk to me, cowboy."

Jake leaned on the door and sighed. "It's stupid."

Tor didn't say anything, didn't move. Traffic passed them by and Jake sighed again. "Just that…well, last year I was alone. Really alone, just me and the Boss's family at Christmas. Been that way for a lot of years, you know? Now I got two sisters, a nephew who calls you uncle, and I'm about to meet your sister, your niece, and your mom— which, yeah, scares the hell out of me." He took a breath. "See? Dumb."

Tor smiled and leaned over, kissing him softly. "Not dumb. Lot of changes. You forgot one though."

Jake frowned slightly. "I did?"

"Yeah. You got me, too. And you don't need to handle any of this alone."

Jake didn't know what to say so he kissed Tor hard and let it go.

Meeting Becky was easy. She said hi and got as far as a polite 'Nice to meet you' and then the room was taken over by Susie. Jake thought that all meetings should have an energetic six year old on hand, just to take the edge off.

Two hours later, Susie was still showing Jake and Tor all her things and talking non-stop. She'd shown them their room, the tree and the presents and was just starting to tell them about the food they were going to have, when Becky finally picked her up and said, "We're going to go get Gram now. Shush so I can talk to Uncle Tor for a second."

Susie squealed and wiggled out of her mother's arms, running for her coat. She was yelling about how she was going to tell her Gram all about the horse Santa was going to bring.

"You coming to the train station?" Becky asked them as she watched her daughter with fond eyes.

Tor shook his head. "No. Momma will understand, tell her there isn't enough room in the car for four adults and Susie's car seat."

"There isn't," Becky answered, rolling her eyes.

"Then why did you ask?"

"'Cause Momma raised me to be polite. You, she raised to clean up after the dog."

Tor chased her down the hall. Jake just shook his head and wondered if he'd ever have an easy relationship like that with his sisters.

When Becky and Susie left, the sudden silence in the house was almost overwhelming. Jake was looking at the tree when Tor came up behind him and started unbuttoning his shirt.

"What are you doing?"

"We have an hour before they're back."

Jake leaned back into him and made a half-hearted attempt to still Tor's hands. "You think this is a good idea?"

"Oh yeah. An hour before I'm stuck in the same house as my mother? Trust me, I want to spend the time getting as relaxed as possible. And being naked with you? Favorite thing."

Jake gave up. He figured it would take a stronger man than him to withstand that kind of pressure.

They were barely out of the shower and dressedwhen Susie burst through the front door, talking a mile a minute. Tor's mom, having raised her own children, seemed to think that just talking over the child was the easiest way to greet her boy, and Jake let himself melt into the background and watch as Tor and his family spent a few minutes trading hugs and luggage.

Tor's mom was tall, only a couple inches shy of six feet, and looked as strong as Tor. Her hair was going gray, strands the color of steel shot through with white, and her eyes were blue, sharp and bright and full of life. Jake couldn't see any signs that she was in failing health, though Tor had hinted at it a time or two.

Finally Tor stepped back and looked over at him, grinning. His smile was teasing, but his eyes were asking questions. Jake took a breath and moved forward.

"Momma, this is Jake Taggart. Jake, this is my mother, Maureen Flynn."

Jake nodded his head, wishing he had his hat on. "Ma'am. Pleasure to meet you."

She offered her hand and waited until he had shaken it to reply. "So you're Mark's man, are you? You two fight much?"

Jake blinked. "Not so much anymore, ma'am."

"But you did?" she persisted.

"Well, yes. Before."

"Fists?" she demanded, ignoring Tor's attempts to interrupt.

Jake shuddered, thinking back to their fight in the rain. "Yes, ma'am."

"You hold your own? Not let him push you?"

"Let him push me too far. That's what led to the fighting."

"What, so now you give in?"

"Now he doesn't push me."

She looked him up and down. "You'll do, then. We'll talk later." She scooped Susie up then and they headed down the hall.

Jake thought his legs were going to give out, but Tor just grinned and kissed him.

Christmas day was chaos, the sort only a six year old could create. Up before light, the presents were unwrapped and breakfast eaten before the phone started to ring off the hook. Becky, Maureen and Tor took turns talking to

185

assorted cousins and aunts and uncles, leaving Jake to teach Susie about the wonders of Lego. Everyone was happy.

Tor had a mid-afternoon nap and Maureen gave Jake a look that meant he was to follow. Jake knew the look, and knew that there was no way to avoid the conversation, so he merely followed her outside and walked along as they toured the backyard.

"Mark ever tell you about what happened before he went to Mexico?" she asked. She didn't look at him.

"Yes, ma'am. He did." Jake kept his voice low and even, wondering where she was going with the conversation.

She sighed and stopped walking, finally looking Jake dead in the eye. "I always thought that if Kincaid had lived, if they had just let their relationship follow its path, that they would have split up. That Mark would have grown out of this. I was wrong, wasn't I? He's not going to change."

Jake looked back. "No, he isn't. He's gay. I'm gay. Did he tell you anything about my family?"

She nodded. "He told me that your momma denied you when she found out. That she lied about you."

Jake shook his head slowly. "That she denied me is an understatement," he said. "She told my sisters and my brother that I was dead, killed in a car wreck. I spent damn near twenty years with no family 'cause she couldn't accept me."

Her eyes widened. "Excuse me?"

"My sister found me about three months ago. I haven't even seen her yet. I can't change who I am so my family will have an easier time of it; Tor can't either. But more to the point, we won't."

Her eyes narrowed. "If you think I'd push my boy away—"

"I'm not saying that. Just saying what happened in my family. But if you don't want to make him unhappy, if you want him to live his life as freely as a gay man can, it would be best for you to try to accept it. It ain't easy, I reckon, but I'm betting it's worth it."

She started walking again. When Jake didn't follow she glared at him until he fell into step. "So, you're together. You love him?"

Jake nodded.

"And he loves you?"

"I–yeah. Yeah, he does."

They walked in silence for another five minutes, around and around the backyard until Jake thought he would get dizzy.

"All right then," Maureen finally said. "I reckon you're a better match than what Becky made, though I did get Susie out of it." Then she headed into the house, Jake half a step behind. When they got to the door she gave him a dazzling smile. "Hurt him and you'll pay."

He didn't doubt it.

Things didn't get really exciting until Christmas dinner was almost over.

"I saw Uncle Tor kissing Jake under the mistletoe," Susie announced around a mouthful of peas.

"Did you, now?" Maureen said mildly. "What did you think of that?"

Susie shrugged. "Looked icky. They were using their tongues and Uncle Tor had his hand on Jake's butt," she said with a giggle.

Jake froze, fork halfway to his mouth.

Susie looked at Tor curiously. "Why were you using your tongue?" she asked.

"Like the way he tastes," Tor said with a wink.

"Tor!"

"Mark!"

"Tor!"

"What? She asked."

"You needn't answer," Maureen said with a frown.

Tor just shrugged. "Rather she heard answers from me than anyone else." He smiled at Susie, and she grinned back.

"Will I want to kiss boys sometime?"

Tor laughed. "I expect so."

"Eww. Nope. That's yucky. Maybe I'll just kiss girls."

Maureen and Becky choked. Jake froze again.

"Maybe," Tor said easily. "But I expect you'll like kissing boys. Kissing girls is okay too, though."

"Did you ever kiss girls?"

"Yep. Long time ago." Tor was still grinning.

"Why did you stop?"

"Met a special boy."

"Who?"

Tor's smile faded a little, but his voice was still light. "His name was Kincaid."

"What happened to him?"

Jake reached a hand under the table and tangled his fingers with Tor's.

"He had to leave me," Tor said simply.

"Did you miss him?"

"Yeah."

"Do you still miss him?"

"Sometimes."

Becky put a hand on Susie's shoulder. "That's enough, hon. No more about that. Ask about something else."

Susie shrugged. "Okay. How come Santa didn't bring me a horse?"

"Won't fit in your room," Tor said, his smile bright again.

"Oh. Momma told me not to tell you that your bed squeaks. But I think you know, 'cause I could hear it this morning."

Jake dropped his fork. Tor, for the first time Jake had ever seen, turned scarlet.

Maureen looked at them both and sighed. "Christmas is always so interesting with you, Mark."

Twenty Five

———◆—◆—◆———

By the time March rolled around Jake had spent a lot of time on the phone with his sisters and had spent one weekend playing telephone tag between Jacob and Susie, both of whom wanted to talk to him about Easter. Jacob wanted to know if he and Tor were going to visit in April or May—they finally settled on late May—and Susie wanted to know if the Easter bunny would leave her a horse if she asked really nicely.

Jake thought he could get used to that. He liked picking up the phone and spending twenty minutes or so talking to 'Lissa and Cath, and he absolutely loved talking to Jacob about soccer and football. He wasn't quite sure where he fit in Susie's worldview, but he liked it when she asked to talk to him when she was done talking to Tor.

Elias had figured out Jake was in touch with family again right after Jake and Tor got back from Christmas. He didn't say much, just smiled and made sure that Jake got his mail fast when it came in.

Kip had finally asked Beth to marry him, defying all odds and waiting until New Year's Eve to do it. He'd also managed to stun them all by calmly announcing that he'd bought land the previous summer and their house was half built already. They'd all spent New Year's Day out at his place, admiring the view and grinning every time Beth looked around her with wide-eyed wonder.

Jake and Hound were in the stable one wet March afternoon, getting two stalls ready for new horses, when a shuffling sound behind them made Jake turn around.

His father stood there, silently watching.

"Jake," the man said, and he knew then it wasn't his father, just his ghost. A man, yes, and real enough to touch, but not his father. His brother.

"James," he heard himself say, his voice calm. He glanced back at Hound, who was still trying to set a board in place. "Hound, get the boys together, yeah? I'm ready for help with the bales." He silently prayed that the kid would get the point and not say anything stupid; they didn't need bales and even if they did Jake wouldn't need help with them.

Hound just nodded and said, "Sure, Jake." He headed out of the barn, not even glancing at the silent intruder, his stride easy.

Jake stood with his back to the stall wall, looking at his older brother. James looked just like their father had, and it suddenly struck him that James was now a little older than their father had been the last time Jake had seen him.

"So, you really are alive," James said conversationally, his hands loose by his sides, less than ten feet away.

"Yeah. How'd you find out?" Jake was only mildly curious.

James shrugged. "Man comes back from the dead, news gets around." He looked around the stable. "You should have stayed gone, Jake. If what I hear is right, you really should have just stayed dead."

Jake smiled. "Why's that now?" He could hear Hound outside in the yard, calling for Elias to hold up.

James looked at him with cold eyes. "World could live without your kind of perversion. You're disgusting."

Jake shifted his weight, balancing on the balls of his feet. "Not hurting anyone," he said quietly.

James sneered at him. "Hurts just to think of you doing—what you do."

"You think I should be dead because I suck cock? What's it to you? I stay here, mind my own business, got nothin' to do with you." James stepped forward and Jake reached out for one of the boards leaning against the stall door. "You spook the horses and I swear you'll regret it."

James froze. "Like you could take me down, faggot."

Jake just gave him a cold smile, which seemed to infuriate his brother.

"You're a fucking pansy, Jake. Couldn't hurt me if you tried, never could."

"You want to bet on that?" Jake didn't move, just stood his ground.

"You and what army?"

"Don't need an army, James. Got what I need." Jake moved out of the stall so they were both in the open, halfway between the wide doors at either end. "Just need a couple of cowboys, and we can shovel the shit right out of here."

He didn't even look, just heard the others move into the barn and fan out behind him. James' eyes went wide, almost comically so, before narrowing.

"So, which of you is taking my brother up the ass?" he demanded, his voice loud and abrasive.

Jake chuckled and turned around, half expecting Tor to say something. He'd expected Tor and Elias and Hound, and he'd hoped Kip would be there too, to add numbers. What he hadn't expected was for them to be joined by the Boss, Bobby Hearn, Tommy and two other day hands. No wonder James looked panicked.

No one answered him. No one said anything, they just stood there, a wall of cowboys backing him up.

Jake looked at his brother. "You won't find anything here but trouble, James. Let it go and head on out, leave me be."

James visibly settled himself. "You're not to see 'Lissa and Cath, and you'll sure as hell stay away from Jacob."

Jake laughed. "Why?"

"You're an insult to proper family values," James said, almost calmly.

Jake could feel anger starting to burn in his stomach, white and hot. "You think? How many kids you got now, James? Three? By how many women? When was the last time you had a conversation with Melissa? You dare come here and talk to me about family after how our parents treated me?"

James leapt forward, one arm raised. "Shut up. Our father was a good man—"

"Our father beat the shit out of us, James." Jake heard his voice rising and lowered it immediately. "Our mother told you I was fucking dead. You want to talk about family values? Fine. You see your kids often? When did you last tuck your oldest into bed? Read to them? They even know each other, or you?"

Jake started to walk forward, fury pushing him. James stepped back.

"You got a problem with me being gay, that's one thing, but you don't come in here shooting your fucking mouth off about family. I got two sisters who want me, a nephew who calls my partner uncle and a hell of a lot of people I can count on. I work hard, stay sober, and live my life. What do you do, James?"

James glared at him. "You don't know nothin' about it."

"Don't have to. Want to hear about what I know? I know the score from Jacob's last soccer game. You know what your kid's favorite book is?"

James stared at him. "You should have stayed dead, Jake."

"Nope. Got too much to live for. You going now?"

James didn't bother to reply, just turned and left. Jake followed him out and stood by the barn, watching as his brother climbed into his truck and drove out with a spray of gravel.

When James' taillights had disappeared he went into the barn and silently shook hands with each man as they left. When he got to Hound he smiled and said thank you, only a little bemused to see how flushed the kid was. Hound ducked his head and followed the others out of the barn, mumbling something about how he was glad to help.

Tor was leaning on the stall door, waiting. As Jake moved toward him Tor braced himself, opening his arms as Jake pressed close, forcing them into the support post.

"What do you need, Jake?" he asked softly, pulling Jake to him.

Jake felt himself trembling, almost vibrating as anger and anxiety leaked out. "You. Need you."

"Got me." Tor kissed him hard, hands holding him and moving over him, turning the twitchiness and need to lash out into something else. Jake didn't even feel them moving, was just aware that they were in the stall instead of out of it and that he had Tor pushed into the back wall.

Tor kissed him and moved with him, hard and eager and as hungry as he was. They bit and tasted skin, tore at clothes for a few moments before Jake just ground his hips against Tor and started sucking a mark up on his neck.

"Jake—" Tor said with a groan. "Oh shit. You want me to—"

"Shut up. Just let me—I need—"

Tor kissed him hard, tongue invading his mouth, then he pushed Jake roughly away. They slammed into the side of the stall and Tor dropped his hands, one holding fast to Jake's ass as he thrust against Tor, the other working their jeans open.

Jake kissed Tor back and let himself go with it. He stopped fighting for faster and harder, and just let Tor do what they needed, freeing their erections and wrapping a hand around them both.

Tor pulled at them, mouth going to Jake's neck. Tor bit down and thrust with his hips, his hands working at their cocks until Jake felt like he was going to pass out. Jake could feel blood being pulled up into a dark mark on his neck, his cock was hard, balls tight and aching.

"Fuck. Tor, please. Need you. Need to feel."

"Feel me, then. Feel me here with you? Feel me next to you at night? See me every day? Not going anywhere, Jake. Family, yeah?"

Jake thrust into Tor's hand and cried out as he came. Tor was watching him, he could see Tor's eyes and see his smile and feel his hand, and then Tor kissed him again, heat spreading as Tor shot as well.

"Family?" Jake said when he could breathe again.

"Yours. Mine. Ours. We're family."

Jake felt dizzy and a little giddy. "Family do this to each other?" he asked hazily, gesturing to their open jeans and the stickiness between them.

Tor leered. "We have a special family. Want to get cleaned up?"

Jake nodded then shook his head and leaned against Tor, kissing him lazily. He was getting hard again. "Want more."

"More I can do," Tor said, easing them down onto the straw. "How you want it?"

"Fuck me." Jake shivered. He could almost feel Tor moving in him already. They wiggled out of their boots and started in on their jeans, but he was too hungry, too needy to wait. He pulled Tor up on top of him, moaning when they slid and rubbed together. Tor was hard against him, hot and heavy and just what he needed.

With a low growl Tor flipped him over and pushed in. Tor took him in a long thrust and then another, going deep.

"Oh God, yes," Jake hissed.

Tor's fingers were digging into his hips, gripping him tightly. "You don't want this hard, say so. Don't think I can be gentle right now."

"Fuck me," Jake gasped.

Tor fucked him, long, heavy cock pushing deep, driving them both. He thrust into Jake with a strong rhythm, pounding into him for ages, both of them grunting and pushing and soaring. It was hot and hard, and Jake needed. He was desperate for more, his hips pushing back, trying to get Tor deeper, trying to get Tor to take him harder.

Tor shifted and pegged his gland and Jake gasped. He wanted to scream, wanted to cry out, and only fear of spooking the horses stopped him. Tor did it again and again until Jake was nearly sobbing, then a hand slid off Jake's hip and pulled at his cock, and it was perfect.

"Oh fuck, gonna come—" He barely got the words out before he was shooting onto the straw beneath them.

Tor kept fucking him, long thrusts that left him shaking. "Tor—"

"Fuck, Jake. Need you so fucking much. Can't do anything without you."

Jake gasped again, head swimming.

Tor froze behind him and he could feel the force of Tor's orgasm crash through them both. They fell onto the hay and Tor eased out of him, turning him until they could hold each other. They didn't talk, just shared long kisses until they could get up and dress and make their way to the bunkhouse.

———————

Jake rolled over in bed, almost asleep. Tor had taken him over the edge twice since supper and he was ready to sleep for a week. He knew he could, too. He was satiated and warm in their bed, and his life was calm. He was thinking about family.

Spring had done its thing and he was going to meet his sisters in less than a week. They'd broken contact with James, had let him know that they were in his court, and he was part of them. He was going to see Jacob for the first time.

He'd gotten a letter from Susie, stuck in with Tor's mail. It was addressed to Uncle Jake.

Tor's mother had called and asked them to visit for the long weekend in July, if they could get away.

Kip had married Beth and moved the week before. They'd rushed the wedding a little, and the house suddenly needed a nursery, but they seemed exceedingly happy about it.

Elias was exchanging long letters with his mother every week, and even Hound was getting closer to his family. It was a bit of a surprise to hear the kid talking about moving to Maine to help his brother build some sort of studio, but it was good that he was going to family. Be a shame to lose him, though, he was a good hand, a good man to have around. But Jake figured that leaving to help out family was about as good a reason there was.

Family was the best reason Jake could think of.

Twenty Six

The auctions were going well and Jake was thinking that it was a fine thing to get away from the ranch once in a long while. He loved the ranch, but it was nice to be with people once or twice a year; get caught up on their lives, trade gossip and lies, get to see some old friends.

He was enjoying the time with Tor, too. They didn't get away much, and the change of scenery seemed to light a fire in Tor, making his humor sharper and his appetites damn near insatiable. Nights were full of conversations with cowboys from all over and laughter that never seemed to stop. Then Tor, dragging him away from the crowds, stolen moments that made Jake burn. Most of the time it was just them, but there were others around, ready to play, and that was okay, too, if everyone was willing. But Jake liked it best when it was just him and Tor, no outside help needed.

Days were busy moving cattle, dealing, making noise. Tor's hands would suddenly be on him, his mouth at the back of Jake's neck or at his ear. Whispers and touches that made Jake ache, make him so hard he had to feel Tor in him, around him, had to taste him.

At the moment though, he didn't know where Tor was. He'd seen Tor at supper, talking to a tall blonde cowboy with tanned skin and broad shoulders. He'd stopped to talk to them, had just been about to find out what this guy's name was, and if he was looking for fun or not, when Elias had appeared, calling Jake away to tend to some paperwork.

Jake had signed the last form and looked around for Tor, who'd vanished into the crowd. Typical. He asked Elias if he knew where Tor had gone.

"Nope, sorry. Expect he's gone off to get a beer, or back to the truck. He's around here somewhere."

Jake nodded and said he figured it would be easy enough to find him, then headed off toward the trucks. It took him almost half an hour to get there, stopping to talk to various people and turn down the occasional offer of a drink. He ran into Elias again as he approached the vehicles.

"Find him?"

"Not yet. Not worried. You headed for the trucks?"

"Yeah," Elias said as he fell into step. "Time to change my shirt, get cleaned up to go see if I can make a new friend somewhere."

Jake laughed. "Lots of lovely friends to make around here, too."

"Oh, shut up. Like I trust your taste in women." Elias grinned at him.

"Just 'cause I don't play with them doesn't mean I can't appreciate the way they look."

They walked down the line of trucks, trading opinions on various women they'd seen the last couple of days. Elias was waxing poetic about a pretty blonde when they turned to walk between two of the trucks in their fleet, and Jake froze.

Elias took two more steps before he saw what had stopped Jake. He pulled up short, an arm reaching back to take a hold of Jake. "Shit. Be calm, Jake. Just don't—"

Jake didn't hear him, didn't even feel the arm on his biceps until he moved forward.

Tor. His Tor, pressed tight up against some cowboy, hips jerking as they dry humped against a truck. Tor's back was to him, the other guy's hands on his ass, pulling him closer. Tor had his mouth fused to the cowboy's, and Jake thought he had never been so close to dying.

Elias still had a grip on his arm. Jake looked at him, waiting.

"Fuck. Jake, just stay cool. You'll hate yourself if you kill him."

Tor hadn't even turned around. He was still going at it like he'd never been laid. Like he didn't need Jake.

Jake stepped forward, not thinking of anything other than the pain in his chest and how he was going to make this asshole pay for touching what was his. He grabbed Tor by the shoulder, tearing him away from the cowboy.

"What the fuck?"

He wasn't sure who said it; could have been him, could have been Elias. Or it could have been either of the two pissed off men in front of him. Neither of whom was Tor.

"Shit." Jake followed up with some sort of apology and took off, leaving Elias to explain. He had to find Tor, and he needed to find him fast.

Bareback

He tore through the trucks and groups of people, scanning the crowds for Tor's face. It took him ten minutes to find the man, and by then he was almost vibrating; he needed to see Tor's eyes, needed to search out the answer to a question he didn't even know he had. His fingers itched to touch Tor, his cock ached. He felt like he could crawl out of his skin. Tor looked up from where he was sitting, still talking to the blonde, and grinned at him.

Jake looked around, quickly rejecting place after place, trying to remember where there was a corner they could hide in. Tor was walking toward him, questions in his eyes, when Jake saw what he wanted. He shot a look at Tor and pointed, then took off, moving fast. He swung around a corner and waited, thanking all and sundry that his memory had been correct. They were almost secluded in the corner created by a side addition to the arena. Almost.

Tor came around the corner. "Taggart? What's—"

His words were cut off as Jake pushed him into the wall and took his mouth in a hard kiss. "Shut up." Jake moved down to suck Tor's neck, his fingers fighting with the buttons on Tor's shirt.

"Christ." Tor sounded surprised, but not unhappy. He put his hands on Jake's hips and pulled him close, rubbing a stiffening cock on Jake. "Let's take this somewhere more private, yeah?"

"No." Jake gave up the fight with the buttons and tore the shirt open, sending the last three buttons skittering off on the ground. "Here." His hands went to Tor's jeans and popped the top button.

"What? Jake, someone could see—"

"Yeah. Shut up and find the lube." Jake got his hand in Tor's jeans and stroked him hard. "Gonna suck you off and then fuck you into the wall." He dropped to his knees and took Tor in his mouth, sucking hard from the start. Jake was in no mood to tease; he wanted Tor's flavor in his mouth, needed to fill all of his senses. Tor gasped and thrust his hips, his hands going to Jake's head.

"Jesus. Oh fuck, Jake." Tor's hips rocked, moving as deep as Jake's mouth would let him. Jake felt one hand drop from his head, watched as Tor tried to get his hand into his jeans pocket. The fabric was folded back and Tor had to work at it, but he managed to get the lube out.

Tor was making rough, needy noises that drove Jake on, faster and harder. He undid his own belt and Tor hissed. When Jake pushed his own jeans open and freed his cock, Tor started to buck, fucking his mouth.

Jake tangled his fingers with Tor's for a brief moment before taking the lube. He slicked his fingers well and pumped his cock a couple of times, moaning around Tor. He lifted his slippery hand, tugging gently at Tor's balls before moving back and thrusting two fingers into Tor's ass.

"Oh fucking shit, Jake!" Tor came hard, hips shoving deep into Jake's mouth as he shot, his cock pulsing and throbbing on Jake's tongue.

Jake swallowed fast and pulled his mouth away, standing on unsteady legs. He spun Tor around to face the wall. "Brace yourself," he said as he tugged Tor's jeans down. Tor barely got his hands to the wall before Jake was pushing his way in.

"No one touches you without my say so," Jake said, fastening his mouth on Tor's shoulder and sucking up a dark mark.

Tor groaned and turned his head, hips pushing him back onto Jake. "No one touched me."

"I know. And no one does." Jake thrust deep and groaned. "Like this, Tor. We can play, but no one fucking goes near what's mine without me knowing." He thrust again. "Right?"

Tor's head was dropped low. He groaned as Jake ploughed into him and nodded. "Wouldn't."

"No. You wouldn't." He thrust again and slid a hand around to Tor's cock, stiffening again under Jake's assault.

He lifted up on his toes and moved forward again, searching.

"Oh fuck," Tor moaned.

Jake did it again, pulling at Tor's cock as he fucked him. He could feel himself getting close.

"You."

Thrust.

"Are."

Thrust.

"Mine." He bit down on Tor's shoulder, hard. Tor threw his head back and cried out, coming again. Jake heard spunk hitting the wall in front of him before he felt Tor's muscles clamp down, and went over himself, pumping into Tor's ass, coming so hard he saw dark spots.

He pulled his teeth away from Tor's shoulders and licked at the mark, then sucked at it again.

Tor moaned softly, his head resting on the wall. "Damn, Jake. Goddamn."

Jake eased out of him and pulled his jeans up. He turned Tor and kissed him gently, then got him dressed. They leaned on the wall together, arms loosely wrapped around one another as they tried to catch their breath.

"What the flying fuck was that?" Tor finally managed.

"You know what it was."

Tor didn't say anything for a moment. "Yeah." He nodded slowly. "C'mon. Let's get cleaned up. Finish this right, yeah?"

Jake stared at him and sucked in air.

Tor grinned, baring his teeth. "Only half done this deal, you know?"

Jake felt himself start to vibrate again. Oh God.

"Right," he managed before Tor's mouth was on his, stealing his very soul.

Twenty Seven

—◆—

Jake stopped on the small porch just outside the bunkhouse and looked down at himself. He knew he was filthy; he couldn't kid himself about that. Head to toe dirt and grime and sweat; he needed a shower in the worst way.

Or maybe he could just stand in the yard and let someone hose him off.

He contemplated his chances of getting through the kitchen, down the hall, through their bedroom and into the shower without tracking enough dirt into the house that

Elias and Tor would have a fit and make him do all the cleaning. Not good. Best to just leave the dirt outside.

He toed off his boots, which were easily the cleanest bits of him, and hung his hat on the stair railing so he could pull his shirts off. Damp with sweat and streaked with dirt and some other crap best not thought about, he wondered if it was worth the trouble of washing them or if they were on their way to the garbage. The T-shirt would probably live to see another day.

The flannel, however, was shot to shit, so he used it to get muck off his jeans, smacking and slapping at his legs until the worst of it was crumbled around his feet. On his socks.

"Damn," he said, under his breath. Should have left the boots on. He peeled off the socks and grabbed his hat, then went into the kitchen. He really needed to get to the shower.

"Jesus Christ, what the hell happened to you?" Elias was sitting at the kitchen table with Tor, staring at Jake with wide eyes.

"What?" Jake had no idea what the man was talking about until he saw the way Tor's eyes darkened. He looked down.

"Uh…oops?"

Tor laughed softly, the sound rolling, hot and sexy and getting hungry.

Jake's chest was covered in hickeys, some dark and fresh, some discolored and half gone. Tor'd been marking him pretty regularly since the auction a week ago.

Elias stood up. "I don't want to know. I really don't."

"It was either that or wedding rings," Tor said.

Jake looked at him sharply, his breath catching when he saw the way Tor was staring at him.

Elias stared too. "Better rings than that, Tor. You'll need to get him a transfusion if you keep sucking his blood like that."

By Chris Owen

Jake decided not to turn around and show off the impressive bite mark on his shoulder blade. He felt himself get hard just thinking about it, could feel where the skin was broken. They'd had to get antibiotic cream after that night. Both of them had bite marks and Tor was freaked about bacteria. Didn't stop Tor from biting him, though, or from claiming him.

Screw the shower. Jake needed to fuck. Now. Maybe they could do it in the shower.

"Wedding rings?" he heard himself say. Well, he sort of squeaked, he admitted to himself. No one had said anything about being married. Not out loud, anyway.

Elias grinned. "Think I'll just leave you two to talk about it. Let me know when I have to have a gift ready, and hey—maybe we can have a bachelor party. Not watching no gay porn, though. Living with you two is close enough."

"Wedding rings?" Jake said again as Elias left the room. He thought for a moment and then added, "Can we talk about it in the shower? Naked?"

"Hell, yeah." Tor started down the hall, already undoing his belt. "Can't promise to talk though. My mouth's gonna be full."

"Shut up!" Elias yelled from the living room. "Still here!"

Jake just hurried to catch up to Tor.

It took them no time at all to get in the shower and Jake wasted even less time pushing Tor into the tiles, kissing him deeply as his hand went around Tor's cock.

"Thought…oh yeah—thought I was gonna suck you," Tor said, his hips pushing his prick into Jake's hand.

"You are. Just not yet." Jake kissed him again and slid his mouth down to Tor's neck. Tor had just as many marks as he did and he added another one as he pulled and stroked Tor's shaft. "Come for me, Tor. Wanna feel you come."

Tor gasped and moved his hips harder, faster, his hand keeping Jake's mouth on his neck. Jake scraped over the

205

newest mark with blunt teeth and Tor grunted, coming in his hand.

"Goddamn," Tor gasped. "Fuck, that feels good; love the way you touch me."

Jake smiled and kissed him again, the water hot on them as the room started to fill with steam. "You touch me now. I really need to soap off—I stink."

Tor grinned at him, lazy and satiated. "Yeah, you do. Not gonna lie. But we can take care of that."

Tor worked up a lather between his hands and started to wash him. Almost immediately Jake started to feel like he was melting, his muscles relaxing under Tor's fingers. Well, most muscles. His cock was starting to throb and he twisted and turned, trying to get Tor to hurry up and touch him.

Tor was being stubborn though, hands slipping over his shoulders, his back, his ass…everywhere but his erection. "Taggart? How do you feel about tattoos?"

"Hate 'em," Jake said, wiggling again and trying to pull Tor's hand to where he wanted it. "The only good thing about the one I've got is that it's on my back. Don't need to see it." He'd gotten the coiled cobra his second year in prison and had regretted it ever since.

"Hmm." Tor finally gave in and cupped his balls. "Elias is right, though. Can't just keep biting and marking each other like this until we're old and gray."

"Why not?" Jake gasped as Tor's fingers slid over him. Old and gray? That sounded… "What the hell are you talking about?"

Jake had to ask, as he was having trouble thinking.

Tor kissed him and sank to his knees, tongue darting out to lick the tip of Jake's prick. "Just talking," he said, then he stopped talking, his lips going around Jake's cock and pulling, his tongue teasing.

All thought fled Jake's brain as Tor set to making him come, made him shake and whimper, hips rocking as Jake tried to get deeper. Tor's mouth was hot and wet, better than ever, his tongue dancing and playing for a bit before he started to really suck. Tor was pulling moans and desperate sounds out of Jake until he flew apart, coming for Tor in a rush, pleasure making his knees weak.

Tor had him moving and stepping out of the shower almost immediately, eyes wandering all over his dripping body. Jake thought that if the man could purr, Tor would have.

"Tattoos are out, then?" Tor said, his hands starting to wander as well as his eyes. Jake didn't mind so much, his own hands sliding over hot skin, across Tor's chest to flick at his nipples.

"Huh?" Jake blinked at him. "Tattoos?"

"Yeah. I asked how you felt about 'em." Tor grabbed a towel and started to dry them both off.

"Oh, right. Yeah, no tattoos. Not just because I hate mine, though. Wouldn't want 'Tornado' on me, because it's not your real name, and wouldn't want 'Mark' because I never call you that." Jake moved closer and teased at a now hard nipple with the tip of his tongue.

Tor dropped the towel and pressed against him. "Could just get a 'T'," Tor said, rubbing on him, one hand going around Jake's waist and dropping down to his ass. "Be the same for both of us."

Jake just shook his head.

"Okay, no tattoos. But I'm not wearing a wedding ring." Tor said it so casually Jake thought he'd misheard him. But then Tor was turning, leading the way to the bed, and Jake couldn't let it go.

"Tor? You got something you want to talk about?"

Tor pushed him down onto the bed and covered him, rubbing nice and slow, leaving kisses wherever he could easily reach. Jake moaned softly, and felt himself start to get hard again, fast. Tor teased his skin with fingers and tongue, and Jake started to thrust against him, nice and slow.

"Want to fuck you," Tor whispered into his ear. "Want you around me."

"Oh God." When Tor talked like that Jake could barely keep it together. Man was pushing all his buttons, going to drive him out of his mind.

"Want you to ride me, Jake, want you on top of me so I can push up into your tight ass."

Jake whimpered, his hips jerking. "Hurry."

Tor hurried. Slick fingers opened him, going deep and making him feel far too good if this was going to last. He pushed Tor back, flat on the bed, and straddled his hips.

"You ready for me?" Tor said, his eyes serious.

"Always," Jake whispered, moving back and down, taking Tor into him.

"Oh God. Just…God, just stay there for a minute," Tor ground out, the muscles in his jaw twitching. "Oh fuck, you feel good."

Jake leaned down and kissed Tor, licking at his lips and sucking softly on his tongue. Tor moaned into his mouth, hips starting to move. Jake pushed back, hunger and need spiraling in him, his cock throbbing.

"Piercing," Tor whispered into his mouth.

Jake froze. "Pardon?"

"Little bits of metal you put through your skin."

Jake sat up, making them both moan. "I know that, idiot. What do you want to get pierced?"

Tor looked him over. God, that almost drove Jake nuts, the way Tor looked at him. Always hot and eager and ready, always wanting. Always caring.

"Here?" Tor said finally, pinching at Jake's nipple until his back arched.

"N–no. Feels—fuck, feels good. But it'd get ripped off, sure as shit. Hauling bales, lifting stuff—either wouldn't, God stop that, I can't think. Either wouldn't wear it, or it'd get ripped out."

Tor nodded and looked him over again, a wicked grin crossing his face. "Mmmm, here," he said, running a finger behind Jake's balls to his perineum, then teasing the stretched skin.

"Oh fuck," Jake arched again, a shudder running through him.

"Like that idea, Jake? Little loop for me to play with? Tease you and make you scream?" Tor teased at him some more, Jake shaking his head even as he rocked and moved, Tor's cock huge and hot in him, making him lose his breath.

"Or maybe here, along your cock?" A finger ran up his shaft and Tor said, "A little series of bars, one after another."

Jake gasped and dropped a hand to his prick stroking himself firmly. "You're doing this too, remember? And you know where I like to put my cock. Think about it."

"Right, no ladder." Tor kissed him again, his fingers tangling with Jake's for a moment, both of them jerking him off, and then Tor pulled both their hands away.

"I know," Tor said suddenly. "I know where. And I don't want you to freak."

"Oh, oh." Jake could feel his balls start to climb their way into his belly. If metal up the length of his cock wasn't the worst Tor could come up with he wasn't sure he wanted to hear this.

Tor's finger teased the head of his cock, then pressed into the slit for a second. "Here. Don't say anything. Just think about it. Think about what it would feel like inside you, a little metal ball on the tip of my cock, slamming against your gland when I fuck you." He matched action to word, planting his feet on the bed and pushing hard, driving himself into Jake.

"Okay," Jake said, his voice harsh.

Tor stared. "Pardon?"

"I said okay. Gonna hurt like fuck getting it done, not to mention we have to go out of state to do it or I'll die of embarrassment, but yeah. Let's do that."

Tor blink. "Oh God. Gonna fuck you now."

Jake didn't say a word, just shoved hard, taking Tor deeper into him.

Tor went nuts under him, hands on Jake's hips as Tor slammed into him again and again. Jake was flying, one hand working his own cock as Tor moved in him, the other braced on Tor's chest. He traced one of the marks around Tor's nipples. He'd done that. He'd marked Tor and let Tor mark him and now they were going to get fucking rings in their cocks.

Jake cried out and came, his orgasm slamming through him at the thought. Tor echoed his cry and thrust hard, then froze as he shot, shudders rolling through him like waves. Jake waited until the last one had passed and collapsed onto him, burying his head in Tor's neck.

"Oh God," he sighed. "That was nice."

"Yep," Tor answered, still out of breath. "That'll hold me until morning, I think."

"We need another shower."

"Can do that. After a nap." Tor wrapped his arms around him and Jake snuggled into him, one leg hooking over Tor's thighs, one arm circling his waist.

"Okay. Nap first. Then shower. Then supper. Then bed."

He'd thought Tor was asleep, he'd gotten so quiet so fast, then he heard a whisper in his ear. "Remember last year? When I ran and came back?"

"Yeah." Of course he did. But he made a point not to think about that period; it was past and things had been dealt with. It didn't matter anymore.

"Said I couldn't promise you forever." Tor whispered, his arm tightening around Jake, hand stroking his side. "Want to now. Forever, anything you want. All of me."

Jake froze for a moment, his head suddenly spinning. "You what?" Jake whispered.

"I want to be with you. Always." Tor shifted a little beside him. "It's like...you claimed me. You marked me and told me I'm yours. And that's good. Then I claimed you, fucked you hard enough you damn near passed out, bit you and said you belong to me, right?"

Jake nodded.

"This time…this time I'm offering. Jake, if you want me, I'm yours. Do anything I can for you, be everything you need. Give myself to you, forever." Tor's voice cracked, and Jake sat up, looking at him.

Jake traced Tor's jaw with a finger, taking in the shining eyes, the curve of his lips, the lines and marks, the tiny white scar just below his hairline.

"I love you," he said.

Twenty Eight

When they got to the motel Jake shucked his coat and boots, tossed his hat on the dresser next to Tor's and flopped on the bed. Tor went to take a shower.

Jake reached over and grabbed the phone book off the nightstand and started looking up tattoo parlors and piercing places, making a mental list of places to call in the morning for hours and prices. When the list got to more than five he got up and hunted for a pen and paper. When Tor didn't get out of the shower he started calling.

By the time the water shut off and Tor wandered out with a towel around his waist, Jake's face was flaming red from asking the questions three times and he'd decided that they could just pick a place from what he'd found out. No way was he asking another stranger how much it would be to get a steel ring through his dick.

Jake threw himself onto the bed again and winced. "That wasn't fun. But I did it."

Tor looked over the sheet of paper and grinned. "You're a strong man, Taggart."

The grin grew wicked as Tor slid a hand over Jake's thigh. "But are you strong enough to do it?"

Jake stared at him. Standing there in a towel, water droplets still clinging to his chest, hair damp, Tor looked delicious. And he looked like he was enjoying Jake's embarrassment a little too much.

Jake sat up suddenly and lunged, tearing the towel away. "Strong enough to make sure *you* do it. Make this real pretty for me."

Tor gasped when Jake's hand closed around him, the sound turning into a moan as Jake played. "You…ah…better enjoy it now; aftercare is going to be a bitch on our sex life."

Jake didn't even look up to meet his eye, just kept stroking Tor's cock, feeling the weight and heat of it in his hand. "Then I better get what I want while I can," he said, sliding his fingers back, over Tor's balls, letting his thumb rub over the head of the rapidly filling shaft. "Gonna be so pretty," he repeated.

Tor swore softly as Jake shifted on the bed for a better angle and started to lick at him. Jake just grinned to himself and nuzzled Tor's balls, lost in the heat and smell of his man. Clean and muted, he could still catch the flavor of him, still find the traces of Tor's scent, hidden behind soap and shampoo.

He felt something uncurl in his belly. Nothing had ever gotten to him as fast as Tor could, just by being there. Naked helped too.

He made a soft noise, heard his own hunger in the sound. Tor must have heard it too, because he dropped a hand to Jake's head, gentle at first as he ran his fingers through Jake's hair, then harder, more forceful as he tried to guide Jake's mouth. "Don't tease," he murmured.

Jake teased. Barely there licks until he was about going mad himself, hard in his jeans, pushing into the bed. He traced the ridge with his tongue, tasting the beginning of Tor's passion, then took the head in his mouth, unable to keep himself going slowly.

"Yeah," Tor whispered, trying to thrust into his mouth. Jake moved his head back, not letting Tor take what he wanted. He sucked gently, playing his tongue over the swollen flesh in light passes meant to torture.

He was taken by surprise when Tor stepped back, pulling away. He looked up, confused, eyes widening a split second before Tor pushed him back. He didn't even try to regain control when Tor kissed him, hard and demanding, fingers working at the buttons to his jeans.

Tor didn't waste any time, undressing him quickly, the movements jerky and as harsh as his kisses, a low growl coming from the back of his throat. Jake responded, his hips wiggling as they peeled his jeans off. He started to pull his shirt off, but Tor forced him back on the bed, moving around him, stroking his thighs and laying down biting kisses on his belly and hips.

"Teach you to tease," Tor growled, then Tor fell on him, mouth hot and wet as it surrounded him in one fluid movement, taking him in deep.

"Oh God," Jake gasped, hands scrabbling over Tor's back, hips pushing up hard. "Good."

Tor made an affirmative noise and sucked him once, then let go. "Gonna make this really fun?" he asked, one eyebrow up.

Jake blinked at him. Fun? Well, yeah. But Tor'd stopped, and that wasn't any fun at all. Then Tor raised the other eyebrow and wiggled his hips, next to Jake's shoulders. When had he done that?

"Taggart." Tor sounded exasperated. Jake felt exasperated. The man had *stopped*. Tor wiggled again and Jake suddenly realized he'd stopped too. Oops.

"You want something?" he asked, and not waiting for a reply—Lord knew the man was capable of getting pissy and might just roll over and go to sleep on him—he made a grab for Tor's butt and sucked that hard cock in, as smooth as he could.

Tor, to give the man credit, didn't play games with him, just swallowed him down and set to making Jake's brains melt.

It was good. It was always good, but this…both of them working together, feeding off each other's hunger, following each other's lead…it was like a sensory loop that made everything more intense, each lick and pull mirrored. Jake could feel what he was doing to Tor, could give back what he was taking. They were in sync, and it was amazing.

Tor's mouth possessed him, tongue and lips and throat working him hard, making his hips move without conscious thought. He figured that was okay though, Tor's own hips were feeding him Tor's prick, the hard flesh sliding between his lips faster and faster.

Tor groaned around him, the vibration settling into his spine. Jake answered it, and Tor jerked. Jake had never been able to take Tor as deep as he wanted—Tor was just better at that than he was, but he relaxed as much as he could, trying to open for Tor.

Tor grew hungrier as he pushed into Jake's throat, his hands on Jake's ass, pulling him in. Jake tried to keep his suction smooth, tried to lick and suck and keep some sort of rhythm for Tor, but he knew what was coming and could already feel his balls draw up tight in anticipation.

Tor's tongue moved over him, fast and hard in that strange twisting motion that Jake could feel in the bottom of his feet. Then he was sucked in, down Tor's throat, and he knew he was going to come, knew there was no way to stop it.

Tor would do it once more, or he would groan, or he would do *something*, and Jake would lose it. He wanted to take Tor with him. He wanted Tor to come with him, or damn near it, and there was no way he was going to be able to manage it, his mouth already sloppy on Tor's cock, his body already starting to shake. He held on tight and willed his orgasm away, just long enough.

His hands slid over Tor's back and hips, clinging and stroking at the same time. He stroked Tor's balls with his fingers, hot and heavy, the skin so soft. Back further, his own hips jerking now, so fucking close as Tor played him.

He teased one hand over Tor's ass, the motion light and fluttering until his fingertips danced across the entrance to Tor's body, and Tor twitched, his own rhythm screwed up for a moment.

Jake didn't hesitate, didn't even really think about it. Tor groaned around him, and he pushed two fingers into Tor's body and thrust hard, so fucking close…

Tor pushed back, his body jerking as he came, a growl sending another vibration through Jake's body. When Jake felt Tor's come fill his mouth he shuddered and stiffened, meeting Tor pulse for pulse as he came as well, the loop feeding itself.

He sucked and licked, tasting and cleaning and loving on his man until he rolled over onto his back and shuddered again.

"Gonna fucking kill me, Jake." Tor's voice was lazy and satiated.

Jake smiled, utterly boneless. "Nope. Just gonna keep you."

By Chris Owen

It'd hurt. Fuck, had it hurt. But not for long, and not as bad as the tattoo did—or at least it faded fast enough that the tattoo seemed worse. But when it was done he'd still let some stranger named Gus (or was it Russ?) stick a needle through his dick and now he had a metal ring at the tip that he couldn't really forget about.

Well, he could. He could move and do stuff, and work, and it didn't hurt, and he didn't really think about it. But if he had to piss? Had to change clothes, take a shower, or Heaven help him, if he kissed Tor? He knew it was there.

Not healed yet, and even Tor wasn't so eager to fuck that he'd rush this. No, Tor was just so eager to fuck that he couldn't sleep in the same bed with him, so he'd taken off to sleep in the hayloft. Stupid cowboy. Could have stayed in bed and watched what Jake was doing.

Jake thought about Tor watching him do this, and he watched the light glint off the ring in his cock, and he thought about the ring in Tor's cock. And his hand moved faster. He watched the little bit of steel, and thought about what it was, what it meant, and he had to bite his lip as his hips began to lift off the bed, pushing himself into his hand. He thought vaguely about what it would feel like in a couple of days, when Tor could fuck him and he'd feel it deep inside him, and he felt empty. Too damn empty.

He didn't stop stroking as he reached for the lube, just slowed down a little. He needed. He was hard, and it hurt, and that piece of metal was going to drive him out of his fucking mind, and he was so goddamn ready to blow all it would take was a stiff breeze across the head of his cock.

What he got was his own thumb brushing the metal, and his own fingers up his ass, but it was enough to make him cry out as he came, and enough for Tor to swear from the doorway where he'd been watching, and it was enough for Tor to buck against air as he tried to undo his jeans before he came. He didn't.

Twenty Nine

Winter

Jake had never been a morning person, even as a young child. His mother—and later his father—always had to drag him out of bed to get him off to school. Eventually, they stopped trying, right about the time Jake stopped trying as well.

In prison he hadn't had the luxury of sleeping late, the regimen of early rising impossible to escape. Over time his body had gotten used to waking suddenly, getting up and starting his day immediately.

When he got to the ranch his early mornings had continued; but where he used to line up for breakfast and wait for the proper time to shave, here he was given a little leeway, allowed to do things in the order that suited him.

Over the years he'd relaxed, and while he still got up early, still headed off to start the day's work before seven thirty, he could appreciate spending some extra time in bed.

Like now. It was almost eight on a Sunday morning and Elias was off doing the early feeding. Jake closed his eyes and let his head fall back on the pillow as Tor moved above him, thrusting into him so gently it was almost sweet.

Yeah, some mornings were better than others.

Sometimes Jake would just look at Tor and know that it was going to be a bad day. The set of his jaw at lunch, or the way his shoulders were tight and set. It was like a big flashing sign over Tor's head that screamed "Bad Mood". Usually, Jake would spend the rest of the day wondering what was wrong, watching the way the others worked around them, trying to see if it was the job, or the weather or what.

If it was his fault.

He never really just came right out and asked Tor; part of him didn't want to know, part of him didn't want them to yell at each other like they did before they got together. Most of him was just willing to let it slide, wait it out. Because moods weren't forever.

Once or twice he'd waited until it looked like Tor was starting to let go of whatever had him all prickly, then

Jake'd just sort of fit himself around his man, rubbing Tor's shoulders or his back, or maybe just bringing him something to drink.

That usually got him a smile and a nod. Usually it melted the last of the tension away. But not always. Not this time.

This time it got a flinch and a dark look, so Jake just sighed and went to the porch with a book, and waited it out. It'd be better in the morning. Always was.

———————•◆•———————

Jake didn't tell Tor the first time he got mail from his brother. He wasn't trying to hide anything, he just…didn't mention it. There wasn't really a point—it was just an envelope full of religious pamphlets about how Jake's soul was condemned to Hell if he didn't shape up and stop sleeping with men. He threw them out and went on with his day.

The second time he got mail from James—more of the same—he dumped them in garbage and made an off hand comment to Tor about it. Tor rolled his eyes, called James an idiot, and they forgot about it.

But now it was war.

Jake was shaking as he slid down the wall, clutching the phone to his ear. "Jacob, calm down. Listen to me, take a deep breath. You there?"

There was a sniffle filled pause, and then the sounds of Jacob trying to stop crying. Long, body-wracking breaths that stuck and caught. Jake ached for the boy, wanted to find out what James had done to him. Why his mother wasn't there, helping him.

"Where's your mom?" he asked, suddenly worried that 'Lissa was either aware of what was going on, or entirely in the dark. He wasn't sure which was more frightening. If James was playing head games with Jacob then 'Lissa should know. If she did know, why was she letting Jacob believe the crap James had been spewing?

"She's at work." He could hear Jacob moving around a little, still hear the hitch in his voice that said he was only a wrong comment away from tears again.

"Okay. Now, tell me what Uncle James said. And trust me, Jacob. I'm not going to be mad at you. Honest."

"He said you're going to go to Hell," Jacob whispered, sounding scared and sad. "He says that what you do with Uncle Tor is wrong, and that God won't stand for it. That if you don't get rid of Tor, send him away and repent, that God will make sure you burn in Hell with murderers and other people who do disgusting things."

"He's wrong," Jake said firmly. "Loving someone isn't ever a bad thing, something that God would punish."

"But it says in the Bible—"

"I know," Jake sighed. "I know. And there are a lot of people who agree with your uncle, and most of 'em are good folk. But when…listen to me, now, this is important. Does your momma know that James has been talking to you?"

"No," Jacob whispered. "He said it was something between us, that women don't understand. That it was up to him and me to make you see—"

Jake interrupted. "Are you supposed to keep secrets from your momma? What did they tell you at school about when a person tells you not to tell something to your parents?"

There was a long pause. "But he's my uncle."

"So am I."

The pause this time was shorter, but long enough for Tor to come in and see Jake sitting on the floor. He raised an eyebrow and Jake shook his head, not willing to interrupt Jacob's thinking.

"Uncle Jake? You think I should tell my mom what he's been saying? She's gonna flip when she finds out he's been calling me."

"Yeah, you should," Jake said, trying very hard to keep his voice even. "Don't keep stuff like this from her."

Tor slid down the wall next to him, questions in his eyes.

"Yeah. Okay." Jacob sounded a little calmer now, thank God. "But what he said–it's not true?"

"I don't reckon so. Some do. It's something you'll have to figure out on your own, Jacob. Decide what you believe. But remember what I said earlier—God don't punish caring."

Tor's eyes widened, and Jake mouthed his brother's name, getting the predictable response. Anger flared in Tor's face, but Jake concentrated on Jacob until he hung up.

Then Tor wrapped his arms around him until he stopped shaking.

———•◆•———

Spring

Jake picked at the label on his bottle of apple juice absently, dropping the shreds of paper on the table. "Yeah, but if we do that then we're short three guys I need on the fences," he said to Elias.

"Damn. How about if we move Kip and Bobby to the fences and get Tor and Jim to…no, that wouldn't work, 'cause Kip's the best man we've got for speed when it comes to shifting that shit, and we need it done fast." Elias took a long swallow out of his beer bottle and turned the list of hands around so Jake could see it better from across the table. "Face it, we need another two bodies, yesterday."

Jake sighed. "Yeah, but with the Boss in the hospital and Missy not able to hire, we're stuck. The fences—"

"Hold that thought," Elias said, standing up. "Gotta piss."

Jake looked at the list as he picked the last of the label off his bottle. Even if they had one more man they could do enough overtime to get the fence line okay, and that meant they could get the rest of the hay shifted and grain brought in. He started picking at the label on Elias' bottle, mixing up combinations of men in his head. Tor was fast on the fences when he had to be, but Bobby was always faster. Kip could shift bales like nobody's business. The rest of them, though…damn. It just came down to everyone having to be at the top of their game all at the same time.

Tor came in just as Jake set the sheet down. "Hey."

"Hey," Tor said, heading to the fridge. Then his head snapped around, staring at the bottle in Jake's hand. "What the fuck are you doing?"

Jake looked down, the label half off Elias' beer bottle. "What? Not like he'll care."

"I fucking well care!" And Tor grabbed the bottle out of Jake's hand, his eyes flashing.

Jake clued in just at Elias came back, looking from him to Tor and back again.

"Uh, bad time?" Elias asked.

"You thought I was drinking?" Jake asked softly.

Tor's eyes widened and he opened his mouth, then closed it again, dropping his eyes. "Sorry."

Jake stared at him, not sure what to say. So he said nothing.

Summer

Jake was almost asleep when Tor got off the phone with Becky and came to bed. "How is she?" he asked, sliding an arm around Tor's waist.

"Becky? She's fine. So's Susie." Tor didn't move, didn't come closer to him. He was stiff, lying flat on his back.

"What's wrong?" Jake asked, not sure if he'd done something to piss Tor off again or not.

Tor rolled over, burying his face in Jake's neck. "Momma's dying. Becky says she might have a few years, or a few months."

Jake held himself still, not sure what to do. Finally, he did the only thing he could do, just held on tight and told Tor he was sorry.

It was supposed to be Lego night, but Elias wound up in the barn doing clean up when one of the day hands quit in the middle of the afternoon, and Kirk was asleep on the couch. Jake would have been just as happy to watch TV or even go up to the barn to help Elias muck stalls, but he had other things on his mind.

Like the frown on Tor's face and the dark looks he was getting that he was pretty sure he wasn't meant to see. Tor's shoulders were square, and even sitting on the floor with Lego scattered around him, Tor's back was ramrod straight.

Jake wondered if this was one of those times that waiting would fix, or if he was in for a night of space between them in the bed and cold stares in the morning. Then he decided he didn't care. Or rather, he didn't care if they wound up yelling this time, 'cause it was obviously something he'd done, judging by the glares Tor was tossing his way.

Then Tor started tossing more than glares, aiming Lego bricks into boxes, not paying any attention if they were going where they were supposed to or not. Jake knew it wasn't exactly a huge deal, but he also knew that Tor was doing it to piss him off; not mixing the Lego was one of the stupider things Jake was insistent about, but it was also the one thing Tor could do at that moment to bring Jake's temper to the front.

"Problem, Tor?" he asked as mildly as he could.

"Yep. But you're not going to hear about it."

"And why's that?"

"My boss is an idiot. And seeing as how I'd love to tell my partner about it, I'm a little upset. Can't seem to get my boss to leave the room."

Ah. Jake sighed, he should have seen that one coming a mile away.

"Tor, you know—"

"Yeah, I know. Fuckwad quit, you got fences down, and I'm good on the fence breaks. You know why I'm good? Because I fucking hate fixing them. So I do it right, and fast, and then I don't have to go back out a week later. But here I am, going out on fences for the next two days, instead of moving the herd. Which, by the way, I'm also good at."

"I know, Tor, but—"

"Jesus, Jake. Stop being the boss. You're my partner. You're supposed to say my boss is an idiot, I never get treated right, and you feel sorry for me. Then you're supposed to offer me a backrub, and fuck me silly."

Jake thought about it for a moment. "Can't tell you that. But I can tell you something else."

Tor glared at him. "What?"

"Your boss thinks you're hot when you get all riled up."

Tor blinked. "Christ, don't let my partner hear you, he's all possessive."

"Of course he is. Look what he's got."

"Good point."

"So, you want to fuck your boss? Even if he is an idiot?"

"Will it get me out of doing the fences?"

"Nope."

"Shit. Think I'll just fuck my partner then. At least I know where I stand with him."

"That works for me."

Kirk rolled over on the couch. "Remind me never to tell you you're an idiot. My ass is so not on the menu."

Jake stared at him, then leered. "Honey, your ass is far too scrawny for me. You'd never survive what I'd do to you."

Tor almost cried he was laughing so hard at the look on Kirk's face.

———•◆•———

Jake was walking past the main house when Missy came out, squinting into the sun. "Got a minute, Jake?"

He turned and nodded, taking the steps two at a time. "How are you doing, Missy? Wedding plans coming along?"

Missy smiled at him, a wide grin that made her look impossibly young, and even further removed from the prick-tease she'd been a couple of years before. "Yeah, slowly. Chris has reached the stage where he just smiles a lot. Momma and I are having fun, though."

Jake laughed. "Good for you. What's on your mind? Hope you're not planning to rope me into the festivities."

Missy rolled her eyes and her nose crinkled. "No, you're safe. Something else." She looked back at the house, then up to the barn, her lower lip caught between her teeth. "It's about Travis."

Jake frowned, but not at Missy. Travis was new on the ranch, had only been there for a couple of weeks. So far he'd proven to be a good worker—strong, and willing to do what was asked of him.

"I just—I know it's none of my business," Missy said. "Lord, do I know it's none of my business. Just wanted to give you the heads up."

"About what?" Jake was confused. If it was anything to do with the ranch Missy would have told her father. If it was about the hands though… "He looking for a fight? Rubbing someone the wrong way?"

Missy shook her head impatiently. "That's just it. He's looking to rub someone the right way. The wrong someone."

Jake stared and she clicked her tongue, looking exasperated.

"He's been checking out your man, Jake. Just think you should…maybe tell him how things are. Keep an eye out."

Jake stifled a laugh before it could get out and insult her. "Okay," he said. "Appreciate your concern."

She nodded seriously and wished him a good day before disappearing into the house.

Jake shook his head and wandered off to tease Tor about his young admirer.

Autumn

They'd been sitting in the truck laughing their asses off for almost five minutes before Jake could see straight enough to drive. "Jesus, I can't believe you did that," he said, pulling away from the bar. They'd just been kicked out of a private party, and Jake wasn't sure if Chris was going to speak to either of them again.

"What?" Tor demanded, wiping his eyes. "Stag party. No women allowed. Didn't see why they should be allowed in the movies either." Tor collapsed back against the seat of the truck, laughing again, laughing until he was gasping for air. "Did you see the look on Tyler's face? Shit, think that boy might be queer."

Jake was just trying to drive in a lawful manner. "I can't fucking believe that you took gay porn to a stag party."

"I can't believe they let me put the tapes in."

"I can't believe they let us live."

"Funny though."

"Fuck, yes."

Thirty

◆—◆—◆

Autumn

"This far enough?" Tor asked.

Jake shifted in the saddle, felt Tor's arm tighten around his waist as he held on. "Nope."

The sounds of the big dance were still floating in the air, happy and bright. The dance was just as good as it always was, and the first night of the party had been just as wild as it was the year before. Tor had met a nice, lonely cowboy for them to take down to the riverbed, and they'd spent the day recovering. Now they were headed out for some peace and quiet. Or maybe not so quiet.

It had been a good summer, spirits were high. So were most of the people, and Jake had grabbed Tor a little earlier than they'd planned. Escape came just before dark this year.

"Little music might be nice," Tor said mildly as they rode away from the ranch.

"Tor, can you hear people yelling?"

"Yeah, a bit. Don't think there'll be fights, though."

"Not my point," Jake said, grinning a little. "If we can hear them yelling, they'll hear you screaming."

This time it was Tor who shifted in the saddle. "Right. Get River to hurry up, will ya?"

Winter

Jake reckoned they looked like something out of an old movie. Both of them on horseback in full riding gear—from leather chaps to riding dusters, boots to hats—heading home in the driving rain. He was all in black, even his leather gloves, Tor in brown; would have been a romantic picture, he thought as water dripped from his brim, except it was damn wet and cold.

Tor and Lug moved easily beside him, River and Lug matching their pace to each other's with ease.

"How's the Boss?" Tor asked, raising his voice against the weather.

Jake shrugged. "Missy says he'll be fine. It was minor for a heart attack, and he'll be home in a few days."

Tor shook his head, water spilling down his back. "Still," he said. "Second heart attack in a year. That ain't good."

"No, suppose it's not," Jake allowed.

Tor looked around them, at the drenched fields. Jake knew he was seeing them as they usually were, green and vibrant, not water logged.

"He'll be looking to sell up in a few years," Tor called to him.

Jake thought about it for a moment. "Missy and Chris—"

"Are talking about heading to Dallas or Austin."

"What?" Jake couldn't keep the surprise out of his voice. "Why would they do that? They aren't city folk, Missy grew up here—"

"Chris doesn't think he's made to ranch. Wants to be in the suburbs. In any case, I don't see them keeping on here, even if they don't go to Texas. Maybe wind up in Little Rock."

"Oh." Jake wasn't sure what else to say.

They rode in silence for a few minutes, the rain picking up enough to stop idle conversation.

When the rain eased again Tor said, "Was thinking that when the time comes we could make an offer."

Jake stared at Tor, feeling like the entire conversation was something he had to be dreaming. "Us?"

"Well, yeah." Tor turned in the saddle to face him better. "I know I don't have as much saved as you, what with sending money to my mother and all, but think about it, Jake. You practically run the place, it's your home—our home."

"I run the hands, not the ranch," Jake interrupted. His gut was starting to knot up. They'd talked about this, hadn't they? Years ago.

Tor raised one eyebrow, the effect diminished by his hat. "Okay, so you keep after the hands and I'll handle the business."

"No."

Tor's jaw twitched. "Listen. Think about it. Aside from being our own bosses for a change, what happens if someone else buys the place? No guarantees we get to stay in the bunkhouse—hell, no guarantee one of us doesn't get fired because we share a bed."

Jake looked through the rain, meeting Tor's eyes. No matter how he turned the idea over in his head he knew Tor was right about that. There would be no promises about anything if the Boss sold to someone with a closed mind.

But it didn't change the fact that the mere idea of buying the spread, taking on the extra work and heartache, made Jake's chest tighten. He just wasn't cut out for it, had never wanted it. He knew himself, knew that owning something that huge with people counting on him to keep it going…well, it would be enough to drive him to an early grave.

"No," he said, his voice low.

Tor searched his eyes for a moment. "Think about it, at least?"

"No."

With a quick motion Tor turned his head, a word lost to the wind and rain. "C'mon, Lug. Let's get home and get dry."

Jake watched Tor nudge Lug into a canter, watched them move off into the rain and the growing dark.

"Damn."

"He wants you."

Jake looked up from his book and grinned at Tor. "Yeah, so he said. Said he wants you, too. Chatty little piece of work."

Tor just laughed and launched himself at the bed. He landed beside Jake, bouncing them both in the air. "What did you tell him?"

Jake shrugged one shoulder as he rolled over to pin Tor to the sheets. "Told him we don't play so close to home."

Tor quirked and eyebrow at him and leaned up to take a kiss. "We don't? The riverbed—"

"Is different, and you know it. Never with anyone who works here, and everyone knows who they were going home with. Kinda think Travis doesn't get that part. Or worse, doesn't much care."

Jake watched Tor's face as he pondered that—it took less than three seconds before Tor kissed him again, strong hands going to Jake's waist.

"Makes sense to me."

"Yeah?"

Tor licked Jake's neck. "Well, sure. If you don't want him, and I don't want him, then there's no point in doing it. And if we did? Get messy, what with seeing him every day."

Jake nodded, sitting up to tug at Tor's shirt. "What did he say to you?" he asked, curious.

"Said you've got a nice ass, and looked real strong. I told him yeah, you are. So he asked flat out if we play around."

Jake nodded again, his hips moving a little as he dipped his head to bite one of Tor's nipples. "Yeah, he told me he wouldn't be adverse to a little action in the loft. You, me and him."

Tor gasped, but Jake was fairly sure it was because of the mark he'd just started to suck up on Tor's chest.

"Forward, ain't he?" Tor said, a little breathless.

"Yeah," Jake agreed, forcing his hand between them to stroke Tor's cock through his jeans. "Not like me."

"Couldn't be like you in a million years, Jake. No one could."

It wasn't until they were almost asleep that Jake realized he hadn't seen that kind of hunger in Tor for ages. That he hadn't even noticed it was missing.

———◆—————

Spring

Jake rode into the yard mad enough to spit, but in control enough not to let it show. He saw Tor heading up to the big barn and called out to him. "Tor! Get your ass over here!"

Okay, maybe not so in control of his temper.

Tor looked over and blinked, his shoulders tightening. Tor walked over to him, eyes flashing, but one hand coming up to rub River's flank as he approached.

"Don't talk to me like that," he said calmly.

"Don't fuck with the work teams, then," Jake shot back. "I've got reasons for sending people where I want them, and they're more important than who's going to be around here for you to have lunch with. Got that?"

Tor's eyes narrowed. "Wasn't that, and you know it. Travis had to—"

"Travis and I talked it over already. What Travis doesn't seem to get is that I'm the Boss here. Not Bobby. Not you. I set the fucking teams and you don't go messing it up."

"Fine. Won't be messing with anything of yours, then." Tor turned and strode away, arms swinging.

"Goddamn right you won't," Jake said under his breath. He urged River to turn and took off at a canter, looking for the scattered remains of his team. Get things fixed around here if it drove him insane.

———◆—————

Jake woke up alone.

It was morning, he knew that much. And Tor hadn't come to bed, hadn't come back to say he was sorry, or to listen to Jake say it, or to even sort out how to fix it.

He found Tor in the kitchen, sitting at the table, a cup of coffee in front of him.

"You been here all night?" Jake asked, pulling out a chair.

"Yeah."

"Why?"

"Didn't see much point in going in. Didn't see the point in yelling anymore, putting on a show for Elias and Kirk."

Didn't want to make up.

Jake thought about that for a bit. "You're still mad."

"Hell, yes. You said you'd book the time off, that you'd take care of it." His voice was low, quiet. Hoarse.

"And I said I was sorry. I am. I screwed up."

"You forgot. I asked you to make sure one simple thing would happen, and you forgot."

Jake kept his sigh inside. "We can trade off, I'm sure. We'll find someone to cover the days—it's only three, yeah? Shouldn't be too hard to get away. I'll ask Bobby if he wants some extra time, and I figure Kip will cover for me—"

"No."

Jake blinked. "Why not?"

"I'll ask Bobby. But don't bother asking Kip. I don't want you to come with me anymore."

———◆———

Summer

Tor always slammed the door when he stalked out during a fight, anger radiating off him in waves. Jake never

236

did. Not that he didn't do his share of storming off, he just didn't slam the door. The rest was the same.

Jake wasn't really worried about Tor not coming back, he always did. He wasn't so much bothered by Tor walking out, either. If one of them didn't take off the fight would get worse, get nasty; turn into more than them having a bad day, tempers high, more than just a release of pressure and tension.

No, what scared the crap out of Jake was that he was getting used to the sound of that fucking door closing on him.

Thirty One

The voices were getting louder, the party gearing up to full throttle. Jake actually felt a little like throttling some of them, but they were just letting off steam, doing what they always did at the end of season dance. The tight feeling in his gut just meant that it was time to get River ready, find Tor, and head out.

Fourth time. The fourth year in a row that they'd spend the night out in the meadow, away from the party. If he could find Tor.

Jake went to the bunkhouse, dodging a few hands and their wives who were too far into drink to make much sense, and stopping to send two little ones back to their tents where their mommas were trying in vain to get them settled. The sun was long down, the kids had done their dancing with sparklers, and it was time for them to be sleeping. Time for him and Tor to get the hell out of Dodge.

He grabbed blankets and food, a couple of juice bottles, and started to leave the house. As an after thought he wandered back into their bedroom and picked up the latest tube of lube, staring at it in his hand like it was something he'd never seen before. Time was, he'd have grabbed it first thing. Now it was just a hope, or maybe a gesture in resignation, and when did he start thinking of sex with Tor as something that may or may not happen, or worse—something that he wasn't always eager for?

He went into the stable still thinking about it, but when the band started up, louder than before, he forced the thought from his mind and started packing the saddle bags, talking softly to River.

"Gonna go soon. Find Tor, and get out of here, yeah? Let that lot out there get the summer out of their systems and go watch the stars. Be nice for us all, right?"

River stamped his feet, apparently agreeing with him.

He hummed along with the song the band was playing until they finished, then he was just happy for the relative quiet. The band was getting better, but they really needed a new soundman. Jake had finished getting River's saddle ready, though not on him, when he heard a noise from just outside the wide doors at the back. He'd heard it often enough—hell, he'd made it often enough—that he knew it right away and paused to grin. Someone was getting slammed up against the back wall and if the grunt of approval was any indication, they weren't fighting.

He shook his head and picked up the saddle, willing enough to let whoever it was have their fun. He tried not to

239

listen, but he could hear it anyway, and part of his mind was trying to sort out who it was. Wouldn't be Kip and Beth—they would be with the tents, Beth getting the baby to sleep and Kip trying to help. Might be Elias, if the looks he'd been exchanging with one of the Thompson girls was any indication.

He was almost to River, had actually lifted the saddle and was about to settle it over the blanket, when he heard it. Probably the only groan on the planet that could make him freeze when heard out of context. With him in a stall and Tor not right there, naked and wanting with him, it was most definitely out of its proper context.

He didn't think, just turned and put the saddle over the stall wall and headed to the doors, not bothering with stealth. He stood in the open doors, knowing he was in full light, and watched.

It wasn't anything like what had happened two years ago at the auction. He didn't feel the rush of anger, the need to run over and stop it, to stake his claim. Maybe because this time he knew for a fact it was Tor. Maybe because he wasn't surprised. This time, when it mattered, he said nothing. Felt nothing.

He watched Tor in the shadows, leaning against the outside wall, his head thrown back as Travis finished undoing their jeans. Listened as Tor gasped when Travis started jerking them both off. Watched as Tor moaned and thrust and begged for more, told Travis to suck him off. When Travis grinned and went to his knees, less than ten feet away, Jake watched as Tor's eyes closed, heard him hiss with pleasure as Travis took Tor in his mouth.

He noticed the way they were just outside the fall of light from the doors, the way Travis knelt with one knee in the dirt, the other leg bent so his boot was planted solid. Travis' jeans were dusty, like he'd not had time to change after playing ball in the yard all afternoon.

Tor had showered and changed, though; was wearing his good boots, and new jeans. The shirt wasn't new, but it was one of Jake's favorites—it was the same blue-gray as Jake's eyes.

Jake noticed other things, too. The ring in Tor's cock and the way Travis played with it. That Travis was noisy, his mouth soft and wet, his lips already swollen, probably from kisses. That Tor had no hesitation in using Travis' name or telling him how nice it felt. That Tor's breath was coming faster and faster, even though he seemed to be in no rush to finish.

He noticed how pale Travis was, how his hair seemed to shine in the less than half-light. How the lean muscles in his back flexed as he moved. How young he looked.

Jake didn't turn and walk away until Tor was thrusting hard, fucking Travis' mouth and Travis was stroking himself off, his hand in rhythm with Tor's hips. Tor sounded like Travis was good at what he was doing.

Jake walked through the stable, from one end to the other, and out into the crowd. If anyone spoke to him, he missed it. He didn't feel anything yet, and that sort of worried him. He should feel something, after all. Anger. Hurt. Humiliation. Anything at all—but he didn't. He just felt empty, like nothing could touch him. Cold.

He walked steadily toward the big tent where the band was playing, the sounds of the music and the people just outside of his awareness. He was pretty sure he wasn't going deaf, which left shutting down and shock as his current state. Jake figured that made sense, but he really only noted it as a point of interest. He was focused on getting to where he was going, and after that…well, he'd see what happened after that.

Jake walked through the groups of people, brushing off one hand that rested on his arm, not knowing or caring who it was. He avoided the lights in the big tent, veering off to the right where he'd seen a large group of lawn chairs and blankets. The portable bar, more or less. People had found that having all the coolers together—at least the ones without food—stopped them from losing their drinks when they were moving around so much. All the booze on the ranch in one handy place, and no one really caring who was drinking what.

He snagged a bottle of water as he rummaged, flipping lids open with the toe of his boot. Someone asked him something—maybe to pass a bottle, maybe what the hell was he doing—and he ignored the voice, moving to the next cooler. He knew exactly what he was looking for, and it wasn't beer. He needed something easy to carry, because despite his new found ability to ignore everyone, he had no intention of drinking himself stupid surrounded by people.

Four coolers later he found it, a bottle of bourbon, mostly full. He snatched it out of the melting ice, then stepped past the coolers into the darkness and started to walk.

He didn't pay attention to where he went, he just walked. In the dark, away from the people, his pace was steady except for when he stopped to swallow another mouthful of bourbon. It tasted like he remembered, which didn't surprise him. He'd known his memories of assorted flavors were true; years of drinking made some things hard to forget.

He wondered if he should pace himself, then realized he was going to throw it all up eventually anyway; the intent was to drink himself unconscious. He walked for what felt like hours, until he'd started to weave and trip over rocks; then he sat and looked around.

He couldn't hear the music anymore, or any yelling. The stars were out, the moon slightly more than half full; all he could hear was his own heartbeat and the cicadas.

He didn't think about it. He didn't think about anything at all, just looked at the stars until he got dizzy, then he looked at the grass. He was hot, the walking and the drink making his body temperature seem higher than it was. It took a little effort, but he managed to get his shirts off and he set them aside, thinking that when he finally threw up he wanted them out of the way.

The bottle was almost empty, only and inch or two left, so he drained it and waited. He waited to feel angry, to feel sick…to feel. He listened to his breathing for a while and got bored.

Finally he made himself picture it, to imagine Tor finally coming down Travis' throat. He tried to hear Tor's voice, picture his face, and it worked to a point, though getting Tor's voice to cry out a name other than his own was work.

Still, he felt nothing, his breathing didn't speed and his hands didn't shake. Dead. Empty. Drained.

He poked at the edges of it all, tried to imagine Tor fucking Travis, and that didn't do it either. He wished he had more bourbon.

He drank the water, the whole bottle in a few swallows and lay back, looking at the stars again, letting himself think of nothing. He must have passed out at some point, because when he started puking the sky was a little lighter, false dawn coming.

He was sober enough to roll onto his side. He may be dead, but he didn't want to choke to death.

He'd forgotten what it was like to be sick on booze, even if he remembered the taste of all the kinds of alcohol he'd ever had. He'd forgotten the way his stomach cramped and the way his throat burned, the way his arms would clutch at his belly.

He'd forgotten the smell, so different from being sick with the flu. He'd forgotten that when he was piss drunk and puking he always got messy, clean shirts off to the side or not. He'd forgotten the stink of his sweat when alcohol tried to get out of his system through every pore.

He remembered the headaches. He remembered the bliss of passing out again. He remembered the way every cell in his body protested when he came awake again, the sun up and getting higher.

He lay on the grass for a long time, waiting for his stomach settle enough that he could figure out where he was. It didn't, and then he got to remember dry heaves.

A long while later, when the sun was telling him it was almost noon, he got to his feet and put on his shirts. He picked up the empty bottles, figured out where he was, and started to walk.

There were people all over when he made it back to the ranch, and he found his hearing was still faulty, or his attention was. He dumped the bottles in the recycling bins and passed a few more hands as he crossed the yard, the smell of breakfast and lunch cooking making his stomach churn.

Someone called out to him, but he couldn't summon the interest to look up and see who. He passed the big house just as Travis came off the steps, his usual friendly smile in place.

He stared at the man, watching as Travis grew nervous, his smile fading.

"Jake? Something wrong?" Travis asked.

"No. Not anymore," Jake said, his voice rough. He wondered if he might still be drunk—there was no other explanation for him talking to Travis.

Travis looked unsure, and more than ready to flee, but something held him where he was. Maybe genuine concern for Jake's well being. "You don't look so good. Do you want me to get Tor?" He pointed toward the bunkhouse.

Jake shook his head. "No. You already got him." He walked past Travis, not bothering to see the effect that had on him, if any. Travis wasn't important. Nothing was, except for getting home. He could smell himself, and only the thought of a hot shower kept him from lying down in the dirt to go back to sleep.

Jake took the steps to the bunkhouse slowly, listening to voices inside. Elias. Kirk. Tor. Wonderful, everyone was home, and in the kitchen. He opened the door and stepped in, walking right through the room as his eyes adjusted to

244

the dimmer light. He thanked whoever had kept him alive so far for making sure he didn't trip on anything.

"Jesus. Bad night?" Elias asked from the table.

"Where the hell were you?" Tor said at the same time.

Jake ignored Tor, which was surprisingly easy. "Had better," he said to Elias, still walking. He barely registered the way Tor was looking at him, his eyes narrowing.

"I gotta talk to Taggart," he heard as he walked down the hall, "y'all might want to leave."

Kirk sighed. "You gonna fight again? 'Cause I gotta say, this is getting tired."

"Just leave." Tor's voice was flat, and then there were steps coming down the hall.

Jake stood by the bed and started stripping off, catching the smell of vomit when he peeled his jeans off. He heard Tor come in, but didn't bother looking up at him, just finished taking off his clothes. He wanted a shower.

"You were drinking last night," Tor said, not making it a question. Jake did look then, met his eyes and saw cold fury in them.

"Yeah. And you were fucking Travis," Jake said, just as a matter of fact. He had honestly expected that saying it out loud would make him feel it, would make him angry, but it didn't. The punch to his gut was apparently still holding back on him.

He didn't even feel a moment of satisfaction as he watched Tor's eyes widen, the fear and guilt shining in them for a few seconds. He watched as Tor figured out Jake had seen, watched as denial was considered and rejected, and truth finally settled on. Then he watched as the color drained out of Tor's skin.

Jake pointed to the bathroom. "I'm going to take a shower."

He locked the door behind him, not wanting to bother with words or whatever bullshit Tor was going to come up with while he got clean. He stayed under the spray a long time, until the water began to cool. He forgot to wash with soap. He just stood and didn't think, then had to wash in the lukewarm water and rinse in near cold. He swallowed a couple of aspirin and walked back into the bedroom with a towel around his waist.

Tor was sitting on the edge of the bed, looking at him. "It won't happen again," he said quietly. A promise.

Jake started getting out clean clothes. "Don't see why not," he said, just as quietly. "Not like you'll ever be fucking me again." The emptiness inside him didn't even waver.

Tor was silent while Jake pulled on his jeans and boots, watching him as he found a clean shirt.

"What do you want me to do?" Tor asked finally, and Jake looked at him, surprised. It suddenly dawned on him, looking at Tor's eyes, the lines in his face, the way he was holding his body…Jake knew that at that moment he could ask Tor to do anything and he'd do it. Anything at all.

Tor had no idea what he'd done.

"Well, I'm going up to the barn to see about River, get the stuff from his saddle bags," Jake said buttoning his shirt and reaching for the doorknob. "You can pack your shit and get the fuck out of here."

Tor looked like he'd been hit. Jake waited, sure that Tor had something to say. He wasn't willing to take this out to the yard or up to the barn. Tor would follow, and Jake, for some reason, didn't want the whole ranch to know what was going on. Not yet.

"Four years, Jake," Tor said, barely above a whisper. "You really going to give up on that?"

Jake wondered why he wasn't pointing out that it was Tor who'd cheated, Tor who'd fucked up. He assumed that if he could feel the hurt and anger he would have done just that, would have screamed and hit and had a fistfight, maybe have hurt Tor really bad. But he didn't.

Jake supposed they both knew that his walking away wasn't entirely his fault—they both knew he wouldn't be if Tor hadn't been with Travis the night before. There wasn't really a point to saying it. Jake didn't care enough to make it a point. He just wanted to get the stuff he'd left in the barn, and go to sleep.

Tor asked again. "You're really going to walk away?"

Jake opened the door and stepped out, then looked back at Tor, sitting on Jake's bed. "Yes, Mark. I believe I am."

He closed the door behind him and left the house.

Thirty Two

When Jake got back from the barn, his arms loaded with the blankets, juice and other things, Elias was on the porch, waiting.

"What the fuck is going on?" he demanded.

"Nothing," Jake said. Still no tone to his voice. He wondered again when it would come back. He was about to push past Elias, his stomach turning, but the shorter man stood in front of him, his eyes flashing and his lips pushed tightly together.

"Tor's moving into the fourth bedroom," he stated.

"Good. Let me in."

"Not until you—"

"I threw him out, all right? Now fucking move so I can get in there and puke!"

Elias stepped to the side, shaking his head. "Damn fools."

Jake didn't bother to argue.

Tor had managed to clear out his things in the half hour or so Jake was gone, and he got the rest while Jake was in the bathroom. When Jake came out Tor stood in the door until Jake told him to leave.

"Jake—" Tor looked lost, unable to find anything he dared to say, or maybe unwilling to say what he wanted to.

Jake gently closed the door on him. "Please. Just go. I don't want to talk about it."

He spent the rest of the day in bed, or in the bathroom, not doing anything. He lay on the bed and stared at the wall, noting the blank places where Susie's pictures had been. Tor left the ones that had "To Uncle Jake" on them.

When it got dark and Jake thought he could keep food down he went into the kitchen and got an apple and some crackers. Tor wasn't around.

"You gonna tell me what the deal is?" Elias asked from the living room door. Kirk was standing just behind him, peering over Elias' shoulder.

Jake sighed. "Not the details, no. All you need to know is that Tor and I aren't together anymore."

"There going to be screaming matches if he stays in the house?" Kirk had retreated already, but Elias was standing firm, his eyes serious. "This is our home too, and I want to know if things are going to settle, or if I need to talk to the Boss. 'Cause I ain't staying here if things are going to get worse."

Jake shook his head. "I don't plan on screaming. Don't even plan on talking much."

That startled Elias, or maybe the flat voice did. He came into the kitchen and swung a chair around, sitting down to face Jake. "No chance you can fix it? I mean—"

"No. I don't think so." Jake ate another cracker and waited for his stomach to accept it. "Excuse me," he said, and went back to his room.

———◆———

Three days later the Boss called him into the main house just after suppertime, and had him sit in the easy chair.

"Anything you want to talk about, Jake?" he asked, leaning back in his own chair and sipping his coffee.

Jake shook his head. "No. Not really."

The Boss nodded. "You look like shit. Sleeping?"

"Yes, sir." He wasn't really. Or not well. For the previous few days he'd gotten up, set the work teams out, and done his job. He could concentrate on that, could function well doing what he had to do. He was willing to admit that he'd shifted things around so Travis got the shit jobs, mucking stalls and doing stuff that everyone hated. He'd also sent Tor out on horseback as often as he could, and if he couldn't keep the two of them working apart, he himself went out to look at the fence line.

Other than that, he went to the bunkhouse at the end of the day, showered and had supper in the kitchen with the others. He and Tor didn't speak. When the washing was done, Tor went out or to his room; Jake really didn't pay attention much, he just went to his room and sat on the bed until his supper inevitably came back up, then he went to bed.

He stared at the walls and didn't think. He didn't feel. He didn't sleep. At one point, the night before, he'd realized he was crying, and that scared him—he didn't remember starting.

Now Doug was looking thoughtfully at him.

"What do you need to know?" Jake finally asked.

"Is it over?" he asked immediately, with no hesitation.

"Yes."

Doug sighed. "Will you tell me why? Do you want him gone?"

Jake blinked. He hadn't thought about it in terms of asking the Boss to fire Tor—hadn't even really thought about getting Travis fired, though he supposed he should have. Now he did think about it. "I don't know. I mean–no. It won't be a problem with him here, I can still do my job, he can do his."

"But do you want him gone?" the Boss pressed. "Do you want me to send him away?"

Jake closed his eyes and for the first time since he'd seen Travis and Tor together he felt something. His chest was tight and he wasn't sure if he could breathe. "I don't know."

They sat in silence for a minute or two and Jake waited for the empty feeling to come back. Did he want Tor gone? Most of him did. Part of him wanted Tor dead and buried. But the idea of firing him, kicking him out of his house, his job, sending him off to…where would he go? Becky's most likely. His mother was living there now, getting sicker. Her health insurance had cut out and there wasn't much money, Tor had been paying for everything, the drugs, the doctors.

"No." The constriction in his chest lessened. "Don't fire him. We'll manage."

———•◆•———

It was dark, the only way Jake knew that evening had passed into night, the room now impossible to see in. He'd just been looking at the ceiling again anyway, and it hadn't changed any in the week he'd spent more or less confined to his room. He'd started making it a challenge to see how long he could keep his supper down. He'd made it to almost an hour tonight.

He had a mirror, he knew he looked like hell. Dark circles under his eyes, lines looking etched into his face. He'd lost weight, his jeans weren't fitting right anymore and his shirts were all loose. He was losing strength too, and that should have been worrying him.

But it didn't. He wasn't worried about anything other than how to stop crying. Now that he'd started he didn't seem able to stop. The feelings he'd expected, the anger and pain and rage had all passed him by; the only thing that touched him was the emptiness, the darkness that filled the other side of the bed.

He had no idea what time it was. He got up from the bed and went into his bathroom to get a wet cloth, cold, for his eyes. He'd discovered that crying in the shower, no matter how much quieter it was, was hell on his eyes, made them red and bloodshot and sore. So now he tried to be quiet on the bed and when he thought he was done, he'd fall into an exhausted sleep with a wet cloth over his eyes.

He stripped naked and climbed into bed, the wet cloth over his eyes, cooling his face. He'd look like hell in the morning, worse hell; it was bad this time, starting right after he'd vomited, and not stopping. His breath didn't even hitch anymore, and he didn't sob. Just a never-ending stream of tears.

He lay in the dark and waited for morning, listening to the silent house.

After a time he realized it wasn't silent, that something was wrong. He got up and pulled on his jeans, swearing when he realized he'd either have to hold them up or find a belt. He gathered the extra fabric in his hand and walked into the hall, listening.

Tor. The sounds were coming from Tor's room. He stood outside the door, one down and on the other side of the linen closet—Tor's original room, as a matter of fact—and listened. A moan. A deep breath.

Jesus fucking Christ.

Then a sob.

Jake walked back to his room and went to bed, trying not to think.

Thirty Three

It was almost two weeks before he said anything more to Tor than "Stick with Bobby and Elias," and when it happened it wasn't what he'd meant to say at all.

They were all at supper, Kirk's turn to cook so it was good, and he was sitting across from Tor, as usual. Some things didn't change.

Jake looked up from his plate and met Tor's eye by accident. He opened his mouth intending to ask for the salt but what came out was, "Why are you still here?" He sounded confused, even to his own ears, but as soon as he said it he wanted to know. If it was just the job that was fine, but they were both falling apart—Tor looked even worse than he did some mornings, though Jake hadn't heard him crying again.

Elias and Kirk froze, then Elias picked up his plate, ready to leave. Before he could even push back his chair Tor said, "Because you're here." His voice was quiet, but he sounded sure of his answer.

"Oh. Pass the salt, please."

That night he couldn't hold his supper for even ten minutes.

Sundays were the worst. They'd had three of them since the dance, and each one had been worse than the week before. The first Sunday he'd spent in his room, still mostly numb. The second he'd fled to the stable and done all the mucking out. The third he'd made an attempt at normalcy, sitting on the porch with his magazines, but the threat of another crying jag had sent him to his room.

Tor spent all three, as far as Jake could tell, moving from his room to the couch and back to his room as soon as he saw Jake. It was getting difficult. More difficult. Jake was edgy and feeling a little penned in, but there was nothing that captured his interest, nothing to keep him busy. He found himself waiting for something to happen, waiting for Tor to do something, say something, to give him a look he could react to, for him to make it easier.

He wanted Tor to do something that would either fix them or make him hate the man. The nothingness was going to drive him mad. But he didn't know what, if anything would do either of those things.

He'd stopped throwing up, which was good, and he wasn't crying every night either. But that was really the only improvement. He didn't want to talk to anyone, didn't want to laugh or joke, or watch TV.

He and Tor had spoken to each other, but nothing of substance. He would tell Tor what his work for the day or the week was, and Tor would nod and go about his business. They'd worked themselves up to speaking a few words at supper, across the table, mostly about the ranch. Nothing more, really, and Jake couldn't bring himself to ask about Tor's mother, or anything else, for fear that once he'd opened the gate he'd find himself asking about Travis, about that night.

Finally, just after lunch, Jake gave up and went to saddle River. He needed to get out, get away from the house, away from people—which, of course, was just what he'd been doing for almost a month, but this was different. He wanted freedom to ride and freedom to maybe feel something.

Freedom to hope for an afternoon.

He rode without direction, giving River his head. At least, he thought he did, but when he realized they'd wound up in the meadow he'd come to think of his and Tor's, he wasn't terribly surprised. He dismounted and ground tied River, giving him an apple from the saddlebag. Then he sat with his back against a tree and looked around.

He picked out four spots that he knew were places he and Tor had either fucked or had important conversations. The spot where he'd told Tor he'd been in prison. The spot where they'd fucked the first time after they'd gotten pierced. The spot where they'd made up after a fight about something he'd now forgotten.

He closed his eyes and let the sun warm him. He almost fell asleep, or let his mind drift far away; the sound of approaching hooves was damn close when he noticed it. He opened his eyes when River whinnied, and watched Tor ride up on Lug.

Jake didn't say anything, didn't move, just watched as Tor settled Lug and gave both of the horses a carrot, then got something else from the saddle bag.

Finally. Finally something was going to happen and he'd either start to live again or at least figure out how far dead he was.

Tor walked over and passed him a bottle of apple juice without a word, then sat next to him, looking out over the field. Jake waited, but Tor didn't seem ready to say anything, so he shrugged and opened the bottle, drinking a little less than half of it.

When Tor still didn't say anything Jake turned his head to look at him and said, "Well?"

Tor took a breath, then looked back. "I'm sorry, Jake," he said quietly.

"I know." And he did know, knew it from the way Tor looked as bad as he did, knew it from the way Tor's eyes were always sad and self-loathing. He'd never doubted that Tor was sorry—sorry he'd been caught, and even sorry he'd done it in the first place. "Just not sure it matters," Jake added softly.

Tor looked at him, eyes searching, questioning his meaning, not the words.

"It's just..." Jake paused, trying to decide how to word what he was thinking. "We were falling apart, anyway. If everything had been all right, you would never have done it. You would've laughed, or walked away, or hit him. You wouldn't have...done that, if we were okay."

Tor nodded slowly. There wasn't any point in denying it, Jake knew.

"Want to fix it," Tor said, his voice rough. "I want to fix us. I can't–I can't keep going like this. Looking at you, watching you. Know I did it to you, Jake, but I want to make it better."

Jake felt something loosen, something he didn't know was tied up in a knot inside him. Maybe. Maybe there was a way to get past it. But the roots were somewhere else, not in Travis. "I just don't know what I did," Jake said. "I keep going over it, the whole day, and I don't know what I did that made you so mad you didn't walk away."

If he hadn't been looking right at Tor he would have missed it. The look in his eye, the flash of pain and regret. The guilt. But he *was* looking and he didn't ever have to worry about what Tor would have done; if he would have kept lying, kept hiding. He saw Tor's gaze slide away from him, the tightening of the jaw, the flash of panic.

And he knew.

He stared and waited for his heart to start beating again, watched Tor crumple into himself, burying his face in his hand for a moment before setting his hat back further on his head.

"How long?" Jake asked, his voice sounding like it was coming from inside a well.

Tor looked at the ground. "Jake—"

"How fucking long was it going on?" Now there was anger, white heat and noise crashing over him, filling the hollow inside him. Taking over. It hadn't occurred to him that what he'd seen was anything more than a one-time thing.

"Almost two months."

Jake closed his eyes and told his stomach that the apple juice wasn't worth throwing up. Two months and he'd not had a clue, not a single suspicion. The idea that Tor could hide it that well for so long stung him, cut deeper than just about anything. Or maybe it was the fact that he hadn't been paying enough attention to notice. It really didn't matter; all that mattered was that it underlined just how finished they were, that they'd been done for a long time now and hadn't even known it.

"Jake, it wasn't—"

"Shut the fuck up. One more word right now and I'll kill you."

Silence, for a long time. Minutes passed and Tor sat next to him, not moving. Jake kept his eyes closed, trying to find something, anything, that had happened which would have clued him in. Any looks, any unexplained time away. Any hesitancy that Tor had had with him. Anything.

Aside from the fights they'd had and the few hours of strain they produced, he couldn't remember anything. Not a smell, a taste…nothing.

Jake opened his eyes and looked at River. "Did you fuck him?"

Tor sighed. "Yeah."

"Did he fuck you?"

"Jake—"

"Tell me."

Another pause. "Couple of times, yeah, but—"

Jake stood up and threw the bottle at the next tree, watched Tor flinch when the glass shattered. He moved to River and took his reins in one hand. "I'm going to talk to the Boss." Tor watched him as he mounted the horse and turned River toward home. "We're done, Tor."

"Yeah. I'm sorry, Jake."

"Too late for that."

"I know."

Thirty Four

———◆◆◆———

The Boss looked up at him from behind his desk. "Want to tell me why?"

"Not really, no," Jake said, fingering the brim of his hat. "But if he stays I go. I don't care if you let him quit with references or if you fire him and kick him off the ranch. But if he stays, I'll be leaving before sunset."

"I'll need something to tell him. Can't fire a man with no reason, and he's a good hand, Jake." But he would, Jake knew. The man in front of him would do it if he knew why.

"He was sleeping with Tor all summer. I want him gone." It didn't even hurt to say it out loud.

The Boss stared. "I haven't heard anything," he said, then shook his head. "I'm sorry, that was thoughtless."

But not surprising. Jake hadn't told anyone why he'd kicked Tor out of the bedroom, and he didn't suppose Tor would have told anyone. Travis might have, but he'd been doing nothing but his job since the dance. It must have been obvious to him that Jake knew what was going on, and Jake suspected that Tor had probably had a word with him, ending it. No one else would have known—Tor had been very discreet.

The Boss crossed to a filing cabinet and pulled Travis' folder. "What about Tor?" he asked, looking at Jake with a steady gaze. "Want him gone now, too?"

Jake blinked. He hadn't even thought about it. He wanted Tor gone, wanted him away, wanted Tor out of his life and away from the ranch. "Yeah. Both of them."

The Boss pulled Tor's file as well, and Jake's. He sat at the desk and rummaged in a drawer, finally producing a list of the current hands that he handed to Jake and said, "You think you can keep things going with the people there? Minus Tor and Travis?"

Jake didn't even look at it. "No. But we can find—"

"Casual labor and day hands. No one like Tor, no one you can count on. We hire two new hands this week and we lose two weeks training them. Now, I know it's slow right now, and we've done it before. But I'd rather not. You say you'll go if Travis stays. Fine, he's gone. But I won't put the extra work on everyone else to get rid of them both, Jake. Not even for you."

Jake swallowed. He knew the Boss had the right, but it still stung. The man was as near he had as a father, and Jake had never asked him for anything. Except, his mind whispered, a place to live, a job, a second chance at a life that should have ended more than fifteen years ago. He owed the man more than a demand to fire people in a fit of revenge. It was Jake's personal life, the Boss's ranch.

Jake straightened his shoulders. "Yes, sir. I understand."

The Boss nodded and laid the three files in a row. "One will go. You tell me which. You, Travis, or Tornado. Personally, I hope you'll stay. You're important here, to the ranch and to me."

Jake tried to smile, he really did. He reached over the desk and picked up the files, knowing Doug was watching him as he went to the cabinet and refilled two of them. He tossed the third back on the Boss's desk and said, "I want him gone, please." Then he left the office.

When he got back to the house Tor was in the kitchen, cutting up tomatoes. Jake was more than ready to keep walking without a word, but as he passed, Tor set the knife down and asked, "Am I leaving?"

Jake stopped and leaned on the wall, looking at Tor's back. Stiff and tight, every muscle tense. "No. Travis is."

Tor relaxed a little. "Thank you. Momma needs the money."

Jake nodded. "I know. That's the only reason you're staying. But I'd appreciate it if you started looking for work in a few weeks, after I can hire some more hands."

Tor nodded, then shook his head. "Jake—"

"Fuck, I don't want to hear it. Not right now, not yet, maybe never." Christ, he was tired. "But I'll tell you this: I'm done hiding. Not going to live in my room for the next few months. Not going to be this…this fucking shell. I won't let you kill me, Tor. You have a problem seeing me, you deal with it. I've got more important things to think about than your guilt."

Tor turned to face him, hands flexing, but his face calm. "Good. Don't want you hiding. I'll deal with it. But I want you to know I still—"

Jake held up his hand, palm out. "Don't you dare fucking say it now. I don't want to hear it from you. You didn't say it before, and I refuse to let you say it to me like this."

He thought Tor might say it anyway, his eyes were screaming it, but he finally nodded and turned away, back to cutting tomatoes.

———◆———

"What is this?" Jake asked from the easy chair. He'd been spending so many nights in his room, and Tor had too, that Kirk and Elias had developed new TV watching habits. The usual schedule seemed to have changed to include a series of cop shows Jake had never seen before.

"Umm…one of the forensic shows," Kirk said. "You wanna watch something else?"

Kirk and Elias were sitting on the couch, tense. It was the first night both Tor and Jake had stayed around after supper and they seemed to be waiting for an explosion, ready to make concessions to avoid whatever it was they thought would happen.

"No, this is fine," Jake said. "Just wondered."

The four of them watched in silence until the end of the program, then Elias stretched and tentatively said, "The new guy seems okay. Learns fast, anyway."

Jake nodded. "He should. Been working ranches for about ten years—he knows what to do."

Tor didn't say anything, simply nodded. Kirk looked from Tor to Jake and back again, his mouth twitching like he wanted to ask something. He settled into the couch instead, and Jake felt a wave of relief. He had no idea what Kirk had been planning to ask, but he was just as glad he hadn't. Jake's only goal for the evening was to make it through the news without saying or doing something he'd regret.

After the news was done Tor stood up and said good night to them all, walking out of the room. Elias followed, and Kirk raised an eyebrow, asking, "You staying up, or should I turn off the TV?"

Jake considered it, but decided he'd best try to get some sleep. His stomach was in a knot, and although he didn't think he'd be sick again, he knew that if he stayed up he'd just stare at the walls in the living room instead of the bedroom.

"No, I'm going to bed, too," he said. "Turn it off."

Kirk hit the button on the remote and reached for the switch on the lamp as Jake stood up. They made their way down the hall in the dark, and just as Kirk opened his bedroom door he said, "Thank you. For…trying to make things normal again."

Jake stopped and turned to look at him. "Ain't gonna be normal again. But you're welcome, anyway."

———————

Jake stumbled out of his bedroom, trying to button his shirt over the white T-shirt he'd grabbed in his rush. He'd managed to oversleep, which on one hand was not a bad thing—at least he was sleeping—but he was still late and not very awake. He'd skipped his shower in favor of chasing down coffee, and was trying to remember if he'd left his coat on the porch or in the closet when he went into the kitchen.

"Coffee?" Tor asked, pouring a mug already.

"Yeah, thanks. Damn alarm didn't go off." He accepted the mug and burned his mouth with the first swallow. "Ow. Fuck."

"It did, you know," Tor said, filling his own mug. "And the snooze went off twice."

Jake blinked. "Really?" He didn't remember that at all. "Why didn't you bang on the door?"

Tor looked uncomfortable. "Wasn't sure you'd thank me for waking you, and the other two were already gone—Elias is on early feeding and Kirk's always up earlier to go for a run."

Oh. Jake put the mug on the table and rebuttoned his shirt, considering it. He probably would have reacted in a less than polite way if Tor had been the one to tell him to shift his ass. "Sorry. And thanks for the coffee."

"No problem, there's more if you need it." Tor looked at him critically. "You might want to put your T-shirt on right side out before you go to work, though."

Thirty Five

Jake had spent a lot of time thinking about himself when he was first on the ranch. He sometimes thought that he fully grew up between the ages of twenty-two and twenty-three, learning all the important life lessons he should have gotten in his teens, and some he should have been taught as a youngster.

He learned to work, and to be responsible. He learned about money; how to earn it, save it, and spend it wisely. Self-control was learned by staying sober, discipline was learned by continued early mornings and hard work. He learned about respect by acting respectably and keeping his promises to Doug Gillian, and by noting that Doug earned respect the same way.

But while he was learning all of those things he was learning about himself, too; about what made him feel good, about what kept him in balance. Being outside. Working with the animals and working his muscles. Rhythm and routine. The seeds of it had been planted in prison, the careful order to every day, each one identical, and he'd been able to adapt it to a larger framework. His own rhythms moved with the seasons, the work that had to be done, the timing of his day.

Then there had been Tor, and a new routine had been added to his life. For four years he went to bed at the same time as before, but there was someone there with him, someone to touch. Four years of doing things together, riding, fucking, watching TV, reading. Playing with Lego. Talking to Susie and Becky on the phone, and later 'Lissa, Jacob and Cath. Fitting together and making their rhythm.

Then it had changed and for a month there was nothing but the walls of this room and the monotony of not thinking.

Jake found it oddly easy to establish new routines after he came out of his room, adapting to the TV schedule and sitting on the chair instead of sprawling on the couch with Tor. He cautiously tested the waters over a few days, seeing how they were going to fit together as co-workers living in the same house, but as men who had every expectation of hating each other if there was a misstep.

He found the idea of hating Tor as unappealing as any other he tried on. He no longer trusted Tor, probably still loved him, but he wasn't about to fill his life with rage again. It hadn't worked when he was seventeen, and he didn't want to try making it work at damn near forty.

It took a few weeks for the edges to wear on the rhythm, for it not to cut in when he sat in the easy chair and not on the couch. He got up in the morning, showered, ate and went to work. He and Tor were at least able to be civil, and the closer it got to Halloween he began to notice that their exchanges, while strictly about work, were starting to be more natural, less stilted. In the evenings the four of them ate at the table, they all took their turns with the cooking and washing up, and then moved to the living room.

Elias had been watching warily, probably waiting for the fall out of living with two volatile men who had obviously hurt each other in a myriad of ways. It showed in his eyes, the way he took longer to relax in the evenings, the times he went to bed early. Jake wasn't looking forward to the conversation he knew was coming when the man followed him into the kitchen one evening, just before the news.

"So. Things are settling?" Elias asked, not meeting his eyes.

"Seem to be," Jake said with a shrug.

"There's not going to be any more shouting? No more fights and extremely loud make up sex?"

Jake stared at him, his hand freezing on the fridge door. Anger started to push up, but he pushed back hard and took a breath. "Been two months. Think if that was going to happen it would have by now."

Elias nodded, still not meeting his eyes.

"You got something to say, say it," Jake said, refusing to look at Tor as he came in from the living room.

Elias looked though, and back at Jake. Tor leaned on the wall, his arms crossed over his chest, waiting.

"Just…it ain't been real comfortable here for the last few months. Not a nice place to live. Want to know if things are going to get worse or better."

"Oh, I'm sorry," Jake said acidly, anger winning for the time being. "Was our not fighting getting on your nerves? Thought you'd be glad we weren't spilling blood." He slammed his hand down on the counter top, the sound sharp. "Fuck, we haven't even yelled at each other—haven't done anything but try to get through each day, what the hell do you expect from us? You want us to rehash it all for you? Give you the constant noise? You want us to put you through hell?"

"No—"

"Then what? Christ. Honestly, your comfort level isn't high on my list of things to worry about lately. You don't like the way we're trying to deal with this you can leave. Just—"

"Jake." Tor's voice was low and tight. "He's right, they live here, too—"

Jake turned on him, furious. "Goddamn it! I'm just trying to get through each day and you think I should give a fuck how everyone else is dealing with it? Jesus, our fucking marriage is destroyed and—"

He froze, the silence in the room ringing. Tor'd flinched, but that was all—Elias was just looking miserable and sorry he'd said anything.

Jake turned and left, quietly closing the screen door behind him. He didn't go far—there wasn't anywhere to go and he didn't feel like wandering all over the ranch, trying to run from what he couldn't. He leaned on the railing of the their small porch and looked at the barn, massive and dark in the night, and waited.

Marriage. They'd never said it, not really. Just Tor giving himself over, swearing to be there forever, and Jake saying that he loved him. But it had been a marriage, even if only recognized by himself and Tor. And now it was gone.

He could hear voices in the kitchen, but not the words. Tor and Elias, a word or two from Kirk. Tor for a longer time then nothing for a while. Elias again. When the door opened familiar steps fell behind him, and Tor leaned on the railing beside him, about a foot away.

"I told them what I did," Tor said.

"Ah, shit." Jake hadn't wanted that, not really. Part of him wanted to call Tor out for being the cheating bastard he was, to make everyone see what he'd done. Part of him wanted the world to spit on Tor and call him a waste of space. Pride, however, came before that—the idea of people knowing what a fool he'd been, how arrogant he'd been…it made him feel ill. And somewhere inside him was a little part that was pleased to know that he was the wronged man in all this, that sometimes other people fucked up his life and this time it wasn't his fault. "What did they say?"

"The truth. Elias called me a fucking idiot and Kirk said I wasn't worth the time to talk to. Both of them made it plain that if I ever hurt you again they'd take me out behind the barn and beat me senseless."

There wasn't really anything for Jake to say to that other than "good", so he said nothing.

"They thought we'd had a fight, at the dance," Tor said quietly. "That you'd gone out and gotten drunk and we'd had another fight about that. That you'd thrown me out in a fit. They reckoned we were just taking our sweet time getting back together, and that things were going to get…messier when we finally did. That we'd get back to fighting and fucking and that it would be even worse than before."

Jake nodded, not really caring what they'd thought. He looked out into the dark again and sighed. "I hate you."

He heard Tor swallow thickly. "I know. I'm—"

"Don't say it. I know."

They stood there for a long time, not talking, not looking at each other. Finally Tor stood up, turned to face the house. "What do you want me to do?"

Jake shook his head in resignation. "Are you still looking for work?"

"Yeah. Not much out there, really, and nothing that pays as well. Nothing with lodging that I can find."

Jake knew that wasn't true, couldn't be true. But he didn't call Tor on it. "Fine. Keep looking. Other than that…we just keep going, I guess. I'm not about to start fights—too fucking old for that shit, and I don't have the energy."

Tor nodded again, kicking at his own boots. "Okay. I– Hell. I can't say anything to you, can I?"

Jake looked at him. "You can. But I won't listen. And I don't want to hear it. But I can't stop you from saying it."

Tor looked like he was thinking about it, weighing the options. "Right. Maybe I'll just think it real loud then."

Jake smiled without humor. "You do that. I'm going to bed."

One evening, a week or so later, Jake was folding laundry in his room with the door open when Tor tapped on the doorframe, looking uneasy.

"What?" Jake said, picking up a T-shirt.

"Can you…um, can you take the phone?"

Jake paused, then folded the shirt. He hadn't heard the phone ring, which meant Tor had called out. The only people he called were his family.

"No."

"Please, Jake? It's Susie, she wants to say hi."

Fucking hell.

Jake looked at him and glared. "No. If she can't understand that we're not together, you'll have to explain it better—"

Tor was looking at the floor, the truth plain on his face.

"You fucking bastard. You haven't told them."

Tor winced. "I will, I swear, but please. Please talk to her, Jake."

Jake walked past him and into the kitchen. He refused to think about it, refused to acknowledge what it might mean. He picked up the phone and steeled himself, made himself sound as cheerful as he could. "Hey, Princess. What kind of trouble have you been causing lately?"

Mercifully, Susie only kept him on the phone for a few minutes. When he was done he turned to find Tor standing against the counter chewing his thumbnail, waiting to take the receiver. As Jake passed it back he covered the mouthpiece and said, "Never again. That was for her, not you. You tell them and you tell them soon. Yeah?"

Tor nodded and took the phone.

Jake was glad it had been Susie and not Tor's mother.

Thirty Six

Jake leaned on the corral fence, watching River. The horse would paw at the ground and take a few steps, then paw again. When he lay down and got back up a few moments later Jake told Tommy to call the vet and went to get River's tack.

He'd been walking River for almost forty-five minutes when Dr. Winters arrived, and River had started to sweat, his attempts to lay down growing more frequent. Dr. Winters agreed that it was most likely colic, and together they moved River to a clean stall so the vet could examine him.

Jake checked the feed and made sure the hay was all right, barking orders at whoever passed by. He wanted to know who'd done the morning feeding, how much River had eaten, how much hay had been given…anything he could find out. Jake hunted up the deworming records while Dr. Winters completed his exam, and soothed the horse as best he could while everyone tried to ease his discomfort.

He hated this. He tried very hard not to show it to anyone, but seeing River hurting, knowing that this was something that could kill him—it wound him up tighter than a watch spring. He wasn't sure if anyone knew it, other then maybe the Boss, who'd have little reason to remember it, but River was the first horse he'd ever ridden, the first week he'd been on the ranch.

Everyone knew River was his favorite mount, of course, same as Elias preferred to take Shelby and Tor liked Lug. He just favored the horse, was all. But he felt attached to him as well, saw River as the first creature he'd ever given a damn about aside from himself. There had been caring and friendships after, of course, but River had been the start of something new for Jake, the start of something good.

And now the horse was hurting.

By the time Dr. Winters had done what he could—a messy and awkward procedure that gave Jake sympathetic stomach cramps—a crowd was in the barn to hear the prognosis.

"No twist in his gut," the vet started to say, and the air was suddenly filled with relief. "And the obstruction has lessened. Not sure what caused it," he went on, looking at Jake, "The feed and hay were fine, you said?"

Jake nodded. He'd checked it all himself, and River hadn't been seen drinking more water than usual either, nor had he gotten too hot from being ridden hard or working, then let to drink water that was too cold.

The vet shrugged. "One of those things that we might never figure out, I suspect. In any event, he'll need to be watched for at least the next day. Walk him ten or fifteen minutes out of every hour, don't let him eat, though he can have something in the morning. If he takes a turn call me back." The vet gave River a gentle pat and left to talk to the Boss, leaving Jake and the others to get back to work. Or rather, leaving Jake to watch the horse and the others to get back to work; there wasn't much that would get Jake out of the stables for the next couple of days.

That night, Jake was nicely settled on a bale of hay when Tor appeared in the doorway carrying blankets and a thermos. He came right over, handed Jake the thermos, and said, "Thought you could use some coffee."

"Thanks," Jake replied, taking the thermos and unscrewing the cap. "Appreciate it."

Tor nodded and went to look at River. "How's he doing?"

"Better." Jake poured out a cup of steaming coffee, wrapping his hands around the plastic cup. "Been quiet, but seems comfortable, and he's been dozing."

"Good," Tor said quietly, almost to himself, it seemed. He walked back to Jake, pulling another bale around for a seat. Still, Jake was a little surprised when Tor sat down, wrapping one of the blankets around himself. He handed the other to Jake. "Thought you could do with some company as well." It was an offer, not a statement, Tor's voice hesitant.

Jake thought about it for a few seconds and nodded. "Yeah. Sure. That'd be good."

They sat in silence while Jake tried to come up with something to say, something mild that wouldn't be taken as an insult or seem too prying. He sipped his coffee, the silence stretching out and reaching the uncomfortable stage, both of them fidgeting and looking around the barn.

"How's—"

"Do you—"

They looked at each other and laughed, the nervousness dissipating once given voice.

"You first," Jake said with a slight smile.

Tor grinned. "Just wondered if you got your holiday plans all set. You know, for Thanksgiving and Christmas—you going to 'Lissa's?"

"Yeah," Jake said with a nod. "Well, for Christmas. Back for a couple of days, then I'm going again for New Year's—Cath will be there, she's going to someone else's for Christmas."

"What about Thanksgiving?" Tor asked, sounding curious.

"Staying here. Everyone else is heading out, someone has to take care of this place," Jake said with a smile. "How about you? Going to Becky's for it all?"

Tor nodded. "Yeah. Thanksgiving, Christmas, New Year's. See Susie…" he looked around the barn and added quietly, "See Momma."

Jake took a breath. "How is she?" he asked softly.

Tor sighed and leaned back, resting against the wall. "She's okay. Well, no. She has good days. And then there are the bad days. Sometimes she can do pretty much what she always did, but other times…some days she can't get out of bed. Becky says most of the time it's somewhere in the middle."

Jake nodded, not quite sure what to say. Maureen had impressed him as a strong woman, probably still was in spirit, if not body. Tor had mentioned her heart problems early in their relationship, but now it seemed that she really was winding down.

"Is it hard on Becky? Having her there?" he asked. He thought about what it would be like for Susie, having her grandmother there, slipping away right before her eyes. Some things a child shouldn't ever have to see.

Tor shrugged. "I'm sure it is, but we've talked about it, and she would rather have Momma there than in a home. Wants to take care of her, you know?"

Jake nodded. "I can understand that."

There was a brief pause then Tor said, "Actually, while we're on topic…" he trailed off until Jake turned to look at him, then said, "I changed my will. And the life insurance thing." He seemed faintly apologetic about it. "Made Momma the sole beneficiary of both, just in case something happens to me. The money—fuck, she'd need the money. Not that there's any chance of anything happening to me before she…before she dies." Tor looked down at his hands, his jaw clenched.

It made perfect sense to Jake. They'd not talked about their wills and such in a couple of years, and Jake hadn't even thought about it since they'd split up. When they'd decided to be together, really together, they'd had their wills made up to reflect that. Jake hadn't had anyone else to leave anything to, so Tor was his only named heir. When he'd been found by 'Lissa and Cath, he'd changed his life insurance to go to Jacob; it was a far larger sum than his savings, so he'd left Tor as the heir in his will. Something else he should change.

"That's fine," he said calmly. "And you didn't have to tell me, you know that."

"Yeah, I know. But I wanted to." Tor gave him a peculiar look, a slight smile playing at the corners of his mouth. "Ask you something?"

Jake raised an eyebrow and nodded. He lifted the coffee cup and took a drink, grateful that he'd swallowed when Tor asked, "You still got your ring in?" just as clear and calm as if he'd asked what the time was.

Jake blinked, then blinked again. "Uh, no," he lied. Jesus.

Tor looked at him out of the corner of his eye, an honest to fuck blush working its way up his neck. "I do," he said, leaning his head back and closing his eyes. "Don't get me wrong, not holding on, just—Jesus, when I think about taking it out, the actual procedure I mean, my balls fucking crawl so far up I get worried they'll never come back down."

Jake choked. "Your fucking fault. Had to get rings instead of those curved barbells. Fucking captive bead rings at that—need goddamn pliers to get it out—" he stopped when Tor turned to look at him, a broad grin on his face.

"You lied," Tor said gleefully. "You couldn't do it either."

Jake stuck his tongue out at him. "Actually got the pliers out once. Scared the crap out of me." It had, too, he'd nearly had himself talked into it until he realized he needed two sets of pliers and three hands if he didn't want to actually damage his cock. Since then he'd put the matter out of his mind as best he could.

Tor grinned at him for a moment then reached for the thermos and took the cup from Jake's hand. He poured the coffee and said, "Oh, forgot to tell you, Hound called earlier, talked to Elias. Said he and Del were planning a trip in the spring, might stop by."

And hadn't that just been a kick in the pants? Hound showing up a year after he'd left, tall, lanky lover in tow. Male lover, a mechanic. Just…weird. Tor hadn't been surprised, which had raised Jake's suspicions about what Hound and Tor had talked about on the phone so many times, but neither of them made a big deal out of it. Jake and Elias though, they'd hauled Hound up to the barn so fast Del looked worried, and proceeded to grill him six ways from Sunday until Hound had pretty much declared undying love for the man and started to describe things that made Elias run and Jake blush.

"You're just full of surprises tonight, aren't you?" Jake said. He wrapped the blanket around his shoulders and settled back. "He's doing okay? Del's still all he's supposed to be?"

Tor nodded. "Guess so. They've been together, what? More than two years now. Still fixing cars, still talking like they're the first two people on the planet to find each other." Tor set the coffee on the floor. "I think it's good. Boy needs someone. Did when he left, anyway. Just glad he found someone like Del."

"What do you mean?" Jake asked curiously, shifting again on the bale. Damn uncomfortable things for sitting on all night, but he was still bone weary.

"He was hurting when he left. Took someone like Del—fun, but solid, hard working, easygoing—to make him whole. Or maybe it was the name change. Swear, if I ever call him Kevin, he'll pass out from shock. Just can't do it. Hell, I can't even remember to answer when someone calls me by *my* real name, how am I supposed to remember *his*?"

"Mmm." Not much to say to that. Jake closed his eyes and pulled the blanket tighter. "Yeah, Del's a good man. Tell me when it's time to walk River, will ya?"

"Sure," Tor said, his voice coming from far away.

When Tor nudged him, Jake came awake quickly but not so fast that he could move before taking note of where he was. Barn, that was easy. Tor. Leaning against Tor, fucking curled up against him, with a strong arm around his shoulders, keeping him steady as he slept.

He sat up slowly and gathered himself together before glancing at his...what? Former lover? Ex? Friend? God, he was tired. Too tired to sort that out. "Sorry," he said. "For—"

"Don't worry about it," Tor said easily, meeting his eye. "You were out of it. I walked River, then sort of propped you up, is all."

Jake decided to take that at face value. "Thanks." He folded the blanket and went to get River out of his stall.

Thirty Seven

It was a mild day for early November, so warm that there was a nice pick up game of touch football going on in the yard. Jake leaned back in his chair, watching Tor, Kip and Kirk get the crap trounced out of them by Elias, Tommy and Bobby. He smiled. It had been a while since things had been easy and light around there.

Jake winced as Elias tripped on something—possibly Tor's foot—and landed heavily on Kip. He groaned out loud when Kirk fell on top of them, making for a very squished Kip. With a great deal of teasing and laughter, the others untangled the three, Tor protesting his innocence loudly to everyone. It didn't look like anyone believed him.

Once they got Kip off the ground and standing up, no one was really surprised to see him check his watch and make his excuses. As a matter of fact, Jake could see money changing hands as bets were won and lost. Bobby spent a certain amount of time explaining that the occasional afternoon away from his wife and son could be a good thing, but Kip just smiled and headed home, saying Beth was expecting him.

"Come on, Jake, you're in. We need another man," Kirk called.

"You've got to be kidding." Jake grinned at him. "Y'all are losing. Why would I join in now?"

Tor sputtered at him, his eyes teasing. "You're fresh, sitting on your butt all day. Got energy we need to win this thing, unless you're worried that the young 'uns will put you to shame and wear out your tired, old—"

Jake was on his feet before the insult could be finished. "Show you old," he said, joining them on the lawn.

Forty minutes later Jake was willing to concede— privately, of course—that he wasn't as young as he used to be. He'd managed to help them even the score a little, but Elias and Tommy seemed to have near inexhaustible stores of energy, wearing even Kirk out.

"Touch football, my ass," Tor groaned from the bottom of a pile. "Christ, this is more like rugby."

"Getting old, Tor?" Jake asked easily, offering him a hand up. "Feeling all of your thirty-seven years?"

Tor scowled and tried to smack him on the ass, Jake stepping away with a chuckle. "Least I'm not forty," he declared.

Jake grinned. "I'm not either. You never could remember my birthday."

Tor rolled his eyes, not really able to deny that particular jibe. "Still," he said as he eyed the others, "can last longer than you. Say, another half hour?"

Jake was about to accept the challenge when Elias and Bobby both rolled their eyes and walked away, saying they were done, finished and leaving before egos got to the point where certain cowboys would need CPR.

"They mean us?" Tor asked innocently.

"I think they're saying we're a little competitive," Jake said, sitting on the grass. "I'm not, though. You are."

"Bet you I'm not as competitive as you," Tor said with a grin, stretching out next to him.

"Idiot."

"Asshole."

"Twerp."

"Dork."

At which point Tommy and Kirk fled.

Jake sat in the sun and laughed, feeling better than he had in ages. Sun, football, jokes…it was nice. Really nice. He was just lying back on the grass to look at the clouds when it suddenly occurred to him that he was horny.

Really horny.

He'd just spent a portion of the day rolling in the dirt with men—he ignored the part of his brain that was screaming "with Tor" at him—and he'd had a few laughs, had fun…and now all he wanted was to get off. Now.

"I'm going to take a shower," he said abruptly, rolling over and getting up.

"Taggart? You okay?" Fuck, but Tor sounded all concerned now, and Jake *really* didn't want him thinking he'd done anything wrong. Not when they'd finally gotten to the point where they could be pleasant to one another.

"Nothing wrong," he said, standing still, but not facing him. "Just going to take a shower."

"Oh. Okay." Tor sounded even more hurt now, and Jake sighed.

He sat back down and looked at the bunkhouse. "Really. Nothing wrong. Just…hell. What were we just doing?"

"Uh, playing ball?"

"Yeah. Playing ball. Having fun. And that's all well and good, but now I've got something I have to go take care of." Jake knew he was blushing and hated every single bit of blood in his body. What wasn't going to his face was headed south rapidly and he really wanted not to be having this conversation. Tor looked at him, a picture of confusion mixed with a bit of hurt still.

"Tor, so help me God, if I have to actually say this out loud I'll have to kill you, got that?"

Tor blinked and gave him a slow once over, then bit his lip. "Oh. Oh, man, sorry. Got it. Off you go, then." And there was the matching blush.

"Let us never speak of this."

"Agreed."

Jake didn't even make it to the shower, stripping down and falling onto his bed, hips and hands already working. He told himself that it was so intense because it was the first time since the dance that he'd brought himself off with anything more than just a mechanical need. But he couldn't lie to himself about the images he came to, the name he called.

———————

"There's nothing on," Kirk said, tossing the remote onto the coffee table. "Why is there nothing on?"

Tor snorted. "Because it's the middle of December, you twit. Nothing good on until the middle of January now. Don't tell me you're sick of the Christmas specials already?"

Kirk just nodded morosely. "How the hell am I supposed to relax after a hard day when there isn't anything good on TV?"

"Read a book," Jake said.

"Bug Taggart," Tor offered, earning himself a stiff finger.

Elias was quiet for a moment, looking thoughtful. "Or. Or, or, or, or. Jake, might be time to introduce the pup to the way we used to relax around here. Back in the day."

Jake caught Tor's eyes and saw comprehension flickering. Elias looked hopeful. Kirk looked terrified, his glance going from Tor to Jake and back again.

"Oh, relax. Nothing kinky—Elias likes it." Jake didn't intend to sound reassuring. He looked at the other two and raised an eyebrow. "You think he's ready?"

Elias shrugged. "Never know 'til you try. Hound wasn't much older than him when he started. Kip…well, Kip never really took to it. Not like the rest of us."

Tor grinned. "Kip just didn't get the novelty of it. Needed to relax." He threw Jake a look and said, "Go get the gear, Taggart. The big ones, I think."

Jake stood up and rubbed at his wrists for no reason other than to see Kirk's eyes get wide. "Three or four?"

"Four. It's early." Tor stood up and started pushing the furniture out of the way.

Jake nodded and went to his room, straight to the closet. Choosing a selection was made easier by the 'big ones' request, so he grabbed four boxes and raced back out to the living room, already predicting the fights.

"Oh, yes! Gimme the Harry Potter one!" Tor thought Snape was cool.

"No fucking way. Mine. You can have the space station—"

"I always get the space station!"

Jake sighed and handed the box to Elias. "Fine. Elias gets the space station, Kirk gets the fleet of shuttles, and you can have the Mars colony. I get Snape."

"Cool."

Jake, Tor and Elias dumped the boxes out on the floor, carefully keeping the pieces from getting mixed up. Kirk, the little shit, didn't even blink, just started building. Tor gave him a thoughtful look, but didn't say anything.

Five minutes later there still hadn't been any comment from Kirk, who was busily looking through his pile of blocks for something.

"Who told you?" Elias asked, sounding very put out.

Kirk looked up, surprise clear on his face. "No one," he said. Then he looked at Jake and grinned, pointing to Snape's Potions Lab. "I have part of the Diagon Alley set. Oh, and I've got a bunch of stuff from when I was a kid— mostly castles and cowboys. Fucking love Lego."

Jake laughed, watching Tor's eyes narrow. Before Tor could try to get his hands on Kirk's Lego, Jake pointed to Tor and said, "Watch him—he likes to mix up the pieces."

Kirk frowned at Tor. "That just ain't right, Tor. Lose stuff that way."

Tor looked thoroughly exasperated. "I give up."

It was suppertime on New Year's Eve when Jake got back to the ranch, out of sorts and tired from driving. Cath had made it to 'Lissa's for Christmas after all, which was good. He'd come back on the twenty-seventh for a couple of days, and headed out again on the thirtieth to find Cath and Jacob in the grips of a very disgusting bout of the flu. 'Lissa had been really sweet about it, pointing out that if he stuck around he'd probably catch it too, so here he was. Home.

Alone for New Year's Eve, which was probably not a bad thing. Kirk and Elias had planned to head into town for the night, and Jake didn't see Kirk's car around so he assumed their plans were going according to schedule. He planned to grab something to eat, go up and feed the horses, then settle in to watch some TV. Nice and quiet night, no one to bug him.

And it wasn't as if the past year had been a good one; no need to have anyone around to watch him wallow in a little self-pity, either. No, the more he thought about it, the more he figured this was going to be just right. Suiting, in fact.

What he wasn't prepared for in the slightest was Tor in the kitchen dumping half a bottle of red wine into a saucepan on the stove, looking at him like he was an unwelcome intruder. Then Tor's eyes cleared, fast enough that Jake wondered if he'd imagined it, and he said, "Shit, I just fucked up the spaghetti for you, didn't I?"

Jake shook his head, hauling his bag in the door. "Not really. Let it simmer for a bit and the alcohol will evaporate out. What are you doing here?"

Tor stirred the pot and made a face. "Susie and Momma both started puking. I ran. Becky said I was useless as a nursemaid and getting underfoot." Tor glanced at him. "You?"

"Same, 'cept it was Jacob and Cath, and 'Lissa said she didn't want me getting sick."

"She's just nicer than my sister, is all. You were useless like me, and getting in the way." The jibe was light, Tor teasing him with his tone.

"Fuck off," Jake returned in kind. "Feed the horses yet?"

"Nope. You've got time before supper if you go now."

Jake went up to the barn, trying to rework his plans for the evening. Spending the night alone in the house with Tor was about as far away from alone and wallowing that he could get, and he wasn't really pleased about it. The past year was looming over him, hurting and angry, ready to crash over him, and there was Tor, making supper and being...nice.

He briefly considered going to his room and pretending that the flu was trying to claim him as its next victim, but he shelved the idea as insulting and low. He didn't want to hide, didn't want to fight. He and Tor had somehow, in the last couple of months, managed to find a place where they were comfortable, if not friendly, and he suspected that a blatant retreat would do more harm than good.

Besides, it was just eating supper, like they always did, and probably watching TV. Like they always did. No need to panic, and if things looked like they could go sour he could go to bed early.

Tor had thought, like Jake, that he'd have the place to himself, so supper was simple. They ate at the table, exchanging bits of family gossip and talking about gifts they'd received; Lego in Jake's case, a rather impressive coffee table book on history of the Southwest in Tor's. "I rented a couple of movies," Tor said when they were done. "Just action stuff—was planning on flaking out for the night with popcorn and mind numbing explosions."

"Sounds fine." Jake gathered up the dishes and took them to the sink. "I'll wash up and grab a shower, you go ahead. Don't bother waiting, if you don't want to."

He did the dishes quickly, leaving them on the rack to dry, then went to his room and stripped. Could be an all right night, he figured. Supper went well enough. When he came out again, showered and dressed in sweatpants and a T-shirt, he could smell popcorn and hear what sounded like Tommy Lee Jones.

They sat down and passed a few hours with Men in Black and Men in Black II, Jake on the easy chair and Tor on the couch. When Tor made more popcorn he came back with the largest bowl they had, filled to the top. "Don't bite, you know. Can sit over here, if you want."

Jake watched Tor put the bowl in the middle of the couch and then go put the next tape in. There wasn't really a reason to move, except Tor had offered. And there wasn't a reason to stay. So he got up and moved to the couch, the popcorn between them, and settled back to watch something forgettable that had a budget of a kazillion dollars for special effects.

Jake found his mind wandering, his concentration floating away from the movie so often that he completely lost track of the plot. He kept his eyes on the TV though, not willing to check and see what Tor was doing. Probably watching the movie. Why wouldn't he be? Still, Jake found himself having to fight to not look over at Tor.

It was stupid, he knew. What did it matter if he looked at the man? Why should it bother him that he wanted to? Why was he trying to find Tor's scent under the smell of butter and popcorn?

Ah, hell.

He shifted on the couch, slouching further down, fidgeting when it occurred to him that slouching made his legs splay out. He could feel himself flush, and was about ready to flee to his room for the night when the movie ended and Tor leaned over for the remote.

"Almost midnight," Tor said quietly. He didn't look at Jake, just turned on the TV and found the celebrations in Little Rock. They watched the presenters talking to people in the crowds, listen to drunken partiers wishing everyone a good year, looked at the excitement as people waited for the countdown.

Fucking year was almost done. Thank God. And may he never have another like it.

Tor sat back on the couch, legs out in front of him, arms crossed against his chest. Jake had a sudden flash of the previous New Year's Eve, in the same living room, the same show on the TV. Tor on his knees between Jake's spread thighs, sucking his cock and happy to be doing it. Jake bit off a moan. He had to get out of there. Except he couldn't really just stand up and go, could he? Even if he was prepared to deal with Tor seeing him, knowing…he wasn't sure he could walk. He felt weak and dizzy, and goddamn he just wanted.

They sat in silence through the countdown, not saying anything, not looking at each other when it was done and the fireworks started. Tor reached for the remote after a few minutes, muting the sound and flicking through the channels, looking for another movie, Jake assumed.

Time to go. Before it was too late.

Jake stood up and picked up the empty popcorn bowl, his mouth dry. "I'm going to bed," he said softly.

"Jake." Only his name, but it was husky and rich and deep, filled with pain and longing and Jake had to look at him.

Tor stood up to face him, eyes dark, arms straight by his sides, like he was bracing himself. And he was hard, so hard he had to ache, and Jake felt everything in him, everything he was, go still at the sight. God, Tor was beautiful, and he couldn't look away.

"Want you," Tor said.

Jake didn't even answer, just moved forward, or maybe Tor did, it didn't matter. What mattered was the kissing, the moans and bites, the hands that seemed to be everywhere but not where they were most needed. They didn't say anything about what they were doing or where they were going, just started down the hall, losing clothes on the way.

Jake knew this was out of control, that he should have taken off about two hours ago, but it was easy to push the thought away. Tor's mouth was on his, the taste of Tor, the heat from his skin; Jake found himself pinned to the wall outside his room, gasping as Tor's fingers dug into his hair and his hips. "Oh God, yeah. Harder—"

Tor ground against him, breathing ragged, mouth leaving a trail of fire along his shoulder, kisses and bites mingling. Jake thrust against Tor, hands going to Tor's ass and finding skin—only his own sweatpants between them, and when the hell did Tor lose his pants?

He dismissed the thought as unimportant, forcing a hand between them to take Tor's cock in hand, fingers finding the hot flesh and wrapping around it easily.

"Oh fuck. God, Jake—" Tor thrust once and backed away. "Bed." Tor reached for Jake, kissing him again even as he guided them through the door and the few steps into the room. They fell on the bed in a tangle, both of them pushing at Jake's sweatpants, and then it was blissful, skin on skin and the air filled with moans as they thrust together, hands pulling and stroking.

Tor was on top of him, panting, moving. Jake could feel muscles working under his hands, the smooth lines of Tor's back flexing as he dipped his head to tease at Jake's chest. It was too much, but not nearly what he wanted, and when he pushed Tor over the man went easily.

It had been months since he'd used lube of any kind, wasn't even sure if there was any, but they found a tube in the nightstand. Then Jake was slick, and Tor was pushing back against his fingers, begging for more, needing more, and Jake wasn't about to deny either of them. Not then, not at that point.

It was fast and furious when he finally pushed his way in, fucking hard and deep, any control they had left in the hallway with their clothes or maybe in the living room with the popcorn bowl. Tor arched against him, crying out, wanting more and harder, and oh fuck, Jake, yes, like that, and Jake gave it to him. Took Tor. Fucked Tor. Made them both cry out at the end, coming in hot gushes moments apart that seemed perfect.

And it was perfect, right up until Jake collapsed across him and Tor kissed him again, then whispered, "Yours."

Ice water couldn't have shaken Jake more. He rolled over on this back, away from Tor and shook his head. "No. Not mine."

Tor blinked at him. "What?"

"Not mine," Jake said slowly, thoughts and images washing over him. Travis on his knees. Tor fucking him,

Jake drinking himself sick. Months of pain and anger. Betrayal and the months that lead up to it. "You're not mine. I'm not yours—"

"What the fuck? What the hell was that, then?" Tor sounded disbelieving and hurt, voice starting to rasp.

"You thought a quick fuck was going to fix us?" Jake demanded, knowing it was unfair and not able to stop the words. Jesus, they hadn't even used a condom, and how fucking stupid was that?

"I thought—fuck, Jake. I thought we were doing good. Working on getting along. I've been trying so fucking hard to be—to be someone you would want. I thought we were doing better." Tor's eyes were starting to shine and he sat up on the bed, drawing his knees to his chest. "I thought we were working it out."

Jake sat up as well looking at the wall. "Tor. God. I know that, I do. And we are doing better. We're getting along, and even having some fun, but..." He trailed off as the truth slammed into him, almost taking his breath away. "But I don't trust you. And I don't think I'll be able to again."

Tor didn't say anything for a long moment. "Ever?" he asked quietly.

Jake shook his head. "I don't know. All I know is that we were thoroughly screwed up before the summer and I didn't see it. I don't think it's fixed yet, and I don't know if it can be. All I know is that I hurt all the time, and I still...God. I still get so angry sometimes. I don't think we're going to get back together, Tor."

Tor looked at him, eyes searching for something he obviously didn't find. "I can't stay, then. I can't stay here with you, not without some sort of hope."

Jake nodded and said nothing. He knew it was coming. Tor got off the bed and left him sitting there in the dark.

———•◆•◆—

On January the second, early in the morning, Tor
loaded the last of his things into the truck and had a quiet
word with the Boss while he waited for Kirk to drive him to
town. Jake and Elias stood on the porch of the bunkhouse,
not speaking, just watching.

Finally Kirk got in the truck, and Tor shook hands with
the Boss. He turned to look at Jake and Elias, and for a few
moments Jake thought he would just get in the truck and
go. Instead he walked over and stood at the bottom of the
stairs. Elias went down and shook his hand, wishing him
well.

Jake waited, leaning on the railing.

Three steps up and Tor stood next to him, one hand
reaching out to cup his jaw. "Take care of yourself, Jake."

Jake couldn't help moving into the touch, though he
drew back quickly. "You too."

Tor nodded once and turned on his heel, clattering
down the wooden steps and striding to the truck not looking
back. Jake watched as Kirk pulled away, turning in the
drive before driving away.

"Only going to say this once," Elias said behind him.
"You're both fucking fools, the pair of you." Elias went into
the house, letting the door slam behind him.

Jake watched the truck turn at end of the lane and
wondered about the truth in that.

Thirty Eight

———◆◆◆———

"So, where's Tor?"

Jake glanced at his watch as he leaned on the counter, waiting to see who got to answer. Not bad, Hound had been in the house less than five minutes, and it was only just a mite over twenty minutes since he and Del had pulled in the yard. Jake had taken one look at the car and known what would happen—he'd just sort of hoped it would take more time.

No one seemed real eager to jump in and answer, and Hound was starting to look around the room, looking at Elias with an eyebrow raised before looking to Jake. Del was trying to look uninterested but he was missing the mark, his face looking more resigned than anything. Jake wondered idly what the hell was up with that before he cleared his throat.

"Not really sure. Gone." He knew very well that the answer was inadequate and invited more questions, but for some reason he'd not really thought that he'd have to be explaining everything to Hound. He hadn't honestly expected the hinted at spring trip, and he'd more or less assumed that Del would talk Hound out of stopping by. Jake didn't really think Del liked him, though it was beyond him why.

"Gone where?" Hound asked, reaching across the table for the bowl of grapes Elias had produced. "Is he gonna be back soon? 'Cause he was so fucking sure I'd never get the Vega road worthy—I have to rub his nose in it."

Jake sighed as Elias and Kirk melted into the background. If they'd turned and left the room it might actually have been better, but no. They leaned back and just let him dig himself in.

"Tor doesn't live here anymore," he said as evenly as he could manage. Damn, five months after Tor had left, and it still made him sound like he was talking through sand.

Hound froze, his hand hovering over the grapes. "What?"

"He moved out at the beginning of the year." Jake crossed his arms over his chest and met Hound's eyes.

"What? Why?" Hound turned a confused look on Elias. "Is he serious? Tor's gone?"

Elias nodded, but didn't say anything, just shifted his weight from foot to foot.

Del leaned back in his chair, resting his hand on the back of Hound's.

Hound bit his lip and looked at Jake. "Why?" he asked, his voice low like he wanted desperately to know what was going on, but at the same time knew that Jake wouldn't want to talk about it. The need to know was winning, but Jake had a feeling Hound was working hard to narrow the flood of questions down to a bare minimum.

"It didn't work out," Jake said evenly. That was about all he ever said about it. Anyone else would have left it alone. Everyone else *did* leave it alone, but not Hound.

"Fuck that. What happened?" There was an edge to Hound's voice that Jake had never heard before, and it took him a moment to realize that the man was furious. Beyond angry, he was almost vibrating, gone from happy and relaxed to barely keeping himself still in less than a minute.

Del saw it, too, had maybe even seen it before, and Jake just stood there while Del handled it, an arm around Hound's shoulders, talking quietly and constantly into his ear. Jake couldn't hear the words but he could see how hard Del had his fist clenched, could see how Hound was listening, his own hands flexing and relaxing.

Hound shook his head at something Del said, and looked down. Jake figured it was time to go, and moved away from the counter, tossing a look at Elias. "Gonna go up to do stalls. Or something. I'll be with the horses." Setting his hat back on his head he left. No one said anything.

It took Hound almost half an hour to show up. Jake was forking hay into River's stall when he heard boots behind him, and he nodded to Hound instead of saying anything. If Hound wanted to talk about it he could start—Jake didn't really feel the need to invite the conversation, but he'd long given up hope of avoiding it. Right about the time the car had stopped, actually.

Hound crossed to River's tack box and picked of the currycombs. He held them, not making a move to go to the horse and Jake figured he was just keeping his hands busy. All the better not to do something stupid.

295

"Del's showing Kirk the car," Hound said softly. "He's a little freaked."

"Del or Kirk?" Jake asked, knowing who Hound meant but not wanting to talk about anything other than surface matters.

Hound ignored his intent if he knew it, and said, "Del. He's not real happy with me. Doesn't like the way I reacted, doesn't want me talking to you about it. He figures you know what you're doing."

Jake grinned. "Del's a smart man, even if he's not a cowboy."

Hound rolled his eyes. "Yeah, well. He also knows that I tend to be pushy and I get a little wound up. He deals. I deal. And here I am."

Jake nodded. Here he was, all right. And soon enough he'd be wound up again. Jake was a little bemused to find that part of him had really missed Hound, wound up or not. He just wished that this once the kid would find something else to be wound up about.

"So, what happened?" Hound finally asked.

Jake looked at him and leaned on the fork. "Elias didn't tell you?" he asked eventually.

"Said Tor was fucking around last summer and you found out. That it was few months before he finally moved out." Hound sounded tired.

Jake nodded. "That's what happened."

"Bullshit."

Jake blinked. "Look, you may not want to believe it—"

Hound shook his head. "Not what I meant. If y'all say that, I'll buy it. Tor cheated. Got it. But what happened?"

Jake stared at him for a moment, then rested the fork against the stall wall. "What do you mean? I kicked him out, he went. Worked out for a few months, then he had to leave."

Hound frowned and tossed the brushes back into the box. "You're not getting it. What happened before he cheated? How come it fell apart?"

Jake sighed and pulled a bale of hay around for him to sit on. "We were fighting a lot. Just got lost, I guess. I found out about Travis, and we split up."

Another frown, and Hound leaned against the wall, just looking at him. "Okay. So you two were fighting and not making up, just letting things slide, right? Then Tor got his head turned. How come he stayed so long after?"

"I really don't want to talk about this, Hound."

"I don't care." And Hound really looked like he didn't, standing there with squared off shoulders, his eyes baffled and hurt—like Jake had done something to him.

"Who are you, and where's the cowboy I know?" Jake said with a slight smile.

"Talk to me, Jake."

Fuck, when did Hound get so stubborn? Jake considered just getting up and leaving, but he got an image of Hound following him all day and that just seemed a little too close to possible.

"What do you want to know?" he finally asked, resigned to talking for at least a little while.

"Why did he stay? If you two were so far apart, how come he stuck around?" Hound shoved his hands into his jeans pockets and stood there, just looking at Jake.

So Jake talked. He told Hound how things were after Tor had switched rooms, told him that he and Tor had gotten to the point where they could talk, where they could stand to be in the same room and not want to kill each other. Told him Tor had been sorry, that he'd tried to fix it, but that in the end it just wasn't going to happen, so Tor had moved out, left the ranch.

Through all of it Hound watched him, nodding and biting his lip. When Jake finished and moved to stand up, Hound held out his hand, palm out. "Hold on. So he stayed 'cause he loves you and thought you'd get back together?"

Jake rolled his eyes and sat down again. "I guess."

"So, he made an effort to attempt to make it up to you? Even though you told him it was over a bunch of times?"

"Yeah." He had, too. Jake had never made it anything other than plain that he thought it was over. Well, except for New Year's Eve, which in hindsight was the stupidest thing he could have done. But Tor had never said anything other than that he was sorry, and had done his best to get Jake to trust him again.

"Okay, let me get this straight." Hound's eyes were dark and his voice was tight again. Jake felt a sudden urge to go find Del. "Tor fucked up and spent five months living in the same house as you, saying he was sorry and doing everything you wanted him to? What did you do? And don't give me any crap about your part being not killing him—I want to know what you did to fix it."

"Me?" Jake stood up. "Don't have anything to fix, kid. He's the one who—"

"Yeah, yeah. Stuck his dick where it didn't have any business being. Got that part." Hound made a gesture with his hand, waiving it off. "Also got the part where you two were heading for trouble anyway. What did you do to fix that part?"

"Excuse me?"

Hound snorted. "Fuck. You figure that just 'cause he's the one who cheated you get off scott free? Goddamn it, Jake. What did you do to fix the actual trouble? What did you do to make yourself someone *he'd* want? Or do you really want to spend the rest of your life without him? Is that it?" Hound walked toward him, eyes flashing now, anger radiating off him. "Your pride worth that much? Jesus."

Jake opened his mouth to interrupt, to say something in his own defense, but Hound had his back up and was starting to pace.

"You two—fucking hell, Jake. You two let yourselves get to the point where Tor would even think about being with someone else, let alone do it, and you think you're an innocent here? The man stays here, where you are, where there's hurt and anger and you hating him, and you don't even bother trying to figure out what you can do? You selfish prick."

Jake knew his jaw was hanging open. Hound rounded on him, his hands flying as he spoke. "Big macho cowboys, ain't you? You think me and Del never fight? Jesus, you should see him when we're working on our cars and I disagree. You should see him when I get going about Daisy. But we at least talk about it. Not enough to just cool off and move on; gotta fucking talk, Jake. Did you even tell him you love him? Even once?"

"Yeah." Jake wasn't sure who was more surprised at the admission, him or Hound.

"Good," Hound said with a nod. Then he added, curiously, "What did he say?"

"Said he'd be mine forever."

There didn't seem to be much to say to that.

Hound sighed and leaned on the wall again, the fight draining out of him. "Look, Jake. You two worked well together. You belong together, and it ain't right that you're not. Think about it, yeah? Try to find him, try to—hell, try to fix it. 'Cause your pride isn't going to keep you warm at night."

Then Hound turned and left the stable, leaving Jake to think and cuss.

———◆———

Jake was not happy. Granted, he hadn't been happy in more than a year, but this time he was really not happy. Elias had finally taken Hound out to ride, saying Lug and Shelby needed to run, and Jake had retreated to the house to think.

Or sulk, as he heard Kirk put it before realizing Jake could hear him.

299

He wasn't sulking, he told himself. He was angry and trying to put it away again, bury everything under cotton where the sharp edges wouldn't poke at him. By the time he'd cleaned his room and made up the double bed in the spare room for Del and Hound, done the dishes and got everything ready to start supper, he knew it wasn't working.

Goddamn the man. Either of them.

He went out to the porch to sit a bit, slamming the door behind him. He'd almost settle his ass in the chair out there when he realized he wasn't alone. Del was sitting on the edge of the porch, leaning on a post. Damn. "Del."

"Jake."

There was a long silence as the two of them looked at each other. Oh, this wasn't awkward. Not at all.

Part of the problem, Jake figured, was that he had no idea why Del didn't like him, or if it was even dislike or something else. When Hound had first brought him to the ranch Jake had thought the man was pretty nice; friendly and easy going, obviously very much attached to Hound and happy to be so. Del had gotten along easily with everyone, especially Tor and Elias, but had seemed to be a little withdrawn with Jake.

Del had been even more withdrawn when they'd arrived that afternoon, and this was the first Jake had seen of him since he'd told them that Tor wasn't going to be coming home. Maybe he'd liked Tor enough that he was willing to dismiss Jake as the reason the man wasn't there.

With a mental shrug Jake asked, "Hound told you what we talked about? Up in the barn?"

Del nodded and looked like he was about to say something, but he stayed silent. Jake considered his options, which mainly consisted of going back into the house, making small talk with the reluctant guest, or fleeing to the barn again.

Jake leaned back as far as he could, tipping the chair onto its back legs and balancing there. "Can I ask you something?"

Del nodded, his eyes wary. "Sure, I guess."

"How come he cares? I mean, what's it to him if me and Tor split up?"

Del suddenly looked very uncomfortable, shifting on the rail and looking down at the ground. He mumbled something Jake couldn't hear, then sighed. "Kevin—he just doesn't like to see people unhappy, you know? And you and Tor were…he just always talked about how right you were for each other. I think it's shaken him up to see you apart."

Jake thought about that for a moment. Hound was always such a happy guy, always concerned for everyone, so that much rang true. But there was something Del wasn't telling him; Jake was sure of it, could see it in the way Del wouldn't meet his eyes, the way he couldn't sit still.

"He talked about us?"

Del nodded and swung his leg around so he could sit facing Jake. "You know why he left here?"

Jake shook his head. "Not really. At the time he said he was going to help his brother in Maine, but he wound up in Utah, so I'm thinking that wasn't quite true."

"He…hell. He was twenty-five and he'd just figured out he liked men. He wanted something special, something real. He wanted a relationship, and he knew he couldn't find it here." Del licked his lips and looked down again, shooting Jake a glance that pretty much screamed he wasn't going to give any more details than that. "So he headed out. Met me. And we found something together, and it's good. But you and Tor meant something, not only to yourselves, but to Kevin, too."

"If you're sayin' I should find Tor and get back together so Hound—"

Del snorted. "Don't be an idiot. I'd do anything to make Kevin happy, but even I wouldn't tell someone to run after their ex just so he'd relax."

Jake blinked, he couldn't help it. That was the most blunt thing he'd ever heard Del say, the first thing he'd ever done to show who he was. "So what are you saying?"

"Just telling you. You asked what Kevin thinks, I'm telling. What you do with it is up to you."

They sat in silence for a few minutes. Jake wasn't terribly comfortable talking about him and Tor—hell, Jake wasn't comfortable talking. And Hound had pretty much said that was the trouble.

Cautiously, he began to explore that, ready to run at the first sign the conversation would go places he didn't want to. "What happens when you fight?"

Del looked at him for a long moment. "Kevin told you to talk more, right? God, you have no idea what it's like. I mean, I talk a lot. Kevin talks a lot. You'd think it would be enough, but no. We have to actually discuss shit when we're done yelling..." He looked out into the yard for a moment and then back at Jake. "But he's right. I mean, we don't sit down and go over everything, but sometimes it's better to say stuff."

Jake raised an eyebrow, hoping to fuck he didn't actually have to ask Del to explain. Thankfully, Del appeared to be an intuitive man.

"Once, we had this huge blow up when we were trying to get some shit done around the house. Turned out the problem was with Kevin's accent—I thought he said something else. Once that got figured out, things were fine. Little shit like that, you know? But there's been times we actually had to sit down with a pot of coffee and go back and forth until something got settled. Like Daisy."

"Who's Daisy?"

"My best friend. Since I was a few months old. She's sort of attached, you know? And Kevin likes her, and she likes Kevin. I thought that was all good, but things were hard for them both when Kevin moved in. Daisy was still my best friend, still coming around, still doing stuff for me like she always did. And Kevin didn't mind each little thing, just the accumulation of everything. Daisy…well, she didn't take so well to me having someone permanent. So they wound up at each other's throats and it wasn't until I finally got Kevin to talk to me that I figured it out. And then I could talk to Daisy. And now things are fine. Usually."

Jake rolled his eyes. "I don't think me and Tor have those kinds of issues."

"So what are your issues?" Del asked. Then he flushed and looked away, jumping off the railing. "Look, I don't mean you should tell me what the problems were before you guys split up, but maybe you should think on that? Figure out what the trouble really was? Then you can decide if you want to find him."

Del moved to go in the house and Jake, without thinking about it, lifted his leg to block his way. "And then what?" he asked softly. "What do I say, just tell him we need to talk? 'Cause we don't talk, me and Tor. We tell each other the big stuff, and we cover our day, but we weren't real big on the emotional conversations. Just not who we are."

Del looked down at him, his eyes serious. "And who are you now? A forty year old cowboy, sitting on a porch trying to figure his life out. Maybe you should try the talking thing. Just once."

Goddamn Hound and his man, anyway. Jake dropped his boot to the porch with a thump, letting Del go.

"Jake? Do me a favor?" Del asked, his hand on the door handle.

"Yeah?"

"Kevin's gonna be twenty-eight next month. Think you can stop calling hi 'kid'? Drives him nuts."

Jake threw back his head and laughed. "Yeah. I can do that."

———•◆•———

Missy and Chris were the final straw.

Three days after Hound and Del left, Jake went up to the barn to find Chris mucking out the stalls. His mouth was pressed into a thin line, and every muscle in his back was tight and rigid.

"Hey, Chris," Jake said mildly, standing back to watch. For all that Chris said he wasn't made to work on a ranch, he knew what he was doing. Quickly and efficiently he cleaned out the stall and got new bedding ready for Shelby before moving on to the next one. His only greeting to Jake was a nod and then he turned himself back to his work.

His unnecessary work. Chris was the Boss' son-in-law, and his involvement with the ranch usually stopped at the bookkeeping. The man had a day job, and plans to move off the land; Jake didn't think he'd ever seen Chris doing stall work before.

"Everything okay?" Jake asked, still watching.

"Nope. But it will be." Chris stood up and wiped sweat off his forehead. "Just having a difference of opinion with Missy. Damn, but that woman is stubborn."

Jake had to smile. "Always has been. Known her since she was a kid, and I don't think I've seen anyone change her mind more than a handful of times."

Chris rolled his eyes and started shoveling horseshit. "Yeah, well. This time she's going to listen to me."

Jake snickered without meaning to. "When you get ready to tell her that give the rest of us a warning, yeah? Don't want to be anywhere in range."

Chris threw him a look and frowned. "Jesus, do I look like an idiot? What do you think I'm doing out here?" Chris scraped the shovel on the stall floor and added, "This is just the cool down phase. The actual talking part comes later, when we're calm enough that no one will actually shed blood."

And there it was. Again.

Jake bit the inside of his cheek and finally gave in. "So, you two always work shit out when you fight? You don't just…let it go and move on?"

Chris didn't even look up, thank Christ. "Well, yeah, I guess. Stuff builds up if you don't get it cleaned up right the first time. Not unlike this mess, so if you don't want to wind up with crap on your boots, I suggest you move."

Jake moved. And then he got River's tack out and saddled up. He always thought better if he was on horseback.

The trouble was, he figured, that he'd not seen a decent relationship before at close range. He'd had lovers before Tor, and a few guys he could best call mistakes, but no one he'd really cared about. His parents had gone for the long silences and hatred approach to fighting. And he'd honestly thought that as long as they weren't actively fighting things were okay.

God, he was such an idiot.

Tor hadn't been much better; his father hadn't been around, so chances were any fights he'd witnessed between his parents were dim memories, and Kin had died. Jake had no idea what Tor's relationships after Kin had been like, but he was pretty sure there hadn't been anyone serious. Toss in the fact that neither of them were given to long talks about anything emotional, and it wasn't a huge surprise that they'd gotten themselves all messed up.

The rest of it, though, was harder.

Jake rode River to the only place he wanted to be while he sorted this out. The only place he really could be for this. He'd long given up doing any serious thinking about Tor anywhere but in bed at night, when the darkness was like a blanket, or out in the meadow where no one would hear him.

It was different this time. He didn't even dismount, just let River walk and graze. Jake looked around, his eyes mostly unseeing; all he could smell was sweet grass and River, sunshine and his own sweat. He set his hat back on his forehead and forced himself to think.

Three hours later he scrubbed at his face and tried to put himself back together. He had no idea if he'd made the right choice or not, but he'd at least thought about everything again, gone over it and over it, and narrowed down a few things.

Decision made, he rode back to the ranch.

Thirty Nine

———◆◆◆———

Jake had no idea where Tor was, but he knew how to find out. Tor still needed money, still needed to work, but no matter where he was he'd have kept in close touch with his sister. Jake rummaged around his room until he found his address book and steeled himself to call her, still not sure he wanted to talk to Tor. But he did know he wanted to find him.

The only trouble was that there wasn't any answer when he called Becky. He let the phone ring about six times, finally giving up and cursing the fact that she appeared not to have an answering machine.

He told himself that it was Friday night and they'd probably gone to the movies or something, and he'd get a hold of her the next day.

He called on Saturday morning, and again late in the afternoon, letting the phone ring for as long as he could stand it. He knew Susie would have school on Monday, but now that he'd made up his mind to at least locate Tor, he hated the delay. Just typical of his life that he'd pick the one weekend they seemed to be out of town.

He called three times on Sunday, just on the off chance Becky and Susie would be home. When he called at ten Sunday night and let the phone ring thirteen times, he knew he'd have trouble sleeping. It was just so damn frustrating. Five months since Tor'd left and Jake was turning himself inside out, not willing to wait even a few more days to start tracking him down.

Sometimes Jake wondered what had happened to his nice calm life, the times when all he cared about were the horses and the cattle. Then he remembered and itched to call Becky again.

On Monday evening he rushed Kirk and Elias through supper, just wanting them out of the kitchen so he could call Becky as soon as the dishes were done. He was up to his elbows in soapsuds when the phone rang, and he grabbed a dish towel while Elias answered. It wasn't the right night for Elias' family to be calling, and Kirk did all the calling to his folks, so Jake assumed it was the Boss.

Elias held the receiver out to him and covered the mouthpiece. "Think it's your sister," he said as Jake took the phone.

"'Lissa?" Jake said, pulling out a chair.

"No," a familiar, if tired, voice said. "Becky. How are you, Jake?"

Jake sat down harder than he'd intended, hitting his tailbone on the back of the chair. He managed not to cuss simply by being too surprised to manage it. "I…I'm fine, Becky. Been trying to reach you all weekend, actually."

"Really?" Becky sounded more distracted than interested in knowing why. Before Jake could really have time to wonder why, she went on, speaking quickly. "We've been living at the hospital since Wednesday. Jake, Momma died this morning."

Jake's chest tightened immediately, a wave of sorrow passing over him. "I'm real sorry to hear that," he said sincerely. He'd liked Maureen a great deal, and knowing how sick she'd been should have cushioned the blow, but it didn't. "How's Susie?"

"She's tired. We all are." Becky took an audible breath. "I know it's a lot to ask, and he'll probably kill me—"

"Where and when?" There wasn't any hesitation on Jake's part, and though a great deal of him knew that it was his new found urge to talk to Tor that spurred him on, he actually wanted to be there. He wanted to say goodbye, and he wanted to help. If Tor didn't want him there…well, he'd just deal with that after the fact with as much grace as he could.

"Here, on Thursday. The church down the block from my place, Saint Paul's. Do you remember it?"

"Yes." Jake grabbed a piece of paper and wrote down the times, making note of the nearest hotel and assuring Becky it wasn't any trouble.

"I'm…I'm not going to tell him I called you," she said softly. "I don't know what happened with you two, but I can't stand seeing him like this, Jake. He needs you."

"I'll be there." Come hell or high water.

"Thank you, Jake."

"Don't. Not yet, anyway. Becky—"

"Yes?"

"She was a good woman."

"She was. Thank you. See you soon."

It hadn't been any trouble getting time off work; the Boss was more than willing to let Jake go for a few days, and let him take the newest truck as well. The drive had been boring, with nothing special to take Jake's thoughts away from where they inevitably strayed.

The first decision Jake had made was that he wasn't going to say anything to Tor about their relationship. It wasn't the time, and it would be beyond cruel to let Maureen's passing give him any sort of advantage. Tor would be hurting and at his most vulnerable; the most Jake intended to do was let Tor know he wanted to talk when Tor was feeling up to it.

The fact that he was scared shitless had little to do with it.

He'd headed out Wednesday night and spent Thursday morning sleeping and pacing, finally taking a shower and double-checking directions to the church. He didn't want to get there late and risk being standing around outside when the family arrived. With any luck he'd get there in the middle of the crowd, and Tor wouldn't even see him until after the service.

That much, at least, went according to plan. He was seated in the middle of the church, surrounded by people he didn't know, when Becky, Tor and Susie finally entered and took their place at the front, along with two older women and a man Jake had never met.

The service was typical. There were hymns and prayers, and a woman who was apparently Maureen's best friend from childhood on up gave a moving eulogy. Jake concentrated on the smell of the flowers and let the words flow over him. He had his own memories of Maureen to take comfort in.

The woman who'd hoped her son would eventually find a nice girl, but who knew love when she saw it. The woman who would fiercely defend her family from anything. The woman who refused to give in to pain and illness until she couldn't fight it any longer.

He sat in the church and listened, his gaze straying more and more often to the family at the front. Susie had grown. Becky looked lost. Tor...well, Tor looked like hell. Worse than he'd ever looked before, he wore his exhaustion like it was part of his clothes, lines deeper around his eyes, shoulders bent.

When the minister referred to the family he called them Rebecca, Susan, and Mark, the names jarring and clashing in Jake's head. He wanted to stand up and correct the man, even though Maureen had always called Tor by his right name. The rest just didn't suit, weren't the people he knew.

Finally it was done, and with sunlight streaming in the windows, the pallbearers rose to carry Maureen's casket from the church, her family following. Tor didn't look to either side of the center aisle, didn't see him.

Susie did, her eyes widening before she quickly stepped into place beside her mother.

When Jake left the church he was relieved to see that the casket was already in the hearse, the cars lined up to go to the cemetery. He'd feared a formal receiving line, and he hadn't been sure how to slip away from it if there was one. But as he stood among the people leaving the church he could see Becky and Tor already in a limo with the older family members, ready to follow.

He asked the person next to him to confirm his directions and went to his truck to wait. Again, he didn't want to get there too early, wanted to be part of the background. He realized as he watched the cars leave that getting directions was a little pointless, and he just slid into

line with the rest, following along and parking on a side
street.

As he walked to the grave, silent among groups of
people who knew each other, he became aware of the looks
he was getting, people trying to place him. He was mildly
uncomfortable as it was, feeling like he didn't really have a
right to be there, and dressed in clothes that weren't his
usual style, to say the least. Still, he knew he didn't look out
of place; his dress pants were tidy and almost new, his one
good shirt was starched to within an inch of its life, and he
had his good boots on. He'd even managed to get his tie on
right, and his dinner jacket, while perhaps a little loose
across the shoulders, was new enough to be in style.

He found a place under a tree, out of the way, and tried
to ignore the looks. He knew they were just trying to figure
out who he was, and he didn't really feel like telling them.

Maureen was laid to rest quietly, her family gathered
around her grave, the rest looking on silently as the
minister said a final prayer for her and committed her to the
Earth. There were muffled sobs from various people, and
Jake watched as Tor wrapped an arm around Becky's
shaking shoulders.

The wind rustled the leaves overhead, and carried the
scent of the flowers to Jake.

After the casket was lowered, Jake stood exactly where
he was, hat in hand, and waited. People more or less
grouped around the family, some leaving and breaking off
into groups before making their way to their cars, others
hanging back and discussing who all was to go on to
Becky's house for the reception.

Jake watched Tor.

Tor didn't look in his direction, far too busy with family
and friends to spare a glance around him. That was fine by
Jake; he just wanted to be there. Becky saw him, however,
and managed a smile. She glanced at Tor and then back at
Jake, a question in her eyes.

Jake shook his head, and she nodded, then someone was hugging her and he lost even that contact.

People left, slowly but surely. Jake stood and waited, not moving, not ready to go forward and put himself on the line. Not here, not yet, and goddamn he was scared. He didn't want Tor to lose it, didn't want to spark off rage and grief, didn't want to be the source of any more pain.

He didn't notice Susie until a small hand slipped in his.

"Hey, Princess," he said, glancing down at her. Not so far down as he would have expected. Soon ten, Susie was almost up to his shoulder. She was going to be taller than her mother, for sure.

"Hey. Are you coming to our house?" She didn't look at him, just held onto his hand, the ribbons on her dress fluttering in the breeze.

"I'm not sure." I want to.

"He'll be mad if you don't." God, she sounded so sure.

"We'll see."

They stood a moment, then someone elderly appeared, taking her away with a hug and promises of sugar cookies. Jake let her go, smiling as gently as he could. "I'll see you soon," he promised. He had four days. He would see her.

Then there were only a few people, and he watched Tor and Becky speak for a moment, not looking at his tree, not acknowledging him. Becky nodded and kissed Tor's cheek, then turned and left, the rest of the people going with her, leaving Tor to stand alone at the foot of his mother's grave.

Jake counted. It was thirty seconds before Tor turned and walked to him, looking at his shoes until he was right in front of Jake. Then he looked up and met Jake's eyes.

"Taggart." Tor didn't move.

Jake raised his hand and laid it along Tor's jaw, his fingers curling around to the back of Tor's neck. "Hey, Cowboy."

Tor leaned in without a word until their foreheads touched, his hand coming up to rest on Jake's hips. Four points of contact.

"Take me home, Jake?"
"Yeah."

They were mostly silent during the short ride to Becky's, Jake taking a few moments to express his sympathy, and Tor thanking him in a low voice. Damn, but the man looked wrecked. Jake drove them through the quiet neighborhood, following Tor's directions through a short maze of one-way streets. When they got to Becky's, they found someone had made sure there was room in the driveway for the truck, cars lining the street.

They climbed out of the truck without a word, Tor leading the way into the house. When Becky met them at the door, Tor grabbed Jake's arm and murmured, "We'll talk later, yeah?"

Jake nodded and tried to let Tor know with his eyes how much he wanted that, but the man was immediately swept away from him, family claiming him and taking him into the living room.

"Thank you for coming," Becky said, her face pale but composed. She looked a hell of a lot better than Tor, tired, but coping.

Jake held out his arms and let her walk into them, holding her for a few moments. "I'm sorry, Becky."

She nodded into his chest. "I know. And thank you." She pulled back a bit and looked him over, giving him a small smile. "You look good, Jake. Come on, come get something to eat."

He followed her into the kitchen, ignoring the searching looks he was getting from the people gathered in clusters throughout the house. She pulled a tray of food from the fridge and uncovered it, telling him to help himself. People followed them in, and before more than a couple of minutes had passed, Becky was deep into conversations with about three different people and Jake was looking for a way to make himself useful.

He took the tray into the dining room where he found more food and more people. He got a warm smile from a woman with dyed red hair when he set the tray down, so he returned it and went back to the kitchen to look for more.

As soon as he stepped through the door someone else handed him another plate, and before long he found himself pretty much in charge of making sure the food made it from the kitchen to the buffet. That was good, he thought. Useful. Helpful. And out of the way.

Too busy to be a pain in anyone's neck, and no one was asking him hard questions.

He set the last plate on the table and picked up one that was nearly empty, reaching past a man with Tor's eyes to do it. The man gave him a long look and finally asked, "Who are you?"

Jake held the plate tightly and said, "A friend of Becky and Tor's."

"Oh. Thought you might be one of the cowboys Mark works with." The man held out a hand and added, "Jackson Dewar. I'm a cousin of Maureen's."

Jake shifted the plate to his left hand. "Jake Taggart. And yeah, I worked with Tor in Arkansas." He waited for a hint of a reaction, anything that would tell him the man knew who he was, but there wasn't anything other than polite interest.

"It was nice to meet you," Jake said, shifting his weight to his other foot. He gestured to the plate vaguely. "If you'll excuse me, I'll just go see if Becky needs any help." He fled to the kitchen, cussing to himself.

He wanted to be there for Tor and Becky and Susie, he wanted to help. He didn't want to talk to anyone else, and he felt like he was on another planet, unsure of what to do or say, not knowing who all these people were and who he should be avoiding, if anyone.

He took the plate to the sink and rinsed it off, glancing out the window as he wiped at it. Tor was in the backyard, talking to yet another man, this time someone damn near ancient. They were alone, just standing by the back fence.

"Go," Becky said, appearing at his side. "Just…go out and be there."

"Not sure that's a good idea," he said, still watching Tor.

"He let you drive him here, right? He's glad you came, Jake. Just…go be where he can see you. Let him know you're still here for him." She put a hand on his arm and squeezed gently. "You are, aren't you?"

He looked at her and smiled a little. "I suppose I am. Not sure he wants me to be, is all."

"He doesn't know what he wants." She smiled at him again and then left the room, leaving Jake to look out the window.

Jake watched for a few more moments, just listening to the hum of people in the house and looking at Tor. Finally he went to the door and out, forcing himself to cross the yard to where the two men stood.

Tor didn't look at him as he approached, but the other man did, and Jake watched as the man took his leave, giving Tor a handshake and a pat on the arm. Jake nodded to the little old man as he walked by and got a grin in return, the man's face crinkling up like an elderly gnome. Jake reckoned the man would be a hellion given enough provocation. Like the word "hello".

Tor had turned to lean one shoulder on the fence so Jake moved beside him, facing him. Standing close, but not touching, he studied Tor's face, took in all the lines, the deep shadows, the gray at his temples. "When did you last sleep?" he asked softly.

Tor shrugged. "Couple hours last night. Maybe three the night before. Been a while."

Jake looked toward the house. "You need to rest."

"Can't. Not in there, not right now. Soon as I step in I'll be surrounded by people all wanting to comfort me. By the way, what the hell are you doing here?" The words were harsh, but the tone was just damn tired and wanting to know.

Jake shook his head. "Here 'cause I want to be. You need to rest, then we'll talk, okay?"

Tor rolled his eyes and turned to lean his back on the fence. "Can't get any sleep right yet, Jake. And I really want to know why you're here. Why now?" There was a catch in his voice and Jake looked at him, saw Tor just about ready to crumple, holding onto control by a thin, worn thread.

"I'm here because I didn't start looking for you soon enough and Becky found me before I could reach you. I'm here 'cause I want to be. 'Cause I want to talk to you, but not right now. Not like this."

Tor blinked rapidly and waved a hand at the house. He looked like he was going to say something, then thought better of it.

"Tor, listen to me. I want…hell, I need to talk to you, tell you some things I finally figured out. But you need to sleep, and you need to deal with family first. I ain't going anywhere unless you send me, and even then I'll be hard to shake until I say my piece. But right now, this minute? Let me help you."

Tor looked at him for a long moment, his eyes searching and apparently finding something he needed to see. "How?"

"I got a hotel room. Let me take you there, right now. You can sleep for a few hours, I'll come back here and help Becky, hang out with Susie or wash dishes or whatever. You call when you wake up and I'll go get you. Or hell, if you don't call in about five hours I'll just go wake you up." Jake resisted the urge to reach out and touch Tor only by shoving his hands in his pockets. "Please? You look like hell. Just get some sleep."

Tor looked around the yard for a moment and turned to him, nodding. When tears welled up in Tor's eyes and started to flow down his cheeks, Jake reached for him, pulling him close and holding on.

"I'm so sorry, Jake," Tor whispered. "God, so sorry."

"I know," Jake whispered back. "Me, too. That's why I'm here. We'll deal with it later."

But Tor still shook, exhaustion and grief making him unstable and given to near silent sobs. Jake just held on and did his level best to be what Tor needed. "Momma...she said...she—"

"Shh. I'm sorry. Come on, let me take you to get some sleep."

Tor finally pulled himself together and they walked to the truck. By the time Jake had gone in to tell Becky where they were going and that he'd be back in less than half an hour to help out, Tor was almost asleep.

Forty

---◆◆◆---

Jake walked back into the house, immediately assaulted by the noise of about thirty people still gathered in the living room. After the quiet of the truck and the muted conversation in the hotel room, the chatter was an adjustment.

He took off his hat and jacket and carried them through to the kitchen, catching Becky's eye and giving her a quick nod. Tor was asleep, and would be for a while.

He made sure there was food still laid out and cleared a few dishes, then went looking for Susie.

Jake found her in her bedroom, sitting on the floor surrounded by books and toys, a few dolls having a tea party at a small table. She looked up at him and smiled, delight written across her face. "You came back!"

"Sure did. How are you doing, Princess?" He moved into the room and sat on the edge of her bed, unsurprised when she scrambled up to sit next to him.

"Okay. Everyone keeps asking me that."

"They're worried. It's real hard to lose someone you love, and your grandmother was a special person. People are just…well, they want to know that you're all right, and if you aren't, they want to help."

She nodded seriously and took his hand, then rested her head on his arm. "Jake? Did you take Uncle Tor somewhere?"

"Just someplace quiet, so he can sleep. I'll bring him back in a few hours." He found himself wanting to stroke her hair. So he did. It felt soft, the loose curls twisting under his hand.

"Thought maybe you were taking him away," she said softly.

He shook his head. "No. But you know that if he did go away he'd always come back, right? He's always going to be there for you, whenever you need him."

She nodded, her cheek brushing his arm, warm breath puffing on the stiff cotton of his dress shirt. "But he went away from you. Was he always gonna be there for you?"

Jake tried not to sigh. He had no idea how to explain what had happened to a ten year old. Or a nine year old. He wasn't sure when her birthday was, or if it mattered for this particular conversation. "That's not quite the same thing, honey. Your uncle and me, we had some problems and couldn't stay together any longer without hurting each other. So he moved out, went to work somewhere else. But it's not like that with you and him."

She looked up at him and frowned. "Why?"

"Why what? Why's it different?"

"Yeah."

"Well, he loves you very much. You're family."

"But your family let you go, for a long time. And I thought you and Uncle Tor loved each other." She looked so small.

"You're right. My family did let me go, but I let them go too, sort of. We found each other again."

Her frown deepened. "Didn't you and Uncle Tor love each other?"

Ah, hell.

"Yes, we did. But we still hurt each other."

She sat up and pulled away from him, then got on her knees beside him on the bed. He looked at her, utterly astonished when she took his face in her little hands and made him stay where she could look into his eyes. "You're here to make it better, aren't you? You want to be my uncle again."

Jake's jaw dropped despite the hands on his face. He had no intention of saying yes or no to that, not to her, certainly not until he'd talked to Tor.

"Susie? What are you doing?" came a voice behind them. "Oh, hello."

Jake turned to see the woman with dyed red hair standing in the doorway. He nodded a greeting as Susie settled beside him again, taking his hand.

"This is Auntie Dot. She's not really my auntie, but I call her that," Susie announced.

Auntie Dot smiled at her and nodded. "I'm one of those hard to place cousins, everyone just calls me Auntie Dot," she said to Jake. "And you are?"

"This is my Uncle Jake," Susie put in firmly.

Dot smiled again and shook her head. "I don't think that's quite right. No hard to place cousins named Jake, and you don't have any real aunts with husbands I don't know," she said indulgently. "Maybe Jake's one of your mommy's

321

friends?" Her expression was pure 'Don't kids say the darndest things?'

Jake opened his mouth, but he was quickly learning that he had to be faster to beat Susie at answering questions.

"No, Jake's married to my Uncle Tor. Or at least, he was. But I think he will be again, and then I can call him my uncle."

Jake watched Dot's eyes go from mildly confused to wider than hell as she figured it out, a dull flush crossing her face. "Oh. Well, then. I guess I'll let you two talk. If you want something to eat, Susie, don't you forget there's a ton of food in the dining room." With an apologetic look at Jake she turned and fled.

Jake sighed. "Susie, that wasn't very nice."

"Why not? She always pretends that Uncle Tor is something he ain't. And Momma always tells me not to pretend and not to be ashamed." She tossed her hair in a gesture that should have been far past her years. "Besides, you're here, and that means you still love him, and that means I might get you back, right?"

Jake rolled his eyes. "Let me talk to your uncle before you start announcing stuff, okay? Man doesn't know which end is up, and you've got him married off. He might like it better without me around, you know."

She shook her head firmly. "He doesn't."

Jake sighed again and looked around the room. "You got any new Lego?"

Susie bounced off the bed and almost tripped over a doll on her way to the closet.

Two hours later Jake stumbled from the bedroom and made his way to the kitchen, noting that the number of voices had diminished considerably. When he peered into the living room he found less then ten people sitting there, all of them comfortable and talking like they were old friends, which he assumed they were.

He retreated to the dining room and cleared the table, had gotten most of the dishes washed and put away when Becky appeared at his elbow.

"My God, what are you doing?"

"Just helping out," he said with a smile. Becky looked better than she had earlier, the stress starting to fade. "Think you just needed to sit."

She still looked shocked and a little displeased. "You're a guest, you shouldn't be doing this."

Jake snorted. "Like I'd rather be out there, dodging questions from Auntie Dot?"

Becky looked startled and then laughed. "What happened? She flew out of Susie's room and headed right for the gin."

"Susie told her I'm married to Tor," he said with a grin.

"That'd do it. She's convinced that he's a gay old bachelor, not just gay." Her smile faded. "What happened, Jake? Tor, he just...he's been empty. Won't talk about it at all, just says he did something terrible and nearly killed you."

Jake was already shaking his head. "No. I mean, no, it wasn't all his fault. The last of it was, the part that made me tell him to go? That was pretty bad. But the start of it was my fault, too."

Becky sat at the kitchen table and waited for him to join her. "Tell me what he did? The way he talks, it's like he took a knife and just cut your heart out."

"Sorry. I'm not going to tell you, it's not my place to spill his secrets. Just...look, it doesn't matter now. It matters, I mean, but—shit." Jake had no idea what he was trying to say.

He took a breath and started over. "Tor and I were having trouble. Then he did something and I kicked him out. But he stuck around, tried to make it better, and I wouldn't let him; too wrapped up in my own pain, too hurt to let him in. But I've recently had my eyes opened to some truths and I want a chance to talk to him, tell him some things I should have said a long time ago."

"So, you're going to talk to him. And tell him what? I mean…God, Jake, if you're not here to take him back, don't even bother. The man's a mess and I don't want him hurt any more than he is." She looked across the table at him, her eyes bright. "I know he did something bad to you, but he's my brother, and I love him. Don't hurt him, please?"

Jake shook his head slowly. "Not trying to hurt him, I swear. And I'm going to do my level best to make him hear me. But don't be surprised if he doesn't want to come back with me. Might be too late for that."

Now Becky shook her head, so hard her hair slipped from behind her ears. "You don't know. You haven't seen him. He loves you so much, Jake."

"I hope so. But I'm not counting on it. Can't."

Forty One

Jake stopped at a drive through coffee shop and got two large. He knew he needed it, and was pretty sure Tor would, too. It was well past suppertime, and he'd finally told Becky that he'd go wake Tor up and bring him back. Susie had kissed him good night and asked him to come back for lunch the next day.

"Depends, kiddo. Gotta see how your uncle feels about that."

He hoped her uncle would still be speaking to him come morning, but he knew there wasn't any guarantee. Only thing he knew was that he wasn't heading back to Arkansas until he'd told Tor what he had to. After that, it was up to Tor.

He let himself into the hotel room, unsurprised to find Tor still sleeping in the bed. It looked like the man hadn't even moved, except maybe to toss and turn a bit. He was still flat out on his back, but the blankets were twisted around his legs, one bare foot sticking out.

Jake set the coffee down on the dresser and quietly looked through his bag, getting out his jeans and a softer shirt. He changed in the bathroom, pretty sure that Tor suddenly waking up to find him half naked wouldn't be a good idea.

When he came out, tucking his shirt in and trying to fix one sock that had gotten twisted, Tor was just starting to wake up, blinking at him blearily.

"Hey," Jake said, fighting a sudden case of cold feet. "Got coffee." He picked up one of the paper cups and brought it over to the bed, setting it on the nightstand. Then he took his own and sat on the other bed, sitting on the edge while Tor sat up, the sheets pooling around his waist.

"Thanks," Tor said, running a hand through his hair. "What time is it?"

"Almost nine."

"Fuck." Tor blinked a few times and reached for the coffee. "Feel like I've been drug through a ditch somewhere."

Jake nodded and sipped at his coffee, belatedly realizing that Tor would probably want to get up and dressed. He glanced at the chair where Tor had tossed his pants, shirt and tie, the suit jacket somewhere else. "Want me to go? So you can dress?"

Tor swallowed a mouthful of coffee and shook his head. "Want you to tell me why you're here."

A hard knot formed in Jake's belly. "Maybe we should wait. You've had a God awful week, at least, and—"

Tor glared at him. "And spending the next few hours wondering what the hell is going on in your head is going to help me how?"

Even Jake could see the point in that. He looked down at his knees and stifled the urge to run. "Yeah. Okay." He looked up at Tor again and nodded, forcing himself to go on. "All right. But if you don't want to hear it all right now, you tell me. I'm not going back until we've talked, but I still think right now is wrong."

Tor rolled his eyes. "Just talk, yeah?"

Jake nodded and set his coffee down carefully, not sure how to start. He'd gone over everything he wanted to say so many times, but the beginning had always eluded him. Finally, he looked at Tor and said, "Hound and Del showed up about a week and a half ago."

Tor winced. "Christ, Hound must be wanting to kill me," he said, closing his eyes.

Jake raised an eyebrow. "No, don't think so. He's not real happy with me, though."

Tor stared at him for a moment, then his expression cleared. "You should have told him what I did. Then he'd be venting about me, not you."

"Did tell him."

"Why's he pissed at you then?" Tor asked, obviously confused. He pried the lid off his coffee and looked at it, his thumb flicking over the rim of the plastic.

Jake sighed and shifted on the bed. "Because I'm an idiot."

That earned him a searching look. Tor drank some coffee, waiting him out.

"Look, it's like this," Jake said, hoping to fuck he'd get all the way through it without losing control. "Hound said a lot of things that made me think, made me take a look at shit I didn't want to. Stuff I'd been trying to bury, but just wouldn't go away."

He looked at Tor and something close to understanding was in Tor's eyes, and it made him keep talking.

"I've not been doing so well," he admitted. "Been working and sleeping and doing what I have to, and just…not thinking. Hound gave me a kick, got me pointed at some things."

"Like what?" Tor asked, his voice low. He was looking at the coffee lid, his fingers tracing the edge over and over.

"Like a lot of things I should have told you before. I've done some fucked up stuff in my day, Tor, you know that. But one of the worst was probably taking you for granted, not telling you things."

Tor stared at him for a long moment, then shook his head. "I don't get it."

Jake bit his lip. "We were—me and Hound, I mean—we were talking. He got me thinking about what happened before the summer, about how you and I got to a point where it could even happen. And it got me thinking about a lot of things, then Del said it comes down to—"

"Del talked to you?" The idea seemed to amuse Tor, though the grin disappeared quickly.

"Yeah, and what is that man's problem, anyway? Half the time he seems okay, then he just sort of avoids me."

Tor shrugged. "What did he say?"

"Said a lot of things; they both did." Jake reached for his coffee and sat back farther on the bed. "Hound said a bunch of stuff about talking to each other, making sure things get sorted right instead of just shoved aside. And when I thought about it I realized he was right—you and me, we just sort of calmed down, but we never really resolved anything."

Tor nodded slowly. "I guess."

Jake decided to take that as encouragement. At least Tor was listening and not telling him to fuck off. Yet. "Little stuff and big stuff, it all just sort of grew. The fights we had—remember when you messed with the schedule? I told you not to do it again—"

"And I didn't—"

"Right, but I never told you why. Aside from it being my job to set them."

Tor looked at him and raised an eyebrow. "So, why?"

The knot in Jake's belly tightened. This was the hard part, the opening up. Fuck, if Hound and Del did this every time they had a fight, they were stronger men than he was. "Because it made me feel like you were taking advantage. Like you knew you could mess with the schedule, get what you wanted, and it was okay because we were together."

Tor's eyes widened. "Fuck, really?"

"Yeah. Made me madder than hell that you would do that."

"But, I didn't—I mean, that's not what I meant to do. I was just…I thought that it would work better, that the work would get done and everyone would be happy." Tor looked around the room for a moment. "I'm sorry," he offered.

"I know you are, and I'm sorry I didn't say anything. You and me—we just assumed the other one would know everything. And we didn't, which is now blindingly obvious. We never got things cleared up, just fought and fucked and went on our merry way."

Tor drew his legs up and rearranged the blankets. "Okay. So we let ourselves get buried in our own shit. Doesn't explain why you're here, talking about it now."

"Didn't realize it until they made me think. You might not have noticed, but I'm really not one for introspection."

"Bullshit. You do it all the time."

Jake sighed. "Okay, how about it was easier to blame you than to think any of it was my fault? And worse, it was easier to blame you, knowing it was partly my fault, and not care."

Tor shook his head. "Was my fault, Jake. I'm the one who—who slept with Travis. I'm the one who cheated and lied."

"Yeah, you are. And that damn near destroyed me, I won't tell you any different. But it was you and me together who made it even possible for you to do that. You think it would have happened three years ago?" Jake leaned forward resting his elbows on his legs. "Point is, we hurt each other a lot. And I know it, now. And I'm sorry I hurt you so bad you looked somewhere else."

"Jake—Jesus." Tor looked stunned, his eyes wide. "You don't have to say you're sorry, not after what I did—"

"The hell I don't!" Jake stiffened, anger coming from somewhere, unknown and unexpected. "You don't get to carry it all. Was me as well as you, and if you can't let me shoulder my part, even though it's taken me an age to see it, than we can't fix anything. Gotta take our own parts."

"Fix?" Tor asked, his voice low.

Damn. That part wasn't supposed to happen yet, he still had too much to say.

"Yeah. If you want to." Jake swallowed hard. "Ain't nothing without you. I ache all the time, I miss you. I want...hell, I want to see if there's a way we can get it back."

Tor didn't say anything for a few long moments, and when he did his voice was hoarse. "You said you couldn't trust me ever again. And I understood that. I accepted it."

"Was before I figured out how bad I'd messed up." Jake put the coffee back down and rubbed his eyes. "Not saying it's going to be easy—we've got too much to talk about, not the least of which is Travis. But I know I'd rather be with you than without you, and I'm willing to do what I can to get you to come back."

Tor took a shuddering breath and let it out slowly. "Miss you, too. More than I'd thought possible." He sat up straighter and rearranged the pillows behind him, then looked at Jake, his eyes serious. "Think we should talk about Travis before we decide anything, though. You might change your mind."

"Doubt it," Jake said with a short-lived smile. "Wouldn't have come all this way, been looking for you for the last week, if I hadn't gotten it sorted. I just…I need to know some stuff."

"You were looking for me?" Tor sounded surprised and Jake smiled again.

"Yeah, called day and night last weekend." The smile vanished. "Then Becky called me on Monday night."

"Oh."

Jake stood up, his legs a little shaky from nerves and tension. When he crossed the space between the beds Tor's eyes widened a little, but he shifted over to make room for Jake to sit.

"What do you want to know?" Tor asked, then licked his lips looking as nervous as a virgin bride on her wedding night.

Jake took a breath and waited until he was steady. He knew what he needed to ask, and if the answer wasn't one that he liked it would be okay. But it would put a serious crimp in what he wanted the rest of the night to be like.

"When you were with him did you—" he paused and shook his head at himself, hating that he was hesitating now, after all that he'd managed to say. "Need to know if you were safe," he finally mumbled.

Tor blinked and nodded. "God, yes. And I've tested clean twice since September." A slow flush rose on his chest. "You think I'd let you fuck me if I didn't know? Jake—"

But Jake was already shaking his head. "That was as much me as you, and that's why I had to ask. Finding a rubber was the last thing on my mind at the time, and I didn't trust you then." He could feel his chest tightening and there was a tickle in his throat. "This is what I mean, Tor. We have to talk about stuff. Shit like this, about things like why I shut down when you said you wanted to buy the ranch, about everything. If this is going to work we need to say things we don't want to."

"Okay," Tor said, his face slowly clearing. "Okay. I can see that. Not going to be easy."

"God, no. That's what I told Del, that you and me don't work that way." Jake looked down at Tor's hand and almost reached for it. "Then he pointed out that you and I aren't together, and I sort of figure that saying hard stuff is a hell of a lot better than being without you."

There was a short silence then Tor did the reaching, brushing his fingers along Jake's jaw and tilting Jake's head up so he would look at him. "Hearing a lot of you saying the hard stuff, Taggart. Only things I've said since you came in are questions."

Jake waited, almost holding his breath. He'd stopped Tor before; this time he needed it.

"Take me home?" Tor whispered.

Jake couldn't speak, the tickle in his throat turning to a lump. He nodded slowly, already cursing himself for a fool. He forced himself to swallow and said, "Yeah. Becky's got supper waiting for you."

"Not what I meant. Take me home, Jake. Gonna take me a couple of weeks to settle things, but I want to be home. With you."

Jake blinked, fighting tears of relief and anger, though the anger was directed at himself. "Oh. Yeah, of course." He turned away, not willing to show Tor how shaken he was. "I'll, um. I'll talk to the Boss and the others, let them know what's—"

"Look at me." Tor moved, shifting in the bed and losing the blankets as he reached for Jake, one hand going to the back of Jake's neck, the other to Jake's thigh. "Look at me."

Jake looked, meeting dark eyes so serious he caught his breath.

"I love you, Jake. Always have. Always will."

Jake didn't bother stopping the sob that welled up as he moved into Tor's arms. It was awkward as they tried to arrange themselves without actually giving up any contact.

Jake didn't care.

He was more or less leaning over Tor, his weight braced on one arm as he tried not to fall off the bed, and it didn't matter. All that mattered was that Tor had one hand tangled in his hair, and the other was on his hip, pulling him down, drawing him closer.

Their first kiss was fierce, possessive. The intensity of emotions and shattered control sweeping them both along, and they came together without any restraint at all, mouths wide and teeth clashing.

When Jake finally pulled back to breathe he found his arm was trembling, threatening to let go and let him fall onto Tor. Tor didn't let him get too far away, the hand on his hip shoving hard, rolling them both over on the bed until they were in the middle, Tor still under a tangle of sheets, Jake over them.

"Need to touch you," Tor said. "Need to, so much. God, you have no idea—"

"I do." God, so long without Tor's hands on him…Jake knew.

Facing each other, they kissed again, hands freely wandering over sides and backs, up arms to trace collarbones and jaws.

He wasn't sure how long they lay there, touching and kissing and trying to crawl inside one another, he only knew when it changed, the kisses becoming less desperate and more about relearning. Gently, almost sweetly, they kissed and tasted, finding each other beneath the coffee and salt of almost tears.

Jake ran his hands over Tor's body, pushing at the blankets, mapping Tor's back and chest. Tor was thin, muscles still hard and skin still smooth, but smaller. Grief and work had taken its toll, and Jake promised himself he'd see them both healthy before the end of summer.

Right then, though, he just wanted to lie there, feel Tor next to him, and hear his voice. They rolled again, unspoken agreement putting Jake on top, straddling Tor's hips. The blankets had shifted out of the way enough that there was only denim and two pairs of boxer briefs between them, and as they moved it was suddenly far too much fabric.

Tor's fingers started tugging at Jake's shirt, pulling it free from the jeans. "You couldn't wear a T-shirt?" he asked with a smile as Jake fumbled with the buttons.

"Too casual. Was a serious conversation." Jake mostly meant it too, though he'd not been thinking like that when he'd packed.

Tor's hips rocked as he sat up and both of them gasped, freezing in place before doing it again, intentionally.

"Oh, God." Jake abandoned his fight with the buttons in favor of leaning down to take another kiss, Tor's hands on his hips to guide their motions.

Tor groaned and broke the kiss, pushing Jake away. "Off," he growled, pushing ineffectually at Jake's shirt. Jake just nodded and pulled it off over his head, ignoring the buttons. Tor's fingers tangled with his own, both of them trying to undo the button on his jeans, getting in each other's way until Jake finally stopped and just let Tor do it. They were both breathing faster, the only sounds in the room their panting and soft sounds that meant hurry up.

"Got anything slick?" Tor asked, trying to push Jake's jeans off his hips.

Jake shook his head. "Wasn't really thinking this far ahead."

"S'okay, we'll make do. The old fashioned way." Tor rolled them again and pulled away, stripping off his own shorts before reaching for Jake once more.

Jeans, shorts and socks gone, Jake moved into Tor's arms with a sound of desperation. He needed. Needed Tor's heat, his body, his mouth. As easy as breathing they moved together, arms and legs wrapping around each other, a low hiss coming from each of them as they started to rock.

Jake licked up the length of Tor's neck and bit down on the soft skin below his ear. "Love you," he whispered. "Never stopped."

Tor shuddered and moaned, his fingers digging into Jake's hips. "Christ."

"Yeah."

Their movements became more and more hurried, more frenzied. Jake felt almost dizzy, the past few months giving way to a time when they were really connecting resounding within him. He kissed Tor deeply, giving Tor forgiveness and welcome, his cock painting need and passion on Tor's belly.

Tor took it all and gave it back, words dropping onto him between gasps and sighs, panted out as they rolled and twisted on the bed. Words Jake had banished from his mind for almost ten months, and hadn't really heard in over a year. Yours. Need. So good, always.

When Tor came it was with a sharp cry, a chanting of Jake's name, repeated over and over as he shook. It took only one more word to send Jake over, the one word he'd not really expected to hear in their time together, no matter how much he knew it to be true.

Sometimes hard things to say got easier with practice.

After, when they were lying together in a sleepy tangle of limbs, Tor kissed him again. "Never thought you'd come for me," he said softly.

"Never thought I would," Jake admitted. "Thought the pain would go away, you know? But it wasn't what you did that was hurting me."

Tor shook his head. "You're gonna have to explain that to me. I saw what it did to you, saw it until I left. The lies, the betrayal—"

"Yeah, I know. What I mean is…" Jake fought to find words. He knew what he felt, but he wasn't sure how to say it; seemed that was most of their trouble right there. Tor's hands rubbed slow circles on his back and he found himself arching into the touch, grounding himself. "Think that the pain of that would have faded. Eventually. But you not being there…missing what we had before—that hurt all the time."

He sat up a little, leaning on his elbow. "Spent a long time in that in-between place. Someone would do something, or I'd read something, and I'd think 'gotta tell Tor'. But I couldn't. And that never stopped, even two weeks ago that happened. You're supposed to be there. And it took Hound and Del to start me thinking that being apart from you was worse than dealing with what happened, that it would be stupid not to see if we could make it work. Because the pain of being apart was too big a price to pay for my pride."

Tor's arms tightened around him. "You're—something. Fuck, I worried about you so much, hated myself so much. I can't tell you how sorry I am, how much I want to take it all back."

"I know. And I thought about that, too. About how different it would have been if I'd said yes when Travis asked."

Tor stared at him. "Oh God. That's just fucked. That…that…I don't even know what to think about that."

Jake shrugged. "That's fine. Just saying that the thought occurred. Not saying it would have changed anything—"

Tor's head fell back on the bed. "God. I want, well, I don't want, but I will. We're gonna have to talk about that. In detail. But I have to think first, yeah?"

Jake nodded and rolled away, his hand trailing over Tor's chest. "Yep. But right now I think a shower is in order, then sleep. You're still wrecked, and we don't have to do this all at once."

Tor grabbed his hand and pulled him back down. "Not all of it. But we can do some of it." He took a breath and Jake steeled himself, seeing determination in Tor's eyes. "I know I've got no right to make rules—"

"Bull. It's us. Two people."

Tor thought about it and nodded slowly. "Okay. Rule. No one but us. No random pick ups, no playing."

Jake almost laughed. He'd be more than happy to never watch Tor enjoy someone else's body again. "Right. You.

Me. Okay." He kissed Tor again and somehow found himself pushing against Tor's hip. "Damn. Shower?"

"Gonna get messy again, anyway," Tor said with a grin, pushing back.

"Yeah, but if we do it right we'll get messy in the shower and then won't have to—oh fuck, do that again."

Tor grinned and ground against him, both of them getting hard as they shifted and rubbed, Tor's fingers finding one of his nipples and tugging it to stiffness. When Tor pulled away and stood up, Jake looked up at him, knowing his own eyes were probably starting to glaze over.

"C'mon, Taggart. Shower."

Jake watched Tor turn and walk away from him, heading toward the bathroom, and decided that watching was almost as good as touching. But only almost.

It took no time at all for the room to fill with steam, Tor's preference for hot, hot water not having changed in the slightest. They washed each other slowly, enjoying the glide of soapy hands over warm skin, and Jake was struck again by the changes in Tor. He was whipcord now, lean and still strong, but not right.

"You have to take care of yourself," he said, sliding a soapy hand down one long thigh. "You're too thin."

"You, too. God, Jake. Have you been eating at all?" Tor turned him around to face the spray, water spilling over his shoulders.

Jake arched into Tor's hands as they slid over his hips, one hand grazing over Jake's erection, the other steadying his hips. He could only nod in response, suddenly breathless and unable to speak.

"Like that?" Tor's voice was husky in Jake's ear, knowing.

Another nod, and Jake could feel Tor pressed against him, heavy and thick against his ass. Strong fingers wrapped around his cock and Tor started sucking up a mark on his shoulder, jerking him off slowly.

Jake moaned and thrust into Tor's hand, bracing himself on the wall in front of him. Water poured over his head, a curtain of steam around him. Hot. Heat everywhere, from the water, from Tor, and Jake felt like he was floating.

Tor's hand sped up, the gently thrust of his hips becoming insistent. Jake gasped when Tor's thumb played over the ring at the tip of his prick, and he could suddenly feel Tor's as well, the metal heated and rubbing against him.

"Tor," he moaned, his back arching. "More, need—"

Tor tugged the ring gently, the hand on Jake's hip moving to stroke his balls. "Fucking sexy, Taggart. Nothing better than you."

Jake cried out, cock throbbing as he came over Tor's hand. Tor held him up, bit at his shoulders until he started to come down, hips still sliding against him gently, slowly.

When Jake could see straight he turned in Tor's arms and kissed the man, fucking Tor's mouth with his tongue. "Hold on," he said with a grin. Then he slid down Tor's body, licking a path from throat to cock.

"Oh fuck." Tor sounded as breathless as Jake had been.

He tasted the same, earth and salt and Tor. Jake didn't waste time, just sucked him in and started working Tor's shaft with everything he knew Tor liked. Long sucking pulls, the full length of Tor's cock, and teasing licks at the head. He traced his fingers, light as a feather, over Tor's balls and played with Tor's ring. It was only moments before Tor was gasping, a few moments more before Tor grabbed at his shoulder for balance and started pushing in deeper, almost ready to come.

Jake sucked harder and made plans to work on their stamina. Ten months apart with only one ill advised fuck in the middle, and they were like teenagers.

Tor pushed deep and Jake swallowed hard, feeling Tor's balls draw up. He felt Tor's cock throb a second before his mouth was filled with Tor's flavor, both of them moaning as he swallowed.

"Damn. Goddamn." Tor reached for the wall, his legs trembling. "Gonna knock me out doing that."

Jake snorted and reached for the faucets, killing the flow before the hot water could start to cool. "You say that now. Give it a month and you'll be fine."

Tor didn't say anything and Jake looked up to meet stunned eyes. "What?"

"Just…just sort of sinking in. In a month we'll be home, and we'll be…us."

Jake was pretty sure that a mirror would show him the same grin Tor wore.

Forty Two

"He called me this morning, asked for his job back."
The Boss was sitting behind his desk, twirling a pen
between his fingers. He'd called Jake into the house as soon
as the truck had stopped in the yard—told him to leave his
bag and come chat.

Jake nodded and settled himself deeper into the easy
chair. He knew what he wanted to happen, but he and Tor
knew what they'd do if this part didn't work out. "He said
he would."

"Told him I'd talk to you first."

Jake grinned. "Told him you'd say that." He could just imagine Tor on the phone, being as polite as possible and inside railing against the wait, even though he knew it was necessary in the Boss's mind.

"I assume you're together again?" The Boss didn't look displeased with the idea. He'd not once said a word against Tor, not even when Jake wanted him to.

"Yes, sir."

But the Boss sighed, sitting back in his chair. Carefully, he said, "You know what kind of turmoil everyone went through last year."

Jake tried not to wince. He and Tor had talked about that too, and had made plans for avoiding the same upset. "Yes, sir. And you know I won't let it happen again."

"If I say no, what happens?"

"I keep working here, but move to town. He'll look for work in town or on a spread that's not too far away."

The Boss shook his head and rubbed his hand over his jaw. "Not sure I trust this, Jake."

"You don't have to. I do."

"That's that, then. I'll call him tonight and tell him to come home."

———————

"We gotta talk."

Elias looked at him and frowned. "Bad trip?"

"Well, there was a funeral. That's never fun," Jake deadpanned as he headed to the fridge for juice. He stared at the bottles all neatly lined up on the second shelf. "Um, not to be an utter idiot, but when was the last time there was actually beer in here?"

"Morning after the dance last fall," Kirk replied. "Tor made it fucking plain that there shouldn't be any booze in the house for a bit. We figured ten months was a bit." He sounded defiant, like he half expected Jake to tell him that he couldn't have beer.

Jake rolled his eyes and grabbed the apple juice. "I never noticed." It was true, it hadn't occurred to him until he'd seen it suddenly reappear. "Want one?"

Kirk nodded warily and Elias whapped him on the top of the head. "If he's offering beer to us he's got something to say that we're not going to much like."

Kirk frowned and Jake rolled his eyes again. "Shut up. It ain't bad."

Elias reached for the beer Jake held out.

Jake took a breath and leaned on the kitchen counter, one hand holding onto it behind his back. "Tor's moving back."

Elias and Kirk stared at him.

"With me."

"Didn't figure he was coming back 'cause of me," Elias said with a snort. "When?"

"Two weeks. Maybe three. Depends on lawyers and his job—and his sister, too, I guess. But as soon as he can manage it." Jake waited, watching Elias think. Kirk was…well, he lived there, worked with him, but Elias had been there forever, almost as long as Jake. And Jake wanted him to deal with this as well as he could.

"Boss know?"

"Of course. Tor called, asked for his job back."

"Which he got."

"Yep."

"He moving in here?" Elias' questions were coming fast now, the ones important to him flying to the surface, which was the way Jake needed it. The points that were important to Elias were the ones he needed most to address.

"We're back together."

"So say yes."

"Depends on you."

Elias blinked. "What?"

"Mean that if you and Kirk are really not happy with it, me and Tor will move out. Drive here every day, home each night."

Elias just nodded and swallowed a mouthful of beer.

Kirk's eyes were wide. "But it's your home. You've been here for what? Fifteen years?"

Jake nodded. "But y'all live here, too, as was pointed out to me last fall."

Elias put his bottle on the kitchen table and looked at Kirk. "You want to talk this over?"

"Me?" Damn, but the man was almost squeaking. "No, whatever. I'm good."

"What happens if things go tits up again?" Elias asked Jake.

"We both leave," Jake said promptly. Tor had brought it up, and though they both knew it wasn't going to happen, they knew everyone else had reason to be skeptical. "The house, the ranch, we're gone."

Elias sighed and reached for his beer again. "Damn. And I'm out of earplugs."

Kirk snickered, but Elias and Jake just grinned at each other.

Forty Three

It had been a long hot day, most of the hands out with Jake moving part of the herd to fresher land. The horses were hot and the men hotter as they made their way back to the ranch, the sun hanging low. Missy had delivered supper to them, but Jake figured there wasn't a body there that didn't ache for a shower and a soft bed.

"So when's Tor getting back?" Tommy asked as they came in sight of the barns.

"Day after tomorrow. He hits town tomorrow night, be out in the morning with Ray and Fred." And not a damn day too soon. Jake had let Elias and Kirk spread the word among the hands, and he'd called 'Lissa and Cath, which was fine. But he'd spent the last two weeks trying not to count days and racking up a long distance phone bill like he'd never done before. And that was only talking to Tor every three days or so. Okay, every other day, but no one was pointing it out. Not where Jake could hear, anyway.

He passed River's reins off to Kirk and went in to see the Boss. One of the perks of being the number two man was that he got to report in and fill in forms while someone else saw to the horses. Usually it grated a little—Jake never really minded spending time with the horses—but this time he was damn near weary to the bone and was happy enough to go sit for a spell before heading to the shower.

The Boss didn't keep him long, didn't even offer him a drink of juice, which was unusual. Jake didn't really think about it, passing it off to the man's own exhaustion. He'd been slowing down a little since his heart trouble, and Jake didn't have much to tell him anyway. Jake filed the herd records and took his leave, pausing only long enough to wish the Boss's wife a good night before heading to the bunkhouse, almost feeling the spray from the shower.

He kicked off his boots outside the door and had his shirts untucked before he'd crossed the kitchen. He was peeling them off when he glanced into the living room on his way past to tell Elias he was going to call it a night, and for a moment he thought it was the flickering light from the TV combined with the fabric sliding over his eyes that made him see the impossible.

He froze and blinked, then grinned as Tor stood up.

"When did you get here?" he asked, throwing the shirts down the hall, vaguely in the direction of his—their—room.

"Couple hours ago. Got away early, hitchhiked out." Tor was walking toward him, his eyes dark.

Elias stood up from the easy chair. Jake hadn't even noticed him until then, and only spared him the briefest of glances. Every muscle in Jake's body was suddenly tense. Hard.

"Can see where this is going," Elias said, walking past them. "At least get down the hall, will you? It's gonna kill Kirk if this goes—"

Too late to take Elias' advice, Tor stepped closer, his hands sliding over Jake's hips and then they were lost, kissing in the middle of the living room, pressing tight against each other.

It had been a long couple of weeks.

Kirk made an indelicate noise and pushed past them, muttering, "Get a room. And welcome back. But God, get a room."

This time Tor seemed to listen, backing Jake down the hall slowly, still kissing him, though his mouth traveled along Jake's jaw and down his neck, licking and tasting.

"I need a shower," Jake said, then shuddered when Tor pressed him into the wall to suck up a mark on his shoulder.

"Room!" Elias hollered.

Jake pushed hard and managed to get them at least inside the doorway to the their room, and Tor kicked the door shut.

"No shower," Tor said, breaking contact only long enough to pull his own shirt off. "Taste like you."

Then they fell on each other, tugging at clothes that for once cooperated and came off with relative ease.

Jake urged Tor back toward the bed, but the man stood firm and solid in front of him, hands fused to Jake's ass and hips.

"Tor—" Jake warned. "This ain't gonna last long, the bed—"

"Can wait." Tor rubbed against him, his cock nestled along Jake's hip. "Just want to—oh yeah."

Jake rubbed back, his hands traveling along Tor's spine from neck to ass, digging in as he tried to stay upright. Tor was back to sucking on his neck, mumbling into his skin. Jake had no idea what the man was saying, but the vibrations were making him breathless. He arched his back as Tor ground against him, panting, all ready. Tor's belly was hard, but it was nothing compared to the rigid heat alongside his prick.

"Tor. Fuck. I'm serious. Bed." It was as easy as leaning over, both of them falling onto the bed. Jake groaned as Tor shifted, their cocks rubbing hard, but nowhere near as much as he wanted.

Tor moved down his body, fast and determined. He looked down to meet hungry dark eyes, then Tor opened his mouth and took him in, sucking hard and doing that weird swirling thing with his tongue that had earned him his nickname.

Jake's head hit the bed with a muffled thunk as his eyes rolled back and his hips thrust up. "Oh shit!"

There was nothing like Tor's mouth, nothing on earth. Only thing better was Tor's cock, buried deep in his ass, and that's what he wanted. Only trouble was, Jake couldn't talk, couldn't think of the words to tell Tor what he wanted. All he could do was ride it, his hips pushing faster as Tor licked and sucked at the head of his cock, then took him deep and swallowed him whole.

A hand on his balls, squeezing gently, rolling them, and Jake was flying, coming down Tor's throat with a strangled cry.

Tor kept sucking until Jake was a shaking mess, his skin tingling, unable to stop the soft sounds he was making.

"Good?"

Jake groaned.

With a laugh Tor crawled up his body, nestled between Jake's spread legs. "No sleeping," he said, just before he kissed Jake.

As if Jake was going to sleep. Not with Tor heavy on him, cock, still hard, pressing against him, and the flavor of his own come on Tor's tongue.

"Fuck me."

Tor groaned and froze, lying perfectly still on top of him. They'd not done that yet, even when they'd finally gotten a hold of lube when they were spending their nights at the hotel. Nothing had been said, Tor just seemed to open for him and that was the way it was. But this time Jake needed it, wanted it.

Tor rolled to the side and reached for his nightstand, grabbing the lube. He kissed Jake hard and pressed the tube into his hand. "Will. In a minute."

Jake was confused until Tor slid down again, lifting his legs and licking at the inside of his thighs, nuzzling his balls.

"Oh fuck, Tor," he gasped when Tor started to lick. His brain kept repeating the phrase, mixing in the occasional round of oh God, yes, as Tor got down to business. His balls were treated to long licks, his ass to licks and sucking kisses, and then there was just intense sensation as Tor rimmed him. Heat flowed through his body and he knew he was making noise, crying out for more and deeper.

He fisted the sheets and rocked his hips, the lube long forgotten. He had a vague idea he'd at least managed to get it in Tor's general vicinity, but he wasn't really worried about it. His cock was filling rapidly, need growing into desperation.

"Tor, please—"

Tor could have been waiting for that, or maybe he was needing, too. Two slick fingers brushed over his skin and the heat of Tor's mouth was gone, just as they breached him.

"Oh God, tight."

Jake gasped and pushed back. "Ten months. You were tight, too. Are. Something, just—"

Tor watched him, finger fucked him until Jake was writhing on the bed. When Jake reached for his own cock Tor slapped his hand away and added a third finger, opening him carefully, avoiding his gland.

"Now, Tor. God, don't make me beg."

Tor gave him a wicked grin. "That's tomorrow."

Then the fingers were gone and Jake could feel the metal at the tip of Tor's prick pushing at him. A gentle push, a rock of his own hips and Tor was in, pushing deep, one long, slow glide that made Jake's toes curl.

Words were gone. Tor filled him, searing him from the inside, claiming him with every thrust, every pull, every kiss. Jake's legs were over Tor's shoulders and the slow pace couldn't last. Tor started to pound into him, the metal ring slamming against his gland with every thrust.

Lost and floating and almost screaming, they moved. Tor's mouth was everywhere he could reach, kissing and nipping, teasing Jake with every breath.

"Oh fuck," Tor groaned. "Fuck, fuck, fuck. Gonna come. Oh shit, Jake. So good, so hot, so fucking—oh God, oh God—"

Jake wrapped his hand around his own cock and pulled, his hips slamming up to meet Tor's, his body on fire. He felt Tor coming, felt heat and pressure and throbbing, felt teeth at this shoulder and heard Tor crying out and grunting.

Jake called Tor's name and shot, spunk flying over his hand, his belly, and all he could smell was Tor's skin and hair around him.

Tor collapsed onto him, arching Jake's back for a moment until they shifted enough for Tor to pull out and Jake could lower his legs. Curled around each other they tried to catch their breath, but kissing interfered. Sometimes it was more important to kiss.

Finally, though, Jake brushed his chin along Tor's, enjoying the rasp of stubble. "Welcome home, cowboy."

Tor smiled at him and took another kiss. "Hey, you."

Jake closed his eyes and stroked Tor's back and sides. Man actually felt better than he had only a couple of weeks ago. Sleep and food and a ton of weight off his shoulders.

"Everyone know I'm coming back?" Tor asked, his own hands mapping Jake's chest.

"Yeah. I told Elias first thing. That sort of took care of telling everyone else."

Tor chuckled. "Yeah, it would. He didn't seem upset to see me, which is good. The rest, though…I dunno."

Jake shrugged. "The rest will deal. No one's said anything to me. And they all know you're a good hand, do your job. None of their business where you sleep."

Tor nodded and kissed him gently. Jake opened his eyes and smiled, taking another.

"Or who I love," Tor whispered.

Jake swallowed hard. Damn, but the man was going to kill him, just saying shit like that. "Yeah. Or who we love."

By Chris Owen

Forty Four

———◆—◆—◆———

Things were fine—better than fine—for about three weeks. Jake had known that the tranquility would end, that eventually they'd stop being sappy and letting their sex drive carry them, and he'd been waiting for it. Problem was, when it did happen, he didn't know what to do about it.

Tor's return went mostly unremarked upon by the others on the ranch, though both Bobby and Tommy had taken a couple of moments with Jake to make sure things were good before they picked up where they'd left off with

Tor. Most of the hands just accepted the dynamic and did their work, though there was some good natured teasing about how Jake wasn't an utter bastard to work for anymore.

But as the days passed and Jake and Tor settled down and got back into their lives, a subtle tension started making its presence evident in Tor. It wasn't anything tangible at first, and it only took Jake a day or so to become certain that it wasn't anger at him or anything like that. It was more a thoughtfulness that would creep over Tor in the evenings, times when he would look into space and his forehead would furrow, his eyes becoming sad.

Jake wondered how he was supposed to handle it. Ignoring it was wrong, not to mention impossible. Asking what was wrong and pressing for answers wasn't quite right, either. He didn't want to push, and more importantly he wanted to show Tor that he knew Tor would handle it in the best way for them both and their relationship. He wanted to show his faith in Tor. In the past he'd just waited stuff like this out, waited and resented. That wasn't going to happen this time.

But on the third night when Tor started looking out the kitchen window at nothing, Jake bit his lip and waited for Elias to leave the room. He had to say something, even if was only to let Tor know that Jake was aware something was going on. But he wanted to give Tor a chance to figure it out, whatever it was, on his own. They were playing on a new field now, and he had to believe that Tor would let him know, when he was ready.

Didn't mean he couldn't let Tor know that he'd noticed, though. That he was paying attention.

Elias finished scraping plates and announced he was going to take a shower; Kirk was already ensconced in front of the TV. Tor reached for the dish soap as Elias left, and Jake stood up, ostensibly to help with the dishes.

"What kind of day did you have?" Tor asked suddenly.

Jake opened his mouth to say his day had been fine, but he paused just long enough for it to click that Tor had phrased the question very specifically. So he thought about it. "Day was okay," he said finally. "Got stuff done, no real hassles came up."

"Want to take a walk after the dishes are done?" Tor asked, looking into the sink. "Ready to talk?"

Jake nodded, his stomach tightening a little. Seemed the honeymoon was over. They did the dishes in near silence, though Jake made a point of not acting stressed or anxious. Tor smiled at him a couple of times, and even kissed him when the dishes were put away. They weren't fighting. They were just working at something.

They left the house and wandered for a couple of minutes, Jake letting Tor pick where they were going to end up. At first he thought they were headed toward the orchard, but Tor veered suddenly, making beeline for the corral.

Tor had his hands shoved into his jeans pockets, his hat low on his forehead, shielding his eyes. Jake listened to the sound their boots made on the hardpack of the lane, feeling every step reverberate through his body; he wondered if the vibrations were what was making his chest feel tight, if the scuff and smack of his boots were making his heartbeat race.

Tor said nothing for too long, looked away too many times, as they approached the fence. By the time they were there, leaning on the fence and watching the horses, Jake's anxiety was turning to anger, fed by frustration. He clamped down on the feeling as tightly as he could, telling himself that this was Tor's show, that something heavy was weighing on him, and it was just as hard for Tor to talk about it as it was for Jake to listen. Or harder, seeing as how it had taken three days to get to this point.

The insects buzzed about them, the only sound other than the slow clomp of Shelby's hooves.

Jake turned to look at Tor, to prod him into speaking, but held his peace. Tor's eyes were locked on a piece of ground about three feet in front of them, his hands clasped together in front of him as he rested his elbows on the fence rail. The despair and self-loathing in his eyes told Jake exactly what they were going to talk about.

He'd sort of thought that once he knew what Tor was thinking about, he'd relax a little, the pressure of not knowing gone. But instead, Jake found himself tensing, his mind slamming useless walls up in self-defense. He took a deep breath and splayed his hands out in front of himself, stretching his fingers wide.

Tor cleared his throat. "Thinking we should try to limit this to one topic at a time."

Jake merely nodded. It wasn't like either of them had the emotional energy for more than that.

"And I'm also thinking," Tor continued, his voice low and smooth, "that there's not much point in going back over every little fight and talking them all over." He shook his head quickly. "I mean, I will, if you want me to, but I don't think I can do—"

"No, you're right," Jake interrupted. He glanced at Tor and saw the broad shoulders relax a little. "How about we just start with whatever's been on your mind for the last few days, and go from there?"

Tor raised an eyebrow and Jake gave him a small grin. "I look at you. A lot. I see things."

Tor smiled a little, then the haunted look came back and he returned to staring into the dirt. "Started thinking about what you said. About how it all could have been different if you'd said yes when Travis first asked to have sex with us."

Jake swallowed hard and nodded. He didn't think Tor even noticed, the man seemed completely focused on just getting the words out.

"Would have been all wrong, anyway," Tor said. "Remember what you said, about us not playing with guys we worked with? That was only part of it. We never slept with guys who…guys we didn't both want, or guys who were just looking for something dirty." Tor shook his head again, sharp and angry. He looked at Jake and said, "I'm not finding the right words."

"You're doing fine," Jake said. He had no idea if Tor was or not, but at least he was talking, at least he was trying to get it out. "Keep going."

Tor looked at him for a long moment and nodded, once. "Like with Ben?" he said. "That was for you and Ben, and me and Jeff just sort of got carried along. We were all willing, we all wanted—and we all knew it was just what it was. Same thing with the others, even the guy at the bar who just wanted you—he knew that we play together, and it was all in fun. Travis wasn't like that."

Tor paused and glanced at Jake, waiting for Jake to nod before continuing. "Thing with Travis was…well, there was a lot with that kid. You didn't want him, for one, that's why you gave him a flat no, yeah?"

Jake couldn't deny the point; Travis hadn't been his type at all; too young, too open, too forward. And considering Tor was his type he figured that was saying something.

"But you wanted him," Jake said quietly. "I could have played along—"

"No, that's just it. Playing was for you and me. Something we did when we both wanted it. Travis—hell, he just wanted to get laid, didn't matter to him if it was you, or me, or anyone else. He didn't get it. Didn't see that us playing with someone else meant anything other than we fucked around. He didn't care that there was a relationship. It just didn't register with him."

Jake's stomach tightened and his chest was constricted again. Tor had known, though, and Tor had broken the rules anyway. "So, what happened?" he asked finally, not able to stop himself, and not knowing if he should even bother keeping the question in.

Tor's jaw worked for a couple of moments and he swallowed hard. "That's…the rest of what I've been thinking on. You sure you want to hear this?"

No. "Yes."

"Jake—" Tor didn't sound anymore convinced than Jake felt.

"Look, I don't want to. But I think you have to say it, and maybe when it's out it'll be better."

Tor gave him a long look, his eyes searching Jake's face. "Okay."

They stood looking into the corral, watching Shelby graze, both of them leaning their elbows on the top railing. Jake flexed his fingers again.

"We were out checking the hay, just the two of us," Tor said quietly, and Jake suddenly knew exactly when it started, to the day. He bit the inside of his lip and stared at Shelby, trying not to react. It hurt to know for sure.

Tor kept talking. "We were having lunch, just sitting in the sun and relaxing for a bit, and he was telling me about some guy sucking him off in a bar—I mean, not like 'So this guy was going down on me' but…describing it. And he's laughing and leaning back, talking about this guy's mouth and hands and what it felt like, and he's fucking hard, rubbing his hand over himself in his jeans." Tor's breath caught and his hands clenched.

"And I got hard, listening to him, watching him." Tor shrugged. "Should have been a no harm, no foul, just laugh and get on with the day, put it out of my mind. Except when he reached over and touched me I didn't stop him. Not when he rubbed me, not when he started telling me what he wanted to do, not when he undid my jeans." Tor's voice was rough, almost too low for Jake to hear. "I didn't stop him when he went down on me."

Jake didn't say anything, just looked at their hands; his own, curled into fists, Tor's white knuckled and twisted together. Jake thought that if Tor stopped now they'd be stuck like this forever.

"He was full of words. Fed me line after line, about how hot I made him, how he wanted me all the time, how he stroked off thinking about me. And I didn't care about any of it, all I cared about was…was not fighting, about taking what he was offering, and living outside of my myself for twenty minutes." Tor swallowed hard and cleared his throat. "Wasn't ever supposed to happen, Jake. Not then, not again. Every single time, it wasn't supposed to happen again."

Tor's voice broke, and Jake took a breath, ready to ask something, to say something—even if he had no idea what. But Tor turned to him, froze him in an instant, and said, "I know it means nothing—it can't—but I never once went to him, Jake, and I said no a few times, promised myself that it was done and I'd never…but I did. Sometimes I chose to listen to him, chose to let him get to me. Gave him what he was after, got myself an escape for a bit. And I can't tell you why I did it, 'cause I don't rightly know, myself. Never cared about him. Never…felt anything for him."

Tor looked away again and sighed, sounding older than he'd ever done before, except maybe the day of Maureen's funeral. "I think you and me were hurting each other, and I wanted to…not to hurt and make it worse at the same time. Punish you, punish myself. Wanted to believe I could turn a kid's head and still have a man beside me. Wanted to self-destruct and wound up destroying us."

Jake tried once more to find words and found himself without any. He watched Shelby, listened to Tor breathing beside him, and looked through his head for his reactions. It hurt, of course. He'd known it would, hearing about Tor and Travis couldn't not hurt. But it wasn't a knife in his gut, and it wasn't the deadness of when he'd seen them together. With a twinge of surprise Jake found that it wasn't actually as horrible as he'd feared.

Tor had taken advantage of Travis' offers because he hadn't been happy with Jake, hadn't been happy in his own skin. That wasn't a surprise, that was what they were trying to fix—were fixing.

Jake was still contemplating the situation when Tor interrupted his thoughts, asking, "Can we get past this? Is it too big?"

Jake stretched out his hands again. They'd get past it; they were already back together and he wasn't letting go. Ever. "Tor, I forgave you for Travis the day I decided to find you. We're past it now."

Or at least close enough that they could move on.

Forty Five

The kitchen was busy, all four of them moving around. Jake put the plates on the table and dodged Kirk, who was enroute with the glasses. "So, 'Lissa wants to know if we can go for a long weekend in September," he said to Tor.

"Yeah?" Tor pulled supper from the oven and set it to cool, then side stepped Elias on his way to the calendar. "She say when?"

"Nope." Jake moved the casserole to the table, and went to the fridge for the salad. "Elias, the salt and pepper?"

Tor flipped the pages of the wall calendar for a moment and grunted. He sat down at the table, reaching for the serving spoon.

"Look okay, then?" Jake asked, pulling out his chair.

"Yeah, anytime's fine," Tor said, his eyes fixed on supper.

"Cool, I'll call and tell her whenever works for her. Jacob's got school and stuff, so maybe Labor—"

"I said fine," Tor snapped, all of his previous good humor gone.

Jake froze, then lowered himself into his chair slowly. "Uh. Okay. Later, then."

Tor scowled at his plate and both Kirk and Elias tensed as silence took over the room. Jake reached for the salad tongs, his cheeks heating in embarrassment and confusion. The meal passed in an uncomfortable silence, no one looking at the others, and as soon as he was done, Tor stood up.

"I'll be back in a bit," he said gruffly. He dropped his plate into the sink and pulled the fridge door open, grabbing a bottle of beer. He didn't look at any of them as he left the house, and stomped off the porch stairs.

Jake and Elias stared at each other for a moment, and Kirk sat there with his mouth open, finally sputtering, "Aren't you going to stop him?"

Jake turned his stare to Kirk. "Stop what? A tantrum?"

Kirk was still looking stunned. "No, the beer. Tor doesn't drink—I thought it was 'cause you both—"

"Oh, that." Jake dismissed it with a shrug. "Nah, that's just me. Tor doesn't drink 'cause I don't like the taste, is all. Not the same thing." He exchanged another look with Elias. "But if he's reaching for beer, something pretty unpleasant is going on in his head. This isn't just a fit of temper."

Elias nodded. "Don't envy you."

Jake shrugged, pushing his own concern and discomfort away. "Part of being together."

By Chris Owen

He had to remind himself of that when Tor came back
an hour later in just as foul a mood, and when Tor made
grumpy noises at the TV, and again when they were getting
ready for bed and Tor bitched about the way Jake squeezed
the toothpaste.

When they finally got into bed Jake made the apparent
error of either waiting too long to loop his arm around Tor,
or it was on the wrong part of Tor's waist, or his body
temperature was wrong. In any event Tor stiffened and
rolled away, taking the last of Jake's patience with him.

"What the fuck is your problem?" Jake demanded.

Tor froze, and Jake was sure he was going to get up and
leave, that the door would slam and they'd be back at
square one again.

Before Tor could move, Jake touched his arm; not
holding him there, just giving him some contact. "Sorry."

Tor was still unmoving, but at least he wasn't storming
off. Jake thought quickly, sure that whatever he decided to
do wouldn't be right, but he had to do something. He had
no idea what Tor wanted him to do, what Tor needed from
him.

So he asked.

"What do you want me to do? If you need some time to
be alone I can go."

Tor looked at him, his eyes unreadable in the dark, but
his body tense. "What?" he finally asked.

Jake sighed and ran a hand through his hair. "I have no
idea what's going on. Give me something here—I don't
know if I did something, or if you're pissed at life in
general, or what. I only know that this is the first time since
you came back that you've come close to leaving instead of
talking, and I don't want to go to sleep wondering what's
going on. This where we have to do that talking shit, Tor."

For a moment Tor didn't move, nothing changed at all,
then his body relaxed and he lay back down. Jake almost
grinned in relief—they were getting somewhere.

"You told me…you promised me this wouldn't happen," Tor said, his voice rough.

Confusion slammed into Jake, a quick punch to his gut. "I never said we wouldn't fight," he began, defenses building.

"Not that," Tor hissed. "Not everything is about you, you know." And then Jake could hear the pain in Tor's voice, the complete agony.

"Tell me," Jake said softly, anger and hurt melting away.

"Do you know what today is?" Tor asked.

Jake remembered Tor looking at the calendar that evening and cursed himself for not cluing in earlier. Quickly, he ran through their family, hoping a birthday or something would come to him. The logical place to start was with Maureen, but her birthday was in the spring. He couldn't remember any possible anniversaries Tor might consider significant for either of them. "No," he finally admitted.

"It's the nineteenth anniversary of Kin's death. Half my fucking life he's been gone, and this is the first time I ever forgot. You said I could let him go and not forget—and I did. I fucking forgot."

Emotions coursed through Jake, one after another as he lay there, but not so fast that he couldn't name them. Sorrow for Tor's pain. Jealousy that a man dead almost twenty years still mattered so much. Shame about the jealousy. Anger that Tor was taking it out on him, and fear that he wouldn't be able to fix it this time.

"You didn't forget Kin," Jake said as calmly as he could, looking up at the dark ceiling. He wanted to touch Tor, but didn't; he knew it wouldn't be welcomed. "You still have him, you just…you remember his smile, right? You remember the way you felt. That's more important than holding onto his death, isn't it?"

Tor was silent for a long moment, then he rolled over to face Jake. "Do you ever fucking listen to yourself?"

"Pardon me?" Jake asked, startled.

"I don't need platitudes, Jake—"

"Then what do you need?" Jake snapped. He wanted to take the words back as soon as he'd said them. Resentment and hurt were leaking out around Jake's edges and Tor was still stiff, holding himself away.

"I need…fuck, I need to know that I'm not losing him." Tor sounded tired now, his voice lower. But his eyes were still angry. "I need you to listen to me, not give me crap about remembering his smile and it being okay to forget the day he died."

Jake sighed. "Fine. You stress yourself out about it, and I'll just lay here, wanting to help, not doing anything. 'Cause everything I try is wrong, when it comes to this. I don't know what it's like, Tor, and I'm glad I don't. But I don't like seeing you hurting, and I'm sorry you are."

Tor didn't say anything, but Jake thought that his eyes softened a little.

"I know he's important to you," Jake said, more softly. "And I know you don't want to forget him. But I think you're being too hard on yourself."

Tor sighed. "You're doing it again."

"Doing what? Trying to get you to see that Kin's so important to you that you're not gonna lose him? Ever? That you hold him so tight that sometimes—" He stopped, horrified.

"That sometimes what, Jake?" Tor asked quietly. Too quietly.

Jake looked away. "That sometimes you get so wrapped in holding onto him that you forget what you do have."

"I don't." Tor sounded sure, but his eyes were searching. "Do I?"

Jake shrugged. "I don't know. But sometimes it seems more important to you that you don't let any part of him escape, and you wind up yelling at me. And I want to make it better for you, take the pain away, but you won't let me."

Tor sighed and closed his eyes. "I don't mean to push you away. And you can't make it better."

Something stabbed through Jake, quick and too sharp. "Why can't I make it better?"

"It's not your job. Not with me, anyway," Tor said.

That just made no sense to Jake. Of course it was his job to make things better. That's what he did. So he said so.

"No, Jake, it isn't. And again, do you ever listen to yourself? It's like you've got this switch—Jake, my partner, and Jake the boss man, always looking to find solutions, to make it all better." Tor sounded calm enough, his voice low and serious.

"I do? I mean…what? Yeah, I'm trying to fix this. Isn't that—"

"Nope." Tor rolled over and touched Jake's cheek lightly. "Just need you to listen. Don't have to fix it. I just need to know that you're here. And I swear to God, I don't mean to make Kin more important than you. I just don't."

"But you blamed me," Jake protested. "It ain't my fault, and I don't want to make it worse, and now I'm fucking talking like a redneck, and I don't know what you want from me."

Tor suddenly rolled on top of him, his hands catching Jake's wrists. "I blamed you 'cause I was—am—pissed at myself. I'm sorry. And I'll say I'm sorry again in the morning. But I need you to be you, not my boss."

Jake felt completely out of control, which was reinforced by Tor's grip on his wrists. "Uh, you wanna be the boss for a bit?" he asked in confusion.

Tor made a noise in his chest and his hands tightened. "What do you think?"

Jake tried to free his wrists and Tor tightened his grip again. "I think…I think I'm getting turned on." He was too, his cock filling as he tugged against Tor's grip. "And I'm wondering if this isn't just you and me fighting and fucking again."

"This is you and me fighting, talking about why, and me being the boss." Tor ground down against him and Jake moaned, friction and adrenaline affecting them both.

"What if I want to be the boss?" Jake asked, knowing full well that he didn't. Not right then.

"Then fight back, Taggart. But it'll be a lie. You like it when I take charge." Tor licked Jake's neck, all the way up to his ear. "Like it when I bite. I can feel you, Jake. Can feel your cock throb when I say that."

Jake moaned, partially from the way Tor was forcing his arms up over his head, partially from the tone of voice.

"Can feel you spreading for me, Jake. Feel your body begging for it. You like it when I do this, tell you what I'm going to do, tell you I'm in charge. You like the words, and you like giving up control to me." Tor was purring, moving against him, and Jake's heart was racing, his prick rigid between them.

Tor pushed a knee between Jake's legs, and sure enough, Jake opened for him, hungry and wanting. He wrapped his legs around Tor's waist and grabbed the headboard, holding on for dear life as Tor got the lube.

He rode Tor's fingers until he thought he'd go insane, his body sweating, his breath coming in ragged gasps as he begged Tor to fuck him. When the hot metal of Tor's ring pushed at him he keened, hips bucking up as he tried to get Tor deep. Tor groaned and gave in, fucking him hard and fast, fingers digging into Jake's hips.

It was all Jake could do not to scream, only the knowledge that their home wasn't theirs alone, keeping him from crying out a litany of words. He had a sudden image of him and Tor trying to fuck quietly in their seventies and would have laughed if he had the breath.

Then all thought fled, words and praise locked in his throat as Tor thrust hard into him again and again, hand pulling him off. "Come for me, boss man," Tor whispered. "Make me feel it."

Jake came, Tor's name a harsh sound that only Tor would hear.

Tor arched, filling Jake with heat. He fell onto Jake's chest, pulling at Jake's arms until they were holding each other, Tor still buried in Jake's body. "I love you, Jake. And Kin is my past, a part I want to remember. But you're my future."

By Chris Owen

Forty Six

Jake walked from the main house to the bunkhouse as quickly as he could, hoping to get there before the rest of them. The day had finished early and he'd spent the last while in the office talking to the Boss. Now he needed to think.

He'd been putting this off for months, all through the summer and early autumn, and now it looked like he'd run out of time. He and Tor had worked their way through an amazing amount of shit since June, starting from talking about Travis and on through various things that had come up. They'd more or less laid Kin to rest. They'd had a couple of discussions about Tor seeing Jake's boss-man attitude showing up at inappropriate times, something Jake was still working on. They'd talked about family, and how to make sure Jacob understood that they loved each other without bringing up the damage that James had inflicted. They'd gone to Maureen's grave together, and they'd even talked about finding out where Jake's mother was buried, but had decided against it.

And through it all, Jake had avoided this one. He didn't even know if it was still an issue for Tor, though he suspected it was. Trouble was, Jake still didn't know what to do about it. What he needed, he thought as he crossed the yard, was a hot shower and half an hour to figure out where to start.

He didn't get it.

Elias was making supper when he walked in, and Kirk was on the phone in the kitchen, talking about a trip into town. Tor was leaning on the fridge, talking to Elias, but he looked at Jake and waved when the door opened. Between the voices and the rattle of pots and pans Jake knew he wouldn't find the peace he was after. And maybe it didn't matter.

He walked through the kitchen and grabbed a glass. "What kind of day are you having?" he asked Tor.

Tor stared at him for a second, his eyes widening and then narrowing as he thought. The phrase had become a sort of code word for them, used when one of them had something on his mind that was important enough to their relationship that they needed to talk, alone, and soon.

"Good enough," Tor said. "Walk after supper?"

Jake nodded and filled his glass with water. "Going to take a shower."

The shower was helpful, but not what he needed; things kept flipping in his mind as he tried to see it from all angles. Finally, he just gave up and got dry and dressed. Tor would talk him through it, and they'd figure it out.

Supper was rushed, on his part and Tor's, both of them ignoring the looks from Elias and Kirk as they wolfed down their meal. That was another thing, Jake thought in the back of his mind. Too many people around, all the time. Normal people could talk things out in the privacy of their own home.

When they'd finished and gotten the dishes washed, Jake went to their room and grabbed a spare blanket. It was a cool night, and he didn't know how long they'd be out there. Tor raised an eyebrow at him, but didn't say anything. The other eyebrow went up when Jake crossed to the nightstand and got the lube.

"Where're we going?" Tor asked as they left the bunkhouse.

"Barn. Hay loft, I think," Jake said.

Tor grinned. "One of those talks?" The grin faded. "Guess not, if you asked about my day."

Jake just bit his lip and led them into the stable.

The loft was fairly full, and night was easing over them, so they only went back far enough that they were nicely hidden to anyone who wandered in, but close enough to the ladder that they'd be able to find their way back out in the dark. They shifted a couple of bales, and Jake spread the blanket, then they settled in, sitting close enough to touch.

"So, what's up?" Tor asked softly.

Jake drew a leg up and hooked his arm around his knee. "Missy and Chris are moving to Austin at the beginning of the month. Chris got a good job, and found a house already."

Tor cocked his head. "Good for them, I guess. They talked about it long enough."

"Yeah. Think they'll be happy. Thing is, Doug's starting to talk about retiring. His heart, Chris going…all of it. He's making noises."

Tor nodded. "Right. So, what do you think?"

369

Jake sighed. "That's just it. I don't know what to think. Or, I know what I think, I'm just not so sure it's right, you know?"

Tor looked at him. "Nope. Not yet, anyway."

Jake wanted to growl. "You know I don't want to leave."

"Right, and I don't want to either. This is our place, our piece of land, no matter who owns it."

"But it isn't," Jake said. "It's Doug's. We work here, I grew up here, really—and there's other stuff, too."

"Like what?" Tor asked softly.

"Like you and me sharing a house with farmhands for the rest of our lives. It's getting…God, it's like we can't ever just be alone. And if we lose the house, we have to find somewhere that's not here to live. It won't be the same."

Tor nodded. "So…?"

"So, it still scares the crap out of me to think about us buying it. I can't…I don't like the thought of having all these men dependent on us. Their jobs, their families…everything can go to hell so fast if the weather so much as gives us two bad years in a row, or the prices drop, or the herd takes ill, or—"

"Jake, how long you been here? And how many times have you seen this ranch almost lost?"

"It could happen," Jake insisted. "Doug managed things just fine, saved the ranch at least twice."

"Sure he did. And you could, too. I could. And the hands? Those men you're worried about? You think they won't do what they have to, for the herd or the land?"

Jake closed his eyes and leaned back, forcing himself to put his fears to one side and to listen to Tor.

"Bobby, Tommy, the six other hands who've been here for more than a few years? They know what to do, they love this ranch as much as we do. Elias and Kirk? It's home to them, too. But you and me? We can make it work. We keep the men, keep the herd, and keep it as is. Only difference is the names on the deed and where we hang our hats at night." Tor's hand found Jake's and squeezed. "And who you're the boss of," he added in a low voice.

Jake grinned at that. It would be a bonus to them personally if that little detail were taken care of. "Partners?"

"Always," Tor whispered sincerely.

Jake turned his head and Tor met him halfway, kissing him fiercely. Jake's mouth opened wide, letting Tor in, even as his hands were pushing Tor onto his back, need flaring out of nowhere, sudden and demanding. It was fast and furious, both of them hungry and moving together on the blanket, hands plucking at clothes. The hands weren't fast enough, however, and Tor managed to wedge his leg between Jake's, giving him just what he needed.

"God, yes," Tor gasped as Jake started moving, rubbing his cock with one hand and biting down on his shoulder at the same time. "Fuck, touch me, Jake."

Jake groaned and tried to get Tor's jeans open, but his own prick was throbbing and his hips moved restlessly as he humped Tor's thigh.

"Oh hell, gonna come," he whispered. "Gonna come, Tor."

Tor grabbed at Jake's hips and thrust hard a couple of times, coming with a groan, wet heat spreading between them.

"Oh fuck, yes!" Jake shuddered and shook, coming in his jeans as he kissed Tor, the smell of sex and hay and horses all around him.

The smell of his land. His lover. His home.

Bareback

Printed in the United States
106531LV00006B/103-108/A